W9-BLS-336

LP FICTION
Sawyer

Sawyer, Meryl.
Play dead

08/10
33950008424076   br

11-6

BR

MANATEE COUNTY PUBLIC LIBRARY SYSTEM
BRADENTON, FLORIDA

PLAY DEAD

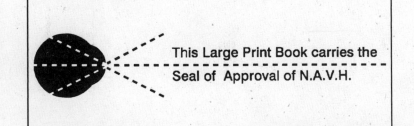

This Large Print Book carries the
Seal of Approval of N.A.V.H.

PLAY DEAD

MERYL SAWYER

THORNDIKE PRESS

A part of Gale, Cengage Learning

GALE
CENGAGE Learning

Detroit • New York • San Francisco • New Haven, Conn • Waterville, Maine • London

GALE
CENGAGE Learning

Copyright © 2010 by M. Sawyer-Unickel.
Thorndike Press, a part of Gale, Cengage Learning.

ALL RIGHTS RESERVED
This is a work of fiction. Names, characters, places, and incidents are either the product of the author's imagination or are used fictitiously, and any resemblance to actual persons, living or dead, business establishments, events, or locales is entirely coincidental.
Thorndike Press® Large Print Basic.
The text of this Large Print edition is unabridged.
Other aspects of the book may vary from the original edition.
Set in 16 pt. Plantin.

LIBRARY OF CONGRESS CATALOGING-IN-PUBLICATION DATA

Sawyer, Meryl.
    Play dead / by Meryl Sawyer.
        p. cm. — (Thorndike Press large print basic)
    ISBN-13: 978-1-4104-2772-4 (hardcover)
    ISBN-10: 1-4104-2772-2 (hardcover)
    1. Artists—Fiction. 2. Murder—Investigation—Fiction.
    3. Large type books. I. Title.
    PS3569.A866P53 2010
    813'.54—dc22   2010014288

Published in 2010 by arrangement with Harlequin Books S.A.

Printed in the United States of America
1 2 3 4 5 6 7 14 13 12 11 10

For Redd,
A Stand-Up Guy.
Thanks for the memories.

The best way to love anything is as if it might be lost.

— G. K. Chesterton

PROLOGUE

"Andy," called Hayley before she remembered he was gone. She walked out onto the third-floor balcony and gazed at the water as the breeze off the bay ruffled her hair. It was way too soon to leave, she decided, but her loft seemed so empty.

She'd been lonely for a long time, she realized with an ache too deep for tears. It was reflected in her paintings, or so she'd been told. Ian never lied. Why would he? Ian Barrington had been the first person to recognize her talent and offer to sell her paintings in his gallery. Hayley's earlier works had portrayed her happy outlook on life.

But in the two years since she'd secretly begun selling her art, Hayley's life had taken an abrupt turn. The familiar sadness, the melancholy seeped through her each day. Betrayal and death changed you radically, she reflected. She thought of her parents and her heart contracted with an over-whelming sense of loss.

"Don't feel sorry for yourself," she said out loud, watching a boat passing by. The guys on the deck were wildly waving to get her attention.

She knew what they saw: a young woman dressed in a short skirt and sleeveless blouse. Her brown hair was streaked with copper highlights, making her look more like the beach bunny she'd been in her teens than the artist she was today.

Maybe she should cut her hair short and stop streaking it. What would it feel like to have short hair? For as long as she could recall, Hayley had worn her hair long. The style made the hazel-green eyes that domi-nated her face appear larger than they actu-ally were.

The needs, the longings for a past that would never come again nagged at her. Time for a change, Hayley reminded her-self. In another few weeks, her life would move in a different direction. This would be a great opportunity for a new hairstyle. The fresh start she'd been planning.

She checked her watch. It was too early to leave. She'd already packed her purse that doubled as a backpack with the few things she would need. She'd placed her treasured set of paint brushes in their wooden box and wrapped it in the shorts and T-shirts she planned to wear.

She realized how much she was counting on her life making a dramatic change. How much she was looking forward to the future. Once she altered the course of her life, there would be no going back.

Bring-bring. From the loft's studio behind her, Hayley heard the sound of the telephone. She decided not to answer; let the machine pick up. She wasn't in the mood to talk.

A shaky voice came through her machine. "H-Hayley, are you . . . you there?"

Hayley charged back into the loft, recognizing the anguished tone of her friend Lindsey Fulton. She was stunned Lindsey was phoning. She never called.

Hayley snatched the receiver from the cradle, saying breathlessly, "I'm here. I'm here. What's happening?"

"Hayley," her friend said, her voice choked with tears. "Oh, Hayley."

"What's wrong?"

"I — I'm at a payphone," replied Lindsey, sobbing now. "I've got to get away. Now! I can't waste a second."

This was the call Hayley had been expecting — and dreading — for so long. Why

11

now? she silently asked. The timing couldn't be worse. Hayley was just hours from changing the course of her own life. It didn't matter, she decided in the next instant. All that counted was saving her friend.

Hayley suddenly realized how she could help her friend while getting a fresh start. The perfect solution, she decided. "Lindsey, listen to me and do exactly what I tell you."

What was taking so long? Hayley Fordham had been in Gulliver's for over two hours, no doubt slurping down cosmos. Didn't she know the hunt was on? Didn't she realize time was running out, trickling away like the last grains of sand in an hourglass? Couldn't she sense this evening was different from all previous nights in her life?

Of course not. The bitch was clueless — as usual.

Hiding at a safe distance, concealed by the trees and the Dumpsters at the back of the trendy restaurant's parking lot, was boring as hell. While the waiting was a total downer, the building anticipation was as heady as a powerful narcotic. Exhilarating. Arousing. The sensation transported the predator to an unimagined height of excitement. Annihilating an unsuspecting victim

12

— just the thought of it — ignited a thrill so profound that it rivaled sex.

Wait.

Just wait. Hayley's charmed life — all thirty-three years of it — was almost over. Charmed? Damned was more like it. She would get what she deserved — in spades.

The killer took stock of the surrounding area, sensing more than seeing the objects nearby and ignoring the rank smell coming from the Dumpster. Death belonged to the night. It always had, always would. Darkness provided a natural shield, especially a moonless night like this. Victims could easily be tailed without the stalker being detected or questioned.

In the light of day, someone from the nearby office building would have spotted a person hunkered down behind the Dumpsters, but not at night. As an extra precaution, the predator had smashed the nearest security light with a rock. There was a security camera at the back door of the restaurant. A quick squirt of Pam ensured nothing but blurry images would be recorded. There hadn't been time to do more than destroy the one light, but then extra precautions hadn't been necessary. Lady Luck had smiled, bringing Hayley to this restaurant and having her park in the rear

— in the shroud of shadows cast by the line of tall, dense shrubs that separated the parking area from the office buildings behind it.

With a deafening roar and whoosh of air, a jet streaked into the sky from John Wayne Airport, which was opposite the restaurant. Convenient. Very convenient. The killer hadn't planned it but Hayley's destination tonight had been perfect. The noise from the airport would add to the confusion, the terror.

A gloss-black limousine pulled up to the rear of the restaurant, its engine purring almost inaudibly. Since Gulliver's faced the busy street across from Orange County's airport, the back entrance was the only way in or out of the restaurant except for the fire exits used only in emergencies. With the stretch limo blocking the view, it was impossible to tell who was leaving. Or was someone arriving?

Not some celebrity. The OC had a smattering of them — nothing like L.A. But the Newport Beach area was filled with people who had money up the wazoo to use a limo at an upscale restaurant like Gulliver's, which was well known for its bar scene. The limo drove into the night and disappeared from view.

The predator waited and waited. A few

groups of people trickled out of Gulliver's. A couple so hot for each other that they almost did it on the hood of his Corvette was mildly distracting, but time ticked on and on. Finally a slim woman with shoulder-length hair emerged, stood on the walkway exit and glanced around warily.

The air shifted with a sense of hushed expectancy. Something seemed to be . . . off. Had she sensed . . . danger?

"No way," the killer whispered. Nothing was wrong. Things were going according to plan. Then why was Hayley just standing there? She usually sauntered along oblivious to everyone around her, glistening brown hair streaked with copper bobbing on her shoulders. Hayley couldn't be waiting for a valet. Gulliver's was a self-parking facility.

Noise exploded from the Acapulco restaurant at the far end of the lot it shared with Gulliver's. A bunch of guys barely out of their teens staggered through the double doors from the Mexican cantina, revealing they'd consumed enough tequila to make them rowdy.

They'd better get to their cars and get outta Dodge in a hurry or — hell, who cared? Killing innocent bystanders wasn't the goal, but collateral damage had been factored into this scheme.

Hayley hesitated, gazing at the group. They were too far away for her to be concerned about them, but the killer thought she might be feeling threatened by something. It showed in the slump of her shoulders and in the way she hurried toward her car. Never underestimate women's intuition. She might have sensed death lurking in the shadows.

Her older model Beamer was parked at the rear of the lot like a black toad, which had made this job a piece of cake. The dark area wouldn't be safe in most cities, but this was Newport Beach. Women felt secure here, and most of the time they were.

Most of the time.

Tonight an ominous undercurrent of danger and death filled the balmy night air. A cunning person could pick up on it the way some animals had realized a tsunami was heading their way. Even the predator's bones could sense the danger and the sensation heightened the anticipation.

Hayley seemed to fumble with the door lock. Was she drunk? It wasn't like her. From this far away and with the lack of light, it was difficult to tell much about the snotty bitch.

Get on with it already.

16

Hayley opened the door and slid into the car. The interior light illuminated her shimmering hair for a second. The killer couldn't help smiling. This would be the last time anyone would admire that shiny mane.

The killer eased around to the back side of the Dumpster for protection and flipped the metal lid backward to act as a shield. A full minute passed. The killer risked a peek around the protective corner of the Dumpster. What in hell was Hayley doing?

The interior light in her car was off. A faint blue glow came from the dashboard. She appeared to be leaning forward, fooling with something. The GPS? Was she programming in her next destination?

"Hayley, your next stop is hell."

A convertible pulled up and a noisy group of guys, already half in the bag, vaulted to the pavement without opening the car doors. *Get inside,* the killer silently warned. They hustled toward the entrance and the driver sped away to find a parking spot. Lucky for him, the guy headed for the open spaces behind the adjacent Mexican restaurant.

Lethal silence. A second later a supersonic crackling — *KA-BOOM!*

The explosion knocked the Dumpster sideways like an eardrum-splitting hatchet blow. The impact of the detonation assaulted every lobe in the killer's brain and blackness eclipsed everything for a few seconds.

"Aw, shit!"

Debris rained down, pummeling the Dumpster lid with shrapnel-like objects. They bounced off the sturdy metal and crashed to the ground nearby. The acrid smell of smoke and burning rubber roiled through the air like a noxious fog. Jolted by the shock wave, nearly a hundred car alarms shrieked simultaneously.

Ears ringing, the killer ventured a look and saw the orange-red inferno that had been Hayley Fordham's BMW. Flames shot out in all directions and lit up the darkness while a cloud of white smoke mushroomed skyward.

Hayley would be reduced to ashes in seconds by the inferno. What remained of her. No doubt the explosion had sent body parts flying. There were something like twenty bones in the human skull. Hayley's head was now in twenty million pieces. The fire would incinerate anything else.

Identifying Hayley Fordham would be a bitch. The killer had foreseen this. Hayley's rear license plate had been removed and scorched with a cigarette lighter, then tossed into the shrubbery behind her car to make it appear that it had been blown off during the explosion. The police would know *exactly* who had died in the car bombing.

Panicked, hysterical people stampeded out of Gulliver's, screaming and holding up cell phones to photograph the geyser of smoke and flames. Others were yelling at 9-1-1 operators. No doubt the emergency switchboard was lit up like the fourth of July.

To the killer, the sounds were muffled, as if they were coming from underwater. *Should have used earplugs.* Even if the chaos couldn't be fully heard, it was exciting. It made the waiting, the planning worthwhile.

Windows were shattered in the cars parked nearby. Some had suffered major damage from the flying debris. Windows and doors in both restaurants had been blown inward by the force of the blast. The destruction was mind-blowing. Worse than expected.

Who knew? Excitement like a live wire arced through the killer. Inching along in the shadows to where the rental car was parked behind the three-story office building to protect it from the explosion, the killer couldn't resist a smile of self-congratulation.

Hayley Fordham was dead. What a trip! Everything had gone *exactly* as planned.

CHAPTER ONE

Trent Fordham took the turn off Pacific Coast Highway in his Porsche at nearly one hundred miles per hour. It was after two in the morning, so no cars were around. He rarely had the opportunity to see what his baby would do. He floored it and the needle shot up to one-twenty.

"Slow down," screeched Courtney from the seat beside him. "You'll get another ticket."

His wife was right, he silently conceded. He could not afford to be stopped tonight. It might result in a sobriety test. Not that he'd been drinking . . . but it was best to be cautious. After all, he was now a CEO of a company. Not a major player — yet — but he was well on his way up the ladder of success. Another speeding ticket was the last thing he needed.

He eased off the accelerator to an audible sigh of relief from his wife and watched the needle drop. They drove in silence — what was there to say? — up to the gated entrance to their exclusive community. He slowed, expecting Jerome, the night guard, to wave as they passed. Instead, the guard signaled for him to stop.

"What's up?" Trent asked.

"The police are waiting for you."

"Why?" He wasn't worried; this had to be some mix-up.

Jerome shrugged. "Wouldn't say." He shrugged again, his voice apologetic. "I had to let them in."

"Of course." Trent tried to sound unfazed, but a yellow flag of caution shot up in his brain. "Thanks for the heads up." That's why he tipped the guards handsomely at Christmas — just for times like this.

He roared through the ornate, twenty-foot-tall gates. He sped by mansions lit up like national monuments. What was going on? he wondered silently.

"It can't be Timmy. The Scouts would have called my cell or yours. Something's wrong at Surf's Up," Courtney said, sounding only slightly worried.

"No way," Trent told her. "Security would have contacted me." His mind was whirling like one of those dervishes he'd read about. Why would the police be waiting for him in the middle of the night?

He stopped at the small park area. The green belt had created open space between mansions that took up most of each lot, leaving little grassy areas. During the day, nannies would be there with children and maids walking neighborhood dogs would be strolling along the meandering flagstone paths.

"What are you doing?" Courtney cried.

Trent turned off the sports car and climbed out, saying, "That was pretty awesome shit we were smoking. I want to hide my jacket in the trunk. It probably reeks."

"*You* were smoking," Courtney said, "with your buddies. I —"

Trent tuned her out. Courtney should talk! She was high on pain pills. All day; every day. He shared a spliff or two with the guys on weekends only.

Bile had risen in his throat; he needed air. He tossed the jacket into the trunk and looked up at the stars. He forced himself to inhale a few deep, calming breaths. The Milky Way slipped in and out, back and forth like a kaleidoscope. He tried lowering his head, then sucking in more air. Better, but not much.

"Oh, my God!" Courtney cried her voice high-pitched. "Maybe something did happen to Timmy. They might not have been able to reach our cells. You know, a tower outage or something."

Trent stood up and rushed back to the driver's side. Their son was with the Boy Scouts at the San Diego Zoo's Wild Animal Park for something called a Roar and Snore sleepover. The kids stayed up half the night to watch the lions feed, then they slept in tents.

A thought hit him, kind of wobbly, fading away almost before he could grasp it. The Scouts required all sorts of emergency information before they took the kids anywhere. He was as sure as he could be when he was this mellow that nothing had happened to his son. "Don't worry, honey. Timmy is fine."

"I hope so."

"Unless," he said as he put the Porsche into gear, "they caught him with dope again."

"Impossible! You know he's being bullied. Those kids planted it in his backpack. None of those little monsters are Scouts."

"Right. So you said." Trent wasn't buying that bridge. He'd been Timmy's age not so long ago. True, his son was just eleven and Trent had been older before he'd first experimented. But today's kids were getting into trouble at a younger age.

The problem with Timothy Grant Fordham wasn't experimenting with drugs. His son was a wimp. How could he grow up in a family who made a fortune from surf and skateboard equipment and not even be able to ride a boogie board? Timmy only used his skateboard when Trent insisted.

The kid should be a surfer or least a skateboard champ, the way Trent had been at the same age, if his mother didn't do her best to make him a sissy. The kid wanted piano lessons. Now whose idea was that? Courtney's. She was a frustrated singer who'd sung backup for a local band before he'd met her. She had music in her blood and claimed Timmy did, as well.

Trent rounded the corner and forced his mind back to the problem. The police cruiser was parked right in front of his house, which, like all the other houses around, was still lit up even though it was well after midnight.

Maybe Timmy had been caught with drugs again. Perhaps the Scout leaders had found his stash and called the police. The Scouts did not like having their name dragged through the muck, so it seemed unlikely that they had called the cops.

Then he noticed the panda car belonged to the Costa Mesa police. Newport Beach patrol cars had ocean blue stylized italic lettering on the sides. Very beachy — for cop cars. Timmy was in San Diego County. If there'd been a problem, the Newport Beach police would have contacted him. Wouldn't they? They lived in Newport, not the lower-middle-class Costa Mesa where Trent had grown up. It bordered Newport but was worlds away financially, socially.

Trent pulled to a stop in his driveway near the rear of the police car and got out. A uniformed officer stepped out of the driver's side of the cruiser while a man in a sports jacket emerged from the passenger side.

"Mr. Fordham?" asked the officer.

"Yes?" Keep it together, Trent warned himself. "Is something the matter?"

"Could we go inside?" This from the suit. Trent assumed he was a detective.

Trent leaned into the Porsche, turned off the ignition and switched off the headlights. Courtney was already out of the car and waiting near him. Tears clouded her dark eyes. She cried so damn easily. Once he'd found it touching. Now was not the time to bawl. Something was really wrong. He needed to be firing on all cylinders, which he wasn't, thanks to the heavy-duty shit he'd shared with his buddies earlier.

"T-Timmy." Courtney's lips quivered around the kid's name. "My son . . ." Tears gushed and Trent put his arm around her, knowing the meds she took often triggered crying jags. She collapsed against him, sobbing softly.

"Mrs. Fordham, this isn't about your son."

Courtney lifted her head. "Really? Timmy's all right?"

"As far as I know," the detective assured her.

There was something ominous about the way the man responded. It was as if the guy thought they should know why he was there. Trent was nervous, which was unusual when he was high. He sucked in a deep breath and held it in his lungs to clear his head. He let it out slowly so no one would notice.

They walked up the flagstone path to the massive double doors that led into the house. For a second, Trent wondered what they thought. The place was impressive, he had to admit, but it wasn't anything compared with the Pelican Point mansion where they'd attended the party tonight. Trent hoped to move there — just as soon as his parents' estate went through probate and he received his share.

If the economy tanked any more, he'd need the money from the estate to keep the company his father started afloat. And pay the mortgage on this house. The cops probably didn't envy him. No doubt they were glad they didn't have this overhead.

Trent unlocked the door and disarmed the security system. The cloying scent of too many roses bombarded his nostrils. Courtney insisted on having five dozen white roses arranged in a crystal vase in the entry hall each week even though he'd told her to cut back. Above the spacious marble entry a vaulted ceiling rose to the second floor. Dead in the center of the foyer was the spectacular floral arrangement on an antique table.

He took Courtney's hand and led the group into the spacious living room that was rarely used. He punched the control panel on the wall to make the low-level lighting in the room brighter.

Trent settled Courtney on one of three sofas that faced a fireplace befitting a castle. The men took chairs nearby. The detective settled back, but the uniformed officer teetered on the edge of the silk chair that some fancy decorator had found, as if the officer believed his gabardine slacks would snag the delicate fabric.

Courtney suddenly began to sob loudly. Now what? Trent wondered.

"Honey, they said Timmy is okay. Stop crying."

"Th-this . . . is b-bad news. I — I can tell."

"Now, Courtney —"

"I'm afraid your wife is correct," the detective said in a level voice.

The words were like a shard of glass entering Trent's spongy brain. This reminded him of the night a little over a year ago when he'd received the telephone call that his father's plane had crashed, killing Trent's father and stepmother. Allison's death was no loss, but Trent had been devastated that his father — his idol — was no longer around to guide him.

"I understand you're next of kin to Hayley Fordham."

It took a second for the words to register. He'd always thought of Hayley as "the step," never his next of anything, but he realized the death of his father and Hayley's mother meant that he was Hayley's closest relative except for her aunt Meg.

"Oh, no," wailed Courtney. "Has Hayley been in an accident?"

Trent didn't have much use for his stepsister beyond her value as a designer for

Surf's Up. That role had taken on greater significance when Hayley's mother Allison had been killed with Trent's father in the plane crash.

He had to admit Hayley had been instrumental in aligning their company with Mixed Martial Arts. Illegal in many states, MMA — the human equivalent of cockfighting — was the fastest growing sport in America. Hayley had picked up on this multibillion dollar business and designed a line of clothes for The Wrath to wear. The Wrath was National MMA champion and one scary dude, but he was to MMA what Tony Hawk was to skateboarding. The MMA line kept the bucks rolling in just when surfboards were tanking, another victim of cheap Asian imports and a nose-diving economy.

Trent might not care for his stepsister, but he admired her business sense. His wife was another story. Courtney adored Hayley. An artist-to-artist thing, he supposed.

"What's happened?" Even as he asked the question, Trent knew this couldn't be a simple accident. A telephone call would have done the trick. His skin prickled with anxiety as reality began to penetrate his usually sharp mind.

"I'm afraid," the detective began in that

same irritatingly level tone, "she's been killed."

"Oh, my God! No!" Courtney jumped to her feet. "Tell me it isn't true."

Trent pulled her back down beside him. Breath gushed from his lungs in short bursts. His mind struggled to get a grip on what he'd just been told. Her death changed — everything. For the better, he had to admit.

"Her car was blown up by a bomb at about eight o'clock this evening," the uniformed officer informed them in a voice barely loud enough to be heard over Courtney's sobs.

"What? That's terrible — a tragedy." Trent shaded the truth. He'd be a hell of a lot richer with Hayley out of the way. "Car bombs happen in the Middle East, not Newport Beach." He tried to keep his mind off the money, adding, "Besides, who would want to kill Hayley?"

"Dear Lord, what is the world coming to?" Meg Amboy asked the nurse who'd brought her breakfast just after dawn. Along with it came her medication and the morning paper. "Did you see there was a car bombing right here in Newport Beach last night?"

"Umm-hmmm," the middle-aged woman

with a chest like the prow of a battleship responded. "It was out by the airport. That's Costa Mesa."

Meg noticed the nurse had dismissed the incident as if it had happened on another planet. Typical attitude around Twelve Acres. The staff had been trained to be elitist. Newport had money and cachet while Costa Mesa, which bordered on Newport, was decidedly middle class with an area that could only be termed a *barrio*. Meg knew most of the help in the kitchen and the housekeepers lived in Costa Mesa or just beyond in Santa Ana.

Meg prided herself on not being a snob. True, she spent her money on the best assisted-living facility she could afford because she knew she didn't have much longer to live. But she remembered with fondness growing up poor and earning her own way. Making a fortune with no one's help.

The battleship nurse, whose name Meg always failed to remember even though Meg had been at Twelve Acres for two years, left. Meg went back to the paper, content to read it until it was time to go downstairs for a second cup of coffee with Conrad Hollister. After they'd finished, she would walk beside his wheelchair to their morning game of bridge.

"Conrad," she whispered and lowered the paper. She stared out at the craggy shoreline framed by her huge window. The rampart-like bluffs had been weathered by wind and the unrelenting surf. Now scrims of early morning mist clung to the shore. Short trees bowed by the elements stooped like hunch-back sentinels along the tops of the bluffs where mansions were perched.

The view was breathtaking but she often experienced a haunting, solitary feeling when she gazed at the sweep of the deep blue sea. It made her lonely, which was an emotion she'd rarely experienced when she was younger, but she had more time to reflect now. Too much time.

"What might have been?" she whispered to herself. What if she'd met Conrad Hollister ten, twenty, even thirty years ago?

Meg refused to allow her thoughts to stray in this direction. At eighty-five, she had the same sharp mind that had guided her as she amassed an empire in real estate. She wouldn't be here if she didn't have a heart that refused to recognize her brain was still young. Why dwell on what might have been when she had accomplished so much?

Conrad was nothing more than an intel-lectual companion. They enjoyed many of the same things, like competitive bridge, but they weren't lovers and probably never would have been. Still, once in a while thoughts crept into her mind and she speculated like an old fool.

"It's people who matter," she quietly assured herself, then realized she'd been talking to herself more and more. There were plenty of folks at Twelve Acres to talk to — besides Conrad — but Meg missed her baby sister. Allison had been killed in a plane crash. Until she was gone, Meg hadn't realized how much she counted on conversations with her sister.

There was Hayley, of course, but her niece had her own life. She visited often, making time for an old woman. Hayley was going to Santa Barbara, then on to San Francisco to buy fabric for the fall line of clothes she was designing. It would be ten days or so before she returned. Until then, Meg would be on her own.

CHAPTER TWO

Farah Fordham pulled her sleek black Ferrari into the Twelve Acres parking lot just after 6:00 a.m. The facility was situated on prime real estate on Pacific Coast Highway, overlooking the coastline between Newport Beach and Laguna Beach. Why they called it Twelve Acres was beyond her; the place was a little over an acre of Cape Cod–style buildings shaded by stately palms.

When Trent had called her at three this morning, he'd insisted she deliver the news of Hayley's death to her old battle-ax aunt. Before he'd gotten that far, Trent had asked, "Did you do it?"

"Do what?" Farah had been engaged in some extremely kinky sex — she loved being the dominatrix — with Kyle, her boyfriend.

"Kill Hayley."

"That's a hell of an idea." Their father's estate was currently in probate. As a CPA,

Farah knew how big a chunk the state would claim, then the rest would be split three ways. Two would be better. One would be ideal.

Despite having a successful business, Farah was overextended and trapped in the economic downturn. To make matters worse, her boyfriend was a residential real estate developer. His career was in limbo and she was supporting him.

"Seriously, Hayley was blown to kingdom come by a car bomb."

"You're kidding." She tried to sound upset but doubted she'd fooled her brother.

"I'm not joking. I've got to go to the station and give a statement. You have to tell Aunt Meg."

Great! Just great! Farah would rather be interviewed by the police than deliver bad news to Meg Amboy. The old crone was giving ninety a hard shove but she was still tough, the same woman who'd turned meager funds into a real estate empire by buying up what people assumed was worthless land east of L.A. Soon urban sprawl drove hundreds of thousands of people to what was laughingly called the "Inland Empire."

As far as Farah could tell, Meg Amboy loved two things. Money and Hayley. The

36

old biddy had a heart condition; the news would probably kill her. The thought made Farah grin as she slithered out of the sports car she really couldn't afford but loved with a passion. What would happen to Meg's money with Hayley gone?

Farah wondered if she could ingratiate herself with the old biddy. Considering the money involved and Meg's lack of relatives, it wouldn't hurt to try.

Meg started at the knock on the door to her suite. She made her way to the door and opened it. Farah Fordham stood there dressed in an expensive suit with a handbag that probably cost more than any nurse at Twelve Acres made in a month. What was she doing here?

"May I come in?"

Meg decided these were probably the first words Farah had ever directed to her other than a polite hello and goodbye at family functions. She eased the door open and watched the young woman saunter in. Meg saw something of herself in Farah — not in the arrogant manner, but in the self-made young woman who'd put herself through college. Her brother, Trent, had ridden on his father's coat tails, going into the family business. Not Farah; she had her own CPA firm.

"Let's sit down," Farah said, looking as if she were facing a firing squad.

Meg's stomach heaved then took a sickening plunge. She staggered backward toward the small sofa where she'd been reading the paper. "Hayley," she cried. "What's happened?"

Farah had hold of both Meg's arms. She eased her down on the sofa before speaking. "There's been an accident."

Relief washed through Meg, leaving her weak; blood pounded like hail in her ears. An accident. Well, she could deal with that. This might mean a prolonged stay in the hospital or special care. That's what money was for; she could help her niece recover.

Then she read Farah's calculating blue eyes. Like a bolt of lightning, the truth almost knocked her to the floor. "Hayley's dead," she managed to whisper.

"I'm afraid so." Farah sat in the wingback chair next to the sofa. "I'm sorry. I wish . . ."

"How? A car accident?" she asked, but Farah shook her head. "How? I want to know."

A suffocating silence filled the room, finally Farah said, "A car bomb."

Suddenly Meg recalled with startling clarity the article in the morning's paper. A car had been blown up in a restaurant parking lot near the airport early yesterday evening. It had seemed so distant, so unbelievable. It couldn't have happened to the one person she loved more than anyone on earth.

In the next heartbeat, Meg's vision became spotty, then all she saw was a tunnel of blinding light. She vaguely heard Farah yelling at her but she couldn't make out the words. Suddenly, the room pitched into complete darkness.

Early morning at the Wedge and glorious sunlight streamed across the ocean and the flawless blue sky. The cool air was turning balmy. Another friggin' day in paradise, Ryan Hollister told himself.

Already a dozen surfers were riding the twenty-foot waves at Newport Beach's famous bodysurfing spot. The Wedge was a unique place. There wasn't any other spot just for bodysurfers — no boards of any kind allowed where giant waves formed.

Ryan ambled along, envying the daredevils, tackling the waves without boards. The surf pummeled the jetty at the entrance to the harbor with such force that spray shot into the air and could be seen on the mainland. All but the most talented bodysurfers were hurled against the shore like a piece of driftwood or hauled under and towed out to sea.

Not that he was much of a surfer but Ryan would like to give those awesome waves a try. When you were successfully riding one, they called it "the green room" because your mind went into a zone where nothing mattered but you and the wave. It was a natural high unlike anything else.

Aw hell, even if he was allowed to surf, the green room wouldn't change a damn thing. *Chill,* he reminded himself. He'd come to the beach to relax, to forget.

He turned his back on the Wedge and ambled along the shore. Overhead a swarm of gulls circled, riding a thermal, cawing, scolding each other. One spotted a fish and dove like an arrow into the waves. Two seconds later it emerged triumphant.

Ryan smiled in spite of himself. There was something about the ocean. It represented the natural order of things — a world bigger than man. The sea could soothe a troubled soul the way nothing else could. He inhaled the briny scent of the ocean and let it fill his lungs. He stared down at the sand pockmarked by crabs' air holes.

He exhaled slowly and walked forward, his beach towel slung over his bare shoulder to hide the scar. He didn't care what people thought, but he didn't want to answer questions. When you got right down to it, he didn't want to talk to anyone.

"For crissakes, get a grip," he muttered to himself.

Garlands of seaweed were being nudged onto the shore by waves that rolled across the sand, tumbling like dice. He kicked idly at a free-floating piece of seaweed. It felt slick as an eel when he flung it back into the water with his toes.

Something in the distance caught his eye. A chestnut-colored dog had just emerged from the waves, a tennis ball in his mouth. The dog raced toward a teenage girl who was clapping her hands.

Buddy, he thought. His breath solidified in his lungs. He'd found his lost dog. Make that stolen dog.

Ryan halted in his tracks. Sand dragged by the retreating waves swirled around his feet. He must be losing it — big-time. Buddy — even if he'd lived beyond normal life expectancy — was long gone.

Dead. Dead for many years.

Buddy had been his dog when he was sixteen and living in Northern California. Part golden retriever, part Labrador, Buddy had been Ryan's best friend in the year following his mother's death and a move to a

41

new town. He'd trained the dog all by himself, using a library book as a guide. Buddy faithfully waited on the front porch every day for Ryan to come home from football practice.

Then one day, Ryan returned and Buddy had vanished. A neighbor reported seeing a strange car in their driveway. Ryan knew Buddy wouldn't have gotten into a car with a stranger. Buddy had been distrustful of anyone but Ryan and his father. Unless Ryan or his father was around, the dog growled at strangers. They figured the dog must have been abused before they adopted him from Cloverdale Rescue.

Ryan put up posters, searched everywhere, checked pounds in the surrounding area, and used his allowance to put an ad in the paper. Nothing. Only the report of the strange car in their driveway.

He'd gone to bed each night, trying not to let his father know he was crying. Sixteen-year-old football players don't cry. He couldn't hold back the tears as he prayed that whoever had Buddy wasn't mistreating him. He was getting good kibble and lots of fresh water. Runs. Sessions with a ball.

No matter who had Buddy, the dog would never be theirs. Ryan had taught him to trust, then taught him a slew of tricks.

Buddy only belonged to Ryan. No one else.

Then there were the nights when Ryan imagined Buddy in a cage too small for his large body. Could be a pound or worse, a lab where they were experimenting on dogs. Ryan could see Buddy's black nose between the bars, his eyes glazed with fear, the way they'd been the day Ryan rescued Buddy. His dog was silently asking: Why did you do this to me?

The thought of Buddy somewhere alone and forsaken haunted Ryan. He kept hearing the dog: Why have you deserted me?

The lingering memory of Buddy had been part of the reason Ryan had gone into the FBI. What would it be like not to know what had befallen a loved one? Thousands of people vanished each year without a trace.

The academy had been a challenge, but he'd enjoyed the training process, the winnowing out of those who couldn't cut it, the air of camaraderie. In a way, it felt as if he were playing football again.

Back then, he'd enjoyed being part of a team. Just when had he turned into such a loner? He supposed facing death day in and day out did that to a person. When death finally arrived and stole the one you loved, you didn't much feel like reaching out, being part of a team.

Reality about FBI work hadn't set in until Ryan's first assignment at a field post in Minneapolis. It was boring beyond anything he could possibly have imagined. He'd watched too much television in his formative years, Ryan decided. There wasn't much action in the field offices.

After two years, Ryan applied for advanced training in the computer sciences unit and was accepted because he'd been a math major at Duke. The training concentrated on white-collar crimes and identity theft. It wasn't what he'd envisioned when he'd joined, but at least he was solving crimes, not pushing paper in some field office.

A bonus had been his assignment to the capital of white-collar crime, Los Angeles. Not only was there plenty of activity, it meant he could be closer to his father, who had suffered a stroke and was living in a facility in Newport Beach, south of L.A.

"Hi," called the young girl with the dog as he approached. Nearby her friends were lounging on beach towels, wearing bikinis no bigger than eye patches. "Isn't Dodger great?"

"He's special, all right."

The dog bounded up to Ryan and offered him the dripping wet tennis ball. Ryan took it and threw it into the ocean with his good arm. The dog was off hell-for-leather after the ball. He splashed through the breaking waves with the same happy abandon that Buddy used to have. Dodger swooped under the water with amazing agility and came up with the ball. He trotted back to the girl.

Ryan marched on; he already had a spot picked out where he intended to stretch out and try to sleep. As he walked away from the girls, he heard one of them call him a studmuffin.

Get outta here, he thought. He was old enough to be her father. He was tall — almost six and a half feet tall — but he no longer had the muscular build of the running back he'd been in college. He was slim now, too slim.

He spread his beach towel on the sand and slathered sunblock on his body as best he could with his left hand. He had a limited range of motion with his right arm but it was quickly improving. Meanwhile, he was getting to be quite adept at using his left hand. He lay down on his beach towel and closed his eyes.

Beep-beep. Beep-beep. The chirping from some distant spot awakened him. Wow. He had been sleeping. A first. He automatically reached for the cell phone in the side pocket of his swim trucks with his right hand. Pain shot up his arm and settled in his bum shoulder. He grabbed for the phone with his left hand and saw Caller ID showed Conrad Hollister. Had something happened to his father?

"Are you all right, Dad?"

"I'm fine. I need to talk to you. It's important."

"I'm on my way." Ryan disconnected and stood up, shaking the sand from his towel with his left hand. He saw that he must have been asleep for some time. It was nearly noon. Dozens of people were now on the beach and umbrellas had sprouted from the sand like mushrooms. The girl with the great dog was gone.

"Weird," Ryan heard himself say, but his voice seemed to belong to someone else. "Car bombs are unusual."

His father hadn't developed a medical problem. He had summoned Ryan to hear this story. Ryan had a sneaking suspicion — hell, more than a suspicion — where this was going. He should just haul ass now, but he needed to let his father down gently. Conrad Hollister wasn't what he used to be. Confined to a wheelchair, his world now revolved around Twelve Acres. And Meg Amboy.

After Ryan's mother's death, Conrad had never remarried, although he'd had numerous girlfriends and plenty of chances. He seemed more attached to Meg than he had to any of them, which was unusual since they couldn't possibly be having sex at their age. Could they? *Don't go there.*

"Hayley was like a daughter to me," Meg said, the threat of tears in her voice.

"I'm sorry." Ryan searched for the right words. "It's such a tragedy."

"I told Meg that you could help us," his father said.

There you go. Ryan would have bet anything that this was the reason he was here. "I'm sure the police are all over this. Since it happened so close to an airport, the Joint Terrorism Task Force must be investigating, too."

His father's lips clamped together in resentment and tears shimmered in Meg's eyes. The air around them was fraught with pain and desperation. Ryan could see that they had no idea of the magnitude of this investigation. He wouldn't add a damn thing.

"The Joint Terrorism Task Force includes the FBI, local fire and police, the Bureau of Alcohol, Tobacco, Firearms and Explosives as well as Homeland Security. That's tremendous manpower focused on this crime. They'll solve the case."

"They're not you." Determination was etched on every time-worn line on his father's face. "This isn't personal to them."

Something inside Ryan clicked, a painful echo of the larger than life man his father had once been. Back then, Conrad Hollister would never have begged anyone for help. A host of conflicting emotions warred inside Ryan. It wouldn't be long, he realized, before he lost the only other person he loved.

"You know I'm not an investigator. I'm a computer jock." He said this more to Meg than his father. Meg knew what he did; they'd discussed it the first time he'd met her. But she looked so stricken, as if she'd keel over any second, that he felt he had to explain.

"I don't trust them," Meg said in a surprisingly firm voice. "They were here to interview me. They don't have a clue. The car bomb has thrown them. The police think there's some foreign connection. I tried to explain Hayley designs clothes. She doesn't have foreign connections, but they wouldn't listen."

"Can't you just look through Hayley's things?" his father pleaded. "See if the police missed something."

The tone of his father's voice triggered a raw ache in Ryan. He'd miss his father as much as — if not more than — he missed Jessica. "The police won't let me waltz into her place —"

"My place," Meg corrected him. "I own the loft. The detectives who interviewed me said they would be through with it this afternoon. I asked because 1 need to find one of Hayley's dresses for the funeral."

Ryan struggled to hold in a gasp. After a bomb, what could be left? He couldn't imagine a coffin with nothing in it but a dress.

Meg rose and walked with surprising agility across her suite, returning to where they were sitting with a photograph in a sterling silver frame.

"This is my Hayley." Meg's voice cracked. "She's all I have."

Kicking himself for getting into this, Ryan gazed at the girl in the photo as Meg handed it to him. It was a candid headshot obviously taken at the beach. Tousled brown hair shimmering with coppery highlights. Clear hazel eyes blazing with happiness.

Pretty. Healthy. Sexy. The typical California girl.

Except for the arresting smile that hit

Ryan like a sucker punch to his gut. She had a mysterious glint in her eyes that made him wonder just what she was thinking. Something told him that there was nothing "typical" about Hayley.

He studied the photograph more closely. Those full pouty lips. Did they taste as good as they looked? And that skin the color of honey. Would it be silky smooth to the touch? His pulse kicked up a notch.

Annoyed at the direction his thoughts had taken, Ryan realized he felt some sort of connection with this woman, which was totally unexpected. Since Jessica's death, not one brain wave had focused on sex for over a year. Why now?

"All right," he said, feeling like a cat who'd just horked up a hairball. "I'll check her place. I'll also make a few phone calls and see what I can find out."

This was like dancing on eggs. He didn't want to give them false hope that he could personally solve this. "It may be hard to tell much at her place. I'm sure the task force has removed a lot of evidence."

"Thank you, son," his father said in a low-pitched voice that couldn't hide his emotion.

"Bless you," Meg added. "Bless you."

Doing this small favor that meant so much

to his father wasn't a big deal, he assured himself. Still, he had the disturbing feeling that he shouldn't be doing this. His sixth sense kicked in, telling him that Hayley Fordham was nothing but trouble.

CHAPTER THREE

"Whatdaya think?" Ed Phillips asked Ryan.

"Too soon to tell, but so far I'm not finding much."

Ryan had arrived at Hayley Fordham's loft to discover the authorities were still there. He wasn't surprised. He'd thought releasing the crime scene as early as Meg indicated was unlikely. His bad luck had not run out when he'd agreed to help Meg. The first person he saw when he walked up was Phillips.

The special agent worked with Ryan in the L.A. office. Phillips was a senior criminal intelligence analyst while Ryan was in cyber crimes, but they knew each other from previous cases. Phillips had been sent to represent the FBI on the Joint Terrorism Task Force that Ryan had predicted would investigate this case. A car bombing so close to an airport was a huge red flag for a terrorist act.

Phillips had immediately enlisted Ryan to check Hayley Fordham's computer and introduced him to the local detectives investigating the murder. He also spoke to the ATF guys, who were still called ATFers even though their official title was now Alcohol, Tobacco, Firearms and Explosives.

"This is the computer guru who cracked the Rosier case," Phillips announced to the team gathered in the makeshift command post set up in the ground-floor garage of Hayley Fordham's loft. This introduction wowed the group. The Rosier case had been a fraud scam that made headlines early last year. The information that hung Carleton Rosier had been encrypted and buried on his corporation's computers. Ryan had figured out how the con artist had created two sets of books on his computers.

"What have they got?" Ryan asked as he kept punching keys and concentrating on Hayley's twenty-one inch screen. Phillips was standing behind him, watching. This was annoying but Ryan didn't say anything because he needed to find out as much as he could about Hayley.

"Nothin' unless ATF finds out something."

ATF bomb experts spent so much time training that even though the FBI had their own team, they took a backseat to ATF. They would be looking for bomb-making equipment, although Ryan thought it was unlikely that Hayley made the bomb that killed her. Yet stranger things had happened. The bomb could have been intended for someone else and she'd accidentally detonated it.

"Nothing like this case on VICAP," Ryan said, referring to the Violent Crimes Apprehension Program that maintained a massive database on crimes at their headquarters in Quantico.

Phillips shook his head. "Whoo-ee, this is one for the books. We get two, maybe three car bombings a year, most of them along the border. Mexican cartels have a buncha' crazy muthafuckers who rig bombs."

Phillips had grown up in Alabama and his roots could be heard when he talked and in the expressions he used, which was unusual at the Bureau. They encouraged the neutral cadence of newscasters. Accent aside, Phillips was one of the sharpest guys Ryan had encountered at the FBI.

"Could Hayley Fordham have been involved with drugs? Should I be looking for something like that on her computer?"

Phillips shrugged. "I doubt it, but *shee-it.* Who knows?"

"Are we sure that it was Hayley who was killed?"

"Ninety-nine percent sure. She used her credit card just minutes before her dad-gummed car blew sky high. The license plate flew off or we wouldn't have been able to ID the car. No body parts. She was vaporized."

Ryan imagined the dress that Meg was coming to pick out tomorrow. Evidently, the poor woman had no idea her niece's body was dust. "What about the security cameras? What do they show?"

"The camera at the entrance nearest the car was on the fritz but the ones in the restaurant clearly show the woman Trent Fordham identified as his half-sister, Hayley. She had drinks with an unidentified female friend, then got in her car and yow-zer. That's all she wrote."

"What does the friend say?"

Phillips quirked one dark eyebrow. "The brother didn't recognize the woman and the locals haven't tracked her down yet." He sounded as if he didn't have much confidence in the police.

Ryan stared at the computer screen as he tapped a few keys. His mind was on the intriguing face in the photograph. Hayley was something else, and according to her aunt, talented and smart. Who would want her dead?

They were on the loft's third floor, which Hayley used as an office/studio. The small desk with her computer was a fire hazard of notes and sketches. There was a work table with some fabric laid out. Two empty easels faced the twelve-foot floor-to-ceiling windows that provided natural light during the day. Racks of oil tubes and brushes were on the wall next to pegs for oilcloth to cover artwork and paint-splattered smocks. Several completed oils were stacked against the far wall.

Ryan again thought about what Meg had told him about her niece. Hayley was the clothing designer for Surf's Up, the family company. Except for the fabric on the table, this place looked more like an artist's studio. But hey, what did he know?

Hayley did have a CADCAM with a clothing design program loaded on her computer. There were lots of designs in the archives; some of them were downright weird. He didn't see much else but he hadn't checked her e-mails or looked for trapdoors.

"We're cutting out," the ATFers told them.

"Any sign of explosives around here?" Ryan asked over his shoulder. "Or drugs?"

"Nothing except a half-full bottle of prescription sleeping pills."

"I think the guys from the office and the police are ready to pull out, too," Phillips told him. "You almost finished?"

He was, but Ryan wanted time alone to look around the place. "Nah. I'll be awhile. Go on. See if you can get me cleared to stay."

"No problem. I already called the office and had you put on the case." He patted Ryan's shoulder. "Guess your vacation is over until you check out this computer. Catch ya later."

Detective Wells, the lead detective with the Costa Mesa police, came up, asking, "Anything?"

"I'm still checking. It'll take me a few hours."

Wells paused a second, then said, "I understand you're a friend of the family."

Ryan wasn't sure where or how he'd obtained this information. "Not the family exactly. My father is close with Meg Amboy, who is Hayley's aunt."

"We interviewed her."

Ryan turned away from the computer to ask, "You personally or one of your men?"

Wells, a dapper-looking older man with silver hair and intelligent blue eyes shrugged. "I sent one of the guys. Didn't seem likely that she'd know much."

"She's a pretty sharp gal. Made a fortune on her own."

"What's she saying in private?"

"She believes it might be a member of the family. They own a local surf store that sells their clothing nationwide. It was started by the father who was killed late last year in a plane crash." He thought Wells knew all this but since the guy hadn't interrupted him, the detective might not have received a report from his men yet. "The three children will inherit the business and other property when the probate is settled. It's a sizable estate."

Wells nodded. "Farah and Trent Fordham have alibis, although it is possible they hired someone. Bomb-making instructions are easily found on the Internet but not many people are willing to risk making one."

"I'm a computer guy —"

"Yeah," Wells said with a knowing smile, "and you played two years in the NFL until your shoulder was ruined after a questionable tackle."

Ryan nodded; he never mentioned his pro career, but buffs like Wells remembered him. "What I'm trying to say is that I'm not an expert, but bombings are usually revenge crimes. The killer wants to obliterate the person."

"I know. It's a strange one all right." Wells pulled a card out of his jacket pocket. "I've got a man posted downstairs. When you leave, he'll lock up. I want you to call me with a report no matter how late it is."

Ryan checked the e-mail log and it yielded only a few interesting items. Apparently Hayley had some sort of business arrangement with an Ian Barrington. He appeared to be an art dealer. He was expecting several oil paintings for what must be a show. That would account for all the art supplies and easels in the room.

He rummaged through the papers on Hayley's desk, assuming the police had already checked them and removed anything important. He found a CD labeled *The Big 3-0*. He popped it into her computer and watched the family barbeque given for Hayley almost two years ago. Most of the jerky footage was of a laughing, smiling Hayley opening gag gifts. There wasn't any sound on the CD but it wasn't hard to tell what was happening.

At her side was a man that most women would call drop-dead gorgeous. Tall, dark hair, lively blue eyes. For some reason, Ryan experienced a pang of something that he didn't want to call jealousy. Why? He'd never met Hayley or the man, who must be her former fiancé. Wasn't his name Chad Bennett? Meg had said Hayley had dumped him after catching him cheating.

He watched the very sexy Hayley blow out a platoon of candles on a cake with the inscription *Over The Hill.* Yeah, right. Hayley was anything but over the hill. Just at her prime was more like it.

She looked right into the camera and blew a kiss as the CD ended. Ryan sat staring at the screen, half-convinced she'd meant the kiss for him. He must be losing it big-time. He removed the CD and forced his attention back to checking her computer.

Since Phillips had Ryan officially on the case, he logged into the network in his L.A. office and let the special software he'd designed run a check for trapdoors on Hayley's computer and see if anything was hidden. It would take half an hour to thoroughly scrutinize all of her files. That would give him time to look around.

He climbed down the high-tech stainless-steel stairs from the third floor office/studio and master bedroom to the middle level, where the kitchen and living room took up the entire floor. He stood still beside the refrigerator, the strangest sensation coming over him. He felt as if he'd been there before. No, that wasn't it. He felt as if he belonged here somehow. It made no sense.

Get real, he thought, kicking himself. Lofts were just huge open rooms portioned off by walls that weren't attached to the rafters. He'd never been in a loft, but he'd seen them on TV. Still, something there spoke to him.

What? He looked around. Honest to God, he couldn't figure out his strange reaction. The entire place was covered with fingerprint dust, a fine charcoal-colored powder. He grabbed a tissue from a dispenser and covered his fingers to open drawers without leaving prints. Not that the crime techs were coming back, but he was too much of a professional to contaminate a crime scene.

The kitchen drawers revealed little except for a utility drawer that had a stash of notepads and matches from various restaurants. There wasn't a personal telephone book, but he didn't find that unusual. Most people Hayley's age kept that info on their cell phones.

He noticed a dog's water bowl and dish on the floor near the refrigerator. The fine dark powder around it indicated that the dishes had been dusted for prints. The local crime scene techs were thorough, he'd give them that.

Stylized surfboard magnets held several photographs to the refrigerator door. One was of a golden retriever with a red ball in its mouth. Another was of a stunning auburn-haired woman — Hayley — sitting on the beach, hugging the dripping-wet retriever. The third was of a weird-looking dude in a T-shirt with the Grim Reaper on it. Obviously, it was a publicity photo. Scrawled at the bottom were the words *Hayley, you're the bomb.* It was signed *The Wrath.*

The Wrath? The name dinged some distant bell in Ryan's brain. Then it came to him. The Wrath was the Mixed Martial Arts national champion. Ryan had watched a few matches while he'd been home with his shoulder injury. It combined boxing, wrestling, kickboxing, judo and other fighting techniques in a no-holds-barred smackdown fight. The barefoot fighters wore shorts and padded gloves. The only rule that governed their fight was no biting or eye-gouging.

Interesting, Ryan thought. Hayley didn't seem like a woman who'd hook up with an MMA fighter, but what did he know? The way Ryan had responded to her blowing a kiss at the end of the CD still had him on edge. How could he react so strongly to someone he'd never met?

He wandered out of the kitchen and into one of two bedrooms sectioned off from it that opened onto a living room overlooking the bay. It was Hayley's room, he realized the instant he entered. The crime techs had dusted everything and removed the sheets from the bed.

Something swept through him, like an adrenaline rush but stronger. Ryan opened the closet door and a delicate scent came from the clothes hanging in front of him. He inhaled deeply. Vanilla, he decided. The perfume Hayley wore had a trace of vanilla in it.

Lavender was her favorite color, he realized. And she didn't own a suit unless the crime techs had bagged one as evidence, which he doubted. Most of the items hanging in her closet were casual clothes. He checked the dresser drawers, knowing they'd been searched but wanting to get a feel for this woman.

Okay. She loved skimpy thongs and lacy bras — size 34C. Not centerfold material, but Ryan always said anything more than a handful was wasted. Honest to God, what was he thinking?

Ryan slammed the drawer shut and stood

there, furious with himself. He caught his reflection in the full-length mirror on the opposite wall. He hardly recognized the image. In his mind's eye, he always saw himself the way he'd looked in his wedding picture, taken just before the season that ended his career.

Time and Jessica's illness had changed him. Even though he was just thirty-five, Ryan thought he looked older. It was because he was thinner than he'd ever been and his face seemed gaunt. Black stubble shadowed the square line of his jaw, making him look more serious than he felt. He tried to smile, the way he once had so easily, but it was just a grimace.

A tragedy, sure, he told himself. *You're still alive. You'll get past this eventually.* He didn't want to get over Jessica. But another part of him must feel the need to move forward with his life. That's why he was reacting so strongly to Hayley.

He forced himself to look through the books and mementos that must once have been artfully arranged on a bookshelf. They were askew now and covered with fingerprint powder. More photos of the dog and Hayley's family.

He flipped open his cell phone and dialed Meg's number. It was late, but Hayley's aunt had assured him that she wouldn't be sleeping and to call with any questions.

"What did you find?" Meg asked the instant he identified himself.

"Not much." This was the truth; he didn't want to get Meg's hopes up. "The police have taken a lot of evidence. They might discover something. I do have a couple of questions. Where's Hayley's dog?"

Two long beats of silence. "With her, I'm sure. She took Andy everywhere. The police said Hayley parked at the back of the lot under the trees. I know it was dark, but it was early evening and still warm. It would have been cooler under the trees. She probably left him in the car while she went inside."

Aw, hell. Just what he didn't want to think about. The dog that Hayley had obviously loved so much — pulverized.

"What was her relationship with Ian Barrington?" he asked to steer their thoughts away from death. "She has several e-mails from him."

"Hayley knew him from design school in San Francisco. I guess they remained friends when she moved home."

Interesting, Ryan thought. The e-mails he'd read clearly indicated a business relationship. Obviously, Hayley hadn't told her

65

aunt everything. What else had she kept from her?

"Did she mention a guy called The Wrath?"

This brought the suggestion of a chuckle from Meg. "Of course, the man who fights in a cage."

True, he thought. MMA fights were held in chain-link enclosures called cages. There was no escape until one man won — and the other lay bloodied on the mat.

"They have clothing sponsors just like other sports figures," Meg told him. "Hayley created a line sold at Surf's Up that The Wrath wears. You know, she had a better head for business than Trent. She knew Tap-something — the designers with the bats on their clothes —"

"TapouT." The only way to end an MMA fight short of getting knocked out was to physically tap on your opponent or the mat to signal you gave up. TapouT clothes had stylized bats on them. The T-shirts were so popular that even Ryan recognized them.

"That's it! Hayley figured the surf craze has peaked. MMA clothes will be the next big thing. Her line has really done well so far."

MMA the next big thing? Who knew? "Did she have a personal relationship with this Wrath guy?"

"N-not really," Meg replied a bit hesitantly. "They're just friends."

He'd asked about current boyfriends and Meg had told him that Hayley hadn't been dating anyone special since her breakup with the sleazy lawyer who cheated on her. There was no evidence around the loft that a man spent time here.

"She hasn't been dating. She hadn't quite gotten over Chad's betrayal."

Ryan thanked Meg and hung up. He sat down on Hayley's stripped bed, thinking. What kind of a man could cheat on a woman like Hayley?

He lay back on the bed and stared up at the loft's industrial-style rafters, imagining himself there with Hayley. He was drawn to her in a way he couldn't explain and it bothered him.

CHAPTER FOUR

Midafternoon two days later, Ryan was standing under the rotunda near the valet-parking stand at the Balboa Bay Club with Ed Phillips. They had just been to Hayley's standing-room-only memorial service at All Saints Church. He was waiting for his father to arrive with Meg in one of the limousines for the reception while Ed spoke on his cell phone to a bomb expert in Quantico.

Phillips clicked off his cell and tucked it into his pocket. "They have a preliminary report from analyzing the bomb debris."

Ryan braced himself to hear about body parts. At the service, there had been a huge photograph of Hayley. Her head had been thrown back slightly as if she were on the verge of a laugh. It had been an even more provocative photo than the one Meg had first shown him. Hayley's haunting eyes followed Ryan no matter where he moved in the church.

"The explosive device was attached with a magnet and a wire to her car's electrical system. It left a two-foot-deep crater under the car and flash melting on metal three cars away. The instant she turned the ignition, the bomb detonated."

"How do they know that?" Ryan asked. He hadn't received any training in bomb-making and none in detection.

"They use infrared spectrography to analyze bomb fragments. The type of device used shows the window of time necessary to place the bomb and where it was located. It was installed after she parked. It didn't take long to attach it but the killer must have crawled at least partway under the car."

"And risk being seen? What about the dog in the backseat? Didn't he bark and put up a ruckus?"

Phillips shrugged. "Maybe. The locals are interviewing people to see if anyone saw anything. So far — nothing. But it does establish the time frame when the killer planted the device."

"*Anything* left of the body?" Ryan hated to ask. When Meg had discovered there was nothing to bury, she'd arranged a memorial service. The elderly woman was devastated and he couldn't blame her. He'd gone through a tough time when he'd buried Jes-

69

sica, but at least he knew where she was.

"Nosiree. Nada. Bits of bone, a few hairs — most were canine. That's all they recovered. The rest was vaporized."

The thought of that beautiful young woman exploding into nothing more than a fine mist depressed Ryan even more. He thought of the CD he'd seen of Hayley's birthday party. She'd been so happy, so alive. So attractive. Suddenly he felt guilty, as if he'd betrayed Jessica in some unspoken way by admiring — and thinking about — another woman.

"Here's what I need you to do," Phillips told him. "Go in there without me. Talk to folks. They oughta tell you more 'cuz you know the family. Know what I mean?"

Ryan nodded; he'd been introduced to the family on the steps before the service. He didn't have a feel for any of them except Meg Amboy. But his connection with her did give Ryan an excuse for being present and he could ask questions without alarming anyone. He'd had the initial FBI training in interrogation but he hadn't really practiced it except for a short time in the field office.

"Check the whole shebang but watch for passion. The Behavioral Analysis Unit profiler who worked on this bets it was a crime of passion."

"Could be the ex-fiancé, Chad Bennett. I haven't met him yet, but I understand he was really pissed off when Hayley gave him back his engagement ring. Meg says he's been trying to get back together with her."

"Anythang's possible," Phillips replied, his twang more noticeable than usual. "Wells, who heads up the locals, thinks it might be related to the family business. Seems the father who died last year was dead set against importing cheap surf- and skate-boards from China the way most of the major companies do. As soon as he was gone, Trent took over the business. The son ordered a container full of boards from Asia. Drugs could have come in with them. Wouldn't be the first time."

"Why would that translate to a bomb that killed their designer?" Ryan asked, but something tripped an internal alarm. Alison, Hayley's mother and Meg's sister, had been the lead designer until the plane crash. Two designers dead.

"Jeez-a-ree, who knows?"

"Are they sure the plane crash was an accident?"

Phillips' dark eyes narrowed as he studied Ryan for a moment. "Where are you goin' with this?"

71

Ryan saw three sleek black limos in the valet parking line. His father would be here soon. "Just wondering. Both designers for Surf's Up get killed? How important are the designers? I could nose around."

"G'wan. Trust your gut instinct." Phillips walked away.

Phillips was a bit of a maverick, Ryan decided. He liked working with him. He dodged the chain of command and avoided paperwork wherever possible. Ryan had forwarded his report — nothing interesting on Hayley's computer — to the L.A. office, the task force and Detective Wells. Ryan was officially off the clock and on his own now. He still had three weeks of vacation before he had to report back to the office. No one except Phillips knew he was investigating this case as a favor to Meg Amboy.

He would find himself in deep shit if his boss found out, but Ryan didn't give a rat's ass. He wasn't sure he wanted to stay with the Bureau. He'd been drifting along, half-heartedly doing his job since Jessica's death. A contact had offered him a job with a private security firm specializing in computer security for corporations. It was right here in Newport Beach; he wouldn't have to slog his way through traffic from L.A. He could see his father every day.

If Ryan closed his eyes, he could see an image forever imprinted on his brain. Conrad Hollister watching with unconcealed pride from the stands at Ryan's football games. His father hadn't missed one game from junior high through a two-year stint in the pros.

His father was going downhill — even though he'd never admit it. Ryan wondered how long his father would live. He had to prepare himself for the worst and see him as often as possible.

An hour later, Ryan was roaming the second floor members-only dining room where the reception was being held. Someone had transferred the photograph of Hayley from the church to the reception. Her compelling eyes kept following him as he moved from food station to food station in the packed room. It was his imagination, of course, but those eyes seemed to implore him to find her killer.

He'd brought his father up the elevator in his wheelchair and had him stationed at a table overlooking the bay with Meg at his side. A constant stream of guests kept offering their condolences to Meg and the other members of the family seated at the table.

"Aren't these shrimp to die for?" asked a

female voice at his elbow.

Ryan realized he was at the seafood station where shrimp were being served in shot glasses of cocktail sauce. Had he eaten any? He'd been so intent on looking around the crowd for Hayley's ex-fiancé that he wasn't paying enough attention to what he was doing.

He turned and flashed a smile at Farah Fordham. He'd met the striking brunette at the church and he'd reviewed her background in the jacket Phillips had given him. He'd checked the files on all the other suspects, too. "They're good, all right."

Farah gazed up at him with inquisitive brown eyes that had enough makeup on them to stock a cosmetics counter. "Are you related to Meg?"

He could understand why she asked the question. Meg had quickly introduced him by his first name at the church. "No, I'm just a friend." His instincts told him to play his cards close to the chest.

Farah reached for another shot glass with a shrimp perched on the rim. "Really? Have you known her long?"

"Awhile." Why was she asking? Ryan wondered. Then the light dawned. He knew from talking with Meg that her only sister, Hayley's mother, was dead, and now, with

Hayley gone, Meg didn't have obvious heirs. He also knew from reading her jacket that Farah was overextended financially. Her CPA firm was doing well, but her lifestyle — and her boyfriend — outpaced her income.

"Hey, babe, here you are." A tall man with a surfer's blond hair and tan strode up to them, his smile revealing perfect white teeth. Phillips would have called them "SoCal teeth" because so many people had invested in braces and teeth whiteners. It was the land of beautiful people with perfect teeth.

"Kyle, this is Ryan . . ." Farah waited for him to supply his last name.

Ryan extended his hand. "Ryan Hollister."

Kyle shook his hand with a firm grip. "Kyle Wilfert."

"You're Conrad's son," Farah said.

Ryan nodded; he could see the light going out of her eyes. He was right; she was checking out possible heirs. He wondered how close she was to Meg. Did it matter? Maybe it did. Phillips said at this stage of an investigation, everything should be considered.

"I'm in real estate development," volunteered Kyle as he grinned at Farah and slipped his arm around her waist. "Not that there's much going on right now with the lagging economy and all."

He'd skimmed the jacket on Kyle and he recalled the file said the boyfriend had declared bankruptcy and moved in with Farah earlier this year. The guy didn't have a pot to piss in — not that you'd know it from his surfer-dude smile.

"What do you do?" Farah asked.

"Computers."

"Oh," Farah said, totally uninterested.

A tall man with broad shoulders and thick brown hair walked up, saying, "I'm so sorry to hear about Hayley. What a tragedy."

Ryan eyed the man who seemed to know Farah and Kyle quite well, but Ryan didn't recognize him from any of the jackets Phillips had given him. The guy didn't sound too sincere, but then neither did Farah or Kyle. During the service the only ones who'd cried were Courtney Fordham and Meg.

"I'm Laird McMasters." The man introduced himself to Ryan with a firm handshake. "I own Rip Tide."

Ryan nodded, recognizing another surf/skate company. It also had a line of clothing that competed with Surf's Up.

"Laird offered to buy Surf's Up," Farah informed him, "but Hayley wouldn't hear of it."

"Really?" Ryan immediately put Laird on his list of people to investigate.

"Now's not the time to talk about it," Laird said. He set his glass on the table nearby. "I'm sorry about Hayley, but I have to leave. I've got a meeting."

"We couldn't sell the company now even if we wanted to," Farah explained even though Ryan hadn't asked. "It has to come out of probate."

"Should be soon," Kyle said.

"Excuse me," Ryan said. "I see someone I need to talk to." He turned away and edged his way through the crowd to where The Wrath was standing alone, sipping a bottle of water with a black image of a hooded Grim Reaper on it and studying the mesmerizing photo of Hayley.

"It's a damn shame, isn't it?" Ryan asked. "A waste."

"Fuckin' A," The Wrath said without looking at him. "Hayley was totally rad."

"Did you know her well?"

The Wrath turned to face him. The guy was tall and impressively built. He must spend most of each day in the gym. His hair was probably light brown like his eyes but it was slicked upward like a rooster's comb and appeared black. Cantilevered eyebrows like caterpillars almost concealed his eyes.

77

"Yeah, we were friends. She was smart —
a lot smarter than the rest of them." The
Wrath looked toward the table where Trent
and his wife, Courtney, were now talking
with an older woman with more wrinkles
than a Shar Pei.

"I understand you went to Surf's Up for
sponsorship and Hayley wanted to back you
while her brother didn't."

The Wrath trained his gaze on Ryan with
obvious suspicion. "Damn straight. Trent
can't see beyond board sports. Surfing or
skating. But Hayley could. Trent's singing a
different tune now that the MMA line
Hayley created for me is raking in the
dough."

"MMA is on the rise. Their products are
hot." He'd read a bit more online about
Mixed Martial Arts since he found The
Wrath's picture on Hayley's refrigerator.

"Who the fuck are you?" The Wrath asked.
His belligerent tone suggested the guy had
testosterone poisoning, but Ryan had played
football long enough not to be intimidated.

"I'm Ryan Hollister. My father's sitting
next to Hayley's aunt —"

"I know Meg." He pointed to the T-shirt
he was wearing under a lightweight black
blazer. It was a stylized Grim Reaper that
Ryan recognized from Hayley's computer

designs. The slogan beneath the macabre face said: *Kick Fear — Believe.* "Hayley's aunt added the 'believe' to my motto — Kick Fear."

"Great idea," Ryan said, and he meant it, although he would never have suspected Meg would come up with a tag word that gave such punch to a design. "Do you have any idea who would want Hayley dead?" Ryan wasn't sure why he'd asked; he certainly hadn't established any rapport with the fighter. It was just a hunch that this man hadn't been involved and could know something.

"Haven't got a clue. But there's something going on with that family. Ask Courtney. She's always high. She might tell you something." The Wrath set down his empty bottle of water that Ryan now realized was The Wrath's own brand when he saw the slogan written in bold black letters beneath the Grim Reaper.

"I'm outta here." He handed Ryan a business card with the same logo on it. "I'm in the cage next week at the Hard Rock Hotel in Vegas. Wanna see me fight, give me a buzz and I'll have ringside tickets at Will Call for you."

Ryan took The Wrath's advice and hung around to see if he could catch Courtney alone, or if Chad Bennett would put in an appearance. He hadn't come to the service. Strange. Meg had told him that Chad still did legal work for the company and was a good friend of Trent's despite the broken engagement.

Finally Courtney left the table, apparently headed for the ladies room, and Ryan intercepted her in the hall. "Excuse me," he said as he walked up beside her. "Are the restrooms this way?"

"Yes. Just down the corridor." Her voice was pitched so low that it was barely above a whisper. The Wrath was dead-on. Courtney's blue eyes were just thin hoops of color around dilated pupils. She was on something, all right.

"I'm Ryan —"

"Conrad's son," she responded. "You fix computers. I met you just before the service."

"Right." He'd instructed Meg and his father to say he was in computers so no one would realize that he was with the FBI. He'd hoped to get more information that way but so far, zilch. "I understand you were good friends with Hayley."

"Yes. We're creative spirits in a family of . . . of . . ."

"Business types," he supplied when she

80

seemed to be drifting.

"Exactly." Courtney paused outside the entrance to the ladies' room. "I'll miss her terribly."

He leaned closer and lowered his voice. "Who do you think killed her?"

Courtney's enlarged pupils welled with unshed tears. "I can't imagine . . ."

She walked into the restroom. Something lingered in the nerve endings of Ryan's skin. His sixth sense told him Courtney knew more than she was saying. Or was it just his imagination? He could be wrong. Anyway, why would Courtney Fordham tell him — a total stranger — anything?

Ryan wandered back into the reception, hoping his father and Meg were ready to leave. He immediately spotted Chad Bennett in a corner talking to Trent. From the looks of it, their discussion was very serious. Ryan went to get another steak on the stick from the beef station and watched the men out of the corner of his eye.

In two gulps, Bennett knocked back a martini with a parade of olives on a pick as he listened to whatever Trent was saying so intently. He munched on the olives.

Bennett was just above average in height but he had an easy smile and long-lashed blue eyes. The man signaled a passing waiter

81

for another martini and Ryan wondered if the attorney had a drinking problem — or was he drowning his sorrow? He was listening to Trent but Bennett's eyes kept straying to the huge photograph of Hayley.

Ryan waited and Trent finally left Bennett when Courtney came teetering into the room. Obviously, she'd done more in the restroom than use the facilities, Ryan decided. The Wrath had been right. Courtney had a problem.

Bennett wandered over to the photograph and Ryan joined him, sipping a glass of sparkling water. Bennett had a fresh martini with another skewer of olives in it. Obviously, the guy thought this was the veggie course.

"Damn shame, isn't it?" Ryan knew he was repeating what he'd said to The Wrath, but he couldn't come up with anything better.

"Got that right," Bennett replied, facing him.

Another set of dilated pupils. *Welcome to the real word, dude,* Ryan told himself. Playgrounds of the rich were havens for drugs and alcohol. *Look on the upside.* Maybe he'd get more out of Bennett like this than he would if the attorney were sober.

"You're Hollister's kid, right?" Bennett didn't slur his words or act inebriated. "I sat next to your father at Thanksgiving two years ago. He told me all about your football career. Your job with the FBI. Computers, isn't it?"

"That's right. I wish I'd known Hayley." He was surprised at how true this was, even though he was merely trying to change the subject. He hadn't been able to get Hayley out of his mind since Meg had first shown him the photo.

"You know Meg Amboy. She's an older version of Hayley. Sharp. Unforgiving." The last word wobbled just a bit as he said it.

"I understand you were engaged to Hayley."

Bennett kicked back the last of his martini and sucked on the olives for a moment before, saying, "Until I fucked up. Then it was over with a capital O. Hayley is just like Meg. Never forgive. Never forget."

Ryan nodded slowly. "Who would kill her so brutally?"

"You've got me." Bennett shrugged and a cord seemed to be pulsing unsteadily in his neck.

The next evening it poured, which was unusual for Southern California in May,

Ryan told himself as he stood in Hayley's loft looking at the rain pounding the dark water in the bay. He'd promised Meg that he would pack up Hayley's personal things. Tomorrow movers would remove the rest of her belongings so Meg could sell the loft.

A flash of jagged-white lightning seared the darkness and a few seconds later a deafening clap of thunder shook the loft. The lights at the Blue Water Grill across the small inlet where the loft was located suddenly went dark. The single lamp Ryan had turned on beside Hayley's computer went out, too.

"Great," he muttered. A power failure. With this storm no telling how soon Edison would fix it. This would make his job harder and it would take longer. Hadn't there been a flashlight downstairs in one of the kitchen drawers? He slowly made his way to the staircase to go to the lower level where the kitchen was located. The freestanding staircase was an accident waiting to happen. A fall could land him flat on his back on the first floor where the tiled entrance and garage was located. It was three floors down — a neck-breaker if there ever was one.

He slowly felt his way down the stainless steel staircase. A noise from below, like metallic creaking, made him stop. What was that? It was hard to tell with the wind-driven rain beating on the bank of windows facing the bay. Probably homesteading rats, he thought. The Cannery, a trendy restaurant, was just a few doors down. A rat magnet for sure, he decided as he continued down the stairs again.

Vaguely uneasy for some reason, he reached the kitchen and felt his way across the granite counter. Beneath his hand traces of the fingerprint dust collected. He reached the bank of drawers near the refrigerator. That's where he thought he remembered seeing a flashlight. He pulled open a drawer and fumbled through the contents. Wrong drawer. He was reaching for the handle on the next, when he heard the creaking noise again.

His attention was drawn from where he was standing to the living area across from the kitchen. He detected movement — a darker silhouette in a pitch-dark room. Shapes were discernible only by varying degrees of darkness.

A form or a trick of the shadows? He squinted hard, concentrating on the far side of the loft. Something *was* there. A man. The killer? Had he returned to remove incriminating evidence or was this a burglary? Often thieves broke into homes of the deceased because they knew they were vacant.

A flicker of lightning in the distance — almost non-existent — faintly illuminated the room for a fraction of a second. The man was short, Ryan saw that much, and he had a weapon in his hand. Ryan thought of opening a drawer and extracting one of the knives he remembered but he didn't want the man to turn and shoot.

He flattened himself against the refrigerator, thankful the intruder hadn't spotted him. From his brief glance, Ryan knew the man wore a trench coat with the hood up. The gun he carried must have at least six shots. Ryan would need to take the intruder by surprise to stand a chance.

This was when years of playing football would pay off. He could sprint across the room and hit the guy with a flying tackle before the jerk could turn around and fire the weapon. In a split second, Ryan exploded into the room and clobbered the man full-force. The air blasted from the prick's lungs in a loud whooshing grunt as their bodies collided.

They both hit the tile floor, a jumble of limbs with Ryan on top. A sharp, bone-deep pain shot through his injured shoulder into his chest, but he ignored it. The weapon the intruder carried bounced across the floor with a thunk.

The little guy was a fighter. He arched his back, twisting and bucking with surprising strength. The gutsy prick swung one leg out and around, attempting what must be some weird move — probably jujitsu or something like it. Ryan immediately thought of The Wrath. Could this be one of his henchmen?

The man was too small to pull off the maneuver and Ryan easily straddled him with his larger frame and pinned him down, but the intruder kept writhing beneath him. Ryan rolled the squirming idiot onto his side. He grabbed for one of the man's arms, determined to pull it behind his back and force the guy to his feet. He fumbled with the raincoat for a second, trying to capture a thrashing arm. He encountered a soft fullness and a fragrant hint of a scent that stunned him. Common sense said to double-check. He ran his hands over the soft mounds. No doubt about it.

A woman.

Couldn't be!

But it was. Holy shit! She moaned and gasped for breath. Women were every bit as dangerous as men, Ryan reminded himself. This one had arrived armed. And tried a martial arts maneuver.

She thrashed and kicked, trying to escape, but he had her trapped by his large body. The more she squirmed, the softer she felt beneath him. She cut loose with a screeching cry that could be heard in Japan. She kept screaming at the top of her lungs even though no one could hear her over the roar of the storm.

"Stop it!" He lifted his body and flipped her onto her back. He had a vague impression of a pale face and light-colored eyes. She yanked at his hair, pulling it with astonishing strength. "Cut it out or I'll have to hurt you."

He grabbed her throat, planning to scare her a little. She responded by biting hard on his hand. "I'm warning you —"

"P-please . . . don't hurt me," she cried. "Take whatever you want. Just don't rape me."

"Rape you?" He stood up, hoisted her upright without letting go. "I won't hurt you if you hold still while I call the cops."

"*You're* calling the police?" she yelled at him, but she sounded scared spitless.

He hauled her with him toward the kitchen's wall phone. "You bet I'm calling them. You were trying to rob the place."

"I wasn't robbing —"

"What about the weapon in your hand?

You broke in armed with a gun."

"Gun? I just had my collapsible umbrella, you jerk! Who are you? What are you doing in my loft?"

Ryan stopped dead in his tracks, holding her close. He was afraid of the answer, but he asked anyway. "Who the hell are you?"

"I'm Hayley Fordham. This is —"

She said something about this being her loft and she was calling the police to report him. Ryan reached for the drawer with the flashlight and pulled it out, still not letting go of the intruder. He turned it on and trained the light on her face.

The brown hair highlighted by copper strands that he'd dreamed about running his hands through hung in damp hanks around her pretty face. The gray eyes that had fascinated him were wild with terror and almost green in this light. The full lips that he'd imagined kissing were trembling.

The girl of his dreams — back from the dead.

CHAPTER FIVE

Panic coursed through Hayley. Her breathing was erratic and she was trembling uncontrollably, fear a high-pitched scream in her veins. This monster intended to kill her. She couldn't see him. The man was nothing more than a looming form and that was going to be the last thing she saw before she died.

The jujitsu kick The Wrath had taught her hadn't worked. This man was too tall, his body too muscular for her to fight off. Her pulse ricocheted against her temples. If she didn't do something, he would grab one of the kitchen knives and slit her throat.

"Let me go," she pleaded, although she doubted it would do much good. Dread and defeat permeated her body and settled in her bones.

In response, he swung her around, his powerful arm just below her breasts. He manacled both her wrists in one fist, his fingers like steel bands. She was trapped by his muscular frame, his height. Even through her raincoat she felt the heat of his menacing body.

He grabbed something out of one of her kitchen drawers. She struggled to wrench herself free by biting him again, but couldn't move. Out of nowhere, a blast of light blinded her and she squeezed her eyes shut — expecting to die in the next second.

"Who the hell are you?" he unexpectedly asked.

She opened her eyes, not able to distinguish anything but the blaring light and spit out, "I'm Hayley Fordham. Who are you? What are you doing in my house?"

His grip relaxed but he didn't let her go. "I'm Ryan Hollister. Your aunt Meg sent me to get your things."

"You're lying! Why would Aunt Meg want my . . ." As she spoke, his name registered. "You're Conrad's son?"

"That's right."

She tried to get a better look at him, not knowing what to think. Her throat was so tight that she could hardly swallow, and her breath came in ragged surges. The strange acrid scent she'd noticed when she'd first come into the loft seemed stronger now.

"I think we'd better sit down," he said,

absolutely calm. "I'll explain what's happening."

"I don't need to sit to hear this." She twisted out of the arm he had around her, but they were still standing nose to nose. The acrid scent wasn't coming from this nutcase. Evidently, he wore a woodsy aftershave. "This better be good."

He'd lowered the flashlight to waist height. In the low beam, she saw he was tall and dark and utterly menacing. His brown hair was damp from the rain. His polo shirt revealed impressive shoulders and a wide chest that narrowed at the waist. A quick glance down told her that he had an athlete's powerful legs. Hadn't Conrad bragged that his son had played pro ball?

She sucked in a steadying breath. He could snap her neck with just one hand. What was he doing here? Just because he claimed to be Conrad's son didn't mean he was telling the truth. She didn't dare trust him.

Abruptly, he pulled out his wallet and flipped it open. He directed the flashlight on a badge that read: Department of Justice. "I'm with the FBI. I'm not going to hurt you."

"What are you doing here?" she managed to ask as she took in the shield and the name Ryan W. Hollister, Special Agent.

"Your BMW was blown to hell by a car bomb. Everyone assumed you were in it. Meg, your family, the police — they all think you're dead. They've had a memorial service, the whole works. Your aunt is too upset to remove your personal effects so she asked me to do it."

It took a second for his words to register. Images of car bombings she'd seen on television burst in her brain. It *could not* be true. "You're making this up. I'm calling the police." She lunged for the wall phone but he blocked her with his powerful body.

"Wait. You have some explaining to do."

"Me? You're certifiable! I haven't done —"

"Where have you been for the last ten days? Didn't you hear about the car bomb?"

Another scathing retort was on her lips but it vanished as she realized he was dead serious. Shock seeped from every pore, spreading through her body with a mind numbing punch. "Car bomb? My car?"

"Didn't you park your car at the back of Gulliver's lot under the trees last Tuesday?"

"Oh, my God!"

Ryan gently guided her into the living room. He eased her down onto the sofa and set the flashlight on the glass coffee table.

The amber light barely illuminated the dark area.

"I've been in Costa Rica doing a huge wall mural in Ramon Estevez's new resort. I lent my car to my friend, Lindsey Fulton." Hayley could barely choke out her next question. "Where is Lindsey?"

Two beats of utter silence from Ryan Hollister. The rain drummed on the glass windows like a flock of pecking birds, but he didn't say anything for a long time. He didn't have to; she knew.

"Apparently she died when she turned the key in the ignition."

Hayley felt as if her breath had been choked off. Holding raw emotion in check, she assured herself this could not be true. But Ryan's troubled expression told her something terrible *had* happened to her friend. "No, please! It's not fair! She had so much talent, so much to live for."

"Everyone assumed it was you. No one knew you were out of town. Why not?"

A paralyzing numbness spread out from her chest. If she closed her eyes, Hayley could see Lindsey. She envisioned the way her friend's eyes would narrow as she stood back and studied a painting. The anxious habit she had of checking her cell phone for messages from her husband. Her toothy, endearing smile.

It took a minute before Hayley could muster a response. "I had a couple of reasons. First, my parents were killed in a small plane crash. I flew down to Costa Rica in Ramon Estevez's jet. I didn't want Aunt Meg to worry about the plane crashing so I made up a story to cover my absence. Second, I didn't want Trent to know that I'm planning a career switch. I've always wanted to be an artist, not a designer."

"Didn't you hear about the car bombing?"

Hayley shook her head. "No. I painted almost nonstop. I didn't watch TV once. I wanted to finish as soon as I could and get back before anyone realized I was gone."

"Okay, but I don't understand how airport security didn't have you on a flight log. There's a whole task force working on this. I'm sure they checked the airport."

"We left from the private Million Air terminal. The limo was late picking me up at the restaurant. I had to run for the plane. No one looked at my passport until I arrived in Costa Rica."

Ryan shook his head, clearly disturbed. "It's lapses like this that leave the country vulnerable."

She barely heard him explaining about security cameras with shots of her and the bar receipt. All she could see was the look of hope in Lindsey's eyes as they had talked about her future.

"Do you know anyone who would have wanted to kill your friend?" he asked.

"Lindsey's husband. He beat her up several times — that I know about. He'd threatened to kill her if she left him."

"She was the woman in the bar with you?"

"Yes. Lindsey lives — lived — in San Francisco but we met at Gulliver's because it was so close to the airport. I was leaving as she was arriving. I told Lindsey that she could stay at my place and use my car while I was gone. When I returned, we planned to figure out what to do next."

"We'd better call the police and let them know. They believe the car bombing has something to do with your family business and drugs. They don't know it was a domestic dispute."

She put a hand on his forearm as he rose and was surprised at its firmness. He tensed powerful muscles beneath her fingers. "Wait. There's no way Steve Fulton could have known where Lindsey was. She took an express shuttle to San Jose then flew from there. That was my idea in case her husband checked the flight rosters out of the bay area."

A puzzled expression appeared on Ryan's face. In that instant she realized how much he did look like his father. They had the same inquisitive blue eyes and angular features. He really wasn't scary looking. He'd just taken her by surprise.

"You can't imagine how closely Steve watched Lindsey. She tried to leave him once before but he found out and beat the hell out of her. It kept getting worse and worse. The last time I saw her, which was a month ago, we sewed one hundred dollar bills I brought into the lining of her jacket. That way she'd have money to get away."

"Why didn't she go to the police?"

Hayley shook her head. "I know it's crazy but Lindsey felt she owed Steve big-time. You see, she'd been hooked on drugs, living on Haight Ashbury's streets when she met Steve. He helped her get clean, paid for her art lessons, then married her. She believed he loved her but was just too obsessive. She didn't want to get him into trouble after all he'd done for her."

He leaned closer to her, looking at her intently. "You don't think the husband had the chance to kill her."

"No. How could he? Lindsey left Wednesday afternoon. That's the day her husband, who's an engineer, goes into the office. He

97

works at home the rest of the week. Besides, Lindsey has relatives in Oregon. Last time, he caught her with a plane ticket to Portland. I'm sure that's where he'd look first."

"He didn't know about you?"

"Not really." Hayley explained how careful they'd been since they'd met at Ian's gallery and become friends. "I always called her on Wednesday when Steve was out of the house. She never called me because he checked the phone bills."

"You're right," Ryan said, his voice measured. "How would the husband get explosives through airline security? He would have had to fly to make it here in time to plant the bomb. It wouldn't have been possible — assuming he could smuggle the bomb aboard — unless he had known in advance —"

"He didn't. Lindsey called me, wondering what to do. I came up with the plan on the spot."

Ryan nodded slowly; it was impossible to tell what he was thinking.

"You don't suppose someone was trying to kill me." The first hint of tears broke in her voice as she expressed the unimaginable.

Again, he didn't answer. She knew what he was thinking. "That's absurd! Why would

98

anyone want me dead?"

"Isn't your parents' estate in probate? Wouldn't Trent and Farah receive a lot more money with you gone?"

"They would never —" She caught herself wondering if it could possibly be true. "I'm an important part of the company. Trent relies on me for designs. Farah has her own successful business."

"People have killed for amazingly small amounts of money."

She just didn't believe it. "There isn't that much money at stake. The business is successful in a small way. It supports us nicely but we're not rolling in dough. Since my father didn't have a trust, the state will get a big chunk." She shook her head, saying to herself, "I can't believe Daddy didn't have a trust."

"What about that Laird guy? He offered to buy the business. Wouldn't selling out generate more cash?"

"That's news to me. I didn't know Laird offered to purchase Surf's Up."

"I thought you opposed the sale."

"No way. Surf's Up was my father's dream. I'd like to get out from under it and concentrate on my art." It occurred to her that this man knew an awful lot about her business. "How do you know so much about my family?"

"Your aunt strong-armed me into using my contacts to investigate your death."

A surge of fondness swept through her. Strong-armed. That was Aunt Meg, all right. If Hayley had died, Meg Amboy would have moved heaven and earth to find the killer.

"Can you think of anyone else who would want you dead?" he asked.

"No. Of course not." Hayley thought about the car bomb and her friend. Her relief at having escaped death was blunted by guilt about Lindsey. If Hayley hadn't loaned her the car, Lindsey would still be alive. "I guess there was nothing left of Lindsey's body or the police wouldn't have thought it was me."

"Nothing," Ryan confirmed.

Her breath caught as her heart lurched painfully in her chest. She was frightened but not as much as she should be. This whole thing had a surreal quality to it. Whoever heard of anyone in this country dying in a car bombing? It didn't seem real, but Hayley had no reason to doubt Ryan Hollister. He was an FBI agent and he was far too serious — and convincing — to be putting her on for some weird reason.

"What about your relationship with Chad

Bennett? Was he angry enough to want you dead after you broke the engagement?"

"No. It was his fault. He'd cheated on me. He keeps trying to get back together. I don't think he's given up hope. He wouldn't try to kill me."

"Somebody did."

"Couldn't it have been a mistake?" It had to be, she told herself. Nothing else made sense. A bleakness, a hollow sensation settled over her.

"That's a long shot. Someone had to get under your car to attach the device. They risked being seen. People are usually careful in those circumstances to make certain they have the right vehicle. Plus the killer deliberately dismantled the security camera that records activity in the parking lot."

"I need to call my aunt right away. I —"

"Not yet." The currents in his eyes eddied and she wondered what he was thinking. "Aren't you concerned about your dog?"

"Has something happened to Andy?" Oh, God, she couldn't lose him, too.

"Wasn't he in the car?"

"No. I didn't want to board him. My neighbors volunteered to take him for two weeks to their place on Bass Lake. I knew Andy would love it."

"Good," Ryan responded. She thought he

looked unusually relieved, considering it was her dog.

"You thought Andy was in the car when it exploded?" She closed her eyes, trying to imagine the golden retriever blown to bits. This just kept getting worse and worse. She was having difficulty putting it all together. Weary from a long plane ride, Hayley didn't seem to be able to think as clearly as usual. All this seemed to be a bad dream. Surely she would wake up and things would be the way they'd been when she'd left sunny Costa Rica.

Estevez had offered her a contract to do murals in several of his hotels. That, combined with the art Ian was selling in his gallery, meant she could start her life over — doing what she loved. Now this.

"The lab found canine fur in the debris. What were they supposed to conclude?"

Hayley tried for a laugh, but it sounded more like a witchy cackle. "I haul Andy everywhere with me. Friends call it 'the fur mobile' because it smells like a rolling kennel. The backseat has a dog liner but Andy sheds a lot."

A blue-white bolt of lightning followed by a crack of thunder that rocked the loft made Hayley flinch. She rose and walked over to the bank of windows facing the bay.

With the power out and clouds obscuring the moon, there wasn't much to see, just rain beating a tattoo against the wall of glass. The fresh scent of rain filtered into the loft.

Lindsey dead. Someone might have wanted to kill her. Hayley was having difficulty keeping her mind on track but she did realize her life would never be the same. Hot salty tears welled up in her eyes and ran down her cheeks like the rain against the glass.

Unexpectedly, the lights came on across the cove at the Blue Water Grill. She heard the snick of a lamp as Ryan turned on a light in the loft. She wiped her wet cheeks with the back of her hand, then turned to face Ryan.

Her eyes swept across her loft. Everything had been shoved out of place and the surfaces were covered with a charcoal-colored dust. "Oh, my God! What happened?"

"The Task Force searched your place, dusted for prints." He walked toward her. "Searched for evidence."

If she'd had any lingering doubts about him making this up, they evaporated. The loft had been thoroughly tossed and dusted. Now she realized the acrid smell was the fingerprint powder. She watched Ryan as he strode over to her.

Ryan Hollister was nothing if not sexy. He had an effortless masculinity that must be irresistible to most women. Where had that thought come from — at a time like this? Considering what she was going through, it was unnerving to realize she was attracted to this man. But she couldn't deny the ripple of heat that swept through her body as Ryan halted in front of her. Close. Way too close.

Now that the lights were on, she had a better look at him than just an initial impression. Evidently, the Hollisters had Nordic ancestors. That would account for their height and masculine jawlines. And Viking-blue eyes. His gaze met hers and Hayley suddenly felt light-headed. What was wrong with her?

"Do you understand how serious this is, how much danger you're in?"

"Yes," she whispered. It had been dawning on her by degrees, but seeing the physical state of her loft made it too real. The hollow ache in her chest would not go away. She was in terrible trouble and didn't know what to do about it.

"Let me help you." He looked into her eyes with an intimacy she found disturbing.

"I'm a pro. I have contacts."

The air was fraught with tension and an undercurrent of something she couldn't define. Maybe this situation was too much for her and she was merely imagining things.

"Can't the police —"

"Come on. I have an idea." He took her arm and she was stunned at how reassuring it was to have him touch her. In a situation that seemed so unreal, this man was a lifeline.

They sat on the sofa again. Hayley looked down at her hands and saw they were smudged with the charcoal powder from where she'd touched things as she came into the dark loft. She self-consciously rubbed them on her raincoat. It helped a little.

He was studying her in that disturbing way of his. What was he thinking? His face was utterly expressionless. If he'd been a card shark, she wouldn't have a clue if he held a winning or losing hand.

"Wait a few days before you tell anyone you're alive. Otherwise you're exposed and the killer might try again. There's a really talented FBI agent who's working on your case. See what he and I can find out. The task force might also be able to solve this without putting you in danger."

"I'm not worried," she fibbed. "I'm sure

the police will provide protection of some sort."

"For how long? Not indefinitely. If this isn't solved, you'll be looking over your shoulder until he kills you."

He had a point, and she couldn't deny it. Catching this maniac was essential for her safety. Even if she had protection, how could she live with someone dogging her every move? "All right. I'll stay out of sight here for a few days."

"Not here. Not only is the place a mess, the cleaning lady is coming tomorrow. It'll take a couple of days to clean up this mess."

"I'll call my aunt —"

"No way. I'm the only one who will know you're alive and where you are or you won't be safe." He said this with such conviction that she couldn't argue.

"How will I pay for a hotel? Credit card activity can be traced, can't it?"

"You'll stay at my father's place. No one will think to look for you there."

"Good idea. If someone should be looking for me, I'm sure they'll check friends and the hotel, not your father's home."

He stood up and reached out a strong hand to help her rise. She took it, wondering if she'd made the right decision. She shuddered, fear rising inside her like a rogue wave about to engulf her.

"Let's get the things you *absolutely* need. Nothing more. We don't want to tip off anyone by removing too much."

CHAPTER SIX

Maybe blowing up Hayley's car so close to an airport hadn't been the most brilliant idea. Who knew it would activate the Joint Antiterrorism Task Force, which included the FBI and every other police agency on the planet, including Homeland Security? They were asking endless questions, looking at all kinds of records and poking into things that were absolutely none of their business.

The good news was the arrogant pricks hadn't discovered squat. They were convinced the car bombing was drug related and were currently pulling Surf's Up's records apart, examining every shipment, every business transaction.

The best news was Hayley Fordham no longer walked the earth. A car bombing might have been overkill but it did the trick. She was dust. There hadn't been enough to bury.

The killer wasn't worried that the forensic team would trace the bomb. The small device had been purchased in Mexico well before the killing. It had been tempting to use it immediately, but waiting and anticipating the murder had been more exciting.

If the authorities did ID the bomb, they would blame one of the Mexican cartels because one of their men had sold the bomb. Making contact with the sleazy Mexican had been a fluke. But fate was like that. It played into your hands, if you were intelligent enough to take advantage of the situation.

A smart person went with the flow. A smart person didn't panic at such an intense investigation. A smart person concentrated on what was important.

Hayley Fordham was dead. That had been the goal. Mission accomplished.

The fragrant aroma of coffee awoke Hayley on the morning following her return from Costa Rica. For a few seconds she didn't recognize the room decorated in tan and black where she had slept. A partially open window brought in the rustling of palm trees and the *whump-whump* of waves battering the shore. She instantly remembered where she was.

Her limbs seemed leaden as she tried to get out of bed. It was like waking up in someone else's body. Suddenly, she recalled the car bombing that had killed Lindsey. Her emotions unraveled like an old sweater as she stumbled out of bed and toward the adjacent bathroom.

A weariness so deep it went beyond the physical gripped her. Shell-shocked. Now she understood what that expression meant. Like a distant star, her past seemed faraway, untouchable. She felt adrift, empty.

She clutched the counter and gazed at the disheveled face in the mirror. Dark circles limned her eyes and her hair hung in tangled hanks around a haggard face. She didn't care. Guilt had a stranglehold on her emotions.

Like a serrated blade, despair ripped through her chest. Lindsey was gone. Someone wanted Hayley dead and had killed her dear friend by mistake. She was precariously balanced on the jagged edge between anger and tears.

"Pull yourself together," she told her reflection. "This isn't helping." She had a purpose — find Lindsey's killer. And save yourself.

She relieved herself and walked back into the bedroom. She found the small suitcase with the few things Ryan had permitted her to take from her loft. *Don't let anyone suspect you're alive,* he'd told her. *Take only what you absolutely need.*

She'd allowed him to bring her to his father's home, not knowing Ryan was living there as well. By the time he'd opened the door of the oceanfront house, her body had shut down, succumbing to weariness and anxiety. She'd realized Ryan was staying there, but she'd merely followed his directions and stumbled into the downstairs guest room while he'd gone upstairs to spend the night.

Hayley had crawled into bed in her underwear, surrendering to her body's demand for sleep. Her eyes had closed immediately as she admitted to herself that having Ryan in the same house made her feel safe.

She quickly showered and brushed out her tangled hair. The situation didn't call for makeup, she assured herself, but she brushed a little mascara on her eyelashes. She walked out of the guest quarters toward the kitchen area, now smelling bacon as well as coffee. Her stomach rumbled.

Ryan stood at the counter, his head tilted forward. Seen in profile, his nose and jawline appeared even more chiseled than they had last night. A hairline fracture in her self-

111

composure opened and a knot of pure sensation formed in her chest. Last night had not been a reaction to her grim plight. *Sexy* didn't begin to describe him. Ryan Hollister was an extremely appealing guy.

The faded blue T-shirt he was wearing emphasized shoulders even wider than she'd remembered. Well-washed navy sweatpants hung low on his narrow hips. She was fairly certain he wasn't wearing anything beneath them. He had a great butt — tight, well rounded. At the thought, she felt herself blushing. Why? She rarely blushed.

Mentally she gave herself a hard shake. *You're in terrible trouble. Forget Ryan is a hottie.* She was grateful for his protection. Nothing more.

"How'd you sleep?" he asked without turning.

"I was out the minute my head hit the pillow." She walked into the room and saw he was beating a bowl of eggs with a fork. "I hadn't slept in almost forty-eight hours."

"Good." He turned to greet her with a smile that would have tested a nun's vows. "Coffee's made. I'm working on scrambled eggs. That okay?"

"Sure. I'm starving. I was the only one on the jet. I didn't want to make the flight attendant mess up the galley, so I just had a soda and yogurt." Hayley hoped she sounded nonchalant but she felt incredibly awkward. Staying with a man she hardly knew — a guy too hot for words — made her uncomfortable.

"Fix the toast, will you? I'll cook the eggs." He moved over to the range and poured the eggs into a frying pan.

She watched him out of the corner of her eye as she placed four slices of whole wheat bread in the toaster. He seemed perfectly relaxed. Well, why not? A guy like Ryan probably had women over all the time.

"There are some newspapers on the counter," Ryan told her. "I pulled them out of the recycling bin so you could read about the car bombing yourself."

She moved to the stack of papers and stared at the picture of the charred remains of cars in the parking lot, then scanned the front-page article. Not that she doubted Ryan, but she wanted to see for herself what had happened. As she read, emotion gathered force inside her like a hurricane. So much damage! So many cars destroyed. It was a miracle only one person had died. Lindsey.

Another wave of guilt engulfed Hayley and she had to force herself to concentrate or she would dissolve into tears. *Why? Why?*

Why? kept echoing through her brain. Why would someone want her dead?

"I'll butter the toast," Ryan said, breaking into her thoughts. She hadn't heard the toaster pop.

"It's okay. I'll do it. I've read enough." She turned, blinking back tears, and removed the slices from the toaster.

They sat at the kitchen table that was already set and had orange juice at both places. From the window, Hayley saw the storm was long gone. The air had been washed clean, the sky a resplendent blue above a wind-ruffled ocean. She'd bodysurfed this area so much as a child that she instantly recognized the stretch of beach near the Wedge. Wow! This was the Gold Coast of real estate. Ryan's father must have made a fortune.

She looked down at her plate of bacon and eggs. Her appetite had suddenly vanished. All she could think about was Lindsey turning the key in the ignition. Hopefully Lindsey hadn't felt any pain.

"Eat," Ryan said. He was shoveling a heaping forkful of eggs into his mouth and holding a piece of bacon in his other hand. His dynamic eyes catalogued her every move.

She tried for a smile and speared some

eggs. "Do you think Lindsey died instantly?"

"Yes. No question about it."

Hayley told herself that she was thankful. If her friend had to die, at least she didn't suffer. They ate in silence for a few minutes. Hayley forced herself to eat half the eggs, a piece of toast and part of a slice of bacon. The food seemed to lodge somewhere in her upper chest like a chunk of cement.

"Do you live with your father?" she asked to fill the silence. She knew Conrad Hollister had been at Twelve Oaks for at least two years because that's when Aunt Meg had moved to the facility and Conrad had already been there.

Ryan shook his head and patted his lips with a napkin. "No. I work out of the L.A. office. I'm just down here rehabbing."

Drugs? Alcohol? He didn't look as if he had a habit but she'd been in Southern California her whole life and knew appearances could be deceiving. Chad Bennett had been hooked on "vitamin R," as the college kids called Ritalin. It wasn't a narcotic but Chad relied on it for a "brain boost" to improve his concentration as had many of her classmates.

When they'd been together, Hayley had told him that he didn't need the so-called "smart pills." But no matter how much she

115

encouraged him to get off them, Chad hadn't listened.

Ryan put one hand on the opposite shoulder. "Physical therapy for my shoulder," he explained. "I had an old football injury that I reinjured in a multicar pileup on the freeway."

"I see."

Hayley gazed out at the blue expanse of water. The house was set back from the sea and separated from the public beach that stretched along the shore by a stand of wild grass, but the crystal blue of the ocean seemed to flow out to the horizon.

She'd come to this part of the beach often as she'd been growing up. Her father had insisted she learn to bodysurf. She'd loved it and took up board surfing at about the same time — to please her father. Even though he was dead, Hayley still felt her father's power over her. Oh, how she'd longed to please him.

Ryan cleared their plates and put them in the sink. Hayley volunteered to rinse the dishes and put them in the dishwasher. He told her to leave everything for now. She could work on it when they'd finished. He took a notepad from the nook beside the refrigerator and returned to the table.

"Okay. Let's make a list of anyone who —

for any reason, no matter how trivial —
might want you dead."

Hayley groaned and tried to imagine who
would be diabolical enough to blow her to
bits. "Honestly, I don't know anyone —"

"Name anyone who just plain doesn't like
you." His expression said only a fool would
believe they had no enemies.

Someone *had* tried to kill her. She put her
shattered illusions aside and tried to concentrate. "I guess Cynthia Fordham despises
me. She's Trent and Farah's mother. She
never forgave my mother for stealing her
husband. She thought I got everything,
while her kids never received enough from
my father, although believe me, he tried to
be fair."

Hayley knew it was more than this that
bothered Cynthia. Russell Fordham had
been just another surfer with a small board-
making operation when he left Cynthia for
Hayley's mother, Alison. Later the company
had prospered, mostly due to the successful
clothing line Alison designed. Cynthia had
been left behind financially because the
money had been earned after the divorce.

Cynthia had taken the whole situation
very personally. The money seemed to be a
huge factor, but there was also a vehement
sense of betrayal. Hayley could relate; she

still experienced a surge of anger when she thought of the way Chad had betrayed her — and they hadn't even been married or had children.

"What about Farah and Trent?" Ryan asked.

"They're like . . . oh, I don't know. Cousins, I guess. They spent most vacations and every other weekend with us, when I was growing up."

The width of the table hardly seemed sufficient to buffer Ryan's penetrating gaze. "How did you three get along?"

Hayley considered this for a moment. "Trent and I were buddies. My father loved it. I was a good surfer and Trent surfed, too, but he became a junior skateboard champ."

"What about Farah?"

Hayley shrugged. "Farah had no interest in sports. She never even tried. She got good grades and concentrated on getting a scholarship to college, which she did. She went to SC and became a CPA. She never looked to my father for anything."

"Commendable, but how did you two get along?"

"Fine. There weren't any problems," she replied, but this man was far too perceptive. She added, "I guess I was a little envious because good grades never came easily to me. I was always more interested in art and sports."

He tapped the pen against the pad. "No arguments with either of them?"

"Not really. I knew they resented me living in a big house when they lived in a small place in Costa Mesa. I went to a private school because it offered art classes while they went to public schools. I don't think that mattered to them. Trent was a skateboard king no matter where he was. Farah qualified for a college scholarship because she was at a public school. But I think they envied the house, the cars."

"What about your aunt? If you died, who would get her money?"

Hayley drew in a deep, shuddering sigh. After the death of her parents and now Lindsey, her throat tightened at the thought of losing Aunt Meg. "I don't know. She told me that she'd split her money between my mother and me, but then Mom died. Aunt Meg reworked her trust. I honestly don't know what she would do if I died."

"But you don't think Farah or Trent —"

"I can't imagine it. They see each other only at Christmas and Easter when the family gets together."

"What would Laird McMasters stand to gain if he bought Surf's Up?"

Hayley remembered Ryan saying Laird had tried to buy their company but she had held up the sale, which wasn't true. "Laird's a rich kid who's never acted like one. Believe me, I've known him all my life. He's always been an overachiever. He was good at everything and excelled whenever he wanted. He went to Yale, became a successful businessman."

"With a surf shop."

"Right. He didn't make boards, though. He imports them from China."

"Why does he want to buy Surf's Up?"

Hayley shrugged; she didn't see what this had to do with Lindsey's death. "Hurley, Quicksilver, Billabong — all the big-name surf companies have gone public. That's meant huge money for the owners. Smaller operations like ours and Laird's can't really compete unless they grow larger."

"Then one of the giants might buy them, right?"

"Exactly. They often do that to shut down competition. I guess Laird would like to cash in on the trend, but with the economy so slow . . ."

"At some point, it'll pick up again and with your MMA line, Surf's Up will have something no one else has."

"We beat them to the punch on that one."

120

"I understand you did it. Trent didn't want anything to do with The Wrath."

"True," she conceded, not wanting to brag, but Trent had been short-sighted. It had taken a lot of convincing to get him to go along. "It paid off big-time. As long as The Wrath is champ, we have a corner on the market. Others can sell their designs but The Wrath is what draws the big bucks."

"I think your Grim Reaper design has a lot to do with it."

Hayley banked a smile. She wouldn't have thought Ryan Hollister would have known what her signature design looked like.

"Tell me what you know about The Wrath." There was an ominous edge to his voice. "Does he have drug or criminal connections?"

Hayley instantly shook her head.

"Really think about it. I know it can be painful to answer these questions, but just remember, your life is at stake here. The more I know about the people close to you, the better."

CHAPTER SEVEN

"Don't you have homework?" Trent asked Timmy.

"He finished it earlier." Courtney spoke up before Timmy could answer.

The boy looked down at his tiramisu. The kid had poked at it but hadn't eaten more than a small bite. What kid liked fancy Italian desserts? Courtney had the maid prepare it to impress Chad, but she could have served Timmy ice cream or cake.

Trent looked at Chad and forced a smile. He'd invited the attorney for dinner so they could have a private discussion.

"More coffee?" Courtney asked Chad.

"No, thanks. Dinner was great. I'm stuffed." Chad turned toward Timmy, who was seated on his left. "Done any surfing lately?"

Trent snuffed a hoot. Surf? The kid was afraid of the water. He barely went in their swimming pool. Braving itty-bitty waves that lapped at his ankles was terrifying. Could this be his son?

Well, no question about it. Timmy didn't have his guts or his personality but the kid looked just like Trent had at the same age. Just went to show you that Timmy's chickenshit genes came from his mother.

"Back still bothering you, Courtney?" Chad asked.

Trent watched his wife nod. Her dilated pupils and slow responses probably hadn't fooled Chad. Courtney was high on pain pills. Chad undoubtedly sympathized. The guy lived on Ritalin and Red Bull. He was pumped all the time. Not physically addicted the way Courtney was but hooked just the same.

Chad had begun taking Ritalin in college. Claimed it enhanced brain activity as did many other guys Trent knew. He thought it was a crutch. Chad was intelligent and cunning. His brain didn't need a boost.

Trent pushed back from the table. "We're going down to the beach to look at the new board I designed."

"Now?" Courtney asked. "It's almost dark."

"We've got time." Trent gave Chad a look that said they needed to talk in private.

"Can I come?" Timmy asked in a weak

123

sissylike voice.

"No. Do your homework." Trent knew Timmy had already completed his assignments, but he hadn't known what else to say to get rid of him. The boy never wanted to go to the beach. Why now?

Chad rode in Trent's Porsche down to the parking lot above Crystal Cove Beach. The attorney complained about the lack of business due to the downturn in the economy. He never mentioned Hayley and hadn't at dinner, either. Chad had been so determined to get back together with her when she'd been alive. Didn't he miss her now?

They parked and took the stairs down the bluff to the beach. The tang of the sea brought back happy memories of times spent here with his father. He had been a great father but not much of a businessman; he refused to change with the times and import surfboards from China.

Chad didn't question why they hadn't brought a surfboard. Trent had already tipped the attorney with a handwritten note that said he thought the Feds might be tapping his phones and planting bugs in an attempt to pin Hayley's murder on him.

Trent stopped just short of the tide line. No point in ruining his shoes. "I don't think anyone can hear us over the sound of the waves."

Chad looked around as if he expected a Federal agent to leap out of the surf. "I guess not. What's up?"

"I'm really worried about this investigation. The Feds are looking into everything. I mean *everything*."

Chad stared out at the sea, which was dappled with gold by the last rays of the setting sun. "I know. They came to see me." He turned to face Trent. "I told them that I couldn't show them any records without a warrant. But I assured them that you had nothing to do with Hayley's death."

"Why didn't you call me and tell me?"

"For the same reason you wanted to talk down here where we can't be taped or overheard."

"Do you think they're onto . . . anything?"

Chad shook his head, looking out toward Catalina Island. "No. I've told you a dozen times. There's nothing to find."

"Right." Trent trusted Chad. The guy was sharp and stayed on top of things. "I'm just nervous with all the scrutiny. They tore the business apart, looked in shipping containers, questioned employees and searched my home."

"What did they find?" Chad started to

125

walk along the shore and Trent fell into step beside him. "*Nada*. You have nothing to worry about."

"I'm concerned about Ryan Hollister. He came around today asking questions."

Chad stopped and kicked at a chain of seaweed. "Is that prick working on the case?"

"I guess. He wanted to know about Laird McMasters and his offer to buy Surf's Up."

"What did you tell him?" Chad's voice was cautious and barely audible above the crash of the waves.

"As little as possible."

As darkness fell, Farah waited at the bar in Duke's, gazing out at the bay with its endless parade of boats, thinking. The popular bar at the Balboa Bay Club resort had been named after John Wayne, who used to frequent the place when he'd been alive. Her mother remembered him, of course, but Farah's only impression of the man came from old movies her mother watched.

Her mind shifted to her boyfriend. Kyle, she thought with an inward sigh of frustration. Why didn't he just get another job instead of surfing all day and playing video games all night? If the sex wasn't so hot, she'd dump him in a New York minute, but

126

it was almost impossible to find guys who were into S & M that she could be seen with in public.

"There you are." Farah's mother interrupted her thoughts. "Let's grab a table by the window before the place fills up."

"Right." Farah took the cosmopolitan she'd barely touched and followed her mother to a table overlooking the bay.

As usual, Cynthia Fordham swanned across the room to attract the attention of the clusters of mostly older males who patronized the bar. Her mother was still very attractive with a great figure, which pleased Farah. She looked exactly like her mother and hoped she still had her good looks when she aged. True, Cynthia had had cosmetic surgery a few months ago, but Farah hadn't thought her mother really needed it.

"How's business?" Farah asked as they settled at the table and Cynthia signaled the waitress for her usual chardonnay.

"I'm a little concerned," admitted Cynthia. "We have sales going all the time but business is still slow."

Cynthia managed The Show, an upscale boutique in the resort. It featured trendy casual clothes and swimsuits that sold to the tourists who visited and the tenants of the Balboa Bay Club condominiums adjacent to the resort. It also catered to wealthy women in Newport Beach, who lunched at the private club dining room on the second floor of the facility.

Farah hated to ask but forced herself. "How are you doing financially?"

"Fine," her mother replied in a tone that was a shade too flip as she reached for the martini the waitress was delivering. "I've got money tucked away."

Farah knew that her mother had saved most of the money from the sale of their childhood home. Cynthia had rented a studio at the Balboa Bay Club condominiums after her children had moved out. She should have enough money to see her through retirement, but it was difficult to tell with her mother. She was often very secretive.

Farah sipped her cosmo and watched while her mother downed the wine in a few gulps, then frantically signaled the waitress for another. *Something's wrong,* Farah decided. Her mother never drank more than one glass of wine when they met every other week for a drink and dinner.

"Mother, is something bothering you?" Farah asked.

Her dark eyes met Farah's. "Not really.

128

It's just your father's death and now this mess with the car bomb."

The plane crash that had killed Russell and Alison had been a shock to everyone, but the way Cynthia had grieved surprised Farah. She knew her mother still had been in love with her father even though she acted as if she hated him. But Farah hadn't realized how deep those feelings went or how much her mother had counted on Russell being around even if she wasn't married to him.

"I'm sure this car-bomb thing will blow over," Farah told her mother. "Have they questioned you?"

Cynthia shook her head. The waitress arrived with the second chardonnay. "Why would they? I don't stand to gain anything from Hayley's death."

But you hated her, Farah thought. *You cursed Hayley countless times.*

"I just don't like the way the authorities are hounding Trent." Her mother sipped the wine. "People are talking, thinking he's guilty."

Farah couldn't deny it. She'd been questioned, but Kyle had provided her alibi for the evening of the murder. Trent had an alibi also, but they seemed to think he had a drug connection that caused Hayley's death.

Cynthia leaned forward and whispered across the table. "Do you think your brother is bringing in drugs with shipments from Asia?"

"No. He didn't place the order until after Dad died. That's not enough time to set up a drug deal." Farah assumed this was true, but she couldn't be sure.

"Could he have hired someone to kill Hayley?" her mother asked.

"No way —" Farah stopped talking when she spotted Ryan Hollister headed for their table. What on earth was he doing here?

He walked up to them with a smile. "Hello, Farah."

She was instantly on guard. Being Conrad Hollister's son was one thing; being an FBI agent was another. "Hi. I'm surprised to see you here."

Ryan pulled out one of the two unoccupied chairs at their table even though they hadn't invited him to join them. Farah's wariness ticked up a notch.

"Aren't you going to introduce me to your handsome friend?" Her mother fairly gushed the words.

Farah had to admit Ryan was drop-dead gorgeous in a rough-hewn masculine way.

He was dressed in dark slacks and a blue polo shirt that made his eyes seem a deeper shade of blue. Even in casual clothes, one look at the man told you he'd been a star athlete. "This is Ryan Hollister."

Her mother offered him a smooth hand crowned by long coral nails. "I don't believe Farah's told me about you."

Farah knew from her mother's tone and the look on her face that she was hoping this man was a replacement for Kyle. Cynthia had never liked Kyle, never thought he was good enough for her daughter. Farah should have listened to her, but had ignored the advice because Kyle was the kind of guy who'd never looked in her direction when she'd been in high school. The cool surfers always chased Hayley, but never paid any attention to a brain like Farah.

"Mother, this is Conrad Hollister's son. You know, Meg Amboy's friend." Farah hoped her mother would recall her mentioning him. Since the divorce, Cynthia never attended family dinners but Farah had told her about them. Her mother had always asked endless questions. She had to know *every* detail of Russell Fordham's new life.

"Weren't you a football star?" Cynthia asked in her most charming manner.

"I played pro ball for two seasons. I'm

with the FBI now. We're working on Hayley Fordham's murder." Ryan's tone was all business.

"Oh, really?" There was a quaver in her mother's voice.

"I don't believe anyone has asked you yet where you were the evening of the car bombing."

Her mother's wine sloshed over the rim as she quickly set it down on the table. "Am I a suspect?"

Ryan shook his head. "We're just eliminating people."

"I — I don't know. I closed the shop at five the way I always do and went home. I live —"

"I know where you live. Did you see anyone, call anyone?"

Cynthia picked up her wine and guzzled it while she thought. "I don't think I called anyone. I know I didn't see anybody that evening."

Anger cracked through Farah like a whip. "My mother didn't plant that bomb. She wouldn't have the faintest idea how to —"

"How did you feel about Hayley?" Ryan asked Cynthia.

"She was a spoiled brat from the second she was born." The venom in Cynthia's voice astonished Farah. She knew her mother despised Hayley, but did she have to sound so vindictive in front of this man? "I had nothing to do with her death, but I'm not sorry she's gone. She got what she deserved."

"Mother!"

"Don't pretend you're sorry she's dead. You never liked her, either. She ruined your relationship with your father."

Ryan drove his rented SUV out onto the peninsula after stopping at the market. His left shoulder still ached from tackling Hayley and hitting the floor. He tried to rotate it the way the therapist did but that made his damaged nerves tingle. He put the pain out of his mind the way he had when he'd played ball.

He'd called Hayley earlier to tell her when he'd be back. She sounded more upbeat than when he'd left this morning. He wished he had something to tell her. He'd poked around all day long — as much as he could without being officially on the case — and hadn't learned much. But his suspicions had grown. He'd developed a sixth sense while playing football. Often he knew which way a play would go before it happened.

He hadn't had much chance to use his precognitive instincts since joining the FBI.

His assignments had been routine white-collar investigations that required more book work than anything else. Then he'd trained for the cyber crimes unit. That relied on facts and little else.

But he had sensed *something* when he'd interviewed Trent Fordham. The guy was shading the truth. He knew more than he admitted.

Follow the money. That was the cardinal rule of most crimes. There had to be a money trail. Since it didn't appear that Trent or Farah, the ones who stood to gain the most from Hayley's death, had actually committed the crime. Evidently they'd hired someone and funds to pay for it must have come from their accounts.

Homeland Security was checking those accounts. The nice thing about having them involved was it didn't take a warrant to access the info. When terrorism might be involved, Homeland Security didn't have to follow regular legal channels. They'd promised to give Ed Phillips copies of those documents.

By inviting Hayley to stay with him at his father's house, Ryan had gone way beyond the professional boundaries that he should have set. He'd wandered into dangerous territory — professionally and emotionally. He could easily be fired for the infraction.

Somehow it didn't bother him the way it should. Perhaps Jessica's death had changed him more than he realized. People were what counted — not rules. He'd been stunned — blown away, actually — to discover Hayley was still alive. It had taken some convincing to make her understand that someone who would go to all the trouble to plant a car bomb wanted her dead. And would stop at nothing.

Last night, when he'd held Hayley in his arms and flashed the light on her face, he'd experienced something that he could only describe as a special connection. Before that moment, Hayley Fordham had been a picture in his mind. The reality was much more compelling.

Aw hell, why was he lying to himself? Tension tightened his nerves as he thought about her. He was attracted to her — wanted her — in a way that surprised him. Since cancer took Jessica, he hadn't been attracted to another woman. But now he was involved — big-time. It was a mistake and he knew it, but he couldn't help himself.

The instant he'd seen Hayley's green eyes wide with panic and her sexy lips set to scream, something inside him clicked. She'd been terrified yet brave. Screaming like a hell cat — kicking and biting. His intense reaction hadn't diminished as he listened to her story. He experienced the urge to help her, protect her. No matter what the cost to himself.

The phone on his belt buzzed and he yanked it off with a quick look around. It was against the law in California to drive and talk on your phone, but since he hadn't bought a new car after totaling his in the accident, Ryan hadn't set up a hands-free system on his father's car. "Hollister." It was Ed Phillips. "Hey, I was just thinking about you. Anything in those bank accounts?"

"Hard to say," Phillips replied. "Trent and Farah both have made sizable cash withdrawals all year long. I'm talkin' in the five- to eight-thousand-dollar range."

Ryan couldn't imagine anyone agreeing to plant a car bomb for that little. "You're thinking drugs?"

"You got it, pard. What else would they continually need cash for?"

"Good question. Something off the books, that's for sure." Ryan hadn't told Phillips about Hayley's miraculous return. He shouldn't have withheld the information. The guy had brought him into the investigation, but Ryan felt he didn't have any choice. He seriously believed Hayley's life was in jeopardy. He didn't want anyone to know she was alive yet.

"Most of the guys think this is some Asian drug deal that has to do with the container of surfboards Trent imported. We're the only ones really looking hard at the family. I got their tax returns and went through them. Sure 'nuf, both Trent and Farah are in debt."

"What about Hayley?"

"Clean. No debt and no large cash withdrawals until the day of her death. Looks like a thousand dollars in cash went up with her."

Ryan turned right and pulled onto the short street that led to his father's house. "I interviewed Trent Fordham today."

"Oh?" Ed didn't have to remind Ryan that he wasn't authorized to investigate. He heard the reprimand in the single word.

"He's hiding something."

"How do you know?"

Ryan pulled to a stop in the alley just behind the garage and pressed the remote control for the garage door to open. "Just a feeling."

"Jeez-a-ree! That's it?"

"Have you talked to him?"

"Nah. I could, but he's been interviewed

every which way already."

The door moved up and Ryan drove into the garage. "See what you get on the mother, Cynthia Fordham. I just ran into her at the Balboa Bay Club." Ryan was shading the truth here, but he didn't want Phillips to order him to stop asking questions. "She admitted she hated Hayley and was glad she was dead."

CHAPTER EIGHT

Ryan opened the door that led from the garage into the laundry room behind the kitchen and yelled, "Hel-looo! I'm baaaack!"

He didn't want to frighten Hayley by appearing unexpectedly. She was skittish enough as it was. At breakfast this morning, the spark of chemistry he thought he'd detected the night before had vanished. She treated him with professional detachment, which was probably the best thing she could have done, if they were going to be alone in the same house.

"I'm in here," Hayley called from the kitchen. "I've made a salad."

Carrying the sack of groceries, Ryan walked in. He'd thought about her all day and yet he wasn't quite prepared for what he saw. Hayley was standing at the island in the center of the kitchen, chopping lettuce. She'd washed her hair and changed into navy shorts and a peach-colored tank top.

She was a knockout, no doubt about it. Those eyes, vivid green with flecks of gold, were captivating. Her lips were full and provocative. Her smile — off-kilter by just a hair — was sexy as hell. Her silky hair swished alluringly across her shoulders as she moved. Her body — *no, don't go there.*

"There won't be a tomato. They were all too far gone, but we've got enough here for a decent salad."

He took a quick — and, he hoped, unnoticed — breath. "That's fine. I bought steaks and stuffed potatoes from the deli case. We can heat them up in the microwave while we're grilling the steaks." He set the bag on the counter. "I'm running upstairs to change. Then I'll come back and light the barbeque."

She nodded with something meant to be a smile. He left the room, heading upstairs, conscious of how much tension filled the air. What was that all about? Was she still afraid of him?

Or — he dared to hope — was she as attracted to him as he was to her?

Get over it! He told himself. *Keep your mind on business.*

It took him a few minutes — moving like a robot with stiff joints — to spare his

140

shoulder and change into cutoff jeans and a long-sleeve T-shirt. He'd worn a long-sleeve dress shirt today to hide the scratches on his arms. Then he returned to the kitchen. Hayley was seasoning the steaks and already had the potatoes in the microwave ready to reheat.

He told her he was going out to the courtyard to light the barbeque. The house was built around a small courtyard with a high wall on the open side. Hayley could be out here all she wanted without anyone seeing her from the public walkway that led along the walk to the beach.

"Did you find out anything?" she asked when he returned after lighting the fire.

"Not really, but I have the distinct impression that Trent is hiding something. Any idea what it might be?"

She handed him a platter with the steaks. "No, but I've been thinking."

He would bet his life on that. He hadn't known her long, but from the moment he'd shined the light on her face, he'd realized Hayley Fordham had a power and depth to her that other women lacked. He motioned for her to follow him and went outside to put the steaks on the grill.

"I like mine medium rare. How do you like yours?"

"That's fine." Something in her expression told him she was apprehensive.

"What were you thinking about? Does it have to do with Trent?"

"Indirectly . . . I guess," she replied as he put the steaks on the grill.

"Go on," he prompted over the hiss of the grill.

"It's about the death of my parents." She led him to the small patio table that she'd already set for dinner and sat down. Ryan took the seat across from her. "I've always been suspicious of the plane crash. My father never radioed that he was having problems or called a Mayday. He'd flown to Maverick's Beach numerous times. Dad was an avid surfer. He learned to fly just so he could get to Mexico or Northern California when the surf was up."

Ryan had been to the beach near San Francisco called Maverick's. Its waves were legendary, favorites of surfers from around the world. And he knew plenty of guys who lived to surf. He didn't get it, but who was he to criticize?

"My father was always so careful about his plane and the way he flew. Their plane hit a hill and the gas tanks exploded. They were incinerated instantly." She clenched her jaw in an attempt to steady the quaver in her voice. "Their plane exploded, my car exploded . . ."

"Do you think a bomb caused the crash?"

Uncertainty shadowed Hayley eyes. "I never thought of a bomb. I did consider some type of sabotage. I mean . . . my father was cautious in the extreme. The Cessna was a new plane when Dad bought it. He had it serviced professionally. It didn't seem likely that a system would malfunction."

Ryan wasn't sure what to think. A plane's gas tanks often exploded upon impact. Or had this plane exploded first? "What did the FAA say caused the crash?"

"The Federal Aviation Administration didn't investigate. Local authorities at the Civil Aeronautics Board handled the inquiry. They said it was pilot error. I don't believe that for a minute."

Ryan didn't remind her that one tiny mistake could bring down the most skilled pilot.

"The Civil Air Patrol found them, using the emergency locator transmitter that my father had installed."

"The Civil Air Patrol is just local pilots who volunteer to search, right?"

"Yes. When my father didn't arrive at the small airstrip not far from Maverick's, the guy who was meeting him to drive them to

143

the beach called to make sure he'd left. After he found out my parents were overdue, he contacted the authorities and the search began immediately. They found them less than three hours later, but the wreckage was inaccessible. They could tell by flying low over the smoldering plane that no one was alive."

The hurt and anguish was evident in her voice. He tried to imagine what it must have been like to wait all those hours — hoping and praying — your parents were alive. He had the impression that it had changed her outlook on life.

"If you were suspicious, who did you think did it?"

Hayley shrugged and her hair swished provocatively across her shoulders. "I — I don't know. I thought it might have something to do with his refusal to purchase part of a container of surfboards with another company. Laird McMasters and my brother tried to convince my father, but he insisted he wasn't going to buy cheap boards from China."

"Why did they need your father to share a container?"

"A container holds thousands of boards. Small companies like ours, like Laird's, don't sell that many. Bigger companies have lots of stores and can handle a full container."

"Trent wanted to import?"

"Yes. That was the only time they fought — over imported boards."

"What did you think?"

Hayley let out a little huff of disgust. "I could see both sides. Cheap imports have killed most American manufacturers. But my father's boards were produced from his custom mold. They were the kind pro surfers ordered. We could keep that part of the business small and grow the rest. We'd still make a lot of money, but we certainly would have made even more with a line of imported boards."

"Do you think Trent had something to do with the crash?"

"No. He worshiped my father. Trent was so miserable after the crash that we were all worried about him."

It was difficult for Ryan to imagine Trent this upset. He didn't seem like the type, but maybe with a sudden shock he'd been more emotional. "How did Farah react?"

"She was pretty stoic, but then she always has been. Farah is the take-charge type. She planned the funeral, arranged everything."

"With your father gone, who runs the business?"

"Trent. He'd been in charge of the day-to-day operations for some time. I did the Internet stuff as well as the designing."

"Internet, meaning you were in charge of the Web site?"

"No. We outsourced that. I started tracking fashion blogs when hardly anyone knew what a blog was. You'd be surprised at how the fashion-obsessed take pictures of their outfits and post them or write about new shoes or purses or whatever strikes them in daily blogs. The blogosphere is a cheap, effective way of advertising. It's really worked for us."

Ryan knew he was one of the most talented computer security experts in the Bureau, but he knew little about blogging. It just seemed like online chit-chat to him. "Do the bloggers make any money?"

"Sure. They get a cut of the profits from links to online stores like Surf's Up. They write about our new beachwear and provide a link. Our system is set up so we can tell where our referrals are coming from."

"Interesting," Ryan responded, and he meant it; although he didn't have a clue about how it related to the attempt on Hayley's life. "Your parents didn't have a will or trust?"

"We assumed there was a trust set up

146

because Dad said they were going to do one. My parents went to Chad Bennett for a preliminary consultation but never completed the trust."

Chad Bennett's name triggered an uneasy feeling. Other than wondering if he'd been high when they met at the "memorial service," Ryan didn't have much of an opinion of the guy. But he did recall seeing the attorney having a heated conversation with Trent.

"Not having a trust means my parents' estate has to go through probate. California is notorious for its high estate taxes."

"Your father would have left the business to . . ."

"Trent, with me as a partner or something. They would have left money to Farah, probably from the sale of the house." She sighed. "They didn't know how much I wanted to be an artist, not a designer."

A crackle from the grill reminded Ryan that the steaks needed to be turned. He jumped up, checking his watch and seeing he'd left them on too long. He flipped them, shaking his head, and found Hayley at his side.

"Why are you helping me?" she asked, her tone low, husky.

A voice inside his head whispered that

he'd been captivated by her picture, but he knew he couldn't tell her this. "Your aunt has been great with my father. I could see how much she loves you and . . . I couldn't say no."

"But you had no idea what you were getting into," she said, and he thought he detected the sheen of tears in the dim light.

"No, but it's an interesting, challenging case." He couldn't resist slipping his arm around her. "As long as nothing happens to you."

He hadn't expected her to snuggle against his chest, but she did. "Thank you. I know I was a complete brat last night, but the whole thing came out of the blue. I'm still trying to come to terms with Lindsey's death. It's taken me all day and hours on your father's computer to read everything and truly comprehend the danger I'm in."

Her head tilted upward so her eyes were looking into his. He felt something sizzle besides the steaks. Was it one-sided, he wondered, or was there mutual attraction? "Ryan, I'm really lucky you're helping me."

He understood Hayley felt scared and alone and cut off from a comfortable, predictable world. Just because she was leaning against his body didn't mean she was physically attracted to him. Still, it

148

was a start.

Her cheek rested against the soft fabric of his T-shirt and he could feel the fullness of her breasts against his rib cage. His arm encircled her shoulders, light, protective. He could smell the fresh scent of shampoo and some elusive vanilla-accented fragrance coming from her warm skin. It was the same scent he'd detected in her closet. He battled the urge to kiss the top of her head.

She looked up at him again, her smoky green eyes framed by dusky lashes. Several beats went by as they gazed at each other, saying nothing. His breathing quickened and his chest hummed like a million bees in a hive. He was beginning to feel *way* too much for this woman. The thing he had to keep in mind was this wasn't a casual encounter. A lot was at stake. His job. Her life.

He slid his thumb gently along the curve of her cheek. Her skin was as smooth and soft as it looked. A hollow, aching need for her crept downward to his groin. They stood together, pressing against each other like two people who met after an absence too long to be bridged by mere words.

One hand on his chest, she pushed away. "I'm sorry. I didn't mean to fall apart." She headed toward the kitchen. "I'll get the salad and zap the potatoes."

With an unusual flash of insight, Ryan decided he'd been alone too long with a deep-seated pain no one could share. Some part of him, some area he'd assumed had died with Jessica was still alive. Ryan forced himself to concentrate on the steaks, which were already too well-done on one side. Behind him, Ryan heard her bringing things to the table. He shut off the grill and removed the steaks.

He sat at the table with a reassuring smile and helped himself to salad and a twice-baked potato. "What was your mother's part in the business?" he asked to get the conversation back to solving the mystery. He munched on the salad as he listened.

"My mother was the brains behind the business," Hayley said with a ghost of a smile. She cut into her steak and Ryan could see it wasn't as overdone as he'd thought. "Daddy had a small shop where he made surfboards while he wasn't surfing. He sold them at Doug's Surf Heaven. Mom made bikinis and tops and board shorts to sell there. That's how they met. Mom convinced him to go into business for himself."

"Did they —" Ryan didn't know how to put it "— fall in love —"

"My father claimed he loved my mother from the first moment he set eyes on her."

Once Ryan wouldn't have believed this happened, but his unusual reaction to Hayley's photograph proved anything was possible. Love at first sight. Chemistry, pure and simple.

"My mother said she was really attracted to him but he was married. She wouldn't have anything to do with him until he left his wife and filed for divorce. Even then she felt guilty because he had two children."

"But she still married him."

"Oh, yes. They were head-over-heels in love. They married the day after his divorce became final. They were like goofy teenagers in love right up to the day the plane crashed." She took a deep breath, as if searching for the right words. Two beats of silence, then she added, "You know, as a kid growing up, I used to feel like a third wheel. They loved each other so intensely that there wasn't much room for me. I actually envied Trent and Farah because their mother loved them with such a passion. Cynthia hated it when they came to stay with us."

Ryan didn't know what to say so he kept his mouth shut. He'd felt loved by both his parents when his mother had been alive.

After her death, his father gave him all his attention. He'd always felt loved and appreciated. He sensed that Hayley never had.

"How did Cynthia feel about you?" Ryan asked without revealing he'd met the woman at the Balboa Bay Club.

"She hated me and my mother," Hayley responded matter-of-factly. "Who could blame her? My mother ruined her life."

"Would she want you dead?"

Nervously, she bit her lip. "Maybe . . . I don't know. Why now, after all this time?"

"The money," Ryan said with a second jolt of insight in just a few minutes. "Cynthia believed the entire estate rightfully belonged to her children — not you."

Uncertainty shadowed her face. "I — I guess it's possible."

An idea had been niggling at the back of his brain all day. He asked, "Did your parents use a computer?"

"My mother did a lot of work on her computer. Designing. Spreadsheets to track the company business and Internet sales. My father rarely used a computer. He had my mother's computer and the ones at the office set up to instantly alert him whenever waves were over ten feet on the California coast or down in Baja. Somebody would have to run and get him when the SurfAlert flashed."

"Your mother's computer was at home?"

"Yes. She did most of her designing on a laptop. That way she could bring it with her and work wherever Daddy was."

They ate in comfortable silence for a few minutes. Ryan kept thinking, trying to decide who had the big three — as they'd called it during his training. Motive. Opportunity. Means. Others could have been paid to have the means and opportunity. But what was the motive? Money was all he could come up with.

"Where is your mother's laptop?"

"At their house." Hayley pushed her plate aside, her steak only half-eaten.

"I think I should take a look at it. Can you get me into their house?"

"Sure. It's just sitting there until the probate is processed."

Ryan wasn't sure checking the computer would do any good but he didn't have a better idea. A drive he couldn't quite explain compelled him to try anything and everything to help this woman.

CHAPTER NINE

Hayley looked over Ryan's broad shoulder as he attached his laptop to her mother's computer. After dinner they'd driven to her parents' home on Linda Isle. The small private island in Newport Bay had a guard at the entry gate. Ryan had phoned the gate in advance, pretending to be Trent, and put his name on the gate list. The guard didn't look twice at Hayley in the passenger seat when they arrived and gave Ryan's name. She'd tucked her hair up under a baseball cap and put on a pair of Ryan's father's glasses. It hadn't mattered. The night shift guard was new and wouldn't have recognized her anyway.

It was the first time Hayley had returned to the home where she'd grown up since the evening her parents' plane had vanished and the family had gathered here to await news. Although the house was still furnished and her parents' things hadn't been removed, the place seemed to have a hollow echo, like a tomb. She tried to remember all the happy times of her childhood, but couldn't. As they crept through the dark house, she kept hearing her parents' laughter as they talked and teased each other. They'd been so in love.

"What are you doing?" Hayley whispered, even though she knew he was removing information from her mother's computer. "Don't you need her password?"

"No," Ryan said, his voice pitched low. "I'm doing what's called a 'wipe-job,' which means I'm using a program on my computer to wipe everything off her hard drive onto a disk so I can analyze it later."

"Good." She knew they didn't want to be in the house any longer than necessary. Linda Isle was a U-shaped island with every house on the water. This type of real estate was so valuable that the homes were very close. They'd parked down the street and entered, using a key that her parents had kept hidden. They didn't want the neighbors to see lights and report them to the police so they'd brought flashlights

"This will take about ten minutes," Ryan said, turning to her. "Let's look through the file cabinet."

On the way over, she'd told him that Trent

and Chad had checked the computer and files after the plane crash, but Ryan insisted on having a second look. Hayley had grown up with Trent and knew he sincerely adored their father. Trent couldn't have had anything to do with his death. Chad was a different story. He'd charmed her, Hayley silently admitted and not for the first time.

What had she seen in him? A smart, handsome guy with a promising future in his father's law firm. He'd been fun — at first. Then she realized how much he depended on Ritalin. She'd researched and found it was an addictive substance. Still, Chad claimed he didn't function well without it.

Later she began to suspect he was cheating on her. Why? They'd been together less than a year. Was he tired of her already? Obviously. The experience had undermined her trust in men. In herself.

Was Chad sorry? He claimed to be, wanted to get together again, but she knew better. If he'd been tired of her within a year, how could their marriage last? Did Chad cry at her funeral? she wondered. Somehow she couldn't imagine him with tears in his eyes.

Hayley kept asking herself why she fell for the lout. All she could come up with was she'd wanted a happy marriage like her parents had. She'd never had trouble getting dates, but she'd never been serious about anyone until Chad Bennett. Why? And why couldn't she get over his rejection? He kept asking her out, trying to make up but her pride wouldn't allow her to forgive him.

"You take the top drawer," Ryan told her as he sat on the floor and trained his flashlight on the bottom drawer. "I'll check the lower drawer. Pull anything pertaining to finances."

"I see a file marked *Chase Visa* and another called *Gas Company.*"

"Just take the Visa. Let's see if there's a pattern in how they spent money."

"The company's charges are in the office at Surf's Up. An auditor goes over those books."

"We'll focus on the personal files."

Hayley paused. "I've heard that nothing on a computer is really erased. Right?"

"Uh-huh. Think of it this way. When you erase, it's like putting the info through a shredder. Not a cheap shredder but one that turns paper into confetti. All the words are chopped up and randomly dumped in the computer's trash bin. We have a program that uses key words and puts the documents together again."

"Wow! That's impressive. Is the technology available to everyone or just the FBI?"

"It's very expensive but firms that specialize in computer security invest in the latest version. Most people don't know about it."

Hayley checked the top drawer and withdrew two other files. Everything else seemed to be household expenses. She glanced down to see how Ryan was doing and saw the linear red scabs on his forearms.

"Oh, my gosh," she cried, forgetting to whisper. "Did I do that to you? I'm so sorry."

"Shh!" Ryan jerked his sleeve down, covering the angry red slashes. He tugged her hand and she sank down beside him. His intense blue eyes gleamed in the backwash of the flashlight.

"Don't be sorry," he told her in a husky whisper. "The best thing to do when someone attacks you is to fight back, try to escape."

"I'll remember that," she said quietly. His intensity alarmed her, but she knew he was right. After all, this was his field. Fight rather than allow anyone to kill you.

Ryan rose to his feet, several files in his hands. "Is there anywhere else that they might have kept financial records?"

"No." She glanced round the shadowy

room. "This was my mother's office."

"What about her personal address book?"

"She kept it in the nightstand next to her bed."

"Let's get it. We'll go through the names and see if there's anyone listed that you don't know."

Using just one flashlight, they went up the sweeping staircase to the second floor, where Hayley's bedroom was located along with two small guest rooms that Farah and Trent used when they visited. The master suite faced the water and had a panoramic view of the bay.

The room seemed to be just as she'd remembered it from her childhood, except now it had a slightly musty smell from being closed up for so long. The bed, facing the water, was still made with the cream-colored silk coverlet and banks of cream and tan pillows with black satin accent pillows. The bamboo shades were down but Hayley could imagine her parents out on the balcony, gazing at the bay and chatting over morning coffee. How incredibly happy they'd been.

She tamped down the surge of sadness and walked over and opened the nightstand on her mother's side of the bed. There was a floral notepad and matching pen but no address book.

"That's funny," she said. "It was here the day of the crash. I know because I had to look up Farah's cell phone number."

"Could it be downstairs somewhere?"

"I guess it's possible someone moved it to the kitchen when we were calling everyone about the funeral."

"Has anyone else been here since your parents' deaths?"

Hayley shrugged. "Just the cleaning lady who vacuums and dusts. She wouldn't take anything. We're not supposed to dispose of anything until the probate is complete."

"Let's check the kitchen for the address book, pick up my computer, then get out of here."

She clicked off her flashlight and followed Ryan downstairs. They looked on the granite counter and in the drawers, but there wasn't any sign of the floral directory in the kitchen.

"That's strange," she whispered. "Who could —"

"Did your father have an address book?"

"Not really. Mom was in charge of social events — not that they did much. Daddy kept a Palm Pilot with his surfing buddies in it. He had it with him."

"Wait while I grab my computer. The wipe

job should be finished."

Ryan raced upstairs and was back again a few moments later. He motioned for her to slip out the kitchen door to the narrow side yard. He followed, closing the door behind them. She returned the key to its place under the stone tail of the lion near the kitchen door.

They didn't speak until they were back in the car and driving off the island.

"Do you have a theory about this?" she asked as they went over the small bridge that connected Linda Isle to the mainland.

He seemed to hesitate and she studied his chiseled profile. "I'm not an investigator. I'm a computer —"

"I know, but you're a smart guy. You must have a theory."

"Well, there are two main ways to look at crimes." He guided the car onto Coast Highway and drove toward his father's home. "We prepare a psychological profile by looking at the crime scene. In this case, there wasn't enough at the scene to leave what we would call a signature."

"Wouldn't the type of crime — a car bombing — tell you something?"

"The Bureau's profiler at the Behavioral Analysis Unit said it seemed to be a very personal crime. The killer wanted you

161

obliterated. It was the sort of thing an antisocial personality would do."

"Antisocial? Like someone who doesn't go out much?"

"No. They often appear to be just as well-adjusted as the average guy. But someone with an antisocial personality disorder is convinced whatever they do is justified. Society's rules don't mean anything to them. They're above the law."

"Dead wasn't enough. I had to be erased off the face of the earth." Just saying the words made her neck go stiff.

"So it would appear."

"I can't imagine anyone who would hate me that much." She bit her lip and looked away. It was a few seconds before she asked, "What's the second way of looking at this crime?"

Ryan sped through the loop from the highway onto the street that went out onto the peninsula. "A geographical profile. It uses an area map and pinpoints the crimes. The theory is the perp has a comfort zone and operates in a neighborhood he knows, but not too close to where he lives, otherwise people would recognize him. We use this for serial killers, bank robbers, rapists — repeat offenders. I doubt the killer will do this again. My guess?" He turned and his intense eyes met hers for a few seconds. "A pro was hired to kill you. Not that it couldn't have been done by an ordinary person, but it seems to have been someone with a lot of nerve or experience. Quite possibly a pro."

Hayley couldn't imagine anyone she knew hiring a killer. Where would they go to get one? "That's why you're concerned about a money trail. It would have cost a lot to hire a pro. But my parents couldn't have paid to have me killed. They were already dead."

"Right, but there could be a clue to the problem in their finances. Maybe they owed money or owned something even more valuable than the business that we don't know about."

"Well, my father did have an amazing collection of surfboards. He hung some of the best, like one of The Duke's boards, in the shop where people could appreciate them."

"The Duke? I didn't know John Wayne surfed."

Despite the seriousness of the situation, Hayley couldn't help laughing. "No, silly. Duke Kahanamoku, the father of modern surfing. You've heard of him."

"Vaguely . . . I'm not sure."

"He was a Hawaiian who won an Olympic gold metal in swimming in 1912, I think. Anyway, back then Hawaii was like a foreign

163

country. Few people had been there. When the Hawaiian swim club told the Olympic committee they had someone for the team, they laughed themselves sick. Then Duke showed up and had the last laugh. People began to travel to Hawaii and Duke and the other beach boys gave surfing lessons."

"How did your father get Duke's board?"

"Duke was a lot like my father. He kept designing his own boards and trying them out. In 1917 — I know because the date is on the board Dad hung in the shop — Duke caught a wave off Waikiki and rode it for a mile and a half."

"Wow! How far out did he go to catch that wave?"

"Not far. There was a big earthquake in Japan that caused huge waves. Duke was off Castle's, a prime surf spot. He caught the huge wave as it angled along toward the shore, that's why he had such a long ride. Lots of people were watching. They called it 'The Big One,' which is where the expression started."

"Your father bought 'The Big One' board?"

"No, that board is hanging in the Bishop Museum in Honolulu. My father bought another of Duke's boards that was very similar. It was resting against a palm tree on

164

the beach when Duke caught the big one. He carved the date in both boards."

"Interesting. How valuable is it?"

"I don't know. Dad bought it when I was two and the shop started to make real money. He bought lots of other boards. Some are at the warehouse where he made custom boards — the best he hung in the shop. I guess Duke's board is worth thousands. I'm not sure about the others."

"People collect anything and everything. I suppose there's a market for vintage boards. I guess it's part of the probate."

Hayley considered this for a moment. "I'm not sure anyone brought the boards to the court's attention. I don't recall them on the asset list. Everyone must have forgotten about them."

"You could have — what? — a hundred thousand in boards. I can't see everyone forgetting about them. Not when a bunch are hanging in the shop."

She was lost in thought the rest of the way out the long peninsula that formed one side of Newport Harbor. The cafés and tourist shops and small hotels that gave the area a beachy ambiance were scattered among cottages that rented by the week during the summer. In the winter students lived here. It was the only section of Newport Beach that was affordable. As they drove toward Peninsula Point, the cottages gave way to elegant single family homes shaded by tall palm trees that swayed in the ocean breeze.

When they arrived, the garage door slowly rolled upward and Ryan drove in, shutting the door behind them. He parked beside an older model Lexus.

She asked, "Do you think I could take a walk along the sand? At this hour no one will be around to see me."

Ryan considered her request. "All right. I'll come with you."

Hayley followed Ryan through the dimly lit house out onto the open-air courtyard. In silence, they took off their shoes and she removed the baseball cap she'd been wearing. She fluffed her hair with her fingers. They left their things on the table where they'd had dinner. He unlocked the gate that opened onto a short path that ended on the sand. After Hayley passed through the gate, Ryan again locked it behind them and shoved the key in his pocket.

The balmy air was just starting to cool, a sure sign summer was almost here. The sand between her toes was still warm and the briny scent of the sea filtered through the darkness like an unseen mist.

Hayley tossed her head back and gazed

up at the winking stars. "How can the world look just the same when everything has changed?"

She asked the question more of herself than him. Until she'd learned about the car bombing, her world hadn't varied much except for her parents' deaths. Life hadn't been the same since that fateful day. The minute she'd heard her parents' plane was overdue, Hayley had prayed for their safety, but had known — deep inside — that they were gone.

After their funeral, Hayley's life had continued, but everything had changed. The disappointment she'd felt at Chad's betrayal became devastation at the loss of her parents. She'd anticipated being sad, believing it would take months or even years to come to terms with the deaths of her parents.

This new — and totally unexpected blow meant she was alone in the world without anyone to trust except a total stranger. She couldn't contact Aunt Meg, who had always been like a second mother to her. She was isolated and had no idea who was determined to destroy her.

"I know how you feel," Ryan said quietly. "After Jessica died, I never looked at the world the same way."

"J-Jessica?" she asked, stunned by the

emotion in his voice.

"My wife. Jess died of myeloma — bone marrow cancer — two years ago."

The unmistakable anguish in his voice sent a depth charge of guilt through Hayley. She'd told Ryan a lot about herself, but she hadn't asked him any personal questions. She'd decided he must be single because he was living alone in his father's house. It had never occurred to her that he might be a widower who even now mourned the loss of his wife.

"I'm sorry," she managed to murmur. "How tragic."

Ryan gazed down at her for a moment, then said, "It is a shame. Jessica's life held such promise, but it wasn't to be. I've learned to accept what happened and treasure the time we shared. The memories."

"Memories," she whispered. For a moment, the rush of the surf against the sand brought with it her parents' laughter. Happier times. Precious memories.

"I know what you're going through," Ryan added. "Just remember, some people will be with us always in the way we live, the way we love. Your parents, Jessica — they're still with us. Life goes on, but memories are forever."

Tears sprang into Hayley's eyes. She never

imagined Ryan could understand her feelings, would feel the same way, too.

Ryan walked beside her as they made their way toward the Wedge. The sound of waves breaking against the beach was louder than usual due to a tropical storm off the Mexican coast that kicked up huge waves. A fine vapor of saltwater spray misted the air as frothy spume from the white-capped waves hit the shore. A silvery wafer of a moon cast otherworldly light on the creamy white sand.

Hayley didn't know what to say. His hand curved around her upper arm — a casual gesture, she was positive, so she pretended not to notice. She walked a few more steps and spotted a couple entwined on a blanket half-naked. Ryan guided her to the right, closer to the water line and around the oblivious couple. Now the sand beneath their feet was cool and hard-packed by the retreating tide.

A nervous need to break the tense silence made her ask, "What made you join the FBI?"

His grip on her arm tightened just slightly, sending a shiver of anticipation tingling through her. "An injury kept me from playing pro football. I'd always excelled in math and was fascinated by computers. A friend from Duke was in the FBI forensic computer program. He encouraged me to apply."

His tone was flat and she had the feeling he'd only revealed the bare details, sharing nothing of his true feelings. He was an interesting man. There seemed to be more depth to him than most of the men she'd met. In other circumstances, Hayley assured herself, they might have become romantically involved.

Wait! Don't kid yourself. This man is still in love with a woman who died two years ago. He's helping you because Auntie Meg has a way of manipulating people.

Ryan stopped, bringing her to a halt too, and pulling her just a little closer. Or was it her imagination? "Why did you want to know about me?"

"Just curious," she told him as lightly as she could.

This time he drew her to him. It wasn't her imagination. "I've been curious."

They were so close that she needed to tilt her head back to see the gleam in his eyes. What was he thinking? she puzzled, suddenly short of breath. The moonlight shone in his dark hair and limned the strong line of his jaw. He was so undeniably masculine, so attractive that she couldn't look away. His lips parted in the suggestion of a smile and she found herself staring at his mouth . . . wondering what it would be like if he kissed her.

Don't go there, she admonished herself, but her body had other ideas. A surge of heat swept through her. Electricity seemed to arc through the air between them. Her heart pummeled her chest just as hard as the waves pounded the nearby sand.

She wrenched her eyes off his lips and met his bemused gaze. "Curious about what?"

"If you kiss as good as you look."

Without thinking, she replied, "There's only one way to find out." She stood on tiptoes and kissed him. In a heartbeat, his arms were around her, pulling her flush against his powerful chest. Her lips plied his, finding his mouth firm yet slightly soft and oh so warm against hers. The tip of his tongue flicked hers and the slow burn inside her kicked up a few notches.

Oh, my, but was he good at this. He'd been wondering. What did that mean? She didn't have time to explore the thought. Her nipples went taut and a throbbing sense of anticipation prickled her skin. His powerful body surrounded hers protectively. His warmth seeped through her clothes and made her snuggle even closer, her breasts pillowed against his torso.

As they kissed, intense heat replaced the warm sensation inside her. Wanting more, needing more, she leaned closer, her fingers now in the silky hair at the base of his neck. Need scorched through her with astonishing speed. Eyes squeezed tight, her head spun and rational thought became impossible.

She'd never known what it felt like to be kissed so thoroughly, so expertly. Of course, she'd been kissed many times, especially when she'd been with Chad, but those emotions had been nothing compared to this. What was happening? Sex had never meant much to her, but now — despite her dangerous situation — all she could think about was how she wanted, needed this man.

She lifted her head, her mouth a scant inch from his. "Ryan," she whispered.

He kissed her cheek and trailed a series of moist kisses along her skin until he found the incredibly sensitive area at the curve of her neck. A cat's paw of wind caught her hair and tossed a strand across her face. "Don't stop." She breathed the words.

"Oh, Hayley," he whispered — low, rough.

She looked into his eyes and found him gazing at her with a fierce energy in his eyes. His mouth slanted over hers. The gentle kissing became . . . more. His tongue slipped deep into her mouth while his hips rocked back and forth with an unmistakable carnality that echoed her own desire.

His hand found its way between them and caressed her breast, running his thumb over her beaded nipple. Through her flimsy tank top the sensation of his thumb on the sensitive nub sent another surge of heat spiraling through her. Toes curled into the sand, a thought hit her. *This man is an expert at seducing women.*

The thought shouldn't have bothered her but somehow it intruded on the moment. She'd been with other men; she knew he'd been married. But some part of her wanted to be the only woman in his life. That was impossible. He still loved the wife he'd lost.

Suddenly, he pulled back, eyes blazing, masculine jaw clenched. He was breathing like a race horse — and so was she. He dropped his arms to his side and gazed out at the ocean. White ribbons of waves cascaded toward the shore.

"Let's keep this professional," he said, his voice hoarse.

Professional? She wanted to scream that he wanted her as much as she wanted him, but pride kept her mouth shut. Somewhere in her muzzy brain came a single thought. *You're in real danger. Now is no time for romance.*

Not that this was romance, she assured herself. This was libido-driven. Sex pure and simple, the kind of encounter that she'd hate herself for in the morning. With a curt nod, she turned and walked back toward the house.

CHAPTER TEN

"Payback's a bitch," the killer whispered. The morning paper did not mention one single thing about Hayley Fordham. Not even a tiny article on the back page.

Nothing. Nada.

What could be better? Gone but not forgotten — so the old saying went. In this case: Gone and forgotten. Who was going to miss Hayley? Well, maybe that ancient aunt of hers would cry over Hayley. Too damn bad. Meg Amboy was almost dead herself. After she was gone no one would remember Hayley.

Nothing could be more perfect. Wiping Hayley off the face of the earth had been the plan.

Mission accomplished.

The killer paused, thinking how often "mission accomplished" had been used to describe Hayley's death. Well, it had been a mission of sorts. It had taken planning and precise execution, like a military operation. The bombing required bravery; not just anyone could obtain a bomb and install it properly. The goal had been accomplished.

"Maybe I'm just jumpy," the killer whispered. "That must be it." Still, using the term *mission accomplished* seemed premature. A lot of details remained to be resolved.

Well, you couldn't think of everything. Getting rid of the hordes of investigators who stupidly thought this was some terrorist act or a drug deal gone bad was a problem that hadn't been anticipated. The mission was *almost* accomplished. *Almost.* Now was the time for patience. *Don't do anything to tip your hand.*

Trent dialed his sister's office number. Farah answered on the third ring. "Where's your secretary?"

"She's part-time now," Farah answered in her usual clipped tone. She always tried to give the impression that he was interrupting something important. "What's the matter?"

"Nothing really," Trent hedged as he rose to his feet and closed the door to his small home office. He was sure Courtney was downstairs listening to Timmy pound away on the piano. Lately, Trent felt someone was watching him, listening to his conversations. He never said anything incriminating over the telephone, but that didn't mean they didn't have sophisticated surveillance tracking him.

No doubt it was the FBI or Homeland Security who was after him. They were convinced the car bombing that killed Hayley was linked to a drug deal. And they were trying their best to implicate him.

"I'm listening," Farah prompted.

"I spoke with the company attorney, Chad Bennett." Trent deliberately used Chad's full name and title. He didn't want anyone listening to suspect how close they really were. "He says Hayley's death will delay probate for about six weeks."

"Which to bureaucrats means eight weeks," Farah said with a huff of disgust. "Exactly what I told you."

Farah sounded irritated that he would waste her time. She was so self-absorbed sometimes that Trent wanted to slap her. "I'm wondering if you know of a way to get a bridge loan of some kind until the probate is finished."

"You're strapped for cash."

Her caustic tone made him lash out. "Don't tell me you're not. Why else would you have your secretary work part-time?"

The hollow silence lasted so long that Trent thought she'd hung up on him.

"You're right," she replied in a conciliatory tone that surprised him. "This economic downturn was unexpected and so devastating. I should have been more prepared."

Trent was stunned that Farah would admit she'd made a mistake. It wasn't her style. "Don't businesses still need accountants?"

"Many do, but others can use computer software to manage their finances." There was only the slightest hesitation before she added, "I could really use money, too."

Now Trent was blown away. Farah, who always handled finances so well, now needed cash. He considered telling her to put that no-good bum of a boyfriend to work, but decided to quit while he was ahead.

"What about Mother?" He hated to bring up their mother. Cynthia Fordham had expected both her children to reject their father after the divorce. The court had granted him visitation rights, but Cynthia insisted this was just a formality.

Russell Fordham was no longer their father; Cynthia insisted she would be both parents now. Farah had followed their mother's instructions. She dutifully visited her father, but she kept herself aloof, never engaging in activities her father loved.

Trent had tried — for a while — then found he loved skateboarding and surfing. And being at the beach with his father. He even befriended the little brat, Hayley, just to please his father.

His actions put distance between them. But one thing they agreed on was that Surf's Up was rightfully Trent's after his father retired. The girls had other interests while Trent lived for Surf's Up, not attending college so he could learn the business.

"Don't you dare ask Mother for money," hissed Farah. "She's broke."

How could that be possible? Their mother had sold the family house before the real estate bust. She'd gotten a bundle for a crappy little house his father had bought just after they'd been married. "What did she do with the money from the house?"

"Beats me," Farah said, her voice troubled. "She won't say, but she's lost all or most of it."

"You're kidding." He couldn't imagine his normally conservative mother risking the money that was to see her through retirement.

"We could get a loan based on the upcoming estate settlement, but I don't think that's

179

such a good idea."

"You're right." He knew she meant they should wait until this mess with Hayley blew over. Looking for a loan right now might serve as a red flag to investigators. His sister had always been smart — smarter than anyone in the family. Now was not the time to think he knew more than she did.

"Can't you borrow against the company's receivables?" she asked.

His stomach clenched like a boxer's fist. "I already have."

The silence on the other end of the line seemed to echo in his ear until she asked, "Can't you borrow from one of your rich friends?"

"Probably," he said, although he knew he'd never approach any of them. It would be far too embarrassing.

Meg Amboy stared out the window of her suite gazing at the picturesque coastline. A cloudless blue sky domed over a sea gilded by midmorning sunlight. "Perhaps if you played bridge it would take your mind off things," suggested Conrad from behind her where he sat in his wheelchair.

Meg stifled the urge to snap at him. After all, Conrad had persuaded his son to help her find out who murdered Hayley, and he patiently listened to her. "I can't concentrate," she told him, turning around. "My mind keeps going over . . . everything."

"When Ryan called you yesterday, he said he was making some progress, didn't he?"

"Yes," Meg admitted, "but he wouldn't say what he found out."

"He's being cautious. Some leads don't prove to be helpful. He'll tell you the details when he has something definite."

Meg nodded and managed a tight smile. She didn't want to seem ungrateful but she wasn't accustomed to waiting while others took the lead. It came from years of being in business for herself.

"It's over a week since Hayley died," Meg said. "Cases that aren't solved within forty-eight hours are rarely solved."

"Where did you hear that?" Conrad asked skeptically.

"I don't know," Meg admitted. "The television maybe."

"That isn't always a reliable source of information," he responded quietly. "The best authorities in the country are working on this case."

"I know, but I still think they're barking up the wrong tree," she said, echoing what she'd said many times, but if her mantra bored Conrad, he didn't show it. "I don't think this was related to drugs."

"But you can't be sure, can you? Hayley could have unwittingly become involved —"

"I'm not buying it." Meg sank down onto the sofa next to Conrad's wheelchair. "I think she was killed for her parents' money."

Conrad wheeled his chair around to face her, their knees touching. "Why now? It's almost a year since Russ and Alison died."

"The economy's worse," Meg pointed out. "I still believe one of the Fordhams — or all of them — were responsible for Hayley's death."

Meg couldn't explain, but this was something she instinctively felt. Or was it an overactive imagination? Since Hayley's death, Farah had been disgustingly solicitous. She'd called almost every day, sent flowers in an obvious attempt to ingratiate herself. Meg knew Farah was after her money. Fat chance. With Hayley gone, Meg planned to rewrite her will so charity would receive her fortune.

"What about Cynthia Fordham?" Conrad asked, breaking into her thoughts. "Ryan was going to see her."

"I only met the woman once when I was at the house and she came to pick up the children after a weekend with their father. Cynthia was beautiful. Bitchy. Not that I blamed her."

"What do you mean?"

Meg shrugged; she felt guilty speaking ill of the dead, but this was Conrad. She could be honest with him, her only friend. "I never approved of my little sister getting involved with a married man, breaking up a happy family. Cynthia hated my sister. I can't blame her."

"Did she hate Hayley, too? Enough to kill her?"

Meg paused; she'd asked herself the same question. "I'm sure she did resent Hayley living in a home on an exclusive island and being with Russell all the time. But enough to have her killed?" Meg stared down at her hands, which were spidered with blue veins. "Again, why would she wait until now?"

Conrad gave her a weak smile. "History is filled with mothers who were ambitious for their children and did whatever it took to put them in power."

"From what I know of Cynthia, I doubt she could have done it herself."

"But she might have hired someone," Conrad suggested. "Ryan will find out. We have to rely on him."

Meg nodded, although she disliked putting her faith in anyone. But what choice did she have?

Ryan stared at the computer screen. His special program had been running all night long, reassembling the files in the trash bin on Alison Fordham's computer. Most of the stuff was fairly mundane, items Alison undoubtedly trashed herself, but this document was different.

The data code indicated it had been scanned into Alison's computer about fifteen months ago. Why had it been deleted? It would take another few minutes to see when it had been deleted. He thought he knew the answer but didn't want to jump to any conclusions, especially when he was a bit hazy from lack of sleep.

It was just noon when he went downstairs to find Hayley. She was in the courtyard going over her mother's files. He paused to watch her for a moment before she noticed him. He hadn't seen her since last night but that didn't mean he hadn't thought about that kiss once or twice. Okay, okay — more than that. Memories of their kiss often interfered with his work. Too often.

Hayley had gripped his imagination from the moment he'd seen her picture. After actually meeting her, being with her,

Ryan's attraction to Hayley intensified. So why had he pulled back when *she'd* kissed him?

Blame it on a ghost. From the depths of his mind, an image of Jessica had appeared. His once stunningly beautiful wife racked by chemotherapy in a hospital bed waiting to die. The memory had forced him to pull away. Recalling such suffering, how could he make love to another woman?

"I'm not finding much," Hayley said as he forced himself to approach her. "What about you?"

Chill, he reminded himself. *Play along.* Apparently she's forgotten last night or she's ignoring what happened. He sat in the chair opposite Hayley, the sheaf of computer-generated papers in his hand. "I discovered something."

"Really," she replied, her tone so pleased that he felt even more reluctant to deliver the bad news.

"Your mother scanned in a document two months before she died. It had been sent to the trash bin."

"What was it? She must have had a good reason for deleting it." A note of anxiety accompanied each word.

"She didn't delete it." Ryan heard the ominous undercurrent in his own voice.

185

"Someone else did — the day after she died."

"Someone tampered with her computer?" Her voice shot up an octave. "What did they destroy?"

Ryan paused and considered his next words carefully. "A signed copy of the trust she and your father had set up."

Her mouth, usually so full and sexy, crimped into a taut, unyielding line. "There was a trust? They couldn't have used Chad —"

"They did. It's on his firm's letterhead and his signature is there along with a witness, Sylvia Morrow, who was also the notary."

"She's a secretary in Chad's office. Sylvia has been around for a long time. Chad's father, who died several years ago, hired her." She paused, then added, "Chad couldn't have known. Destroying trust documents would violate his professional ethics and —" Hayley's mouth snapped shut as if she realized how naive she sounded. "Ethical attorneys. An oxymoron, right?"

It was a rhetorical question so Ryan didn't answer.

Her tone became as matter-of-fact as if she were discussing the weather. "What happened to the copy Mom scanned? It should have been in her files."

"I suspect it was removed when they erased the copy from her computer."

"They?"

"It could have been just one person," Ryan told her, "but Bennett had to know about it. Another copy of the trust has to have been on file in his office. Either Farah or Trent persuaded him to keep his mouth shut. Otherwise he would have come forward to avert probate proceedings."

Hayley's face still revealed no emotion, no hint of her inner thoughts. "What was in it that they didn't want known?"

Wondering how she would respond, he quickly drew a breath. "Your parents left you Surf's Up. They split the proceeds of their other property between Farah and Trent."

"Oh, my God," cried Hayley, clearly devastated by the news. It took another minute before she added, "That would have given me two-thirds of the total estate."

"Right. By destroying all traces of the trust, a probate court would have leveled the playing field by splitting the estate equally among the three of you." He proceeded to state the obvious. "But someone, or both of them, wanted . . . more."

Hayley attempted a laugh, but it came out

more like a derisive snort. "Ironic. I didn't want the business. Trent lived for it."

"Why wouldn't they have left the business to Trent? He was already running it with your father, right?"

"True. I can't imagine what changed Dad's mind."

"Their minds. Your mother would have had to agree."

"Mom always backed up Dad on anything to do with the business." Hayley considered the situation for a few seconds. "I can't imagine what my father was thinking. He adored Trent. He won all sorts of skateboard tournaments when he was young, the way Dad once took prizes for his surfing. Trent was a budding Tony Hawk."

"Hawk? The skateboard champ? Trent was that good?"

"*Almost* that good. He never made it to Hawk's level. The guy's still around, hyping video games and appearing on the circuit."

"Trent worked at the shop and I helped Mom with designs. It just seemed understood that Trent would inherit the business."

"You, too. I guess."

Hayley shrugged. "Art was my first love. I guess I should have been more insistent that I wasn't interested in a career as a designer. I just didn't want to disappoint them until I could prove I had a future as an artist. Even after they died, I didn't tell the family I wanted out of the business. If I had spoken up earlier, none of this would have happened."

Ryan had his doubts about that. Greedy people weren't so easily satisfied. "That doesn't explain why your father left you the business."

"I guess he must have been convinced Trent would change it from a custom shop to just another board store loaded with surfboards imported from Asia, which is exactly what has happened since my father's death."

Ryan stared up at the bird trilling from the coral tree in the corner of the courtyard. "You don't seem too surprised by my discovery."

Hayley gazed directly into his eyes. "I'm not. I was awake all last night. I kept thinking about the disappearance of my mother's address book. No one could have gotten into the house except family. No one would profit from my death except Trent and Farah. I finally accepted the truth. What you discovered merely verifies it."

"I guess we'd better notify the authorities." He didn't want to give her up. Honestly, he didn't, despite the fact he'd been the one to end their kiss. He enjoyed being alone with Hayley and getting to know her. But he realized now was the time to reveal what they'd discovered.

Chapter Eleven

Ryan and Hayley had worked out their story. If he wanted to keep his job, they had to make certain no one found out he'd been hiding her. Hayley didn't like to lie, wasn't good at it, but she owed Ryan this — and more.

"The first thing I must do is see Aunt Meg," Hayley told him. "She's been upset long enough. Then I'll call the police."

"Remember, this won't mean you're safe. The police will need to do more investigating before they make an arrest. You'll be in danger. Don't tell anyone where you'll be staying — not even your aunt."

"Okay, I won't."

They'd agreed that Hayley would continue to live there secretly. It was a desperate move and he knew it, but this was the only way he could protect her until the crime was solved.

The cell phone in Ryan's trouser pocket

vibrated. He pulled it out and checked caller ID. Ed Phillips. "Hollister here."

"Looks like the locals were right," Phillips said immediately. "The ATF lab in Quantico IDed the bomb fragments. *Hecho en Mexico.* Made in Mexico, as they say."

"Really?" Ryan said, stunned, then decided he shouldn't be surprised. Southern California was close to the border.

"Get this. The ATF guys are really good. No wonder they're now Alcohol, Tobacco, Firearms and *Explosives*. This bomb was made by the Sinaloa cartel. They're an established cartel that's quite professional, considering smuggling drugs is their business. They don't sell bombs or post how to make them on the Internet. ATF's thinking Hayley or her family crossed them somehow."

"How could they tell?" Ryan was amazed. He hadn't had much training with explosives. That was assigned to a special team who only worked on that. But the bomb fragments he'd observed at the scene were tiny. He'd doubted they would be of any use.

"The ATF team used infrared spectography to analyze bomb fragments. A copper wire coated in blue plastic is a signature of the cartel. That's how they traced it to the

Sinaloa gang."

"Tell me about them." All Ryan really knew about the cartels was what he'd read in the newspaper or had seen on television. His work focused on white-collar crime that involved computers.

"The Mexican cartels go in for a lot of kidnapping, torture, brutal murder. Chopping off heads, dumping bodies in acid. They often don't hit the target directly. They kidnap and kill a family member. Siblings, cousins, kids. It's a warning."

"Who do you think they were warning?" Ryan asked, although he had a good idea what Ed would say.

"Looks like they were putting Trent Fordham on notice."

"I understood there was a drug connection with Asians that piggybacked their shipments in containers of surfboards."

"That was the theory, but this puts everything in a new light."

Something didn't jive, Ryan decided, but he couldn't pinpoint what was troubling him. "What happens now?"

"We squeeze Trent Fordham. See if he admits his involvement."

"We?"

"The locals," Phillips responded. "Apparently this is going to be their show. With

Homeland Security and ATF involved plus the Bureau, it's a real clusterfuck, but the local police are claiming jurisdiction."

"I might be able to help. I found something on a disk I took from Hayley's loft."

"What?"

"I'm not quite sure yet," Ryan hedged, aware of Hayley's intent gaze on him. "I'll know in a few hours."

"Call me," Phillips instructed, "before you alert the locals."

Ryan closed his phone, still not knowing what to make of this development.

"Whatsamatta?" Hayley asked in a *Sopranos* imitation that was surprisingly good.

She was so damn cute that he couldn't help smiling. He knew he shouldn't reveal what Ed Phillips had told him, but he'd already jeopardized his career for Hayley. What could this hurt?

"The bomb has been IDed as a Mexican cartel's. That's who blew up your car and tried to kill you. The Sinaloa gang."

She stared at him, her captivating eyes mystified. "Why?"

"By killing you, they were sending a warning to Trent."

"Trent involved in drugs? No way. He hangs with a group that party a lot. Marijuana and cocaine," Hayley countered in a harsh, raw voice. "That's it. Party stuff."

Ryan didn't want to remind her that she hadn't believed Trent would want to kill her, either. "I'm not suggesting he was using. I'm wondering if he saw an opportunity to make a lot of money. You weren't at Surf's Up on a daily basis, were you?"

"No," she admitted. "I went in every other week or so to deliver my designs and to check the computer to see what was selling in my current collection. I worked out of my loft most of the time. That's why I knew I could go off to Costa Rica without being missed."

"So it's possible Trent was doing something you didn't know about."

"It's possible," she conceded reluctantly. "Maybe Dad suspected and that's why he left the business to me."

"Could be. It wasn't difficult to access your mother's computer. Someone could have discovered the trust and decided to delete it. Do you know if Cynthia Fordham is familiar with computers?"

"Yes. My father's ex works in a boutique that does inventory control, employee scheduling, and all that sort of thing on a computer. I know because Trent insisted Surf's Up needed the latest version of that software."

"Was Cynthia at your parents' home after they were killed?"

Her expression was tight with strain. "Yes. A lot of people were coming and going. It was a madhouse. We were trying to plan the funeral, dealing with so much . . ."

"How it happened doesn't really matter —"

"Why not? I'd like to know who wants me dead."

Without thinking, he slipped his arm around her, saying, "I realize how upsetting this is. I assume the original plan didn't include killing you. They just didn't want you inheriting two-thirds of the estate."

"What changed?" she asked, echoing his thoughts. "Months later they wanted me dead."

"Good question," he responded, dropping his arm. He really shouldn't be touching her — no matter how much he longed to pull her into his arms. "One thing is certain. Chad Bennett had to be in on destroying the trust documents. He must know who is behind this."

Hayley didn't say a word but he detected the hurt clouding her eyes. He knew she had to be upset. Even though they'd broken up, they'd been engaged. She must have loved him — and still might for all he knew.

196

■ ■ ■ ■

Meg stood on her balcony overlooking the craggy coastline and inhaled the tangy salt-air cocktail that usually cheered her. The early afternoon sunlight blazed down on the water. The sun-spangled sea washed against the pristine beach. This stretch of the coast had no public access from the high bluffs above it. This was nature as God had intended it to be, yet it seemed lonely and forlorn somehow. She squeezed her eyes shut to make the world go away.

She heard a soft knock on the door behind her. It had to be one of the staff, she decided. Conrad was with the physical therapist now.

"Come in," she called over her shoulder. The front door was rarely locked.

A minute passed and Meg realized the staffer hadn't spoken, which was unlike them. To hold down a job at Twelve Oaks, a staffer had to be sickeningly cheery at all times, opening with a comment on the weather like: "Hi there, how are *we* feeling? Beautiful day isn't it?"

We? Who did they think they were kidding?

Meg slowly turned, trying to quell a vague

sense of unease and squinted into the shadowy suite behind her. A huge, constricting knot of pain tightened her throat. *These old eyes must be playing tricks,* she thought. The silhouette near the sofa reminded Meg of Hayley. Meg realized her grief had metastasized into depression, sadness so black and so deep that words couldn't express her feelings. She rarely came out of her room now — not even for Conrad.

"Who's there?" she called.

"It's me, Auntie."

Auntie? What damn fool stunt was someone pulling? Only Hayley called her "Auntie" and had since she was a toddler. For a handful of aching heartbeats Meg stood there.

The form moved out of the shadows.

Hayley! Oh, my God! She'd lost her mind, Meg thought. Suddenly she was aware of shortness of breath and a heart thumping like a caged animal trying to escape her chest.

Meg pressed a hand between her breasts to slow down her heart. She swayed slightly as the woman rushed forward, arms outstretched. Hayley. It was Hayley. Meg decided she must be hallucinating. The finality of her niece's death, of never being able to see Hayley again had triggered this illusion.

The woman threw her arms around Meg, saying, "I didn't mean to frighten you, Auntie. I'm so sorry."

Meg closed her eyes and let the woman guide her from the balcony into her suite. *She even smells like my Hayley,* Meg mused, unwilling to open her eyes and destroy the dream.

"I'm alive, Auntie. I didn't die. I wasn't in the car," the woman said in a low voice as she lowered Meg to the sofa.

A tendril of hope unwound inside Meg's heart. She cautiously opened her eyes. Could this be her beloved Hayley — the daughter who should have been hers, not Alison's?

"It really *is* you." She reached out and touched Hayley's soft cheek.

"It's me," her niece assured Meg. Hayley sat close beside her. "I'm still alive."

Meg gazed up at the ceiling, tears beading her eyelashes. "Thank you, God."

"It's quite a story," Hayley told her and Meg listened as she explained about the trip to Costa Rica and the mural she'd painted. She'd returned home, not knowing everyone believed she was dead.

"You didn't tell me about your trip because you thought I'd worry," Meg said when her niece had finished. Hayley nodded and her expressive eyes shimmered with unshed tears. Meg admitted she'd brought this upon herself. She would have insisted Hayley not fly on a small plane — not even a state-of-the-art private jet.

"I've been back two days," Hayley said.

Her words siphoned the air from Meg's lungs for a second. "Why didn't you call —"

"When I found out someone tried to kill me, I thought it best to hide out for a day or so. I was hoping the police would discover who wanted me dead."

"Where were you?"

"You remember my neighbors, Max and Jim?" Something flickered in Hayley's eyes. "I hid out at their place. They're up at Bass Lake near Yosemite. They didn't hear about the bombing, either. They were working on the cabin they'd bought. The cable isn't installed yet."

Meg hesitated for a second; Hayley had never been a good liar. She wasn't positive the girl was lying now but she suspected she wasn't telling the whole truth. Why? She decided not to challenge her. It was enough to have Hayley with her again.

"Did the police find out anything?" Meg

asked. Detective Wells should have called her if they had.

"I don't know. I haven't contacted the authorities yet. I wanted to see you first to let you know I'm okay."

Meg's mind processed the facts just as quickly as she had when she was young. Conrad's son would have called them if the case had been solved. Hayley was still in danger. "Why don't you hide out for a while longer? Give them time to solve the case."

"The boys are coming back tonight. They kept Andy for me. I can't stay with them, but I am going to keep my whereabouts a secret until this is sorted out."

"What about money?" Meg asked. "You can't use credit cards. Those are too easy to trace. I can get you whatever you want."

"Thanks. I may need to take you up on it." Haylcy paused. "Auntie, when you heard I'd died, who did you think had done it?"

"One of the Fordhams," she responded without hesitating. "Who else would gain from your death?"

"That's what I thought, too. All of them or just one of them?"

Meg shook her head. "I don't know. I've gone over it a million times in my head and still can't decide. I even hired Conrad's son, Ryan Hollister, to help, but he hasn't come up with much, either."

"Really?" Hayley's eyes shifted to the floor, then back to Meg's. "How could he help?"

Meg explained about Ryan Hollister's position with the FBI and the wild-goose chase the police were on, believing there was a drug connection with the car bombing. Hayley nodded as Meg spoke, but she didn't get the impression that her niece was really listening.

As she had all her life, Meg forged ahead with sheer determination. Hayley didn't seem to grasp the extreme danger of her situation. Meg had to take over. "I'm calling my lawyer. He'll recommend a criminal attorney. I think you're going to need one."

CHAPTER TWELVE

Garver Browne led Hayley out the back entrance of the Newport Beach Police Station to avoid the media swarming around the front. Her aunt, Conrad and Ryan were waiting in a Twelve Oaks limo. It was nearly midnight but the area behind the station was brightly lit by security lights. The chauffeur opened the Mercedes' door. Hayley and the criminal attorney climbed into the air-conditioned limousine.

"What happened?" asked Aunt Meg with a welcoming smile.

"Those jerks aren't interested in Lindsey." Hayley knew she sounded shrill but couldn't help herself. The last several hours had been grueling, beyond anything she'd imagined. Anger combined with devastation over Lindsey's death left her frustrated. The police didn't care an innocent woman had died. "They're positive this is drug-related."

Aunt Meg's smile dissolved. "That's

203

ridiculous! You never —"

"They're suspicious of me. They wanted me to take a lie detector test."

"Of course you agreed." Conrad Hollister was seated near the rear door in his wheelchair in the specially modified limousine.

"No," Garver Browne answered for Hayley. "They have no right to ask."

Silence roared through the limousine. Hayley ventured a quick look at Ryan. He would understand why she refused to take the test. She'd explained everything except where she'd been since returning from Costa Rica. "With a friend" was all she would say. How could a little white lie hurt her when she'd told the unvarnished truth about everything else?

Not everything, she silently amended. She hadn't mentioned the trust data on the disk someone had discarded in her mother's computer trash bin, because it could cost Ryan his job. He was going to funnel the information to the authorities through his friend Ed.

She felt guilty about not telling her aunt, either. If it hadn't been clear to Hayley before, Aunt Meg's reaction to her "back from the dead" appearance assured Hayley that her aunt was the only person on earth who truly loved her. But Ryan had convinced Hayley that telling could jeopardize his career, her life.

"Listen, everyone," Garver said. "Hayley is not going to discuss this until the police have completed their investigation." He turned his head slowly and looked at each of them before saying, "No one talks to the press. No one. If the police want to interview you, insist that I be there before you say *one* word."

Garver Browne was a criminal attorney who'd taken his private helicopter from L.A. to Orange County so he could accompany Hayley to the police station. She'd begged her aunt not to spend the money, but after the rigorous interrogation, Hayley was thankful she'd had the lawyer with her. The police had grilled her as if she'd been the one to plant the bomb.

Conrad said, "I don't think anyone will ask me —"

"Bet on it," Browne insisted. "Someone at the station alerted the press about Hayley's return. That's why there's a flock of carrion eaters gathered out front. The media will do *anything* to get a sound bite on the news."

Garver was in his late thirties — a few years older than Hayley and Ryan, but his prematurely gray hair made him seem much older. His hairline was creeping upward above a ladder of lines on his forehead, which gave him a scholarly appearance. The lawyer had a self-assured way of holding himself, of speaking, that complemented his reputation as the go-to attorney in SoCal if you were in trouble — and could afford him.

"Garver's right," Ryan said, speaking for the first time. "Our response to questions about Hayley should be *no comment.*"

"What about family?" Meg asked. "They'll want information."

Garver considered this for a moment. During their initial meeting at Aunt Meg's place, they'd explained that the rest of the family wasn't very close to Hayley. "Stick to the basic facts. Hayley was in Costa Rica doing a mural and had no idea what had happened. Other than that you don't know anything."

Hayley doubted her so-called family would really care. She told herself that she'd been prepared for what Ryan had found on her mother's computer and to some extent she had been. In other ways, it was difficult to imagine two children you'd grown up with, played with — shared a father with — would destroy trust documents, then try to kill you. And what about Chad, who claimed to love her even though she'd broken up with him? She forced herself not to think about the depth of his betrayal.

"Be certain to say you don't know where Hayley is staying," Ryan added.

"That's a fact," Aunt Meg said with a trace of anxiety that made Hayley feel even more guilty for what she'd put her aunt through. Aunt Meg's heart was weak and this stress certainly wasn't helping.

"Have you rented a car and bought an untraceable cell phone for Hayley?" the attorney asked Ryan.

The two had conferred at Twelve Oaks before Hayley and the attorney went to the police station. They'd agreed that nothing should have Hayley's name on it. For the time being, they were going to keep her whereabouts a secret.

Ryan handed her a small cell phone without looking her in the eye. Hayley could tell by the way he used his left hand that his shoulder was still bothering him. She couldn't help wondering what he was thinking. Was he sorry he'd gotten involved?

"I'm the only one who'll have your number," Garver told her.

"What about me?" Aunt Meg wanted to know.

"Sorry," Garver replied unapologetically. "Hayley will have to phone you. That way no one can force you to reveal her number."

A swift shadow of alarm swept across Aunt Meg's face. "Is she in so much danger that I should be careful?"

"We *all* need to be careful." Again, Garver took his time and looked at each one of them in that direct way of his. "What you don't know, you can't tell." He turned to her. "Don't drive for a few days. You have a place to live where no one will look for you. Stay indoors — don't let anyone see you."

Hayley nodded, careful not to glance in Ryan's direction. She gave her aunt credit for being a smart woman. Why tip her off that there was something between them? Not that there was.

"What did you think about Ryan and Hayley?" Meg asked Conrad.

They were still in the limousine on the way back to Twelve Acres, having driven around a lot to be sure they weren't being followed, then dropped off Hayley, Ryan and the attorney in a parking structure near the airport so Garver's pilot could helicopter him back to Los Angeles.

"I think we're lucky to have such great kids." Conrad's smile wavered. "For a while there we assumed you'd lost Hayley." His hand covered hers. "I'm thrilled she's back even though there's a lot to settle yet."

Meg nodded; she could see how weary Conrad had become since she'd called him to her suite before sunset and introduced him to Hayley. He'd immediately phoned his son and Ryan had come over. Meg hadn't waited to hear Ryan's advice. She'd called her personal attorney to get the name of a criminal defense lawyer.

This whole situation was perplexing. She wasn't buying the theory that Hayley was involved with drugs. The Fordhams were another matter. They could be up to anything. She'd never trusted Cynthia or either of her children. But she had no idea what was really going on. Her duty was to protect Hayley.

Seeing her niece again had been the greatest gift Meg Amboy had ever received. Just holding her, knowing she was alive was nothing short of an answer to her prayers.

So what if Garver Browne was a disciple of that great philosopher Jerry "Show me the money" Maguire? Browne's retainer had been outrageous, but Meg had immediately authorized a wire transfer to the attorney's account. What good was having a fortune if you couldn't help someone you loved?

"Is that what you meant about Hayley and Ryan?" Conrad asked, breaking into her thoughts. "What good kids they are."

Meg shook her head. "No. I was thinking about them as a couple."

"A couple? They just met under horrible circumstances. How could they be attracted to each other? They barely had a conversation."

"True." Meg knew Ryan Hollister had the kind of masculine good looks that gave women cardiac arrest. Even in a crisis, a woman would notice him. Not Hayley, apparently. She'd paid little attention to Conrad's son other than to listen to his recommendations about her safety.

Meg had watched them carefully. She'd tried to gauge Ryan's reaction to Hayley. There was something odd about him, as if his mind was elsewhere.

Why? Most men found Hayley very attractive and always had. But not Ryan. Could he still be grieving over his wife? She'd been gone for some time now.

Maybe the situation — the car bombing, the drugs, being presumed dead — had them both off-kilter. It was an unusual situation, to say the least. Under the circumstances, why would two unattached people notice each other? They probably wouldn't.

Still, something seemed strange to Meg. It was an unprecedented state of affairs, Meg acknowledged. She'd lived a long life, seen a lot, heard many unusual tales, but this beat all of them. Even so, the situation wasn't bothering her as much as Ryan and Hayley themselves. Something wasn't right.

Trent was diving underwater, catching a wave at the Wedge. He surfaced on the backside of the breaker and turned to body-surf the incoming wave. He could hear the smaller waves — which came in sets of three when surfing was at its best — crashing on the shore. The sound — usually background noise — distracted him and he missed his opportunity to ride the perfect wave onto the beach.

He bobbed beyond the break line and surveyed the water in the distance for "bluebirds" — the next set of waves. The noise of the crashing waves seemed unusually loud. He turned and looked toward the shore. No one was there. No one at all.

He sat up, sweating and breathing hard. He wasn't in the ocean, he realized. He was home in bed and the phone on the nightstand next to him was ringing — not waves crashing. He glanced at the clock beside the phone. Almost two in the morning. He grabbed the phone before it woke Courtney, even though she showed no sign of stirring. Pills had her out cold — again.

"Trent," Farah said the moment he pressed the receiver to his ear. He mumbled something and she added, "Go somewhere you can talk."

Trent put the phone on Hold and stumbled down the hall to his office. Why was Farah calling in the middle of the night? He could tell by her voice that she was upset, which was out of character. Even as a child, Farah hid her true feelings and over time had become almost inscrutable to those around her.

"What's happening?" he asked as he picked up the telephone on his desk. He quietly closed the door as she spoke.

"Are you sitting down?"

"Yes," he replied even though he was standing next to his office chair.

"Hayley is alive. She didn't die in that car bombing."

He swallowed hard, striving to control his jellied knees. "You're shitting me." He swiveled the chair around and dropped into it like a sack of lead.

"Don't I wish this was a joke." The cold edge of irony cut through each syllable. "Kyle went to the police station to bail out a friend of his. There were television cameras everywhere. It seems that little Miss Hayley Fordham and her frigging attorney

212

— Garver Browne, no less — waltzed into the station to tell them she was alive."

Trent stared out the window at the ocean where a sailboat's mast light bobbed in the water. "Unfuckingbelievable! Who died in her car?"

"Kyle couldn't get the details. The police were questioning Hayley."

"Why did she have a lawyer with her? What's going on?"

"Good question." Farah's voice hardened. "I'll bet that battle-ax aunt of hers is paying Garver Browne's fee. The prick doesn't come cheap."

"For sure." The thought of money triggered a gut reaction. "Now probate will have to be recalculated *again*." What in hell was he going to do?

"At least we'll be splitting it in thirds. Hayley won't get control of Surf's Up."

Trent wondered if there would be enough left of the company to worry about. His creditors were circling like sharks with blood in the water. He had to feed them money — soon.

There was a long pause before Farah spoke again. "Look on the bright side. They can't pin the car bombing on us." There was a thin chill in her voice that Ryan didn't like.

213

"So? Nothing seems to be stopping them from trying to implicate me. Not us. You're in the clear. Just me."

"Let's not discuss this on the telephone," Farah cautioned. "Go over and meet with Chad in person. Maybe he'll have a few helpful ideas."

Trent rang the bell of the mansion on Harbor Island where Chad Bennett lived. The island was even more exclusive than nearby Linda Isle where Trent's father had lived, but it didn't have a guard at the gate. A card key was all that was needed to access the island. Of course, the metal bar didn't rise to admit your car without one. This hadn't bothered Trent. He'd merely parked on Harbor Island Drive and ducked under the steel arm.

It was nearly 3:00 a.m. now. Few lights were on in the yards of the thirty homes on the private island. They must use timers, Trent thought as he leaned on the bell again. Through the leaded glass door, he saw a light go on upstairs.

This home had belonged to Chad's parents. His mother had passed away long ago and his father had never remarried. Chad inherited the mansion when his father died, along with his father's law firm. It was a huge place for one person to kick around in, Trent thought, but then Chad was rarely alone.

He saw Chad taking the stairs two at a time while cinching a robe around his waist. Chad turned on the porch light and peered through the glass before unlocking it and saying, "What's wrong? It's the middle of the fucking night."

"Hayley isn't dead." Trent kept his voice low. Land on the small islands in the bay was so valuable that lots were not much bigger than a parking space. They were just a few feet away from the neighbors. Trent didn't want any of them calling the police about a disturbance. "She's back and she's hired a lawyer — Garver Browne."

Chad stared at him as if Trent was speaking in tongues. He grabbed Trent's arm and pulled him inside. "Browne? No shit?"

Trent waited for Chad to close the door before saying, "It's true."

Chad's brow furrowed and he pointed upward, then put a finger in front of his lips, indicating he had a woman upstairs and they should keep their voices down. "Where's she been? Who was in the car?"

"I don't have all the details. Farah and I thought I should come here to tell you rather than use the phone and leave a record."

"Good thinking." Chad ran his fingers though his hair. "This certainly fucks up everything."

"How long do you think it will take to recalculate the probate?" Money wasn't Trent's only concern, but it was his most pressing problem.

"The lowlife bureaucrats almost had it figured out for three. They've just started on dual calculations. Now they'll have to start all over."

"What? Can't they go back to what they originally had?"

"No. It doesn't work that way. Papers were filed, including the death certificate. Now that will have to be corrected and appraisals of property resubmitted. Guaranteed to take —" he shrugged "— who knows how long?"

Just what Trent feared. What was he going to do?

"Still need a loan?" Chad asked, then added without waiting for an answer, "Try Laird McMasters. He's hot to be involved with Surf's Up."

"Might have to," Trent admitted. He hated the thought of dealing with Laird, but what choice did he have?

Chad cracked the door, a clear sign for Trent to leave. "Don't worry about Hayley's reappearance. They can't prove squat."

"I'm not so sure . . ."

"Trust me." Chad opened the front door. "I'll take care of everything."

Trent walked outside without another word. Trust Chad? Did he have a choice?

CHAPTER THIRTEEN

Barefoot, Hayley silently walked across the tile floor in an oversize T-shirt and panties to the bank of floor-to-ceiling windows that faced the beach. A scythe of a moon gave off pale light that bounced across the waves and highlighted the sand in front of Conrad Hollister's home. A window nearby was open and the fresh scent of the ocean filled the room. The wind chimes hanging from the roof danced in a whisper of a breeze along with the lulling sound of waves breaking on the beach.

It was the middle of the night and she couldn't sleep. Hayley had believed meeting with the police would solve her problems. It hadn't. If anything, the situation was now more complicated.

The police couldn't tie her to the drug cartel but that didn't mean Trent wasn't involved. By association she could easily be implicated. Once she would have laughed at the thought. Those things only happened on television, but now she knew better. Look at all the bizarre events surrounding her lately.

White-hot anger mushroomed inside her. The soothing sound of the sea that usually calmed her didn't help. She didn't have much of a temper. Most of the people she'd known always described her as "laid-back" — a typical SoCal expression. She might have been mellow once, but no longer. A single thought kept ringing in her brain: Someone wants you dead. It was frustrating as hell not to know exactly who and why.

"See anyone out there?"

She whirled around, her heart thumping. Ryan. Sitting in the shadows on the sofa facing the magnificent view. But even as the thought registered, telling her that she wasn't in danger, it was impossible to steady her erratic pulse. Someone had tried to kill her. Was she ever going to feel safe again?

"I — I w-wasn't looking for anyone," she managed to say, remembering how little she was wearing and wondering if he could see she was nearly naked. "I just couldn't sleep."

"I know what you mean." Ryan patted the seat next to him.

A now familiar shiver of awareness swept through her. In the dark room his features were hazy, but she could make out the strong line of his jaw and his glossy black hair. Her heart fluttered wildly as she ventured toward him.

She sat, putting an appropriate distance between them. A professional distance. He was so compelling; his vitality captivated her. He didn't feel the same way. *Get a grip,* she silently instructed herself. *You're in real trouble.*

"How's your shoulder?" she asked to fill the awkward silence.

"Okay. Sports teach you to ignore pain." His teeth flashed white in the shadows and the ambient light glinted in his eyes.

"I've been thinking."

"Uh-oh," he said, his tone light. "Thinking about what?"

"Playing this a different way. Not hiding."

"Got a death wish —" he leaned toward her "— or what? Your attorney told you to stay out of sight."

"Hear me out." She ignored the flutter in her chest brought on by his closeness. "What would I do if I didn't know about the erased CD of my parents' trust?"

"Well, I suppose you'd go about your business, thinking the bombing was a mistake of some kind."

"Exactly. I wouldn't hide. I'd take some

precautions. Obviously a vicious cartel has *mistaken* me for someone else."

"Hold on, sweet cheeks."

Sweet cheeks? Her eyes were adjusted to the hazy light and she could see his expression. He was concerned about her. Was "sweet cheeks" a term of endearment he used with his wife and it just slipped out? Undoubtedly. *Easy, Hayley, let it go. This man is trying to help you.*

"I have my doubts about the cartel angle even though the ATF traced the bomb to them," Ryan told her. "I think Trent and Farah — possibly their mother — and maybe Chad Bennett are the real threats."

"Agreed, but what good does it do to hide forever?"

"It's not forever. It's just until the police get the copy of the CD and realize the trust was altered. They'll put the pressure on the Fordhams to get a confession."

"Possibly if it were just Trent, but I think Farah is too smart and Cynthia too conniving to admit anything. The CD you're going to give your friend Ed is a copy of a CD that my mother *supposedly* gave me along with several design CDs that I never bothered to look at. The Fordhams will claim I made a fake CD. Chad Bennett will back them to the hilt rather than risk being

221

disbarred for his part in the scheme."

They'd decided to pretend the CD had been among the group of disks Ryan had taken from Hayley's loft. Otherwise, they would have to admit they'd broken into her parents' home and found the info on the hard drive. This was the only way to reveal the information while protecting Ryan.

Warily, she watched him consider what she'd just said. His jaw tightened and she could almost feel the sudden tension in his body. For an instant, she thought he was going to grab her and shake some sense into her. Fierce determination filled every cell in her body. He could be as persuasive as he wanted, as demanding — as anything — but she'd made up her mind.

She noticed him shudder as he drew in a sharp breath and hunched his shoulders forward. "You know, Hayley, you're onto something. There's no way to prove when that CD was made. A hacker could have altered it."

Now she leaned closer to him. "Exactly. Chad would claim I took stationery from his office when we were engaged. I used it to create the disk and make it appear legitimate."

"You're probably right. Unless the authorities have your mother's hard drive checked by an expert, they won't know the document is real."

"While I'm returning to my usual routine, couldn't you get the police to examine my mother's computer?" she asked.

"It's not that easy. A regular technician used by most police departments to examine criminals' computers isn't skilled enough to find this file."

"What should we do?" The minute she uttered the word *we* Hayley regretted it. This was her problem — not his. He'd already jeopardized his career for her. She couldn't let him take another risk. "I'm not hiding. I'm going to find out who's behind this."

He rubbed his injured shoulder for a moment. "What do you intend to do?"

"Go to Surf's Up as if I don't know a thing. Plant a bug in Trent's office —"

"Where would you get the bug?"

"Online from the SpyShoppe."

"Spare me! Too much television. Too much Internet." Ryan threw both hands into the air, palms up. "If you could get something on Trent — and that's a big 'if' because devices sold on the Internet are notoriously unreliable — what would you do with the info?"

"Take it to the authorities. Hopefully, he'll implicate the others involved."

He turned to her; even in the shadowy light she read the skepticism in his expression. "You would have obtained it illegally and it couldn't be used in court."

A sourness flared in the pit of her stomach. Had she been thinking, she would have realized this. She had no idea what she was going to do, but she refused to hide. A thought hit her. "You must know where I could buy reliable equipment."

His eyes were so assessing that it made her uneasy. "I do, but it still won't solve the evidence problem."

"I feel like I'm stuck in quicksand. I want to know who exactly is behind this and why. Then I'll know what to do."

"I understand," he replied.

"I can't help thinking that it's more than the money motivating someone."

"Why?"

She could feel her throat closing up, and quickly said, "A hunch. That's all."

"Has to be two people at least," he responded. "Bennett didn't stand to gain anything by denying there was a trust —"

Hayley shot to her feet. "Oh, my God. I have an idea. Let's contact Sylvia Morrow, the secretary in Chad's office who notarized the trust. She could back up what you found in the computer's trash."

"I thought of that but I assumed she was in on this or she would have come forward."

"True," she agreed. Hayley had only met Sylvia a few times when she'd been in the office with Chad. She didn't have a feel for the older woman.

Ryan reached up and took Hayley's hand, then gently pulled her down beside him again, closer this time. "Do you know how a bug works?"

"Sort of." This near him, she couldn't ignore the heat of his body, the masculine planes of his chest under the T-shirt. "It picks up conversations and they're recorded . . . somewhere."

"So where would you hide the recorder?" he asked, unaware of the effect he had on her.

"I don't know. Nearby. In the bushes behind the shop."

"Great, so kids could come along and grab it."

"It's not much of a plan," she admitted. "But I'm not going to hide. Garver said it could be months before the estate was settled. At that point, no one will have a reason to kill me — if that actually *is* the reason. I refuse to wait — hiding like *I'm* the criminal — until the probate is completed. I'm not going to do it." She knew she sounded petulant but couldn't help it. She'd made up her mind. Nothing her aunt or anyone said would change it.

He seemed to sense her need for reassurance. He slipped his arm around her shoulders and drew her flush against the solid wall of his chest. His arm was warm and strong. She inhaled the clean, fresh scent of soap. He must have showered after they'd come home.

Being in his arms felt so right that she snuggled closer. For a fleeting second she remembered the way he'd rejected her yesterday, but then the thought evaporated. She needed to feel connected to someone. Even if Ryan was only a friend, it didn't matter. She'd always put a distance between herself and others. Oh, she had friends, but Lindsey had been her only close friend other than Aunt Meg.

Aunt Meg was family. She'd been programmed to love Hayley because Hayley was her sister's child. Lindsey had become a close friend because she had confided in Hayley — drawn her into her life. Maybe that was what had been wrong with her relationship with Chad, Hayley reflected. They'd been engaged but somehow they'd never been truly close.

Now she needed a friend, someone who

would understand what she was up against. Ryan's sheer size was comforting in a way that she hadn't expected. She knew he didn't agree with her plan, but at least he listened to her, discussed things. Unlike Chad, who was a man who wanted an audience, she realized.

"I can help you," Ryan said. "What you need is a professional bug that can be picked up far away — not in the bushes nearby — and will record on a CD, not a tape that has to be changed all the time."

"Is that how it's done?" she asked, realizing she knew little about high-tech surveillance.

"Yes. I can get a chip for any phone, even a cell phone."

"Great." She gave him half a hug with her one arm before the light dawned. He was volunteering to help her. She couldn't allow him to do anything more to put his career at risk.

"You've done enough for me. I can't let you get into trouble. If you just tell me where to go and what to get —"

"It's too technical. I'll take care of it." The concern she detected in his eyes startled her. "I've decided to resign. I can't get into trouble for helping you."

She gasped, alarm coursing through her.

"You did? Why?"

His arm still around her, Ryan rested his head against the back of the sofa and stared up at the ceiling. In the shadowy darkness, she couldn't read his expression. Oh, God, she didn't want to be responsible for ending his career. Then she recalled the way he'd acted last night. She didn't mean that much to him. Something else had to be going on that she didn't understand.

"It's complicated," he finally said, lowering his head and looking into her eyes again. "I haven't been on track with the Bureau's program for some time now. Even before I reinjured my shoulder, I didn't like the way career advancement means moving to another city when you get a promotion."

There seemed to be some unspoken yet intangible link between them. She didn't dare speak and break the spell. It occurred to Hayley that she knew very little about him. Maybe she was foolish to trust him. The thought vanished before it could settle in her brain.

"When I return to work in two weeks, I expect to be promoted and sent to Quantico, where the main office has a world-class computer forensics team. That would mean leaving my father. I can't. He won't be around forever. I want to share what time we have left."

"I understand," Hayley replied in a whispery voice that she hardly recognized. "When my parents died, I would have moved to San Francisco, but I couldn't leave Aunt Meg." She had the feeling there might be more to his story than he was telling her, but now didn't seem to be the time to question him.

Ryan silently gazed down at her. His look was so galvanizing it sent a tremor through her. His grip on her tightened as his attitude became more serious. "My priorities have changed. I'm going to help you through this, then I'll reevaluate . . . things."

He pulled her closer, both arms around her now. Her cheek rested against his T-shirt and she could feel the firmness of his torso, the powerful beat of his heart. She circled her arm around his waist, feeling protected and desired.

Desired? Was she imagining it? After the way she'd misjudged him last night, Hayley couldn't be sure. His appeal was devastating but maybe he just wanted to comfort her. She was just plain stupid to allow herself to imagine this to be something it wasn't.

She tilted her head up so she could look directly into his eyes. In the shadows, his gaze roved over her face. The smoldering spark she saw in his eyes was startling. A ripple of excitement danced through her. There was no mistaking his intentions.

He cradled her face with a warm hand, sweeping away all her doubts and fears. His touch was almost unbearable in its tenderness and the surge of passion it released in Hayley. Her feelings for him were intensifying with every beat of her heart. Her whole body seemed to be filled with wanting — and waiting. Tonight he had to kiss her first.

His lips pressed against hers, then gently covered her mouth. His grip on her tightened as he pressed her flush against his chest. Her pulse quickened and a hot ache built inside her. The velvet warmth of his kiss became slightly moist as his tongue sought hers. She returned his kiss with reckless abandon. Her nipples tightened and her body did a slow burn.

Dizzy with excitement, she dug her fingers into the solid muscles of his neck, careful to avoid his injured shoulder. His lips slanting over hers, his tongue invaded her mouth and his grip on her tightened. Her senses reeled as if short-circuited.

He eased her backward, still kissing her, until they were stretched out on the sofa, his powerful body half-covering hers. A riptide of pure desire swept through her at the mind-blowing kiss. The magnitude of her own feelings stunned her. When had she ever wanted a man like this?

Never.

Until now, until Ryan Hollister. She arched her body upward so her breasts could revel in the warmth of his chest and her lower body could cradle his burgeoning arousal. *Oh, my.* Her body had been made for him.

His lips left hers, but hovered a scant inch above her mouth. His eyes were as hot as the molten sun. "You're so damn sexy. It's eating me alive."

She touched his cheek, the emerging stubble rough against her fingertips. "Am I?"

"Damn right," he replied, his voice suddenly hoarse.

She tried to smile but his lips were already on hers again — more possessive this time. Feverishly she kissed him, nibbling the tip of his tongue, then sucking on it. A groan came from deep in his throat; inwardly she smiled. His fingers slipped under her tank top and up her rib cage, stroking and caressing. His large hand fondled the fullness of her breast as his thumb circled her nipple. Her head spun with excitement and she quaked beneath him.

Some inner voice echoed in her brain: *Slow down. You don't know this man. Now isn't the time for sex.* Good advice, but who cared? She wanted Ryan — and she wanted him *now!*

The sweet spot between her legs throbbed and her toes curled into the sofa's smooth leather. What was happening to her? In a distant part of her mind, Hayley realized she was out of control but she couldn't help herself.

Ryan levered himself upward and shucked his T-shirt in one swift movement. In the pale light from the window, she saw the dense thatch of chest hair that arrowed downward in a vee then disappeared under the waistband of his shorts. What right did one man have to look so heart-stoppingly masculine, so handsome?

The lean muscles on his broad chest were ripped and his arms bulged slightly. A white welt of a scar marked his shoulder. An athlete's body, complete with battle scars, she thought.

He had her tank top off before she realized she was helping him. The cool ocean breeze through the window swirled over her beaded breasts. Her nipples became hard as marbles. Heart reeling, she pulled him down on top of her again. She kissed him as if he were the only man she'd ever wanted to kiss.

Arms around his neck, she arched upward to feel his rough nest of curls against her sensitive breasts. Oh, yes, she thought as her nipples instantly responded to the coarse feel of his chest and the firmness of his arousal pressing into her.

She was so engrossed in the marvelous sensations that it took a few seconds to realize the buzzing sound wasn't in her sex-crazed brain. Ryan's telephone was ringing and vibrating at the same time near her thigh.

Ryan broke the kiss and jammed his hand into the side pocket of his cargo shorts. Breathing audibly, he told her. "It must be Ed. I have to take this."

They disentangled their bodies as Ryan answered in a raspy voice that wouldn't have fooled anyone. Hayley searched for her T-shirt and found it on the floor beside the sofa. Ryan's conversation barely registered, but she knew he was telling Ed that the disk had turned out not to be important.

She shrugged into the flimsy shirt, realizing the call had saved her. This was a mistake. She couldn't get involved with a man right now. She wasn't sure if what she was feeling was a reaction to a prolonged lack of sex, or had it been ignited by the danger of her situation?

Taking time, making sure was the best course of action. *Don't jump into anything, especially with a man still in love with his deceased wife. You won't ever live up to the image he has in his mind,* she reminded herself.

She stood up while Ryan was still talking. Now he was telling Ed that he expected to go to work for a private security firm as soon as his shoulder fully healed. The situation was awkward, to say the least, she thought.

The last thing she wanted was to face Ryan and acknowledge what had — almost — happened between them. Or take up where they'd left off.

Mumbling, "Good night," she headed toward the bedroom she was using. Once inside, she locked the door. Hayley half expected Ryan to come to her room, but he didn't. No doubt he'd come to his senses, too.

CHAPTER FOURTEEN

"What the fuck happened?" The killer hated that word — fuck. It was so overused, but in this case it described the situation to a T. "How could that bitch still be alive?"

Asking the sun just peeking over the horizon was useless. Same for the ribbons of white clouds against the pale sky. Mother Nature had the answer to many questions, but not this one.

The killer squeezed out a furious growling sound. Shit happened. The woman who climbed into Hayley's car looked *exactly* like Hayley. Didn't she? Thinking back to that night, it was hard to be sure. It had been so dark, so shadowy.

Who wouldn't have mistaken the woman — whoever she was — for Hayley? *Fuck. Double fuck.* The woman had gotten into Hayley's car and put a key in the ignition. At that point there was no way to stop the explosion.

"Let it go," the killer whispered, hatred flaming from every pore. "Forget about it. Move forward. Come up with a new idea."

Don't allow one lousy snafu to end the plan. This was merely a roadblock. The screeching wail of a siren, sounding like a cat in heat, filled the air. It reminded the killer of a more pressing problem. Now everyone from the media to the authorities was watching . . . investigating. Hayley's return from the dead — nothing short of miraculous — intrigued everyone.

Welcome to the real world. It might be total bullshit, but the public loved a mystery, a conspiracy theory. They'd be howling to see this case solved.

At this point, taking out Hayley wouldn't be prudent. *Prudent.* What a word. The killer savored it. Some might have used *smart* instead, but not the killer. Thinking at a higher level had deceived even the cleverest of investigators. So far.

Who would have imagined Hayley was alive? Not one fucking person.

Who was the woman who died? Not that it mattered to the plan. But if she happened to be someone important, the authorities would bully everyone to solve this. Eventually, they might figure out what was really happening.

Do something to sidetrack them. But what?

The killer stared at the sky, now painted dazzling blue by the morning sun. A trio of gulls flew over, circling, cawing. An idea slowly began to form in the killer's mind. There were obstacles — mere details — to be worked out, but this might be the answer. The killer considered various possibilities. What had to be done became crystal-clear and the killer was jazzed, wired.

Hayley Fordham didn't have nine lives. She couldn't escape death twice. She was as good as dead. *So* dead.

Trent sat on the deck of the Beachcomber Café and sipped a cup of coffee, inhaling the bracing scent of the sea as he gazed out at Crystal Cove Beach while he waited for Laird McMasters. The gentle swells that broke on the sugar-fine sand became choppier whitecaps closer to the horizon. This wasn't a good surfing beach, but it was a favorite of families.

Crystal Cove was one of the spots in Newport Beach that Trent liked best. No other beach boasted a café within a few feet of the surf. Fine dining could be found on the bay, but none right on the ocean like this. When you got right down to it, even foodies admitted you couldn't beat Mother

Nature's beauty.

"Hey, dude. Been waiting long?" Laird appeared at Trent's side.

"Not long." Laird pulled out the chair opposite Trent, and Trent couldn't help wondering — not for the first time — why Laird seemed so anxious to become a big name in the surf business. No one had ever seen him surf.

Laird could easily have gone into his father's commercial real estate business, but no. Right out of Yale with a degree in finance, Laird had used a trust fund from his grandfather to open a surf shop.

"Coffee for me. Black. And blueberry waffles. Hold the whipped cream," Laird told the cute redhead who'd appeared out of nowhere when Laird sat down. The guy was a chick magnet. The only girl who hadn't fallen all over him since junior high was Hayley.

Trent ordered an omelet while Laird pulled off his Ray Bans and tilted his face up to catch the rays of the morning sun. The light glinted off his gelled brown hair. "What's up? You said it was important."

Trent wanted to ease into this; he didn't want to sound desperate. "You heard about Hayley."

Laird's head snapped down and he looked

at Trent. "What about her?"

Trent knew by Laird's expression that he hadn't heard. Hayley's reappearance was all anyone could talk about. "It wasn't Hayley that died in that car bombing."

"No shit!"

"What planet have you been visiting? It's all over the news."

The animation had left Laird's face. He didn't seem to notice the waitress bending low, giving him a look at her breasts as she brought Laird his coffee and refilled Trent's cup. This wasn't like Laird. He was an ass man from the get-go. That's why Trent had always been secretly glad Hayley hadn't fallen for him. Even after her lowest point when she'd broken up with Chad, Hayley just had a few dates with Laird. He knew without asking that Laird hadn't gotten Hayley in bed. Good. Life was too easy for the prick.

"I was on the *Hail Mary* in Catalina." Laird's tone sounded strained as he referred to his Donzi. The speed boat had been christened *Hail Mary* because it went so fast that those aboard prayed when Laird was at the wheel. "I'd just returned when you called."

That explained it. Laird had undoubtedly been banging some chick on the boat all night, then headed home from the island at dawn. The damn boat was so fast it took less than an hour to cross the channel.

Trent leaned back, valiantly trying to hide a smirk. It wasn't often that he was one up on Laird McMasters. "Seems Hayley went down to Costa Rica without telling anyone. She just returned and found out we'd buried her."

Trent couldn't stifle a laugh. He chuckled loudly and several people at nearby tables glanced their way. Laird's answering smile was bleak, tight-lipped as he shot his hand through his hair.

Trent realized that what he suspected was true. Laird still had a thing for Hayley. Always had; probably always would have. Trent didn't see it, but that didn't matter. What was important was how he could take advantage of the information.

"The police, the FBI, everyone was looking for her. Why didn't her passport show up on a computer security check or something?"

"I don't have all the details, but apparently she flew there on some guy's private plane. A Falcon X7." Trent had heard this on the morning newscast.

That got him. Laird had an eighteen-hole tan so he couldn't turn green, but a flash of jealousy sparked in his dark eyes. Only the richest guys could afford such an expensive plane.

"Don't they have CNN down there?" Laird asked, bitterness underscoring each word. "Didn't she hear she'd supposedly died?"

"Apparently not." Trent raised his eyebrows, hoping to give the impression that Hayley had been too busy in bed to turn on the news. Why in hell had she gone to Costa Rica, of all places?

The waitress arrived with their food and set the plates in front of them, again giving Laird a full view of her boobs. The guy had it bad; he didn't look.

Laird didn't even glance up when the bell clanged three times and a male waiter shouted that a whale had been sighted in the surf. The tourists sprang to their feet — as usual every table was full — to see one of the pods of whales migrating north from Mexico to Alaska. The locals, accustomed to the sight, just gazed at the passing whale.

"You wanted to have breakfast with me to tell me about Hayley." Laird sounded as if he'd been eating a dog turd instead of the Beachcomber's famous waffles.

"No. I assumed you knew." Trent had to be careful here. Laird was irritated and maybe now wasn't the time to bring up money. His temper, when crossed, could be almost uncontrollable. Trent was sorry he'd mentioned Hayley.

"I didn't know," Laird replied with his usual self-confidence, "but I'm glad. She has an eye for our business and she's a good person."

This gave Trent the opening he'd been praying for since leaving Chad last night. "You're right. She has great business sense."

"Like her mother."

Trent almost choked on his bite of spinach omelet. He forced himself to say, "True." He felt as if he'd stabbed his mother in the back. The woman always deluded herself by believing Russell Fordham alone had built Surf's Up. No one dared mention to Cynthia Fordham that Alison had been the brains behind the operation.

"What's going on?" Laird sounded like his old self now.

"We're in a bit of a bind," Trent replied, easing into this. "The DEA has a hold on my shipment of surfboards from China. The economic meltdown. We're strapped for cash."

Laird put down his fork and his dark eyes pierced the distance between them. "Isn't the company in probate?"

"Right. We should be out soon." He didn't tell him that refiling the papers when they thought Hayley was dead had delayed the process considerably. "We need cash now." He deliberately said "we" because it was obvious Laird had a soft spot for Hayley. "Could you advance us some money short-term?"

"Is that legal? I mean shouldn't the receiver — or conservator or whoever oversees the probate — be handling this?"

"Yes," Trent conceded. "This would be off the books."

Laird shoved his half-eaten waffles aside. "You know, Hayley has the right take on our business. Smart girl, like her mother."

Trent struggled to keep his face neutral. Allison Fordham again. And Hayley. Why wasn't Laird discussing the money?

"Remember that meeting at Tommy Bahama's a couple of weeks before your father crashed?"

Trent nodded, hiding his bitterness. How could he forget the lunch on the sunny patio of the Caribbean-style restaurant a few doors away from Surf's Up? He and Laird had planned to convince his father that importing boards was a great idea — the future of the business. He'd brought Hayley along; she'd had other ideas.

Laird leaned across the table. "Hayley was dead-on, you know. Sports in America have changed. I hadn't thought about it until Hayley mentioned it. Skateboarding has been the fastest-growing sport for the last —" Laird shrugged "— dozen years or so. Since we were kids. Right behind it is mountain biking, kayaking and snowboarding. All individual sports — not team sports."

Trent managed a nod. He'd heard all this before — several times. What Hayley had pointed out that day made their father reevaluate his business.

"Team sports aren't growing," continued Laird. "They're too competitive, cause too many injuries to young players and they've become too . . . too corporate. College ball has been decimated by guys who leave for the pros without finishing school. Then they make outrageous amounts of money and it pisses off the public big-time."

"True," Trent agreed, although he had once hoped to make his fortune as a pro skateboarder. He had talent, but others were more talented, and he was smart enough to realize it.

"Know what I read the other day? There was a survey in some flyover town like St. Louis or Kansas City. The fifteen- to twenty-

244

five-year-olds questioned couldn't name more than two of the pros on the local football team, but they knew the names of five or more MMA fighters."

"I'm not surprised. Hayley saw that trend coming." He despised the sport, but no question the gear with The Wrath's logo — designed by Hayley — was kicking butt even in a depressed economy.

"I think Hayley is right. Surfers changed the country. Clothes, vocabulary, attitude, but we're on the downstroke now. Sure, there'll always be the need for boards and clothes, but it's not the growth industry it once was."

Laird and Hayley were probably right. In fact, checking the company's numbers proved they were onto something. But that didn't mean Trent had to like it.

"How much do you and Hayley need?"

Trent shook his head regretfully and told him. Laird's smile morphed into a shit-eating smirk.

Trent left the Beachcomber and took the tram that was new — but made to look like a fifties Woodie — up to the parking lot. Crystal Cove was a state beach now, but once it had been home to locals who'd built wooden cottages along the shore back when not everyone had two or three cars. Now only service vehicles were allowed down to the area where one large cottage had been converted into The Beachcomber while the others were rented to tourists. They paid big bucks to be right on the water in "cottages" that were little more than shacks.

On the drive to Surf's Up main shop in the Corona del Mar shopping center, Trent reviewed his options. He did not want to be in business with Laird. The sleaze would find a way to bilk Trent out of major dough. Laird and Farah were both smarter, more educated than Trent, but Trent figured he had his mother's craftiness. He reviewed his options as he pulled into the huge parking lot.

It was only nine-thirty — early for the beach in summer — but the area was crowded with cars. Then he noticed the horde of people outside his shop. They hadn't had this large a crowd since the last Christmas sale two years ago, before the economic meltdown.

Wait a minute. Why weren't people inside? The shop had been open for half an hour. A van with a satellite dish on top caught his eye. *KABC News* was in metallic letters along its side. They were filming a live remote.

Hayley, he realized. Not customers. News media. They were here no doubt for a comment on Hayley. What could he say? He didn't know squat.

He swung his Porsche into the space reserved for him and shut off the engine. No one had spotted him so he was tempted to go home. Who needed this?

Home made him think of Courtney and Timmy. Trent would bet his life his whiny son was banging away on the piano or in his room reading a book. Jesus H. Christ. At Timmy's age, Trent had skateboarded his way to the beach carrying his own surfboard. Could the kid be gay? Trent brushed the thought aside. This was Courtney's doing. She was making a wuss out of Trent's son.

Trent knew he should divorce Courtney. Her pill problem wasn't getting any better, but he couldn't afford a divorce right now. If Hayley had died and the estate had been split two ways, he would have been able to divorce Courtney at the end of this year. The way things were going, he wouldn't get rid of her in the foreseeable future.

At times like this, Trent wished his father had opened a corporate office. Then Trent could hide out in a high-rise somewhere until the dust settled. But no, his father, like the other surfers who'd turned their passion into a business, chose to stay close to their customers. A spacious office was in back of the retail store.

Face your problems, Trent told himself. He glanced at the crowd in front of his store. Was that The Wrath standing there?

"I'll be a son of a bitch," he swore as he climbed out of the Porsche. *Don't go off half-cocked,* Trent warned himself. Sales of MMA gear were keeping the company afloat. Trent hadn't anticipated the trend, didn't like The Wrath and all his steroid-pumped bully boys who lived for cage fighting, but enough people idolized the prick to spend money on clothes — even when dollars were tight — that carried The Wrath's logo.

With a measured, purposeful stride, Trent walked toward the swarming horde at the door to Surf's Up. No one paid any attention to him as he elbowed his way forward until he was almost abreast of the gaggle of reporters who had a bouquet of microphones thrust to The Wrath's face.

"Yo, Trent," called The Wrath.

Bulky cameras burdening the shoulders of the men with the flashy reporters swung in Trent's direction. Reporters scrambled to reposition themselves. Microphones jabbed at him.

"Isn't it the *bomb?*" The Wrath asked. "Hayley is alive."

Bile rose in Trent's throat and he forced himself to smile and nod. "The whole family is thrilled." A bald-faced lie. Only Meg Amboy was truly happy.

"Were you surprised? Where had your sister been? Why hadn't she called? What's going to happen now? Who was the woman in the car? Has her family been notified?" Like machine-gun fire, the questions bombarded him.

Trent suddenly remembered the brief clip he'd seen on TV of Garver Browne. "No comment," he said as he shouldered his way past the reporters toward the two shopping-center security guards stationed at the entrance to his store. If he left them panting for more, Surf's Up would be on television for hours. Couldn't hurt business.

The Wrath followed at Trent's heels. "I had to talk to Hayley myself. See that she was okay."

Trent halted and The Wrath nearly bumped into him in front of the counter fashioned from old-time surfboards. He cautiously asked, "You talked to her?"

"Sure," the muscle-bound hulk replied

with his trademark sneer. "She's in the office."

My office! Trent stopped himself from shouting this out loud. What the fuck was she doing here? The Hayley he knew would be hiding out until this situation was resolved. Obviously, someone had tried to kill her. What was she doing sashaying around? Camping out in *his* office?

What should he do? What should he say? How should he act? Shit! He should have gone home. There was no turning back now.

CHAPTER FIFTEEN

Hayley pretended she didn't hear Trent coming toward the office. She tinkered with the computer, looking at sales reports that she'd already reviewed. Could she pull this off? She'd never been much of an actress, and was worse at lying.

Your life depends on this, she reminded herself. When Ryan had dropped her off before the shop opened, she'd spotted the reporters and slipped in the back door. The young clerks — who surfed on days off — had been thrilled to see her.

Hayley had expected Trent to arrive any moment, but he hadn't, which was unusual. The man had an admirable work ethic. Trent had refused to attend college because he felt he could learn more on the job. Hayley's mother hadn't agreed, but Trent's mother backed him all the way.

Cynthia had always wanted Trent to own Surf's Up. Hayley hadn't spent much time around her father's ex, but when she had, Hayley could tell the woman saw Trent as the rightful heir to the surf empire his father had built. It hadn't bothered Hayley because she wanted something different for herself.

Hayley had told a clerk to call the center's security guards to keep the media vampires thirsty for fresh blood out of the shop. They swarmed outside the door, anxious for Surf's Up to open. A few seconds later insistent banging on the front door had caught her attention. She'd peeked from behind the rack of board shorts where she'd concealed herself to see The Wrath.

She had the clerks let him in and he strode right up to her, then engulfed her in his powerful arms. "I heard you were back. I couldn't believe it. I had to see for myself."

The MMA fighter who could make opponents quake with a single scowl was genuinely glad to see her. When she'd been thinking about her lack of close friends, Hayley hadn't realized Carleton Cole — The Wrath — had become a friend, not just a business contact. She took him back to the office and gave him the story that she and Ryan had agreed upon.

Ryan hadn't come into her room last night as she'd half-expected. Half-hoped. She was confused; her own emotions baffled her.

How could she be so attracted to Ryan when less than a week ago, she'd been telling herself to get over Chad Bennett? She was over him all right, but what had she gotten herself into now? Her life was proof positive she was a crummy judge of character.

Hayley recalled some psychologist on television saying women tended to pick the same kind of man over and over. Was that what she was doing?

Was she setting herself up for another heartbreak by falling for a man who must still be in love with a dead woman?

There was no way to compete with a ghost, she realized. That person had died and could no longer do anything wrong. Jessica Hollister had been immortalized in Ryan's mind. Otherwise he would have moved on after two years, right?

Wait a minute, she told herself. What made her think Ryan hadn't moved on? He could have a girlfriend in L.A. or somewhere. After all, his excuse for breaking off the kiss was to "keep this professional." Considering Ryan had ignored professional standards in hiding her, Hayley believed this wasn't the real reason.

Something she'd heard in his voice, seen in his eyes when he'd discussed his wife made Hayley believe Ryan's reasons were personal — not professional. Technically, it was impossible to be unfaithful to someone who was no longer among the living, but maybe Ryan didn't feel that way.

On some level, he was attracted to her. *Get real,* she thought. *Remember what he said:* "You're so damn sexy. It's eating me alive." Last night may have meant *something* to her, but to Ryan it had been all about sex. He might worship his wife's memory, but he had physical needs. No doubt anything in panties would do. Well, not these panties.

She had to keep her priorities in mind. Finding out exactly *who* wanted her dead and *why* trumped anything else in her life. Next came her aunt and her career. Sex finished dead last.

"Hayley!" Trent called from the doorway.

She lifted her head, acting as if she hadn't heard him arrive. The Wrath was at his side, smiling. She'd thought The Wrath had left for his morning training session, but now he was here again.

"I'm baaack!" Hayley cried, striving to sound upbeat. She rose from the computer and awkwardly walked into Trent's outstretched arms.

"Oh, my God! I can't believe it!" Trent

bear-hugged her. "I — I thought . . . w-we thought — everyone thought you were dead."

A croaking sob burst from Trent and hit Hayley like a punch worthy of The Wrath. The anger simmering inside her instantly cooled. Uncomfortable, she pulled out of his embrace. Were those tears pooling in Trent's eyes? His reaction was the last thing she'd expected, and it left her totally unprepared.

"Everyone's stoked that you're okay," The Wrath said.

"Where were you?" Trent asked, his tone concerned. "Why didn't you let anyone know you'd be away?"

"It's a long story." She didn't want to have this discussion in front of The Wrath.

"Gotta run," The Wrath said, instantly solving her problem. "I'm late. Just came back to tell you the reporters know you're in here. Now they have the rear entrance covered."

"Thanks," she said. "It was great to see you."

He reached out and brushed her cheek with his big hand. "Anytime, babe. You're the bomb. Don't wanna lose you." He sauntered toward the door. "Remember, you're coming to the exhibition fight."

"Count on it," she replied, then ventured a look at Trent. He was more composed now, but there was no mistaking the emotion on his face. He'd acted the same way when they'd been told their parents had died.

Could she be mistaken about Trent? Perhaps it had been Farah or Cynthia who'd conspired with Chad. It was possible, she conceded. In her experience, women were much more capable of deceit than men.

"Sit down." Trent still looked shaken. "Tell me all about it."

The office had two desks with computers and a bank of filing cabinets and display stations for mock-ups of gear they were considering producing or purchasing. The larger desk had belonged to their father, but after his death, Trent had taken it over. The other desk had been her mother's until Trent came to work full-time. Then she began to do more of the designing at home. Since the plane crash, Hayley had used the desk.

Hayley sat in the chair next to her father's desk and studied Trent for a moment. "I went to Costa Rica to paint a mural for Ramon Estevez's new hotel."

He gazed at her with reproachful eyes. "I didn't realize you knew Estevez."

Hayley explained about selling her art in a gallery in San Francisco where she'd met Estevez and agreed to paint a mural. "I've always wanted to be an artist. Surely you knew that."

Trent shook his head. "I thought it was a hobby, like golf or tennis."

"Didn't you want to be a pro skateboarder? Isn't Surf's Up a second choice?"

Trent rocked back in the swivel chair and stared at the ceiling for a moment, then he looked at her again. "Sorta. Not second choice. I just thought after my pro career, I would come into the business. I've always liked it." He waved his arm to indicate the shop in front of the office. "I thought you did, too."

This wasn't going the way she'd imagined. Hayley could see her revelation — instead of making Trent free to claim the company as his own — disappointed him. Now, she really questioned his involvement in the destruction of the trust documents.

"I want a career as an artist. Doing this mural raises my profile in the art world. I flew down there secretly because I didn't want Aunt Meg to worry. You know how much she hated Dad's plane. Then when they were killed, she made me promise not to fly on small planes."

Trent sighed heavily, his voice filled with anguish. "You could have told me."

For a moment, she was baffled. He cared much more than she could possibly have imagined. Why not? They'd been raised together — part of the time anyway — and he'd helped her father teach her how to surf. She would have been just as upset if he had died. "I should have, but I wanted to make *sure* Aunt Meg didn't find out. Her heart's so weak."

"I see," he slowly responded, but it was clear that he didn't.

"Somehow the air crew didn't run my passport through the system, or the authorities would have realized I was out of the country," she rushed on to change the subject. "When I returned and found out, I hid until I decided what to do."

Trent arched one eyebrow as if she lacked her full share of brain cells. "Who was the woman killed in your car?"

"Lindsey Fulton." Just saying her friend's name, imagining her gruesome death, caused a sense of loss too deep for tears.

Trent frowned. "Do I know her?"

"No. She was an artist from San Francisco. She'd flown down and met me at Gulliver's where I'd parked my car. She was going to use it and stay at my place until I returned." Hayley didn't bother to explain about Lindsey's crazy husband.

"Jesus H. Christ! Talk about being unlucky. Wrong place at the wrong time."

He was just a little too flip about Lindsey's death, she decided, but didn't call him on it. If they kept discussing Lindsey, she was certain she would begin to cry. That would put her off track. She'd come here for a reason.

She'd installed the two state-of-the-art listening devices Ryan had given her. One was in Trent's office phone. Another was hidden in the rim of his desk. She had a third to slip into his cell phone — if she had the chance.

"Why'd you hire Garver Browne?"

"That was Aunt Meg's idea. I went to see her first, intending to call you next," she fibbed. "She insisted I needed an attorney. She was right."

"What do you mean?"

"The police acted as if I were the criminal." She went on to tell him about the aggressive questioning. "They even asked me to take a lie detector test."

"Really? They're holding up my container from China, but they didn't mention the test to me."

"Be careful what you say," she warned

him. "Don't talk to the press. That's what Garver told me. Let's see what charges they file, if any."

Trent hesitated, measuring her for a moment in a way that made her even more uncomfortable. "Didn't Browne tell you to stay out of sight? If he didn't, he should have. What if the killer tries again?"

As casually as she could manage, Hayley fibbed, "Garver thinks it's a drug mix-up. Happens all the time. With all this publicity, they'll realize their mistake and leave me alone."

Trent nodded thoughtfully. "Probably."

Actually, when she'd called Garver to tell him she wasn't going to play dead and hide, the attorney told her that she was "wacko." He believed that someone would try to kill her again. She asked one of the questions troubling her. "You haven't let anyone ship drugs with the company's orders, have you?"

"Of course not," he shot back immediately. "Hell, they had drug sniffing dogs all over the store, the warehouse, the container. Then they tore everything apart, but they didn't find shit. I'm not sure why they think it's drug-related."

She felt his sharp eyes boring into her. If Trent was lying, he was better at it than she

260

could possibly have imagined. "It seems the way bombs are made give them a certain signature. The police told me the ATF identified this bomb as belonging to the Sinaloa cartel."

"Really?" His eyebrows shot up. "You haven't —"

"No. I never have done drugs." She couldn't believe he was asking her, since he'd tried over the years to get her to smoke pot or kick back tequila shooters with him and she'd always refused.

"What about The Wrath and that crew? They're a bunch of dick-swingers pumped on steroids. Who says they aren't involved in some major drug scam?"

"That's ridiculous," she cried, then told herself Trent had a point. She'd gone to the local gym where he worked out. It was in the seedy part of Costa Mesa near Santa Ana.

A lot of odd-looking guys hung out around the gym. They seemed friendly enough, she thought, recalling The Wrath showing her a few moves to ward of an attacker. Not that it had done much good when Ryan mistakenly jumped her. A crowd had gathered to watch her lesson. Just because they'd been smiling and laughing didn't mean they weren't involved in illegal activities.

Suddenly, she recalled something else. On the morning of the car bombing, Hayley had gone to the gym where The Wrath was training to get his approval on some designs. Was it possible the bomb had been planted while she was inside the gym?

"I suppose you could be right," she admitted, still wondering about her trip to the gym. "There's a lot of money at stake in MMA fights."

"No kidding. Joe Hunter just bought a twenty-plus million-dollar estate on the ocean in Laguna."

Hayley knew "Mean Joe" Hunter was an MMA promoter who'd bought the rights to televise the sport when the bouts were unknown beyond the back alleys. Joe had made a fortune when MMA hit the big time and television was the next step. She hadn't realized the promoter had moved to the art colony just minutes south of Newport Beach.

"Fights have always attracted a certain . . . element," Trent said. "Fixing fights. Mobsters. The works."

"What would that have to do with me?"

Trent threw up his hands. "I haven't a clue. I guess it doesn't compute. Garver Browne is probably right. This was a mistake."

"Let's hope the police come to the same conclusion — and the media. Then we can go about our lives." Hayley tried to inject as much sincerity into her voice as she could. "Tell me what's been going on with Surf's Up. I checked the sales reports. Swimsuits are still selling at last year's level. Same for board shorts. MMA merchandise sales are up — way up."

Trent held the tip of his tongue between his teeth, the way he had when he'd lost a skateboard competition when they'd been kids. Being a man, her father had claimed. Trying not to cry.

Why was he so upset? No one had tried to kill him. An odd twinge of heaviness centered in her chest, turned to lead. She'd grown up with this man. Hayley was friends with his wife. His son was her nephew and she loved him as if he had been her own child.

"Something the matter?" she asked in a ragged whisper.

"We could lose Surf's Up," he replied in a low voice taut with anguish.

His words caught her off guard. "What?"

"You heard me. We could lose everything Dad —" he inhaled a sharp breath "— and your mother built."

Her pulse began to beat in double-time as

his statement registered. "Why? How? Isn't the court overseeing the probate?"

"Sure the court is in charge — so to speak." A bitter laugh erupted from his pursed lips. "But we're running the company. They're just trying to decide its value so they can settle the estate and scarf up the state's cut. The economy tanked our profits just when we were set to take off."

"You mean the container you're — we're sharing with Laird?"

His expression darkened, and she sensed bad news coming. "We're not sharing that container. It's all ours. Not that we could sell all those boards in this economy, but with them impounded we can't even try."

We? She wanted to scream at him. Their father had warned about cheap imported boards. He'd made Surf's Up's name on custom boards from his own molds. They didn't have enough stores to sell half a container of inexpensive boards in a great market. What was Trent thinking?

"We need cash — now — to meet payroll, pay for shipments, rent. You name it."

Her chest felt as if it would burst, but she couldn't yell at Trent. It was clear how devastated he was. Trent had a family depending on him. She'd anticipated this discussion all night, but in the various scenarios she'd envisioned this had never occurred to her.

She'd believed if she met with Trent face-to-face she would know if he had been involved in the destruction of the trust and — possibly — the car bombing. Now she could see that Trent was distressed about his mistakes. He wasn't out to get her. His concern was the company.

"What can we do?" she asked.

CHAPTER SIXTEEN

"What can we do?" Trent replied. "Good question. We need money so I met with Laird McMasters this morning. He's agreed to help, but he wants part of the company."

Hayley groaned inwardly. She'd known Laird since high school when he'd moved to Newport Beach. He was smart — attended his father's alma mater, Yale — and charismatic. Girls adored him. Except Hayley. They'd gone out several times when she'd been younger, but she'd never felt comfortable with him. Then she'd refused to date him despite persistent calls.

When he'd left for Yale — with a big send-off party — she thought Laird would stay back east after graduating. But he hadn't. He'd surprised everyone by coming home and opening a surf shop.

What was that all about? everyone wondered. The guy didn't surf. He was a golfer and his father was a real estate developer who also loved golf. All the big names in the business, from Hurley to Quicksilver and, of course, Surf's Up, had been founded by surfers.

She had to give Laird credit. He'd learned the business and become successful. She'd been with her father when he'd met with Laird to discuss importing surfboards together. Laird was ambitious. Maybe a little too ambitious. He was willing to cut corners to make money.

After she'd broken up with Chad, she'd again gone out with Laird. She was older now; he no longer intimidated her the way he once had. Still, she didn't enjoy his company and stopped dating him. Maybe she'd been too upset by Chad's betrayal to take an interest in any man. She wasn't sure, but she didn't regret her decision.

"Are you comfortable with Laird?" she asked.

"No. Are you?"

She couldn't help giggling at Trent's candor. He'd never liked Laird. She couldn't imagine him *wanting* Laird to be a partner. The situation must be truly desperate. "No, but do we have another choice?"

Hayley hadn't looked closely at the books. She should have. There was no excuse for not checking. That had been her mother's job. With her death, Hayley should have been more hands-on.

Instead, she'd turned inward and focused on her art. She cranked out surf designs that were little more than a recycling of earlier work. Her only innovation had been with the MMA line.

She'd believed Trent was more business savvy than her father, whose interest had been limited to custom boards. Trent had been very involved, but obviously not cautious, as he should have been.

"I've tried everything," Trent assured her. "Banks aren't loaning to retail operations right now. Private equity has dried up."

"Can't the court —"

"I asked. Raising money isn't their job. Unless you count raising money for the state in a probate."

Hayley thought of all her parents had built, their lifetime of happiness represented by Surf's Up. She recalled the years she'd spent at the shop, running up and down, trying on equipment and clothes. She'd suffered her own insecurities, but it was about as happy a childhood as she could have known. To lose it or have it taken over by the likes of Laird McMasters seemed like an insult to her parents' memory.

"Didn't Laird offer to buy Surf's Up once

before?" she asked, recalling what Ryan had told her.

"Yeah. How did you know?" There was an edge to his voice now.

Hayley shrugged as if she couldn't recall. "What did you tell him?"

Trent lifted his brows and blew out an exasperated breath. "I said you didn't want to. I was too chicken to tell him that I was hoping one of the big guns would buy us out for more than he was offering, so I blamed it on you."

He wasn't lying, she thought. This was what Ryan had told her. "You never mentioned anything about Laird or hoping anyone would buy us out."

Trent slowly shook his head. "It was a crazy time. Dad had just died and the economy hadn't tanked. I don't know what I was thinking. But today Laird's hurting for money just like the rest of us. He has enough to see us over this hump but not enough to buy us out. It's partners or nothing."

Nothing, Hayley silently vowed. At least Trent was being up front with her, and she knew how he felt. Their parents' deaths had thrown everyone into a tailspin. Out of nowhere, the answer came to her. "I could ask Aunt Meg to help us out."

He stared at her in utter disbelief. "I thought you wanted out."

"I do, but . . ." She realized this meant her art career would go on hold again. "I can't let Laird McMasters take over. And that's what he'll do. I know Laird. He won't be satisfied until he's running the whole show."

"You're right. That's what I'm afraid of."

Hayley gave him an encouraging smile. They were in this together. How could she have thought he was behind the attempt on her life or had concealed the existence of the trust? That left Farah and Cynthia. One or both of them were behind this.

"Do you think your aunt will help?" His mood seemed suddenly buoyant and she knew that she had let him carry the burden of the store alone too long.

"She might. I'm going to ask her right now." She rose to leave, then remembered the reporters. "Is the side door to Peet's still working?"

"Are you sure you want to do this?" Ed Phillips asked.

They were sitting at Java City, having coffee and muffins while Ryan waited for Hayley to contact him. She'd been in the shop, which was less than five minutes away,

270

for a long time now. It had been over an hour since she'd sent him a text message saying Trent hadn't come into work yet.

He'd met Phillips and discussed Hayley's situation. Phillips was blown away by her unexpected reappearance, but he let it go. The FBI had been pulled off the case. With the AFT, DEA, Homeland Security and the local agencies still involved, the director thought the FBI could be put to better use.

"Yes. I'm sure I want to resign. I've written the letter already, I just need to see Dawkins in person to tell him."

"What are you going to do?" Phillips asked.

"I'm planning on joining a friend's computer security firm. Corporate work mostly. It's right here in Orange County."

"They could use you in Quantico." Ed finished off his coffee-cake muffin.

"I know." Ryan couldn't help feeling a bit guilty. The Bureau had trained him and now he was bailing when he could be of real use. "I'm up for a promotion and you know that means a transfer."

Phillips smiled blandly. "So?"

"I don't want to go back there. My father's not well. He's all the family I have. I need to stay close to him."

Phillips nodded. "I didn't realize. I certainly understand."

"I'll be working on stopping botnets."

"Say what?"

Sometimes Ryan forgot three-quarters of the people he met used computers but didn't know squat about how they operated. "Botnets. Masses of computers like yours or your kid's that are secretly hijacked. Hackers send messages through those computers without the owners ever realizing it. Those messages can send spam or denial of service attacks that overwhelm Web sites."

"Ya mean like what happened to Twitter a while back?"

Ryan nodded and swigged the last of his coffee. "Exactly. So much traffic is sent to a site that it shuts down. Denies service. Not a major problem if you're Twitter, but if you're a bank or brokerage or business, it can be a disaster."

"Jeez-a-ree. Terrorists or spies could also use it."

Ryan put down his empty cup. "That's what I want to stop. I'll be willing to consult with the Bureau and just charge a base fee, but I'm not moving back east right now."

"Think you can solve the problem?"

"Not really. The true problem is the Internet was developed as an experiment by the military. It wasn't perfected, but it was so

272

good that business latched on to it. And it took off big-time. The infrastructure supporting the system hasn't had an upgrade since the mid-eighties. That's a recipe for disaster."

"Russia and a buncha' those 'stan' countries have packs of hackers sitting all day trying to tap into the Pentagon's system."

"I know. It's a huge problem for the government, for business. And getting bigger every day." Ryan grinned at Ed. "Of course, you've never forwarded a chain letter e-mail. Have you?"

"Naw. Hate those things."

"Even if it's a good joke or supports cancer awareness or recognizes the importance of God and it comes from someone you know?"

"Well, I mighta," Ed admitted. "Some jokes are just too good."

"That's another part of the problem. Chain messages often have hidden tracking cookies. It gives the original sender a whole new list of e-mail addresses for spam or a botnet."

"*Yow-zer.* That's butt-ugly. Guess I'm not forwarding anything." He finished his coffee. "Are the Bureau's computers safe? I'm told they are."

"Yes. They're encrypted. That means

they're harder to hack into — but not impossible. I'm looking forward to working on this exclusively."

Phillips smiled. "And here I thought you were quittin' because you'd fallen for Hayley Fordham."

It was all Ryan could do not to flinch as if he'd been slapped. "You're good. I'll give you that. How did you know?"

Phillips shrugged and ran a hand through his shaggy salt-and-pepper hair. "Your father, her aunt. You askin' about the plane crash that killed Hayley's parents. Her turning up, saying she'd been alone in some guy's place before she came to the police. I figured she contacted her aunt, met you and somethin' else went on before she came to the police."

"You're close. Real close. I did know she was alive." Ryan decided to leave it like that. He trusted Phillips, but thought it best if no one knew the facts. "But she's not the reason I'm resigning. I've been thinking about it. Now's the time — while my father is still alive."

"Okay by me." Phillips stood up. "I contacted the Bureau. They're looking at several pieces of the wreckage from the crash that killed the Fordhams. The whole shebang was in a warehouse in Riverside. When I get a report, I'll call you."

Ryan rose, glancing at his watch. What was keeping Hayley? "I owe you."

"Don't worry. When I need a computer guy, I'll call you."

Phillips started to walk toward his car, but Ryan stopped him, saying, "I know why you haven't gotten rid of your accent."

"Get out!"

"Jist so'z ya' know," he mimicked Ed. "You didn't want to be promoted. You like living in L.A. You don't want to go back east any more than I do."

Phillips aimed a finger pistol at his head and fired. "You got me!"

Farah waited at a small table on the sidewalk outside Café Panini for Trent. He'd called her and insisted she meet him as soon as possible. He'd said not to come to the store because of all the reporters. She watched him drive up in his sleek Porsche and let the valet take the car.

"What's happening?" she asked the second he sat down.

"Hayley came to see me."

A wave of apprehension swept through Farah, heightened by the troubled expression on her brother's face. "She's not in hiding?"

"Nope." Trent signaled the waitress for coffee and Farah nodded that she would have the same. "She thinks it was a mistake. She assumes she's safe."

For a moment, she was too surprised to do more than nod. "Hayley was never the brightest bulb in the chandelier."

"No. That was you." Trent's words were laced with sarcasm. "You were always the smart one."

"So you couldn't tell me this over the phone? You had to drag me all the way here?"

"I don't trust phones. They're too easy to bug."

The waiter appeared and they both ordered turkey paninis. Farah waited until the girl had left before speaking. "There are parabolic microphones that can pick up conversations from waaay off."

Trent leaned closer, whispering, "That's why I wanted to come here. I checked on the Internet. Heavy background noise like waves and —" he gestured toward the cars streaming by on the Coast Highway "— traffic sounds make it impossible to hear if people are speaking in low voices."

Farah though her brother was becoming increasingly paranoid, but then he'd never been really brave. Oh, he thought he was so macho for his high-flying skateboard tricks and riding monster waves, but when it came to real courage, he was a zero.

"Hayley hasn't a clue," Trent told her, his voice still pitched low. "She's going to ask her aunt for the money to save Surf's Up."

"You're kidding."

"No way. She doesn't want Laird McMasters to get a piece of dear ole Dad's business."

Farah's body vibrated with silent laughter and she put a hand over her mouth. It was a moment before she could ask, "How did you manage that?"

Her brother flashed a Cheshire cat grin. "I don't know. I guess I'm a better actor than I ever imagined. Son of a bitch! I was so surprised to see her that I didn't know what to do.

"I hugged her to buy time, then thought what would I do and say if this had been you back from the dead. I went with it. All tenderness and astonishment. It worked. I even managed — hell knows how — to tear up. She bought it and I took it from there."

Farah decided she should have given her brother more credit. She might have it over him in the brains department but he had the same intuitive way of reading people that their mother had. And fooling them.

"Great. You're the best." She toasted him with her water glass. "I guess you're thrilled to dodge Laird — again."

"You got that right. He's gonna be pissed. He's always wanted to get his hands on Surf's Up."

"What if Hayley can't talk her aunt into loaning the money? That old bat didn't make millions because she's dumb."

"True, but she has a soft spot for Hayley."

CHAPTER SEVENTEEN

"You what?" Meg Amboy cried. She simply couldn't believe her niece was standing there telling her that she'd waltzed into Surf's Up this morning. "Didn't Garver Browne say not to go anywhere? You were supposed to hide. Even I don't know where you're staying or what your new cell phone number is."

"That was last night. I spoke with him this morning. The whole thing is a case of mistaken identity." Hayley sounded confident, but Meg wasn't buying it. "The ATF proved the bomb had been made by the Sinaloa cartel. I've never had anything to do with drugs. Obviously, the car bomb was intended for someone else."

Meg gulped. "You can't be serious. You asked me who I thought was behind the bombing. I said the Fordhams and you agreed."

"That's true, but in light of the discovery

of the origin of the bomb, I think it rules them out."

"Think again! You may not be involved with drugs but Trent or his sister could be."

"Trent gave me his word that he hasn't."

"His word." Could this be her Hayley? What was she thinking? Meg drew in a breath and attempted to relax. She reminded herself that when she rose from bed yesterday, she would have given everything she had to have Hayley back.

They were standing on the balcony of Meg's suite. She gazed out at the magnificent stretch of coastline visible from her balcony. When it came to nature's marvels, people were insignificant.

Hayley lightly touched Meg's arm. "Let's sit down."

Meg lowered herself into one of the two wicker chairs where she often sat drinking her morning coffee or enjoying the sunset with Conrad. No doubt this car bombing had been a life-altering experience for Hayley. It came less than a year after her parents had been killed, which had been followed by Chad's betrayal. No wonder Hayley wasn't thinking clearly.

Hayley turned to Meg; her niece's eyes were more hazel than green under the awning that shaded the balcony, but there was no mistaking the seriousness in them. "Trent had nothing to do with this. I'm positive. When he saw me this morning, he hugged me and there were tears in his eyes. He acted just the way he did after Daddy died."

Meg was sure he did. Splitting the estate in thirds rather than in half was enough to make a grown man cry. She tried to think of how to respond, since her niece obviously didn't perceive the situation the way she did.

"I know you're concerned, but I don't want you to worry. We're taking precautions."

We? Surely she hadn't forgiven Chad Bennett. That cheater was never good enough for Hayley, but befriending her now could persuade soft-hearted Hayley to forgive him. She kept her face neutral — she hoped — asking, "We?"

"Ryan Hollister. You and Conrad asked him to help me. He's been great." Her words were infused with a slight tinge of excitement.

Something's going on between them, Meg thought, pleased. She knew they'd be a perfect couple. All they needed was time to discover it for themselves. "What precautions are you taking?"

"I'm still not telling anyone where I'm staying or giving out my new cell number."

"Why not, if you're positive the bombing was a mistake?" Meg challenged, but took care not to sound too critical.

"Ryan says . . . just in case the police are wrong, I shouldn't be an easy target."

This was straitjacket territory, Meg decided. Either that or she was truly succumbing to senility. Why half hide? It was like being half pregnant. Either you were or you weren't. Something else was going on here. She'd had this feeling since Hayley had first returned from the dead.

Hayley stood up, took two steps forward, and clutched the balcony railing with both hands. Facing the sea, Hayley said, "We're going to lose Surf's Up if I don't do something."

A jumble of confused thoughts and feelings assailed Meg. What was really going on here? How could Surf's Up be lost? Hayley seemed stronger now, yet different. Had Ryan caused the change or was it escaping death while losing a close friend?

Meg concealed her inner turmoil with a deceptively calm voice. "What do you mean? Is the company in trouble?"

Hayley turned to face her. "Yes." Her voice echoed her concerned expression. "We need money so much that we may have to accept Laird McMasters as part owner."

"Really?" Meg was astonished. Surf's Up had been a cash cow. It had supported Russell Fordham's whole family. Some of its products were sold in sport shops around the country. True, Alison had been the brains behind the business, but it had been less than a year since they died. "What happened?"

Hayley sat down again and gazed steadily at Meg. "It's my fault."

Strange and disquieting thoughts began to race through Meg's mind. This had to be financial and she'd bet her life it was Trent's problem. "It can't be your fault. You've just been filling in for your mother — designing."

"I should have been watching the books the way my mother did." There was no mistaking the self-deprecation in Hayley's voice.

"I thought Trent had a handle on things. It seemed to me he was more interested in the business than his father. Without your mother's encouragement Russell would have spent the last twenty-five years in a garage making boards, not building a famous company." Meg had never spoken disparagingly of Russell. After all, the man had been Hayley's father.

"My father and mother contributed a lot. Not just to their shop but to the whole culture. When they started, no one knew much about surfing. Now you can go to any town in the Midwest and find Surf's Up merchandise."

Meg had to admit that surfing had certainly taken off since her sister married Russell Fordham, but she wasn't sure she would give them much credit. They rode a wave that had already formed — thanks to others.

Hayley must have detected the skepticism in Meg's expression. She continued, "It's not just the clothes or the boards. It's a style of life that's caught on even where there's no ocean to surf."

"The big breakthrough was Nagano," Meg added, recalling those winter Olympics clearly because she'd been lucky enough to attend them. "Skateboarding was featured for the first time. After the games, your father couldn't produce and ship boards fast enough. As I recall, Nagano also caused a revolution in surfing. Surfers saw the fancy tricks skateboarders were doing and began trying them, which called for new surf-boards."

Happiness shone in Hayley's eyes for the

first time since her return. "My parents were part of a cultural revolution. Outlines of three waves, the last one being three times bigger and the words *Surf's Up* became a brand magnet. We're about to blow everything they worked so hard to make happen."

Meg had never thought about it in quite these terms, but Hayley was right. Alison — her little sister — had been part of something larger, more important. Of course, it would have happened without them, but they had been prime movers.

"When I was in Costa Rica painting the mural, I took a break one afternoon because it was unbelievably hot. The hotel isn't open yet so the air-conditioning wasn't running. At the beach, I saw a teenage girl wearing board shorts. I recognized the pattern," Hayley said, the threat of tears in her voice. "My mother and I designed it together at least fifteen years ago. The fabric had faded but the logo with the three waves and the words *Surf's Up* in brilliant blue were still as bright as the day someone purchased those board shorts."

"I know. I've seen your mother's designs all over the world." Meg was grateful that she'd taken the time to travel when she'd been younger. Now she was just an armchair tourist.

"I don't want Surf's Up to be ruined because Trent made a simple mistake, then the economy tanked. This is like a rogue wave. We can ride it out and reinvent the business."

"Reinvent? I think the wave has — how do you say it? — clamshelled. There will always be surfing and a certain number of boards and clothes will sell, but I think it has run its course."

"Maybe," Hayley conceded, "but I have some ideas. Mixed Martial Arts is just taking off and Southern California is the epicenter just as it was for surfing. My designs for The Wrath are booming despite the weak economy."

Meg frowned; she hadn't known much about MMA until she'd met The Wrath, then watched a fight on a cable channel. Three rounds with barefoot fighters wearing lightly padded fingerless gloves and trying every move imaginable from boxing punches to jujitsu moves disgusted Meg. There was no escape for the fighter. The ring was octagonal and enclosed completely in chain link. A human cockfight, the announcer had called it. The description fit to her way of thinking.

"I find it barbaric." Meg knew she sounded old-fashioned, but she couldn't help it. Suddenly, the world seemed to be moving faster than ever — and beyond her understanding.

"Violence has always sold," Hayley commented. "Right back to the Romans watching the Christians battle lions for entertainment. It's a testosterone thing. Male bonding."

Meg couldn't stifle a laugh. "You may be onto something. I watched one MMA fight and the announcer said it's a billion-dollar-a-year business, which I found hard to believe. But I checked it on the Internet and discovered he was correct."

"I want to put MMA products in our store and market them with the surf/skate products that we sell to other companies. This Friday is the annual surf competition. We have a booth. I want The Wrath to be there along with some of his buddies to meet the kids."

"Will you be selling MMA T-shirts and stuff?" Meg asked.

"Yes. We're expecting huge crowds."

It sounded hot and boring to Meg, but then, she'd never been one to stand around and watch surfers compete. Obviously, she was in the minority. She'd been to enough competitions with her sister to appreciate the huge crowds they drew. "Where does

Laird McMasters fit in?"

Hayley rolled her eyes, then sat down beside Meg again. "I haven't spoken with him. I honestly don't want to have another partner. It's hard enough for Trent and I to agree."

Meg nodded; she understood completely. Early on in her career in commercial real estate, she'd taken in a partner. It had been a dreadful mistake. After she extricated herself, Meg didn't purchase any property she couldn't finance alone. "Don't do it then."

Hayley huddled in her chair without responding. Something clicked in Meg's brain. Hayley wasn't here to discuss the business. She needed money to keep Surf's Up afloat. *Well, I'll be,* Meg thought. *She's afraid to ask me for the money.*

Last month, Meg might have refused even though it would have been difficult to turn Hayley down. But a lot had happened since then. Meg had believed she'd lost the only person left on earth that she truly loved.

What was money for? This loan would be only a blip in her funds. Everything would belong to Hayley at some point anyway. It was a fact that Meg hadn't been able to face. Death was her shadow.

Knowing this made her wish to see Hayley

288

happily married. Settled on a career path she loved. She'd believed Hayley was anxious to follow in her mother's footsteps as a designer, but she'd been wrong. Or had she? Hayley had claimed going to Costa Rica secretly had been a career move, but now she sounded as if Surf's Up was her passion. Did she know her own mind?

"What about your career as an artist?" Meg asked Hayley, who was staring out at the ocean.

Hayley faced her. "It will have to wait until I get Surf's Up over this hump. I can't desert Trent. He has no one to help except Courtney, and she isn't interested in the business."

As far as Meg was concerned, the wheel was turning but the hamster was dead. Courtney had never been the same since she started taking pills for her back injury. She needed to go into rehab, but Meg wasn't the one to suggest an intervention.

"Why don't I lend you the money?" Meg said as casually as she could manage. She didn't want her niece to have to ask for the money. And she did want to save her sister's legacy. She wasn't sure this would be successful, but she had to try.

A cry of relief broke from Hayley's lips. "Really? You'd do that for us?" she asked, her voice thick, unsteady.

"For you. I'm doing it for you. I love you dearly." Meg wasn't comfortable saying this; she never had been one for displays of emotion. When Alison had died in the plane crash, Meg realized she'd never told her sister how much she loved her. Meg believed Alison knew. Hadn't she been the big sister who raised Alison after their parents died? Still, it would have been nice to have said the words.

"I love you, too," Hayley whispered, tears trembling on her dusky lashes. "You've always been like a mother to me." Hayley left her chair to hug Meg, saying, "Sometimes I felt you loved me more than my mother did."

Meg hugged her back. "We both loved you," she assured her niece, although she had her doubts. Hayley had never been told but she had been an accident. Her parents had come close to getting rid of her. Alison and Russell had been so much in love that there really hadn't been enough room for another child, when Russ already had two. At the last minute, Alison decided she wanted the baby and Russ went along to please her.

Hayley sat down again and swiped at her teary eyes with the back of her hand. "You won't regret lending the money. I swear."

Meg hated to lecture but now was the time to make this point clear. She should have discussed her financial situation right after Alison died. "You must never trust anyone except yourself with finances. Even now, when I can't go in every day to oversee my business, I check the books. Having managers is fine, but never allow them total control."

"That's what happened with Trent," Hayley admitted. "My mother *always* kept her eye on the finances. When I went away to design school, she insisted I take several business courses."

"I know," Meg responded. She let her niece believe it had been her mother's idea, but Meg had persuaded Alison to convince Hayley that she needed to take business courses.

After the Fordhams had been killed, Meg had assumed Hayley was checking on things. Trent took after his father; he was a bit of a loose cannon. Was he also a killer? Meg couldn't help but wonder.

CHAPTER EIGHTEEN

"Andy's just excited. That's all," Hayley assured Ryan as her golden retriever raced around Ryan's father's house, tail wagging.

"He's calming down," Ryan said, although it was hard to tell. The dog had stayed with Hayley's friends. He'd been so excited to see Hayley again that he'd almost knocked her over when she came to get him. On the drive back to the house, Andy had hung over the backseat and tried to lick Hayley all the way.

"He's housebroken and everything."

"Don't worry about it," he told her. "We have bigger problems. Andy will calm down. He just needs to become adjusted to a new home and having you again."

She plopped onto the sofa and released an exhausted sigh. He took a seat beside her, but avoided getting too close. After last night, he didn't know what to think. Obviously she was as confused about her feelings as he was. Where they went from here, he didn't know, but he was right about one thing. They had bigger problems.

"Having second thoughts about asking your aunt for the money?"

Hayley had told him how difficult it had been to request a loan to save Surf's Up. It wasn't just the money. Putting her career on hold bothered her as well.

Ryan was more concerned about someone killing her. He didn't trust any of the Fordhams but he could understand Hayley's thinking — up to a point. Playing dead and hiding out wouldn't work for him either, if he'd been in the same position. Still, he hated exposing her to unnecessary risks.

Hayley looked at her watch. "It's nearly ten o'clock. Do you think John's guy will have checked the bug on Trent's phone?"

John Holmes owned the corporate security firm Ryan planned to join. They specialized in corporate security and had the capacity to monitor the bugs he'd given Hayley to place in Trent's office.

Ryan pulled his cell phone from his pocket. "I'll see." He touched the app to bring up the e-mail transcripts of the two bugs in Trent's office. He moved closer to Hayley. "Here it is. The info from the office. Nothing from his home yet."

"How is it working?" Hayley wanted to know.

"State-of-the-art devices like the two you hid can be transmitted a considerable distance — unlike the cheapies sold on the Internet. With the depressed real estate market, we got lucky. There's a nearly empty office building across the street from Surf's Up. Conversations are recorded there and sent by e-mail to John's operative who's working this case. Now he's e-mailed me a transcript."

Together they scrolled through the transcript. Within five minutes of Hayley leaving Surf's Up, Trent had called his sister and asked her to meet him at Café Panini.

"Do they lunch often?" he asked.

Hayley pulled away from him. "I really don't know. I wish I could have bugged his cell phone, but it was impossible."

"Could be helpful, but I know how difficult it is." He pocketed his own phone. "It's hard to find an excuse to use someone's cell long enough to take it apart and insert the chip. John sent technicians to Trent's house, posing as cable television men there to upgrade the system. His home phones are now bugged. Just wish there was some way to plant one in his cell."

"It probably doesn't matter. Like I told

you, I don't think Trent had anything to do with the car bombing."

Her hair piled up under a baseball cap, Hayley had slipped out of Surf's Up by going through the hidden door into Peet's Coffee next door, then walking into the parking lot where he was waiting. The media had been too busy staking out the entrance and exit to the shop to notice anyone in Peet's busy patio area behind them.

Hayley had astounded Ryan when she told him that she felt Trent was innocent. He'd argued with her, but she'd been adamant. She'd been there; she'd seen Trent's reaction. She insisted Trent was not involved.

Ryan wished he could have been with her. He had a sixth sense. He'd felt Trent hadn't been completely honest when he'd interviewed him. But he might have been concealing something other than his part in the car bombing as Ryan had then suspected.

Still, he had doubts. This transcript made him wonder even more. Why call his sister so quickly? Both of them stood to gain from Hayley's death. Both could be plotting another attempt.

He didn't like it one damn bit. At least they didn't know where Hayley was staying. If they tried to kill her again, it would have to be out in the open. He intended to be her bodyguard and see if he could catch the killer.

Andy finally wound down and settled at Hayley's feet. Ryan couldn't help inwardly smiling. The reddish-colored retriever reminded him of Buddy. Dogs were great companions and right now Hayley didn't need to feel any more isolated than she already did.

He rested his head against the back of the leather sofa and watched Hayley stroke Andy's back, then fondle his ears. Ryan had tried all last night — barely sleeping — to figure out how he felt about Hayley. It was more than sex; he knew that for sure.

He was back among the living.

Somehow Hayley had breached his carefully built defenses. Life had been hell since Jessica's death, but oddly enough, it was a predictable place. His heart ached and he knew why. Jessica was gone forever. His private misery was a comfortable place where he could tend his wounds.

And wouldn't be hurt again.

That's what he'd been trying to escape. He didn't want to take a chance he would fall for someone, only to suffer. Hayley made him shove those encumbering feelings aside and take another chance.

Jessica's memory hovered in his mind. He

knew she'd tell him to go on with his life. Hadn't she said that a dozen times when she'd been dying? Ryan hadn't thought he could resume his life again — until he'd seen Hayley's picture.

But how did Hayley feel about him? Physically, she wanted him, but something kept holding her back. Could it be Chad Bennett? Or someone else? Hell if he knew. Women had always been a mystery to him. With them, his sixth sense failed to work.

Hayley tilted her head to one side and her hair fell alluringly across her shoulder. She gave him a sensual smile that tilted the corners of her mouth provocatively. It sent a surge of heated longing through his body. "Ryan, do you think . . ."

"Think what?"

"Think that we could be friends?"

Friends? Not on her life. Friends — the kiss of death; the last thing on his mind. Okay, sex had commandeered his brain, but, hey, he was only a guy. And he had more than sex in mind with Hayley. Much more.

Obviously she didn't feel the same way. *Great! Now what?* The way she'd kissed him last night, rubbing her sexy body against his, hadn't been "friendly." It had been a total come-on. Then she'd bailed. What was she thinking?

Ryan didn't think Hayley was playing a game. He decided she was genuinely confused about her feelings. Maybe she didn't trust herself. An experience like Chad's betrayal could produce lasting insecurity. The way Ryan had broken off their first kiss certainly hadn't helped. How could he make her understand that he truly cared about her?

"Ryan, why aren't you saying anything? Don't you want to be friends?"

"No." The word came out like a shot before he could think. "That's total bullshit after what went on last night."

"My mistake," she whispered. "It didn't mean anything."

"Prove it." He grabbed her so quickly that her hands were crushed against his chest. "Let's see. Show me how little this means."

Before she could utter a word, his firm mouth covered hers and the force of his body pushed her into the sofa's cushions. Blood thundered in his brain, blocking out the sound of Andy's tail wagging and slapping against the coffee table in front of them.

Ryan's tongue slid into her mouth and mated with hers. A surge of liquid heat pooled in his groin. Without breaking the kiss, he wove his fingers through her silky hair. The floral scent she was wearing filled his lungs. She pressed against him — unable to get enough. A total turn-on.

He couldn't get enough of the way she tasted, the softness of her skin beneath his hands, the little moan from low in her throat.

His lips left hers to explore her neck, her throat, with a trail of hot moist kisses. He edged his hand between them to cradle her warm breast. Another sweet moan of delight escaped her lips.

Damn! He'd been right; she wanted him as much as he wanted her. Maybe more, he decided, recalling that she'd kissed him first during their walk on the beach.

Abruptly, he broke the kiss. "Tell me to stop and I will."

"D-don't stop," she cried in a low voice.

He gazed at her and saw her green eyes were smoldering with desire. "Friends, huh? I don't *think* so."

Her sharp intake of breath was followed by a sigh of surrender as he again kissed her. His throbbing loins tightened as she thrust her breasts upward and wiggled enticingly. Through the sheer fabric of her blouse he felt her tight nipples pressed against his chest.

Sexy as hell.

"Know what?" he said. "You're really something." He rose, keeping her in his arms; her arms circled his shoulders and she snuggled her face into the crook of his neck. Her bedroom was the closest, he decided and headed to the back of the house, Andy trotting along behind them.

He found the bedroom and shouldered his way through the half-open door without turning on the lamp. The shade was up and pale moonlight revealed a double bed covered with a floral comforter. He laid her down on the bed as gently as his jackhammering pulse would allow, then stretched out beside her.

"Hayley." His voice was suddenly raw with emotion. "We're more than friends, right?"

"Right," she murmured, pressing closer to him, molding her soft curves against the taut length of his body. She made no attempt to hide how turned on she'd become — so quickly.

Her fingers traced his jaw, the lobe of his ear and ended twined through his thick hair. His scalp tingled. Hell, more than that tingled. His erection was pressing painfully against his fly, begging to be released.

He somehow managed to remove her clothes. Damn, she was gorgeous, he thought as the faint light of the moon played across the soft curves of her body. His eyes roamed over her and he couldn't keep from appreciatively smiling. Her golden tan against fair skin made it appear that she was wearing a bikini. An X-rated bikini.

"You can change your mind," he joked, his breathing ragged.

"No way." She kissed him, flicking her tongue against the seam of his lips and arching her back with a little shimmy that jiggled her breasts provocatively. His hand found one peaked nipple and rolled it between his fingers, squeezing just slightly.

"Don't stop," she whispered again as he drew back for a second. "Don't even think about it."

He almost chuckled, but she was kissing him again, more urgently this time. His hand swept down the smooth curve of her waist to the fullness of her hips. Man, oh, man. She was perfect.

Still kissing her, Ryan skimmed across her flat tummy to the juncture of her thighs. His fingers caressed a cluster of moist curls.

"Oh, God," Hayley cried, panting. Had she ever been this aroused? The exquisite pleasure elicited by him touching her there brought tears to her eyes. He wasn't even undressed yet, and she was ready to burst. Wouldn't that be embarrassing — to have an orgasm before he'd really gotten started?

Andy barked from beside the bed.

"H-he thinks it's a game," Hayley muttered.

"Hasn't he ever watched?" Ryan's voice sounded hoarse.

"No," she told him, thinking that Chad hadn't liked dogs. Andy had spent most of his time in the yard when Chad had been around.

Ryan stood up. "Okay, boy. Watch closely. This is a new trick."

Heat seared through Hayley even though his body was gone and the cool air of the room wafted over her. She should have felt totally exposed, she thought, with him gazing down at her as he unbuttoned his shirt, but she was too turned on to care.

She heard herself cry, "Get on with it!"

"Yes, ma'am." He saluted, his shirt hanging open to reveal dark crisp hair fanning across his broad chest, sheltering flat brown nipples. He shrugged out of his shirt and flung it into the corner of the room. Andy bounded after it, tail wagging.

Hayley watched Ryan as he toed off his loafers and shucked his socks. His belt clinked as he removed it. The zipper purred softly, then he used his thumbs to peel off his pants and briefs in one swift motion. Andy was back at his side, tail wagging, offering Ryan the shirt he held in his teeth.

"Good boy," Ryan said and gave the dog a quick pat.

Hayley couldn't take her eyes off Ryan. She tried not to look at the puckered white scar on his shoulder. The skein of dark chest hair tapered to a thin strip at his slim waist then arrowed down, becoming denser around a rigid erection that jutted out from between powerful thighs. He was so virile, so effortlessly masculine that she sucked in her breath.

"Andy, pay close attention," he teased the dog.

Andy stood, the shirt still in his mouth, watching while Ryan climbed in beside her. The bed gave under his weight and she raised her hand touch his shoulder.

"Does it still hurt?" she asked.

"A little, but don't worry about it."

He settled over her. The iron heat of his sex pressed into her stomach, hotter and harder than the rest of his body. He kissed her gently and slowly, as if for the very first time. Her lips parted and her tongue sought his with a rush of heated longing that filled her whole being. She arched her back to bring her soft mound flush against his erection.

Her hips wiggled, showing him she wanted more — now. For a few seconds he just went on kissing her, then his tongue plunged deep into her mouth and his body provocatively rocked against hers. She wrapped her arms around his neck and kissed with more intensity than she'd ever kissed any man. She'd never made love like this.

Woof!

"Quiet!" Ryan commanded. "Sit. Watch." Chuckling, he smothered his laughter against her breasts.

It tickled and she laughed, too. When had she ever laughed during sex? Never. Some small part of her mind wasn't on sex and she realized her life had changed in so many ways.

His large hand slid under her bottom and levered her upward. With the other hand he guided himself into her opening, pushing and slowly stretching her. Halfway in, he stopped to kiss her again with fierce intensity. Hard and hot, he thrust into her. She opened her mouth as he filled her — more than filled her — to cry out with pleasure, but he again covered her mouth with his.

Oh, wow! He was just too good at this. A low groan rumbled from deep in his throat, and she hoped he was enjoying every second the way she was. She prayed he wasn't thinking of his wife. Comparing them.

Slowly, rhythmically he withdrew, surged forward, withdrew, surged forward as if he couldn't get enough of her. She wrapped her legs around his and moved with him. Dizzy with passion, she helped him drive her wild. What choice did she have? Every fiber of her being wanted him — now.

Each movement caused a searing rush of pure sensation that was more powerful than any drug. She lifted her hips to meet each thrust, clinging to him with both arms. Seconds — or maybe minutes — later undulating waves of pleasure swept over her. Inside she clenched and convulsed until her world fractured in a burst of pure pleasure.

"Ryan!" she heard herself scream.

Weak and spent, she managed to hold on to him while he continued to pummel her. With the most powerful surge yet, he thrust deep and threw his head back, exposing the length of his throat. Eyes squeezed shut, his face contorted with an expression that might have been mistaken for pain except he cried, "Yes!"

The following instant, he collapsed on top of her, taking most of his weight on his bent forearms. Unexpectedly he rolled onto his back so she was on top and gazing down at him, breath rushing out of her in long, satisfied gasps. Still buried in her, Ryan hugged her to him.

Hayley clung to him a satisfied lassitude sapping her body of its usual strength. She'd made love to other men — very few actually — but those she assumed she loved. Yet with a start, she realized she'd never given herself fully and completely the way she just had.

She couldn't help wondering how Ryan felt. He must have made love to numerous women. Most probably had a lot more experience than she did. And what about his wife? Unquestionably he'd loved her. After all, he'd mourned her for two years.

How did he feel about her? Hayley silently asked.

A sound broke into her thoughts. For an instant she thought it was Andy barking again, but it was the William Tell Overture playing from somewhere nearby. Ryan's pants, she realized as he rolled her to the side and scrambled for the phone.

CHAPTER NINETEEN

"Was Laird upset when he found out Meg Amboy is going to lend Surf's Up the money?" Farah asked Trent.

"Naw, I think he was relieved. Sure, he wants Surf's Up big-time, but the economy's in the crapper. If he loses the money he inherited, Laird's father will be all over him."

Farah nodded; Elliot McMasters was a tough businessman who owned a great deal of commercial property in Southern California. He'd openly scoffed at his son's venture into the surf business. "Small potatoes," he'd called it. She doubted he was so critical now with real estate taking such a mega-hit.

"Did you tell Laird that the loan was Hayley's idea?"

Trent chortled, a short grating sound. "I sure as hell didn't say I maneuvered Hayley into asking her aunt. I don't want him pissed at me. I told Laird that Hayley didn't want any partners."

Farah sipped her cosmo. Just like her bro, she thought. Trent had always been one to shift the blame whenever it suited him. And take all the credit when that put him in a better light.

They were on the deck overlooking the inlet at the Blue Water Grill, having an early dinner. The restaurant was situated across the water from the loft where Hayley lived before the car bomb. Farah wondered where Hayley was staying.

Trent had called her from work this morning and said Hayley had been able to convince her aunt to loan the company enough money to tide them over. In typical Trent fashion, he'd insisted they meet rather than discuss the details on the telephone. She thought he was being paranoid but played along.

"How's Kyle?" Trent asked.

She mustered a smile. "Fine. Just hanging out until the economy gets better." Which meant he was surfing and smoking weed all day while she worked her fanny off. She planned to dump the jerk as soon as possible, but she didn't want to discuss it with her brother, so she broached another subject. "I found out what happened to Mother's money."

Trent signaled the waiter for another scotch. "Really? She told you?"

"No, but one of my clients accidentally revealed the info." She finished the last of her second cosmo but decided against having another. She was wound too tight these days; drinking too much. And not getting enough kinky sex. "Several rich women who shopped at Mom's store were speculating on real estate in Newport Coast. Buying houses, staging the homes, then flipping them. Mother gave them money to invest."

"When?" Trent looked as shocked as Farah had been when she'd learned this. It wasn't like their mother to put her money into anything the least bit questionable.

"Over a year ago, just before the market tanked. It looked like a sure thing. The bank now owns the houses those women bought." She forced herself to say the words. "Mother lost all her savings."

"Oh, shit!" Trent took his drink from the waiter before the woman could put it on their table. "Why didn't she marry a rich man when she had the chance?"

It was a question they'd often asked each other. Cynthia Fordham had been a beautiful woman who'd married young. She'd still been pretty, with a knock-out figure, when

Russell Fordham had divorced her. Over the years several men had been interested, but Cynthia refused to get serious with any of them. She kept saying marriage had taught her a lesson.

"Mother's still attractive," Farah said, "but I doubt she'll ever remarry. I guess this means she'll have to work until . . ."

"She's too old and we'll have to support her." Trent knocked back more of his scotch.

"We owe her," Farah said, even though she had no idea how she would come up with her share of the money. She could only hope the economy would improve and along with it her business. Before that happened, she needed to ditch Kyle. He was a useless drain, but the time wasn't right.

"So that's it? All you have to tell me?" Farah would rather have spent the time trolling the Internet for someone to substitute for Kyle when she finally had the opportunity to give him the big kiss-off.

"No, I wanted to run something by you. Get your opinion."

Farah was flattered. Despite being close, Trent rarely asked her opinion. She wasn't sure why not. Obviously she was smarter and had more business background.

"Hayley is going to be a lot more involved with the company. She wants to expand even more into MMA gear. This weekend is the Board Wars Contest."

Farah couldn't make herself smile. The signs for the surf contest had been up for weeks. Every surfer who could afford the trip — and zillions of beach bunnies — would show up at the Newport Beach pier for the three-day event. What a waste of time! Nothing could make her attend.

"Wait a minute. I thought Hayley had decided to be an artist." Farah couldn't keep the sarcasm out of her voice.

"She has, but she feels obligated to help Surf's Up since her aunt is lending us the money." His lips thinned with irritation. "Hayley wants The Wrath to have his own space in our booth at the Board Wars to sell clothes and shit. That muscle-bound prick will be there all day signing posters."

Farah waited for her brother to say more but he didn't. "Okay. So?"

"So what do you think? MMA and surfers? Not a good mix."

As far as she could see, they were all on a macho trip. "Don't they appeal to the same crowd? Young males."

"True." Trent put down his empty glass and frantically signaled the waitress for a refill. "But get this. Hayley wants to sell dog leashes and onesies with The Wrath's logo

311

on them."

"It's just a few days until the event. How can she get them made in time?" Farah had to admit it was a gutsy plan. One of her clients made baby clothes with outrageous sayings on them. The woman was cleaning up even in this economy.

"Are you kidding? With the meltdown, there are plenty of machines sitting idle. They'll be ready. I just not sure about sales and Surf's Up's reputation."

Farah opened her mouth to respond but saw Chad Bennett coming across the deck toward them. "Did you tell Chad we'd be here?"

"No, but the Blue Water is a popular spot." Trent turned around and waved Chad over even though the guy was obviously coming to their table. "Don't mention what I just told you," her brother whispered.

"Hey, you two," Chad said as he came up to them. "What's happening?" He swung out one of the empty chairs at their table and sat down.

"Not much," Trent said smoothly while the waitress delivered his third drink and took Chad's order for his usual — an extra-dry martini with three spicy olives.

"What's going on with Hayley?" Chad asked. "I saw on the news last night that she was at Surf's Up yesterday. No one was able to get an interview."

"Hayley believes the bombing was a mistake. It was intended for someone else," Trent told him.

"The so-called bomb experts said it had been made by the Sinaloa cartel," Farah added. "They assume it was a drug deal gone bad."

Chad seemed on the verge of saying something but the waitress appeared with his drink. Farah thought Chad was as boring in person as he was unimaginative in bed. But for some reason she couldn't understand, women adored him. She wouldn't put up with the jerk — if she had a choice.

"Got Hayley's number?" Chad asked. "I need to tell her something."

"She isn't giving out her number or where she lives," Trent responded. "Just in case it wasn't mistaken identity. But she'll be at Surf's Up tomorrow. Should I give her a message?"

Chad swizzled his olive-laden pick through his martini. "I was at the police station this afternoon, bailing out Tom Everett *again*. Third DUI in eighteen months. Guy's going down this time." He swigged his martini while they waited for him to continue. "A cop I know told me that Steve Fulton is in town."

Farah asked, "Who's he?"

"Husband of the woman who was supposedly killed by the car bomb." Chad munched noisily on an olive. "Claimed his wife didn't know Hayley."

"Why would Hayley make it up?" wondered Farah.

Chad shrugged and sucked on his two remaining olives. "The police checked Hayley's story and found Lindsey Fulton had taken a flight from San Jose down here. The SF police just checked local airports after the woman went missing. No one thought of her leaving from San Jose, but there are express busses from the city every hour."

"The husband didn't know Hayley?" Trent asked, and Farah noticed his pupils were dilated.

"That's right. The guy insists his wife didn't know Hayley, either."

"Why tell Hayley this?" Farah wanted to know. "She's already been interviewed by the police."

"Steve Fulton insists on talking to her." Chad sipped his martini. "He's sure his wife isn't the woman who died."

"The police showed me the security tape

314

of Gulliver's bar on the night the car blew up. Hayley did have a drink with a woman, but I didn't recognize her."

"Husband saw it, too. Claims it isn't his wife."

"Something doesn't sound right about this story," Farah said.

"For sure," Trent agreed. "Somebody's not telling the truth."

"Chad! Chad! There you are." A sultry redhead in a micro-miniskirt that showed off endless legs paraded across the deck toward them. Her breasts — oversize implants — spilled out of her halter top.

"Got to go," Chad said, standing and taking his martini. He left without bothering to introduce them to his hot date.

"Where does Chad find them?" Trent wondered.

"They're everywhere," Farah replied. The waitress arrived with the calamari appetizer. She set it down between them and asked if Farah was ready for a refill. She wasn't; tonight she was Trent's designated driver.

"You know, I've been thinking," Farah said after they'd eaten over half the house specialty. "About Hayley's idea. What could it hurt to let her try? Have Hayley at the booth to hear what people say about bibs and onesies with the Grim Reaper logo on them. Let her see for herself it isn't a great idea. Don't alienate her. You need dear ole Aunt Meg's money."

Trent was silent for a moment. "You're right. Pissing off Hayley isn't a good idea." He gave Farah an affectionate pat on the shoulder. "That's why I wanted to talk to you. You've got a head for business."

"With any luck, Hayley will see this is a stupid idea and go back to her murals or whatever. She'll be out of your hair."

"I could use some luck right about now."

Farah watched Chad over her brother's shoulder. He was at the bar, his arm around the slutty redhead. "Did you hit Chad up for a loan?"

"Been there, done that. The guy's set on keeping his father's house."

"I can understand. Billionaire's island. He's not just another lawyer on the make if he lives there."

There were several islands in the harbor — all of them exclusive. Linda Isle, where Farah's father and stepmother had lived, was just one cut beneath Harbor Island. Cynthia Fordham had always resented Hayley growing up there while Farah and Trent's visits were limited to weekends and vacations. The small house they'd grown up in was nice for Costa Mesa — but it wasn't

Newport Beach.

"Chad could live at Pelican Point. That's even more exclusive than Harbor Island." Trent sounded soused now and bitter, which wasn't like him. Her brother was easygoing most of the time.

Farah could have argued that Pelican Point merely had spectacular ocean views — none of the mansions with their enormous manicured grounds could boast of being beachfront, but she had to admit they were awesome. Several of Trent's buddies lived there and she knew he was determined to move there one day. In contrast, Harbor Island homes were closer together but all of them had docks for large boats, which made them very desirable.

"I doubt Chad's business is doing that well," Farah commented. "I have several clients who are lawyers practicing contracts and trusts like Chad. Business is off — way off. Chad's father is no longer around to pull in clients. The guy's gotta be hurting."

"If he is, he won't admit a damn thing."

The killer checked the third television news broadcast. Nothing on Hayley. That didn't mean the police had dropped the case. No frickin' way. It just meant the media didn't have anything new to report. Other stories took over.

Hayley was waltzing around town like she didn't have a care in the world. What the fuck was that all about? Obviously she didn't believe the car bomb had been meant for her.

How fucking stupid could she be?

The killer considered a moment, gazing at the wash of dying sunlight glazing the ocean a shimmering amber. Maybe it was some sort of trick. A ploy to lure the killer into making a mistake.

That's gotta be it.

Stupid people made mistakes. Intelligent people took precautions. Now was the time for taking precautions. The authorities weren't on the right trail — yet. But never underestimate them.

Placing the bomb in the car when it was parked so close to the airport hadn't been smart. It had brought down a shitload of investigators. Some of them were the best in the world. If they detected anything unusual and took a second look, there would be hell to pay.

Taking precautions; covering tracks, leaving no traces was the solution. Just how to do this and when remained unclear. But the solution would present itself. It always did.

CHAPTER TWENTY

"Not what I expected," Ryan whispered to Hayley. The dilapidated building smelled fruity somehow — as if it had once been used to process strawberries or some other fruit.

"Me, either. I've never been to an MMA exhibition fight, but I have seen their televised fights."

They'd driven to the City of Industry east of Los Angeles in the early evening. Their destination was an unused warehouse that had been set up with temporary bleachers around an octagonal ring for the matches. The ring was encased on all sides and across the top by double-gauge chain link.

Throngs of people — more men than women, but a lot more women than Ryan had expected — were crowded onto the bleachers. Klieg lights had been temporarily strung from the ceiling. The ring was blindingly bright, but much of the spectator area was in shadows.

"Why so much chain link?" Ryan asked Hayley.

"The fighters use lots of moves from every fighting sport imaginable — kickboxing, jujitsu, judo, wrestling and God only knows what else. Sometimes the fighters fly through the air. The chain link keeps them from landing on spectators."

"Good to know," Ryan said, thinking how pretty Hayley looked in the sexy black blouse cut low enough to get a peek at the swell of her breasts and white cutoff denim shorts that showcased nicely tanned killer legs.

Sleeping with her had been both a good idea and a bad idea. He was more attached to her now and knew it wasn't just sex. He was even more worried about her than before. Nothing suspicious had happened since she'd resurfaced, but that didn't mean Hayley was safe. He needed to stay vigilant, watch everything, everyone, which was damn hard with Hayley so close that he struggled to keep his hands off her.

"I tried to use a jujitsu move on you the night you tackled me in the dark," Hayley told him in a teasing tone that made him want to kiss her. Hell — everything she did made him want to kiss her.

"You need to practice that move some more." He winked. "I'm available."

"You think? After the fight, The Wrath is going to show me a surefire move to take someone down — even someone your size and weight."

"This I've gotta see."

"You will." She looked around at the bleachers where not a single seat was left. A throng of late arrivals had been forced to stand shoulder-to-shoulder to watch. "Look how many of my T-shirts are out there," she said.

Ryan nodded; he'd already noticed all the stylized Grim Reapers with The Wrath's logo: *Kick Fear — Believe.* Other shirts had different logos on them, but it was apparent The Wrath was a crowd favorite.

"Wait until you see how many I sell at the Board Wars. I'll have a baby line, pet collars, shorts, caps and hoodies with The Wrath's Reaper on them."

He didn't like her plan to be in the booth with The Wrath. It exposed her to a crowd of people. Anything could happen. It was two days away. With luck, this mess would be cleared up and they would be getting on with their lives.

The crowd screamed and stomped as a bare-chested fighter with dreadlocks like a nest of snakes bounded into the ring, followed by another fighter with every visible inch of his body — even his shaved head — tattooed with skull and crossbones of various sizes. Both fighters wore shorts and lightly-padded fingerless gloves. Neither wore shoes or shirts.

"How long's a round?" Ryan inquired.

"Fifteen minutes."

"No kidding?" He was dumbfounded. "Pro boxing just has a three-minute round."

"True," Hayley responded with the cute off-kilter smile she often had. "But they have twelve rounds. These guys just go three."

Ryan couldn't help being impressed. He'd seen part of a match on television but hadn't paid much attention. He'd switched channels before the fight had been completed.

"There are very few rules," Hayley continued. "No poking eyes or biting. There are weight classes like in boxing. There's a referee but he isn't in the cage. If a fighter wants to give up, he just 'taps out' and the match is over. That's how TapouT, the most successful of the MMA lines, began." She inclined her head toward the section next to them. "Surely you noticed the big-boobed blonde in the TapouT T-shirt."

Of course, he'd picked up on the blonde. He'd secretly kept his eye on everyone, checking for someone who might hurt Hayley. Two-thirds of this crowd appeared suspicious. Apparently they did it on purpose.

Butt-hanger jeans or shorts on guys with enough tattoos to cover the navy. Too many had fast-food guts beneath cage fighters' T-shirts. Women with so many body piercings they could set off a metal detector from fifty feet away. Most of their breasts weren't original equipment. Humanity's resale rack, for sure.

"I see the woman you mean. The TapouT logo reminds me of a bat."

"It's supposed to. Punkass uses a lightning bolt. PimpIt uses a red outline of a rattler as a logo. I came up with the Grim Reaper idea for The Wrath. It takes a little more designing but it's way cool."

Hayley was proud of herself and he couldn't blame her. She had more talent than most designers, and more guts. What she needed was a break. If he could just find out who was after her. Where was the bastard? A cold-blooded killer didn't just plant a bomb, then give up.

Didn't make sense. He would try again. He? Ryan watched the cage fighters warm up by jogging around the ring, pumping fists at the cheering crowd. Why did he think it was a man? It could have been a woman. They had the capacity to be just as evil as men and more of them were committing violent crimes. But somehow he believed the bombing had the mark of a pro. Professionals were usually men.

Ryan scanned the crowd surrounding the ring. Most of the spectators were under thirty-five and didn't look like pros. Not that he knew what he was looking for exactly. He was merely checking to see if anyone was watching Hayley.

There was a man in the far corner of the bleachers opposite them who might be staring at Hayley, but it was hard to tell because he wore sunglasses. Odd, Ryan thought, keeping the man in sight without directly looking at him. The guy shoved the shades to the top of his head. He was concentrating on the ring, not Hayley.

"Did you get a look at people's shorts?" Hayley asked.

"Sort of. Mostly camouflage stuff or denim cut short."

Hayley smiled her approval. "Good eye. Shorts are getting shorter, even on surfers and fighters. The gangsta look with baggy shorts that flap around the knees is going out. Short is back."

"I guess designers keep abreast of trends."

"Not trends. Microtrends. Small changes that seem cutting edge. Most people don't notice them or think it's an aberration. If you're going to be successful you catch the wave — so to speak — before it maytags."

"Maytags?"

"Sorry. A surfer term for a wave that breaks and spins you around like you're in a washer. You want to ride the wave, not be maytagged. That's why my summer collection has shorter board shorts in it. I'll repeat that in the fall line. Let other designers chase me."

Hayley's green eyes sparkled as if she was playing a game, but Ryan knew how serious she was about her work. She'd already told him the first thing she'd checked when she'd gone into Surf's Up and accessed the computer was how her clothing line was selling. She had an eye for fashion and a good business sense. He wasn't sure where this fit with her ambition to become an artist.

A bell signaled the start of the fight. With whoops like Confederate soldiers, the fighters charged each other. They went at it like lunatics on meth — kicking and flipping with astounding swiftness. One would hit the mat, then rebound to throw a punch worthy of a pro boxer followed by a karate chop. Wild grunts and sounds like a jackal's cry rose above the shouts of fans cheering them.

The dreadlocked fighter threw a punch and a geyser of blood shot from the other fighter's nose. It squirted onto fans in the first row and the women among them squealed in delight.

"The ref's not going to stop it?" Ryan asked. A bad cut would halt a pro boxing fight until it was fixed or the ref called off the fight.

"There's no stopping unless a fighter taps out."

"Aw, hell," Ryan said. He'd seen enough injuries on the gridiron to inure him but most women hadn't. How could Hayley watch? he wondered. He shot her a sideways glance and saw her eyes were squeezed shut.

Now the guy with the scorpion tattoos kicked with his leg. It snapped around like a bull whip and caught dreadlocks in the solar plexus. The guy hit the thin mat on the cement floor with a wet sound like a load of sand. But he hadn't been knocked out. Dreadlocks grabbed his opponent's leg and hauled him off his feet.

They grappled on the floor, now using

wrestling holds Ryan recognized, and stayed there while the crowd, hyped on bloodlust, chanted, "Kill! Kill! Kill! Kill!" Neither seemed to have an advantage as they furiously battled to get the upper hand.

Ryan checked his watch. Less than five minutes had passed. How in hell did these fighters go three fifteen minutes? Just then the rattler-tattooed guy was thrown against the chain-link fencing. It gouged his back and rivulets of blood oozed out of his skin.

Ryan leaned closer to Hayley and asked, "When does The Wrath fight?"

"He's third on the card," she responded, now opening her eyes. "The primo spot. Two others follow but they'll just be beginners. After all, it's only an exhibition, which is a glorified practice, not a real fight."

A tragedy, for sure. Ryan would hate to see a real fight. Whoever called it "human cockfighting" was dead-on. "The fighters make money?"

"Absolutely. Not on an exhibition fight, but real fights have huge cash prizes. MMA is the darling of pay-per-view sports right now. Megabucks."

Ryan was about to say more when his cell phone pulsed. A quick check of Caller ID revealed Meg Amboy was trying to reach him. "It's your aunt," he said before he answered. "Ryan Hollister."

"Ryan? Where are you?" Meg asked.

He put his hand over his other ear. "Hold on a minute." He stood up and signaled Hayley to let him out. They were near one end of the makeshift bleachers. He jumped to the warehouse's floor from the third row up. That put him behind those standing to watch the fight.

"Can you hear me now?" he asked. He went to the back wall where he could still keep his eye on Hayley. He doubted she was in any danger. A killer who took such pains to hide an explosive device probably wouldn't attempt to hurt Hayley in front of so many people. But you never knew.

"Yes. I hear you fine. I wanted you to get a message to Hayley."

Ryan leaned against the wall. He was positive Meg knew that he and Hayley were together. She may have even guessed they were staying at his father's home, but she pretended that she didn't suspect a thing.

"What kind of message?" He heard the wary note in his own voice.

"A man named Steve Fulton came to see me."

Uh-oh. Lindsey's abusive husband. "What did he want?"

"He claims his wife didn't know Hayley.

He believes his wife is still alive and wants to know why Hayley made up the story."

"What did you tell him?"

"I had to calm him down. Poor man was beside himself with grief. I think he's in denial. He knows his wife must be dead but can't admit it. He insists she didn't know Hayley."

Hayley had told him all about Lindsey's relationship with her husband and how Hayley had encouraged her to leave many times. Hayley had met the husband at a gallery in San Francisco, as Ryan recalled. What man wouldn't remember Hayley?

"Steve Fulton wants Hayley to call him at this number."

Ryan memorized the number. "I'm not sure Hayley talking to this guy is a good idea."

"I'm not, either," Meg told him. "The man seems . . . I'm not sure how to put it. Unstable, I guess is the best word to describe him. Should I contact the police?"

"Let me call them. I need to talk to Detective Wells anyway."

The fight was over apparently. The guy with snaky dreadlocks was parading around the ring, pumping his fist. Ryan looked at Hayley and saw she was watching him. He held up one finger to let her know it would be another minute. He scrolled through his call list to retrieve the phone number for Detective Wells.

"Dave Wells," the deep male voice said after the third ring.

Ryan started to explain who he was, but the detective immediately recognized his name. He could tell by Wells' tone that the guy was busy. Ryan quickly explained about Meg's call. "She's really concerned that Steve Fulton might harm her niece."

"The man's damn upset. He has no idea who Hayley is. Claims his wife never knew her."

It sounded as though Detective Wells agreed with Steve Fulton. "Lindsey was trying to get away from him. Wasn't Lindsey on the bar's security tape? Didn't you show it to him?"

"True. Fulton claims the woman isn't his wife. The tape is pretty grainy. It's hard to be sure."

Yeah, right. And pigs fly. "Can't you make Fulton stay away from Hayley — a restraining order or something?"

"No chance. Not unless he threatens her personally. Just looking for her and wanting an explanation isn't enough."

"Okay, but you're on notice." Ryan figured he'd have to take care of Fulton himself.

Although it might not come to that. Hayley wouldn't be that easy to find.

He was set to thank Wells and hang up when the detective said, "Interesting report came in today. Seems the cleaning service that services the Fordham house on Linda Isle reported a robbery."

"What was taken?" Ryan asked, although he had a fairly good idea what the detective would say.

"Electronic gear. Television, Blu-Ray, computer and color printer."

"Umm-hmm," Ryan responded. He'd guessed correctly. Someone wanted Hayley's mother's computer. Probably discovered the computer hadn't been totally wiped clean and didn't want to chance incriminating evidence being found by one of the high-fliers from Washington who were circling the case like vultures.

"Doesn't the house have an alarm system?" Ryan asked, recalling Hayley resetting the alarm after they'd wiped the computer.

"It does, but some thief was smart enough to cut out the glass on a sliding door to the water side. Came and went from there without triggering the alarm."

"Sounds like a lot of risk and work for some electronic gear that has to be at least a year old, if not older." Ryan decided other things had been taken to cover the computer theft.

Ryan said goodbye and was putting his cell phone away when it vibrated. It was Ed Phillips. "Yo, Ed. Whassup?"

"Very funny, Hollister. You don't really sound like a redneck. More like a dickhead."

Ryan watched Hayley. Her attention was now on the ring where another pair of fighters was warming up for a bout. After this fight The Wrath would be in the cage. Hayley planned to see him after the fight, then they could go home.

Get your mind off sex, he told himself. But it was difficult. Hey, he was just a guy who'd been without sex for too long. Now that he'd found the right woman . . .

He checked himself. Some small part of him still felt disloyal to Jessica. He knew she wouldn't have minded. She would have liked Hayley, but he still felt a twinge of guilt.

"Something else came through on the car bombing," Ed said. "Since we're not involved any longer, it was forwarded to the DEA and the local police."

"Okay, shoot." Ryan was pleased Ed had contacted him despite knowing he was quitting the Bureau. No doubt the guy wanted to make sure Ryan would give him any computer help he needed in the future.

"You know there were over two hundred thousand fragments collected after that bombing."

"I guess that's not surprising, is it?" Ryan had zero experience with bombs but he thought an explosion of that magnitude would generate thousands if not millions of tiny pieces.

"No. The ATF guys were immediately able to ID the bomb as one built in Mexico by the Sinaloa cartel."

Ryan had been half favoring a scenario with Steve Fulton hiring a pro to take out his wife. Come to think about it, that didn't seem likely. How would a software specialist in San Francisco come in contact with a cartel member who possessed a bomb or could be hired to do a bombing?

"This morning ATF also found pieces of a GPS tracking device. The cheap kind you can purchase at any electronics store. It must have been attached to the car with a magnet — probably under the bumper or wheel well — where it would be easy and quick to hide. That way they could have tracked Hayley to the restaurant without arousing her suspicions."

"Right. Thanks for the update." As soon

as he clicked off, another thought hit him. Hayley had told him that she'd been to see The Wrath about new designs on the morning of the bombing. Maybe the destruction of the trust and the bombing were two unrelated issues. The Wrath couldn't give a rat's ass about Hayley's portion of the trust. But he could be upset about something else. Or he'd been planning to use Hayley in some way.

CHAPTER TWENTY-ONE

Farah returned to the Irvine Terrace house she shared with Kyle. It was after ten and she was bone-tired. Driving Trent to his Newport Coast home had taken longer than she'd anticipated. Courtney had met them at the door. Her brother's wife had been so excited that their son had been accepted by a noted piano teacher.

Her usually mellow brother, fueled by too much scotch, exploded. He'd yelled that Timmy was becoming a sissy and it was all Courtney's fault. Farah didn't agree. She thought Timmy should pursue his own interests.

In a way her nephew reminded Farah of herself at the same age. Her father had taken unmistakable pride in the way Trent followed in his footsteps, surfing and skateboarding like a champ. Later silly little Hayley had tried to please their father by surfing. Farah had known she was best at intellectual pursuits and hadn't bothered to solicit her father's admiration.

Being ignored had hurt, but Farah had learned to appreciate academic accolades from her mother. And to rely on herself. Just one of life's important lessons.

It had taken a bit of talking, but Farah had managed to calm Trent down. As usual Courtney had been stoned on pain pills. Farah left, doubting this marriage would last.

"Kyle, are you home?" Farah called. The house was dark but his car was in the drive.

She tossed her keys and purse on the entry console that was nothing like the antique table in Trent's grand marble foyer with its massive arrangement of snow-white roses. Her home was older, but recently updated to feature the postcard-perfect view of the bay. It was a prime address, but not nearly as opulent as Trent's exclusive gated enclave. She didn't care; part of Trent's problem was impatience.

Impatience and greed did not make a good combination. Farah wanted to make money as much as her brother did, and this economic downturn had stalled her plans. She knew things would straighten out with time. Trent wanted to move into one of Pelican Point's Italianate villas with parklike gardens and breathtaking ocean views. He was determined to keep up with the guys he envied — right now. His ambition might force him to take unnecessary risks.

She walked out onto the terrace overlooking the bay and stared at the sparkling lights of the Pavilion opposite Balboa Island below Irvine Terrace. The Victorian-style Pavilion had been built early in the twentieth century as a railroad terminus for a line coming south to the beach from L.A. The rails were long gone and now the Pavilion was a fancy restaurant festooned with lights that illuminated its graceful lines.

"Hard to believe," she said out loud. Farah had always admired the way the early founders saw the possibilities in the area. Saw the future.

Back then, Bay Island had been the only natural island in the harbor. Actually, there was no harbor, she mused, gazing at the sparkling lights of what was now one of the largest pleasure boat harbors in the country. It took dredging to clear the harbor and build the islands. It took imagination and foresight, she thought.

Newport Beach had been a three-hour drive from L.A. on rutted roads that would become a freeway — over fifty years later. The freeway opened up the area and fortunes were made on real estate once considered not particularly valuable.

"Look ahead, not back," Farah whispered to herself.

She had to admit that's what Hayley did. She had the ability to project into the future and see where the business was going. Surf shops like Surf's Up sold the California lifestyle. But styles changed. Hayley, she hated to admit, embraced the change the way her mother had. Trent didn't see beyond board sports — just like his father. Their father.

Despite her assurances to her brother that Hayley's line of MMA gear wouldn't sell at the Board Wars competition, Farah believed it would. She'd read MMA fights were attracting huge numbers of fans. She hoped Hayley was right. Keeping Surf's Up profitable was in her best interest.

Farah didn't care about saving her father's company. She needed the money for her own dream. Working as a CPA, even with her own firm, wasn't going to make a fortune. A good living, but not the kind of money Farah wanted. She needed to be ready to invest as opportunities presented themselves. She had lots of ideas but no cash.

A sea lion barked; it was mating season. The male was warning off competitors, but sound traveled over water, often being magnified. Up on Irvine Terrace, the honking barks seemed to be coming from the next yard, not the bay below.

Farah went inside and wondered if Kyle had gone for a walk. That wouldn't be like him. Surfing passed for exercise, not walking. In their bedroom she kicked off her shoes and peeled off her panty hose.

She heard a noise and paused, set to remove her skirt. Was that Kyle laughing? It sure sounded like it. Where was it coming from?

She hurried into the kitchen, thankful that all Irvine Terrace homes were one story to preserve their harbor views. She didn't envy Trent his opulent two-story mansion on days like this when she'd spent too long in high heels.

Another laugh. All the windows were open as usual in the summer to let in the cooling ocean breeze. Kyle's laugh was coming from outside. He was in the shop behind the garage.

What was he doing back there? Kyle wasn't the least bit handy. Unplugging his blow-dryer was the extent of his expertise.

Barefoot, she walked out the back door to the shop behind the double-car garage. Through the window in the door she saw

Kyle standing by himself. Chuckling. Great! No doubt he was smoking pot. He'd recently discovered Red Rover, a new strain that was more potent than others, yet smooth. Farah had no use for drugs. She was afraid of their power. She didn't want anyone controlling her.

Farah opened the door and walked in without saying a word. There was an open box of cold pills with the empty inserts strewn across the worktop. An instant-ice pack was on the table beside scissors used to cut it open.

Kyle spun around with a two-liter plastic bottle in his hand. She'd expected to see a spliff of Red Rover. "Hey, babe. What's happening? I thought you were having dinner with your brother."

"It's after ten. We finished two hours ago."

"Really? What time is it?"

Farah didn't bother to check her watch. It was clear from his glazed eyes that Kyle was high, even though she didn't detect the usual sweet herbal smell. "It's nearly ten-thirty. What have you got there?"

Kyle held up the plastic bottle that had once been filled with root beer. Now all that was left at the bottom was a disgusting looking brownish sludge. "A surefire way to make money."

Farah glanced around at the small area that was neatly filled with tools and hardware that had been left when she'd purchased the house. She noticed at least a dozen empty two liter bottles newly lined up on the shelves.

Kyle showed her a packet of crystal-like granules in a plastic container. "I'm making meth to sell at the beach."

A scorching surge of anger ripped through her like a column of fire. "In my house? No way! You'll set the place on fire or blow it up. Meth labs are always going sky high!"

Kyle flashed the smile that had once captivated her. Not tonight. Methamphetamine was almost instantly addicting. You could smoke it, snort it, or inject it and the result was the same. You were irrevocably hooked.

"Are you using meth?" she asked.

"Of course not, babe," Kyle assured her.

Farah didn't know if she could believe him. Not that he was a liar, but addiction did strange things to a person. Kyle always hid how much pot he used.

"I'm just trying to make money to help out."

Once she would have given him a blow job on the spot for accepting *any* responsibility for their finances. But this was different. Did he seriously believe making meth was the answer to their problems?

"This is the new shake-and-bake method," Kyle continued, oblivious to her disapproval. "It takes less pseudo-whatever —"

"Pseudoephedrine. The decongestant in those cold medications." She pointed to the worktable where the empty boxes were scattered.

"Right. This takes less so no one is busted for buying restricted cold pills. Then you add a few household cleaning chemicals — just a bit — not much and then you need ammonium nitrate, which is found in these instant-ice packs." He held up the open ice pack. "Put it all in an empty bottle and cap it. Shake for five minutes and presto! Crystals begin to form. The whole process takes fifteen minutes."

Farah hadn't realized meth could be produced this way. The method she was familiar with called for "cooking" the brew, which required a ton of cold capsules and chemicals to boil in pots over an open flame. She understood it took several days to produce a batch.

She was caught off-guard at the vibrancy of his voice. Kyle was truly proud of himself, thrilled that he knew something she didn't.

"How did you figure this out?" She was certain he didn't come up with this on his own.

"One of the guys was making it in the back of his SUV after we finished surfing. I got the formula from him. I'm going to make a lot —" he gestured to the empty soda bottles lining the shelf "— and sell it at the Board Wars."

"I don't think that's a good idea," she said quietly. She hated to stop any moneymaking venture Kyle was willing to try, but this could mean big trouble for her as well as him.

"The guys say to just keep one packet on you at a time. That way if you're caught, it's not enough to bother prosecuting. And if they should check here, there won't be anything to find. All of this stuff won't fill more than two grocery bags. I'll throw them away tonight."

"Not in my trash," she said.

"I already planned to take it to Balboa Island and dump a little here, a little there in trash cans on the main drag."

"Okay," Farah replied reluctantly and turned to leave. She really had to get rid of this guy. As soon as everything was settled, she would. Meanwhile let him make a little money on the side. If he was caught, she could always claim she knew nothing about it.

Ryan followed Hayley as The Wrath led an entourage of wannabe cage fighters and half-dressed groupies to his dressing area. It was after eleven, but it had taken this long for The Wrath to leave the ring area. In the first round, he'd easily won his fight with a guy with a mug like a gargoyle. The Wrath had taken a seat ringside to watch the last two fights, which both went three painful rounds with no tap out. Hayley told him that meant the fighters would be rematched next time in a professional fight.

The makeshift dressing rooms were in what must once have been the main office of the warehouse. All the furniture had been removed, but the partitions that divided up the cube farm remained. Each fighter had his own station in the cube. The Wrath's was the largest and filled with more groupies than a rock band.

"Do you want to leave?" Hayley asked when it became apparent that the entourage was going to hang around for some time.

"No. Let's wait and talk to The Wrath." He had more than a few questions for the fighter, since he'd learned about the tracking device discovered in Hayley's car. He hadn't told her about it because the noise prevented serious conversation. He glanced around but didn't see a place for a private discussion.

"You want to see if The Wrath can teach me a move to take you down, don't you?" Hayley teased.

"I double-dog dare you."

"You're on!"

He hugged her, wishing they could always be this carefree. Take time; enjoy life. Really get to know each other.

Ryan reminded himself to keep his mind on protecting Hayley. He checked the cube farm that was now swarming with fans. No one seemed to be paying any attention to Hayley. But then, that's what he would expect. Someone was cunning enough to place a GPS tracker on her car and plant a bomb wasn't going to be easy to spot.

Everyone looked suspicious and no one looked suspicious. In wrinkled khaki shorts and a well-worn blue T-shirt, Ryan was the closest to a *GQ* look any guy in this crowd would get. Clearly these men lived to watch *mano-a-mano* combat. The women were better dressed. Many were attractive, but the fawning looks of adoration they gave the fighters and their simpering giggles made them seem shallow.

He couldn't help comparing them to Hayley. Many of these women were blondes with fried platinum hair. Hayley's silky chocolate-colored locks streaked with shimmering copper were much prettier — more natural. She wasn't just attractive; she had brains and personality. A winning combination.

"Notice how MMA has religious overtones," Hayley said.

"Religious?"

"Sure. Look at the religious symbols on a lot of the logos. Celtic crosses, regular crosses, angels' wings, Gothic lettering. You know, that sort of stuff."

"I guess." All right, all right, Ryan said to himself. Another part of Hayley's appeal was her ability to make him think.

Keep your mind on business. Ryan again scanned the large room to see if anyone was targeting Hayley. The crowd was thinning out; tomorrow was a workday for most of these folks. "I also see a stylized Grim Reaper, skull and crossbones, swords, flames that must represent hell."

Hayley lifted her chin and met his gaze straight on. "Right. I spoke to a lot of fighters when I was trying to come up with a logo for The Wrath. They see cage fights as a struggle between good and evil. Some of them represent good, or God, while others go for the evil of the devil."

"Which is The Wrath?"

"Stands for The Wrath of God."

Well, hell. Why not? Ryan figured it could go either way, depending if you believed in a wicked or forgiving God.

The Wrath chose that moment to shrug into one of Hayley's black zip-up hoodies with the Grim Reaper on it and flames licking The Wrath's name. He sauntered up to them, leaving the groupies behind.

"Let's go over to my gym," The Wrath said. "It's right around the corner. We can talk there." He winked at Hayley. "I'll show you a surefire move."

"Okay," Hayley said for both of them.

Ryan put his arm around her and took her back through the now empty warehouse where a team of men was breaking down the bleachers. He stepped outside ahead of her. He carefully looked both ways before allowing Hayley into the alley. The area was well lit, but he didn't take any chances. He hustled her into his car.

Ryan checked the car's frame for a hidden GPS.

Nothing.

CHAPTER TWENTY-TWO

Ryan's patience would have worn thin after watching Hayley spend over half an hour learning a jujitsu move that could knock over the strongest opponent, but Hayley was so determined. So damned sexy. Every move — even when she fell on her cute butt — was worth seeing.

"She's got it now!" The Wrath had hit the ground after Hayley skunked him with the maneuver and actually flipped him. Amazing.

"Let me try it on you," Hayley said to Ryan.

"Later, sweetheart. I need to talk to The Wrath." He felt like an idiot calling the guy by his fight name. "What's your real name?"

"Carleton Cole." He threw back his head and roared with laughter. "See why I go by The Wrath?"

"Gotcha," Ryan said.

They were in the most professional

private-training facility Ryan had ever seen. There were several boxing-style rings and an octagonal stainless-steel chain-link cage for practice fights. Weight rooms, a sauna, massage room with several tables and a huge granite shower with enormous showerheads that on their own must contribute to the area's water shortage.

Sophisticated television cameras recorded practice rounds for review later in the small screening room adjacent to The Wrath's office. Everything in the building was new and smelled like antiseptic. When Ryan had walked in, he'd decided it must have taken The Wrath a considerable amount of money to convert this old warehouse into a state-of-the-art gym. The way he'd showed them around revealed how proud The Wrath was of his facility.

"You want to talk about something? How about I show you a few moves?"

Ryan put a hand on his shoulder. "Bad shoulder. An old football injury that I recently injured again in a car accident."

"Another time." One of The Wrath's unruly brown eyebrows arched.

"I want to know about the morning of the car bombing. Didn't Hayley come here to show you some designs?"

"You know I did," Hayley said with a note

of protest in her voice.

There were times when he wished Hayley was just a dumb blonde. He ignored her and looked at The Wrath for a response.

"Yes," he said smoothly. "There was only one tank top design I didn't like. She agreed to redesign it."

"How could she redesign the Grim Reaper? Seems as if it needs to look the same each time. It's more stylized with fewer lines than most Reapers, but how can you change your brand mark?"

"It needed to be made smaller." This from Hayley; he could tell she was getting pissed. "The Wrath was right. It overwhelmed the tank."

God forbid. Ryan waited a beat before asking The Wrath, "How long was Hayley here?"

"I dunno. I was in the ring —" he gestured to the boxing ring nearby "— working on some kickboxing moves." He turned to Hayley with a gaze that wasn't purely professional. "You waited — what? — ten minutes or so?"

"About that. Then we went to your office, had some Red Bull, and went over my sketches for another half hour or so." She looked at Ryan as if to ask what business it was of his.

"You were here less than an hour." Ryan knew it would only have taken seconds to hide a GPS tracker under her car. The devices used a powerful magnet to stick to metal. Someone could walk by and slap it under a bumper or wheel well without breaking stride.

"That's right. What about it?" The Wrath appeared tired, as if he'd been running on adrenaline and was ready to tap out.

Ryan knew Hayley was going to bust his chops for not telling her this first, but he went on anyway to gauge The Wrath's reaction. "The ATF team analyzing the bomb found that a GPS tracking device had been planted, probably under her car."

"What? You never told me," she retorted with a look meant to frost his cookies.

"I just received a call telling me this during the fight."

"You've had plenty of time to tell me."

Ryan didn't want to argue with her. He needed to see if he could detect anything in The Wrath's response that would implicate the fighter.

"You think it might have been put on Hayley's car while she was in here?" asked The Wrath.

As far as Ryan could tell the guy seemed concerned — not the least bit guilty. "Possibly. It's impossible to say how long the device had been there. Hours, days, weeks . . . Who knows?"

Suddenly Hayley was less upset with him as the gravity of the situation registered. "You mean someone was following me — for who knows how long?"

"That's right." Ryan turned to the fighter. "I'm no longer with the FBI. I don't give a damn what you may be doing on the side. I'm just asking if there's anything — anything at all — going on that might make someone want to kill Hayley to get to you."

The Wrath dropped onto a nearby weight bench and stared off into space for a second. "I'd like to help," he said with all the enthusiasm of a man receiving the last rites. "But I have no idea."

"Think again. Consider even the wildest possibility."

Suddenly, The Wrath's face lit up like a spring sunset. "Hold everything! I have security cameras all around the building."

"You do?" Ryan had looked but hadn't spotted any.

"Sure." He stood up. "I bought the latest. An industrial park with half the buildings deserted because of the economy isn't the safest place." He motioned for them to follow as he walked back toward his office.

"Also, I don't want any of my rivals photographing or videotaping my practice bouts."

There were shelves with neat rows of CDs behind The Wrath's chrome-and-glass desk. He checked the dates and pulled one out. "This is the recording of the exterior of the building on the day Hayley visited."

"You don't erase them and rerecord?" Ryan asked. This was standard practice with most security systems. As soon as the disk was full, it was erased and used again. They weren't saved unless there was a good reason.

"We save them for six months." Again, he gestured for them to come with them. "Just in case someone is loitering or appears too often. They could be casing the place. I have a lot of valuable stuff in here."

They went to the media room that was usually used to review tapes of fights. They sat in theater-style seats while The Wrath fiddled with the equipment. The screen came on with the date and time in the lower right corner. The fighter fast-forwarded the CD from just after midnight on the day of the bombing through the dawn hours — nothing much was happening except for a few rats foraging in the Dumpster. At daylight a cleaning crew appeared followed — at eight o'clock — by The Wrath. Soon several other fighters appeared and parked their cars.

There were five cameras taking pictures from various angles. This was much more than most companies used unless they were some type of financial institution or had something valuable to protect.

At eleven thirty-three, Hayley drove up in an older model blue Beamer. She took what appeared to be an oversize sketchbook and went into the building. She walked briskly — all business — but she still managed to look sexy.

Ryan carefully studied the tape. Several cars arrived with more guys. One of them was butt ugly, with jaws like bowling pins and a body like a tombstone. He stared a Hayley's car for a moment but didn't go near it. "Who's that?"

"KickAzz. A fighter from up north. Not very good," The Wrath said, "but he tries hard. Trains a lot."

They watched every frame of the tape. Nothing else happened until 12:17 when Hayley came out, still carrying the sketchbook and drove away.

Hayley said, "The tracker wasn't put on here."

The Wrath got up and turned off the machine. He removed the CD. They followed the fighter back to his office where he returned the disk to the shelf.

Ryan said, "Sorry to be so suspicious. It's just —"

"No apology necessary," The Wrath assured him with a broad smile for Hayley. "I don't want anything to happen to my marketing genius."

So what else was new? The Wrath was as taken with Hayley as most men. Too late, Ryan told himself. They belonged together.

The Wrath turned toward Ryan. "You see, I was a champ but I lacked a concept, a brand that drew my fans. Hayley came up with the idea. The saying was her aunt's. Hayley made the whole enchilada come together."

"No big deal," Hayley said a little self-consciously.

"I don't want anything to happen to my marketing guru. When I thought she'd died, I was totally bummed," he told Ryan. "If there's anything I can do to help —"

"I don't think she should be in the booth with you at the Board Wars," Ryan responded.

"Do you think I'd let anyone walk up and take her?" The Wrath's face turned red. "Ain't gonna happen."

Ryan could see the guy was sincere and

believed he would protect Hayley. "This person is sly and clever. No one would have expected a bomb. The next attempt will take us by surprise."

The Wrath didn't appear convinced. "They have to get to her, right? I'll be with her and so will PimpIt. He's an up-and-comer who trains here."

"I want to be in the booth," Hayley insisted. "I need to see for myself how people react to my new items. It's a huge investment risk for Surf's Up. Trent doesn't want to do it. I promised him that I would drop it if people aren't really enthusiastic."

"You can tell by the numbers if it's selling."

"It's still not like being there and talking to customers."

Hayley was as stubborn as a Kansas mule, Ryan thought.

"No one will get to her," the fighter assured him. "I guarantee it."

"What about a sniper? A sharpshooter can blow your head off from a mile away."

Hayley touched his arm and the affection he saw in her eyes startled him. "Ryan, all the booths have covered backs and face the ocean. A sharpshooter a mile away would be out at sea. No one's getting on the sand carrying a gun. There's always security at these events."

"Umm-hmm." Ryan didn't give two nickels for rent-a-cop security. "Remember the two Somali pirates holding that ship's captain at gunpoint on a small boat?"

"Sure," Hayley said and The Wrath added, "I remember that."

"Two SEAL snipers took out the pirates. Both boats were bobbing in heavy seas. This time the target will be on land. Makes it a helluva lot easier."

"They were lucky the pirates didn't fire when they were hit and kill the captain," The Wrath said.

"Luck had nothing to do with it," Ryan explained. "A sharpshooter aims for the head, for the brain stem. The minute the bullet hits — the brain can no longer send any messages to the body. Firing is impossible   the guy drops dead."

"Really?" said Hayley. "I didn't realize that."

"Neither did I." The fighter shook his head. "Pretty amazing."

"I think you're overreacting," Hayley told him. "Those were the best in the world, right? Where would someone come up with a sniper that talented?"

"Where did they come up with someone to make a bomb?"

The Wrath said, "I thought bomb-making instructions could be found on the Internet."

"They can," Hayley insisted. "I checked."

Ryan silently admitted an amateur with nerve could produce a bomb. It took years of practice and talent to become a world-class sniper, which the shooter would have to be to hit a target from a boat off the shore. His phone vibrated and he pulled it out of his pocket. It was a text message from John Holmes, saying to call him immediately. It was after midnight; this must be important.

"Gotta make a call," he said. "I'll be right back." Ryan went outside the building and dialed the number and John answered on the first ring.

"You know that woman, Sylvia Morrow?"

"Of course." Ryan had asked John to use GorillaTrace.com, a compilation of databases available only to law enforcement that searched for missing people. Ryan had tried to call the woman after discovering she'd left Chad Bennett's firm about the time the Fordhams had died in the plane crash. He'd been unable to find her, but knew John subscribed to GorillaTrace.

"I sent an operative to the apartment she was renting in Tustin. Morrow was dead.

ME said it looks like a heart attack. She's been dead less than twenty-four hours."

For a moment the silence around Ryan was so thick it was suffocating. How could Sylvia Morrow be dead? Since Sylvia had left Bennett's firm, Ryan had counted on her to verify witnessing the Fordhams' trust. Now he couldn't prove a damn thing. If he didn't have such bad luck, he'd have no luck at all.

"Have you got any influence with the coroner? Can you get him to run a full battery of tests, including an advance tox screen?"

"I'll try. You thinking this wasn't natural causes?"

"Let's make sure."

Ryan clicked off and leaned against the wall for a moment. Sylvia Morrow had quit after being with the same firm for years, sold a nice home in Costa Mesa and dropped out of sight. Why? Something about this didn't add up.

CHAPTER
TWENTY-THREE

"I've got it!" Ryan shouted.

"G-got w-what?" Hayley mumbled.

It was nearly dawn. They'd been with The Wrath until after two, then returned to the beach house. On the way back they'd talked, and Ryan explained everything he'd recently learned about her case. She forgave him for not telling her first about the GPS, but cautioned him not to leave her out of the loop again.

At the sound of voices, Andy, who'd taken to sleeping beside the bed, began to wag his tail. It thumped on the carpeted floor like a kid lazily tapping a drum.

"I have an idea about where we might find a copy of the trust," Ryan said quietly, then kissed the soft curve of Hayley's neck.

"You think Chad kept a copy in his office or on his computer?" Hayley asked, fully awake now.

"I doubt it," Ryan replied. "Even if he did,

getting a search warrant wouldn't be easy. He probably switched the office computer's hard drive or purchased a new computer rather than risk disbarment." Ryan paused before saying, "I'm wondering if your mother used the clouds."

"Clouds?" muttered Hayley, sounding sleepy again. "What are you talking about?"

"Cloud computing. You've heard of it."

"Yeah, but I didn't pay much attention. What is it exactly? Why —"

"The new PCs that are so small and lightweight aren't using their own personal systems to back up data. They're sending it out over the Internet — into the clouds, so to speak. It's backed up on a huge server somewhere that's maintained by a company. Trouble is they could go out of business or hackers could access the system and steal information. The user might not realize his personal info was stolen until something happened, like identity theft."

Hayley sat upright and positioned her pillow against the bed's backboard, saying, "Designs could be stolen. Right?"

"Possibly. So far the systems have been remarkably safe, but we're just on the leading edge of this new technology. It's been my experience that there isn't a system around that hackers can't get into, given enough time. Hell, even supersecure sites like the Pentagon have suffered attacks that nearly took them down."

"Mother always backed up her designs on disks. I don't think she would have trusted the cloud thing."

"Maybe not, but she was on a newer model Dell. Right?"

"Yes. She bought it a month or so before she died."

Ryan gazed at her face, barely visible in the moonlight. "It's possible that she took advantage of their SafeSave service without realizing she was sending info into the clouds. The technology's new enough that many people don't realize how it works. Your mother could have used it without realizing what she was doing exactly."

"It's possible. I guess."

Hayley didn't sound convinced and neither was he. This was a wild shot in the dark. But if something didn't turn up, Ryan planned to go to the police and tell them what he'd illegally found on Alison Fordham's computer. He risked being arrested, but after learning about the GPS on Hayley's car and Sylvia Morrow's death, he felt too much was happening that he didn't understand. He didn't want to conceal anything that might help solve the case.

"It would be great if I could get into the cloud system and find the document again. That would prove to the authorities that Chad and others had concealed the existence of the trust."

"I've been thinking," Hayley said.

"Uh-oh. I was afraid of that."

"Kidding aside." She sounded deadly serious. "I don't want you to go to the police. If they know you made a copy of info illegally, they might jail you. Right?"

"Possibly, but unlikely. It's not the crime of the century. Like I told you, I was worried about my job with the Bureau. That's why I didn't want anyone to know. Now I'm not concerned. John Holmes won't care if I hacked into a system. My new job is safe."

"Please don't go to the police," she said in a choked voice that surprised him.

He scooted closer and put his arm around her. "What's the matter?"

She buried her face against his throat, then whispered, "If they arrest you, I'll be all alone."

She was afraid; not that he could blame her. After all they'd learned today, it was clear something was going on — but what? *Who* — exactly — was a better question.

"Go back to sleep," he whispered. "I'm going to work on the clouds and see what I can find."

Her expression darkened with an unreadable emotion. "I've made up my mind about something." She didn't wait for him to respond. "I want to talk to Steve Fulton."

A warning voice whispered in his head: *Don't let her do it.* "Why?"

"I owe him an explanation. I —"

"Look, the guy was abusive. Lindsey was afraid of him, right?"

"True, but . . ." Tears bordered her eyes. "He saved Lindsey from heroin addiction. He loved her, truly loved —"

"She believed he was going to kill her."

"Maybe Lindsey was . . . overreacting." Her tone seemed strained and a glazed look of despair swept over her lovely features.

Her reaction brought him up short. He recognized something he'd seen in himself, felt in his heart for over two years. Guilt. The crushing weight of the burden he carried over Jessica's death almost buried him alive at times. He tamped down thoughts of Jessica and what should have been — but never would be. Hayley blamed herself for Lindsey's death in a similar way that he'd felt responsible for Jessica's.

"If —" he let the word hang there for emphasis, even though he knew he could do nothing to stop Hayley once she'd made up her mind "— you talk to Fulton, what would you say?"

"He seems to be in denial," she replied in a voice filled with anguish. "I want him to understand several things. Lindsey loved him and appreciated everything he'd done for her. Getting someone off heroin isn't easy."

"No, it isn't," he admitted. Ryan considered himself to be a sympathetic man but he couldn't imagine what it would take to turn around an addict's life.

"Steve was too controlling, in a scary way. He wouldn't allow her to have friends —"

"Maybe he was afraid they'd lead her back to drugs."

Hayley nodded and a wisp of coppery hair fell across her cheek. She brushed it aside. "That's true. He blamed her friends for her addiction, and her family for not doing more to help her. He was so close-minded about it that she didn't dare introduce me, even though I've never done drugs."

"Okay. What else do you want him to know?"

"That Lindsey left him because she was afraid of him. She planned to stay at my place and file for divorce. I gave her the keys to my car, not knowing someone had hidden the bomb that killed her."

"He needs to know this because . . ."

"Steve doesn't seem to believe Lindsey is dead. Once he realizes she's gone, he can put the past behind him."

Easier said than done, Ryan silently told himself. Much easier than Hayley could possibly realize. He thought about Jessica less often since meeting Hayley, but his wife was still in his thoughts.

"Eventually, Steve will meet another woman. I don't want him to make the same mistake again."

"You said he beat her up several times and when she left him it was because he was going to kill her. Right?" When Hayley nodded, he continued, "I don't see how that translates to the type of personality change this man will require. It would take extensive counseling."

She took a deep breath, gazing at him defiantly. "You may be right, but I believe Lindsey would want me to try."

He knew it would be futile to argue with Hayley. She had a soft heart and she was more stubborn than any woman he'd known. No chance she'd change her mind. But for reasons Ryan really couldn't explain, the thought of Hayley with Steve Fulton seemed dangerous.

Hayley saw Steve Fulton approaching the fountain outside Peet's Coffee and Tea where she was waiting with Ryan. She would rather have met Lindsey's husband alone, but Ryan refused to allow her to be by herself. He wouldn't even consent to watching from the window of nearby Surf's Up. He insisted on being at her side.

They'd decided to meet near Surf's Up so they could quickly get back and pack items to be taken down to the booth at the beach. Tomorrow would be the first day of Board Wars. Hayley wanted to arrange her display items personally.

Steve stopped a few feet from the small round table where she and Ryan were sipping coffee. "I know you. I met you at some gallery."

"Ian Barrington's gallery."

Steve shrugged as if to say: Who cares? He pulled out a chair and stared at Ryan with narrowed eyes filled with hostility and contempt. He was older than Hayley remembered. Steve Fulton appeared to be a little over forty, with black hair burnished at the temples with silver and deep-set brown eyes. He was tall — almost as tall as Ryan

— and whipcord lean, like a long-distance runner.

"This is my friend Ryan Hollister," Hayley said. "Would you like some coffee? Peet's has the best in Newport."

"I'm not here for coffee," Steve snapped, barely holding his anger in check.

Hayley felt Ryan lean forward slightly and knew he was going to put Steve in his place. Under the table, she squeezed Ryan's knee. She could handle this. "I owe you an explanation about what happened to Lindsey."

Just saying her friend's name nearly made Hayley choke up. If only she'd encouraged Lindsey to go to a women's shelter, she might still be alive. Instead, she'd insisted Lindsey fly down here where Hayley could make sure she was safe. Safe? What a joke. She'd been so naive; no one had the power to keep another safe — if a killer was determined to eliminate them. But Steve wasn't that kind of man. His crime was obsessive love that in the end drove Lindsey away.

"Okay, so talk," Steve said brusquely.

Hayley cut a sideways glance at Ryan. "It was two years ago that you and I met at Ian's gallery."

Steve shrugged. "I guess. I didn't recall your name. When the police said Lindsey had come to visit you, I didn't believe it because I didn't remember you. I know all her friends."

"Did she have many?" Hayley asked, careful to keep her tone level. No telling what might antagonize this man.

"A few."

Hayley waited to give him time to name them. From what Lindsey had told her, Steve hadn't allowed her to associate with anyone.

"I was her best friend," he continued, his tone softening.

"I was her friend, too," Hayley added when it became clear that was all the man would offer on the subject. "We had art in common. Lindsey loved to paint. She appreciated the lessons you paid for her to take."

The look that crossed his face said she'd stepped into verbal quicksand. Maybe Ryan had been right. This wasn't such a great idea. Still, she felt she owed it to Lindsey.

"Is that where you met Lindsey — in class?"

"No. I met her when the class came to Ian's gallery. She was there and we began talking, then went for coffee. We had a lot in common."

Something glinted in the depths of his

brown eyes that Hayley did not like. "A lot in common, huh? You're an addict, too?"

Keep it together, she told herself. He's deliberately trying to antagonize you. "No. We were both interested in art but didn't think we could sell enough to support ourselves."

"Lindsey didn't need to support herself. She had me."

The man gave Hayley a half smile that was really a sneer. This was going nowhere, she decided.

"Lindsey loved you very much, but you were too controlling. You wouldn't allow her to express herself, have friends. That's why you didn't know about me. She was afraid to tell you, afraid you'd beat her up again."

Steve jerked back as if she'd slapped him. "What are you talking about? I never touched Lindsey."

Hayley didn't want to argue so she kept quiet.

"Never. I — I loved her too much to hurt her." Steve stared at the stone fountain with water undulating rhythmically over sea creatures like starfish and turtles into the pool below. "Did she say I hit her?"

Not trusting her voice, Hayley nodded. A quick glance at Ryan told her that he was a perplexed as she was. She could sense the controlled power in his body. She was really glad he'd insisted on coming with her.

"How well did you know my wife?" Steve asked.

"We talked every week on the day you went into the office. I called her because she said you checked the phone records and wouldn't approve of her calling me."

"I never check the calls unless our bill is unusually large."

He sounded so sincere and appeared so truthful that Hayley didn't challenge him. Clearly the man was delusional.

"Did Lindsey come down to see you last week the way the police claim?" he asked as if he couldn't believe it.

Hayley nodded and felt the welcome warmth of Ryan's hand on her arm. "She was nearly hysterical when she called — afraid of you. She thought you were so angry this time that you might kill her."

"What?" He slapped the table so hard their coffee cups jumped.

"Take it easy," Ryan cautioned in a voice that only someone with a death wish would ignore.

"I advised Lindsey to take an express shuttle to San Jose and fly from there to John Wayne airport. That way I could meet her and give her the keys to my car and my condo. She was going to hide out and think things over. When I returned, we planned to talk. Then she'd make a decision about what to do next."

Steve Fulton stared at her as if she were speaking an unusual foreign language. "What do you mean?" he asked in a voice so low that it could barely be heard above the burble of the fountain and the chatter from nearby tables.

"I think it's clear," Ryan said when she didn't reply. "Your wife was considering a divorce."

"Why are you making this up?" He shoved his hands into the pockets of his corduroy trousers, his shoulders hunched forward.

"She's not making it up," Ryan said.

"We were happy. She wouldn't have left me." He flushed a deep crimson.

"Lindsey did love you," Hayley said softly. "She just needed a little space. I wanted to meet with you so you would know exactly what happened and how sorry I am. Lindsey was so young, so talented."

An unexpected sob burst from the man. "She never said she was unhappy. I gave her everything."

"Why would your wife make up a story like this? Coming here got her killed."

Steve noisily sucked in air, took a minute

before saying, "I have no idea. It wasn't like her to lie."

Stunned silence enveloped them. Steve Fulton rose and quickly walked away. Hayley wanted to call him back, to comfort him, but she had no idea what to say. She'd wanted to comfort the man, to let him know what really happened so he could get on with his life. Instead, she'd given him more to be upset over.

"Do you think he's psychotic, delusional?" she asked Ryan.

"No. He could be telling the truth."

"No way! I spoke with Lindsey. I knew how afraid of him she was. We'd talked about it for two years. I'd been encouraging her to leave him. She finally did and look what happens." She was dismayed at the magnitude of her own sorrow. She'd believed she could fix things but it seemed impossible.

"Did you ever see Lindsey after he'd beaten her up?" Ryan wanted to know.

She shook her head. "How could I? We were miles apart."

"I just thought you might have been in town on one occasion," Ryan said in a troubled voice. "Did she file a police report?"

"Of course not. Lindsey didn't want to

cause a problem for Steve after he'd done so much to help her."

His compelling eyes riveted her to the spot, but he didn't utter one word.

"What do you think?" she asked.

"Maybe Fulton is telling the truth."

Hayley couldn't believe it. "You didn't see Lindsey that night. She was scared to death."

Ryan nodded slowly and took her hand. "Okay, but was it her husband that had her so spooked?"

"Yes." But some small part of her did wonder.

CHAPTER
TWENTY-FOUR

Death is the one constant in life, thought the killer. *Time flows along to one final, inevitable point.* There were defining moments in a person's life, but the last heartbeat was the same for everyone.

Death.

The world could take its time. Death might not arrive for years and years. But for some it came sooner. The Grim Reaper couldn't eliminate Hayley fast enough.

Stupid bitch! She thought the Grim Reaper was such a clever logo. It was a sign — if there ever was one — that she was destined to die.

The killer didn't like being forced into action, but the road of life had created a pothole — make that a landmine. But it had been handled. Alison Fordham's computer had to go. Who knew incriminating evidence had been left behind when the files had been erased? That was the problem with technology today. There was no getting away from it.

With luck the police wouldn't realize why the computer had been heisted. Taking other electronic gear should have made it look like an ordinary break-in except — of course — it had been on Linda Isle.

A small island with a guard gate and water surrounding it should *not* be a robber's target unless the thief had the ability to come in from the waterside, using the house's dock. So many boats came and went from all the private docks in the harbor that no one paid attention to who was on them.

The house had the added impediment of a security system, but it was easy to foil by cutting through the sliding door's glass and not tripping the alarm. Carrying the televisions and the Blue Ray player out had been simple under the cover of darkness. No one noticed. The police wouldn't have been called for days except the gardener next door noticed the hole in the sliding glass door.

Shit! Why didn't nosy people mind their own business? Never mind. It had been for the best. Having the police snooping, asking questions, meant Sylvia Morrow had to die. Life often provided such moments of epiphany.

The old woman had gone to a lot of trouble to hide. But all she'd really done was drop out of sight. Anyone with any tenacity at all could have found her. The elderly secretary's death was sure to be ruled a heart attack.

It was doubtful anyone would connect the two incidents. What would a robbery on exclusive Linda Isle have to do with a heart attack in Tustin?

Meg Amboy was straightening her skirt, getting ready to go down to lunch, when she heard a knock on the door to her suite. She hesitated. Who could it be? The last time someone had unexpectedly come to her door it had been Steve Fulton searching for Hayley.

She cautiously approached the door and looked through the peephole. Nothing. Maybe the knock had been next door, where Gus Miller lived. She turned away to go run a brush through her hair. Another knock, louder now.

Again she checked. This time she caught a blur at the bottom of the fisheye. Conrad, she realized. In a wheelchair he was too short to be fully seen from the peephole. She swung open the door and saw the breath-taking bouquet in his hands.

Two dozen red roses.

"What?" she cried.

"For you, Meg." He held out the crystal vase with the clusters of fabulous rosebuds.

"Why?" She motioned for him to come in and he pressed on the electric button that moved his wheelchair forward. "It's not my birthday."

He zipped by her and stationed himself beside the sofa where they often sat to talk. She placed the magnificent arrangement on the coffee table in front of them and took a deep breath of the fragrant bouquet.

"They're fabulous. Thank you." She sat beside him with a delighted smile.

"I'm glad you like them." His voice held a rasp of excitement.

"Like them? You know red roses are my favorites." She leaned over and gave him a light kiss on the lips. "I give up. What's the occasion?"

Now his smile seemed mischievous. "I passed my physical the other day with flying colors. Other than my balance problem — which is a short-circuit in my brain — I'm in great shape for my age."

"I'm sorry. I forgot to ask," she said, ashamed of herself. "With Hayley and all that was going on, it skipped my mind. I'm thrilled. I wouldn't want anything to happen to my bridge partner."

"What about a life partner?" He pulled a small blue Tiffany's box out of his pocket and handed it to her.

Meg's fingers trembled as she opened it. Inside was a magnificent diamond, its multicut facets winking in the light. She felt herself color fiercely. Did this mean what she thought it meant?

Of course it did. A life partner had to mean marriage. It wasn't the first time a man had asked her, but it was the only time she wanted to be asked. Was she too old? she wondered.

"What do you say?" Conrad asked in a lower, huskier tone. "How does Mrs. Conrad Hollister sound?"

"W-wonderful." A rush of tears startled her; she'd never been the type to cry. "It's just that I'm too, too . . . old."

"No, you're not," he assured her. "I'm older than you are. We might not have a lot of time left, but we still can be happy."

Blood pounded in her temples, thundered through her heart and made her knees tremble. "Yes, oh, yes. We can be happy."

He held out his arms and she moved toward him. It was a bit awkward with him in the wheelchair but they made it work. Why hadn't he come into her life years ago?

she asked herself.

You can't turn back the clock, she decided as she hugged him. *Be grateful for what you have today.* They kissed with a tenderness Meg hadn't considered possible. "Mrs. Conrad Hollister sounds wonderful."

"Where are we going to live?" he asked. "Your place or mine?"

Meg eased herself back onto the sofa. She'd been so taken aback by the proposal that she hadn't considered anything else.

"You know, just because I'm in a wheelchair doesn't mean . . ."

Another rush of heat rose to her face. "I — I understand." A strange inner excitement filled her suddenly. "What about one of the new cottages they're building? They're almost finished."

Twelve Oaks had acquired the land just below the existing buildings. They had constructed single-story cottages to keep from blocking the ocean views from the main building where Meg and Conrad now lived.

"They're bigger," Conrad said, "but the views aren't as good. We could go down there and look —"

"Views don't matter. Being together is what's important. You still will be able to see the ocean, just not the sweep of the coastline toward Laguna Beach."

"Yes," Conrad said softly. "Being together is what really counts. Let's not wait any longer. Let's get married as soon as possible."

Meg nodded her agreement, but her mind was on Hayley now. She wanted her niece to be there. Until this mess was resolved, a wedding didn't seem possible.

"Having second thoughts?" he asked in a teasing voice.

"Of course not. I was just thinking about Hayley."

"You're wondering if she ends up with my son — will two Mrs. Hollisters in the same family cause confusion."

Now Meg couldn't help laughing. "No. I would love it if they decided to become serious. I've been impressed with Ryan since I first met him. I just want them both to be at the wedding. With all that's going on I don't know when that will be."

Conrad considered what she'd told him for a moment before responding. "I think we should have a justice of the peace marry us as soon as possible. After this thing is straightened out, we'll have a big celebration at the Balboa Bay Club. The whole works — flowers, dinner, dancing."

"Sounds great," she said, a catch in her

voice. "Really special. I can't wait to tell Hayley. She'll be so happy for me."

From the Surf's Up stockroom, Hayley watched Cynthia Fordham escort a woman with an obvious face-lift. They sorted through the racks of tees and board shorts. Trent had gone out as soon as his mother had appeared, then returned, saying Cynthia was helping one of her clients select a wardrobe for her granddaughter's surf camp.

Hayley could have told her old tees and board shorts over a bikini with straps that wouldn't easily break were all the "wardrobe" a surf camp required. Anyone with too new clothes and flip-flops that weren't two seasons old would be branded an outsider.

Hayley was packing the boxes of clothing that she'd rush ordered for the Board Wars. As soon as they were finished, she and Ryan would join the others at the beach to set up the booth. She watched Cynthia, still wondering about the GPS tracker placed on her car and the bomb. Others might write off Cynthia, but Hayley gave her credit for being a very intelligent, cunning woman. She would have made much more of her life had she been able to let go of Russell Fordham and concentrate on a career.

Instead Cynthia never gave up on watching his every move. It had been clear for a long time that she still loved him despite the fact her ex had remarried, fathered a child and was very happy. When Hayley's father had been killed, Cynthia had been crushed. She'd been even more upset — outwardly — than Russell Fordham's children.

Right now, Cynthia was pointing out the replica of Duke's famous surfboard to her friend. The surfboard made Hayley think of all the other valuable boards decorating the shop. There was certainly more money involved than Hayley had realized.

There were also the custom molds her father had created for world-famous surfers. They could be modified slightly and used again as an authentic Fordham Board. That could be priceless.

No doubt Cynthia believed Hayley's charmed life on Linda Isle and education at a private school represented more than her fair share of the estate. Had Cynthia coveted the money so much that she'd destroyed the trust Hayley's parents had written? Had she arranged for the car bomb? Cynthia could be sneaky, Hayley decided. No telling what she was capable of doing.

She put Cynthia out of her thoughts. There were no answers to these troubling questions. It just made her mind whirl. She concentrated on packing the few remaining boxes while Ryan helped nearby with the surf stuff that Trent wanted in the booth.

Ryan's closeness was so male, so reassuring. She'd come to care for him more than she wanted to admit. It had happened so fast, so unexpectedly.

Thinking about Ryan reminded her of Chad. No matter who was behind the destruction of the trust, Chad must know about it. They'd been fighting over his inability to keep away from other women when her parents' plane crashed. Losing her parents had brought into focus their loving relationship and Hayley realized she couldn't settle for anything less.

"How's it going?" Ryan interrupted her thoughts.

"Almost finished."

She watched him out of the corner of her eye. Ryan had loved his wife deeply and remained committed to her even after she was gone. Would he ever feel that way about her?

Wait a minute!

How do you feel about him? She'd never been so attracted to a man. The way she felt about Chad couldn't compare to her intense feelings for Ryan. Her feelings for him had nothing to do with reason. But did she love him or was this merely about attraction and sex? So much was going on in her life that Hayley didn't know which way was up most of the time.

Ryan was a lover, a protector, a friend. She had to give this relationship time to develop, she decided. She needed to be living a normal life to see what she wanted — and who she wanted to spend that life with.

She saw him pull out his cell phone. "You get more calls than a teenage girl," she told him.

He winked and checked the caller ID. "It's your aunt. Wanna bet this is for you?" He answered then handed her the telephone.

"Aunt Meg, how are you doing?"

"I'm getting married."

Hayley sank down onto the nearest sealed box. "You're kidding!"

"No. Conrad and I plan to marry as soon as possible." Aunt Meg sounded totally serious and very happy.

For a moment the shock wedged words in her throat. "I'm so glad for you," Hayley finally managed to say after a long pause. She couldn't imagine her aunt, who'd always been single, getting married so late in life. And to Ryan's father, of all people.

"Your father wants to talk to you," she told Ryan after Meg asked her to give him the telephone so his father could explain the situation.

Hayley studied Ryan as he spoke with his father. She expected him to frown at the news but instead his face glowed like a kid on Christmas morning. "Hey, Dad, that's great!" He gazed at her and gave the thumbs-up sign with a smile.

They chatted a few more minutes, then Ryan said goodbye. "How do you like that, Hayley? We're going to be related."

She attempted a smile, but she wasn't sure she did like it. What if something happened and they were no longer a couple? She would have to face Ryan at family functions. "Don't you think they're a little old to marry?"

He crossed the small space cluttered with boxes and pulled her into his arms. The warmth of those arms and the affection in his eyes affected her deeply. "No. They're not too old to marry. My father says he loves Meg. I believe him. We're a lot alike. He never remarried after my mother. If he's finally found love, I'm all for it. I want him to be happy."

Conrad Hollister had remained single for

over twenty years, she quickly calculated. Did that mean Ryan would mourn Jessica for that long?

"You're wondering if my father can have sex, aren't you?"

She wasn't, but she couldn't discuss what was really on her mind. It was far too early in their relationship to seem so . . . so possessive. "Umm," she mumbled.

Both hands on her shoulders, he gazed directly into her eyes. "Marriage isn't just about sex. Companionship has a lot to do with it. They already spend a lot of time together. Maybe they'd like to wake up in each other's arms or go to sleep talking about things."

Hayley had never stopped to consider Aunt Meg being lonely. She despised the "all about me" syndrome. Had she fallen into that trap? "You're right. They deserve to be happy."

"You have no idea how lonely you can be living alone when you've been accustomed to having someone you love next to you in bed. How lonely it gets wandering around an empty house that once buzzed with activity." Gathering her close, he held her snugly. "My father has a balance problem. I doubt it interferes with his ability to —"

"I get it! This is none of our business.

Anyway, there's always Viagra."

Ryan laughed, a deep masculine sound that vibrated in her chest. "Somehow I doubt Dad will need it."

The apple didn't fall very far from the tree, she decided. Just the thought of making love to Ryan sent a ripple of anticipation through her.

"Son of a bitch! It's my cell phone *again*." Ryan reached in his pocket, pulled out the cell phone, and checked Caller ID. "John Holmes. I've gotta take this."

He pulled away, saying, "Hollister."

Hayley watched as Ryan listened. He frowned and pursed his lips. Whatever John Holmes was telling him was not good news. She leaned away so she could see through the stockroom door. Cynthia Fordham and her client had left the store, but Chad Bennett was standing at the entrance talking to Trent.

Why wasn't he at work? she wondered. It was the middle of the afternoon. A coating of ice formed inside her. How could she have ever believed herself in love with that man?

A debilitating wave of bitterness assailed her. She was angry with Chad, but she blamed herself even more. Something about Chad should have tripped an alarm. But it hadn't. *Go slowly,* she reminded herself with a sideways glance at Ryan, who was still on the telephone. Don't rush into anything.

He pocketed the cell phone, saying, "You're not going to believe this. Sylvia Morrow didn't die of a heart attack. A comprehensive toxicology screen showed selenium poisoning killed her. It mimics a heart attack."

"Oh, my God," she said, her voice barely perceptible over the voices coming from the store. Someone had ruthlessly murdered the woman. She would be foolish to believe she was safe. The knowledge twisted and burned inside her. The world seemed to be closing in and she was powerless to prevent it. She tried weighing the whole structure of events for connections, but nothing made sense.

"Do you know what selenium is?" he asked. When she shook her head, Ryan said, "It's a trace element in our food from the soil. Too much of it is toxic."

"How did she get too much?"

Ryan shrugged. "They're still checking. Selenium can be purchased over the counter in pill form at health food stores and places like that. It's easily disguised in food and drinks."

"Do you think her death had something to do with the trust?"

A tense silence enveloped the small room. After a few seconds, Ryan said, "I'm sure someone wanted to silence her."

"How did the police get the info so fast?" she wondered out loud. "Doesn't it usually take days or weeks to get back a tox screen?"

"Usually, but Tustin isn't a high crime area. They don't have a lab, so they outsource it. Since the lab rarely hears from Tustin PD, they put a priority on it to show how it pays to use them."

"I'll bet the killer never counted on anyone doing a screen."

His unexpected bark of laughter lacked humor. "I wouldn't count on anything with this maniac. He's used a bomb, which is unusual, and selenium, which is difficult to trace. Expect anything. This guy is tricky."

"Almost finished?" Trent asked from the doorway. By the expression on his face, Hayley doubted he'd overheard them.

"Just about," she replied, forcing a smile. She believed Trent wasn't involved in this mess, but now she wasn't sure she could trust her instincts.

"Chad's here," Trent said gently. "He wants to talk to you."

CHAPTER
TWENTY-FIVE

Hayley leaned back against a table of folded men's swim trunks near the entrance of the store. "You wanted to talk to me?" she asked Chad.

"Could we go somewhere more private?" Chad asked with the smile she'd once considered charming. Now she saw too much whitener had made his teeth look like piano keys in his tanned face.

"We have to talk here. I've got work to do." Hayley didn't add that Ryan refused to allow her out of his sight. He was keeping an eye on them from the storeroom. Ryan didn't trust anyone, and at this point, neither did she.

"I just wanted to say how happy I am the car bomb didn't kill you," he said with what might have been mistaken for sincerity.

"It was a mistake," she replied as glibly as possible. The GPS tracker on her car had convinced her that the bombing hadn't been a mistake. She'd been deliberately targeted, but they hadn't told anyone about the tracker yet.

And no one knew about their discovery of the trust. Chad had to have been involved. He knew her parents had signed the document. His signature as well as that of the now-dead witness, Sylvia Morrow, was on the trust.

It was possible he'd given his former secretary the fatal dose of selenium. It could have been disguised in food or a tablet or injected. The medical examiner hadn't seen any signs of needle marks, but Ryan believed it was possible a pediatric syringe had been used. In that case the puncture hole would be too tiny to detect.

"Mistaken identity. That makes sense," Chad told her. "No one would want you dead."

She wasn't buying that line — not from him — but replied, "One of my closest friends was killed." Lindsey's death and her husband's odd behavior caused a painful blockage in her chest. Hayley couldn't shake the feeling that she was responsible for her friend's death. She kept telling herself she wasn't to blame, but she still couldn't get the thought out of her mind.

"I'm sorry about your friend." Chad

reached out and touched her arm.

She resisted the urge to snatch her arm away. He gazed at her with a loving expression that sent her temper soaring. The man always counted on his charm to manipulate her. Well, not this time. "If there's nothing else, I have work to do."

Without hesitating, he said, "I think it would be a good idea for us to start over. We were a great couple once. We could be again."

Cripes! The man had an endless supply of self-confidence. Did he seriously expect her to forgive him? Fool me once — not twice. Even if Ryan hadn't been in her life, she was finished with Chad.

"Tell me something, Chad."

"Anything, sweetheart."

Sweetheart? She almost slugged him. Instead, she lowered her eyes as if flattered. Then she raised her head, looked directly at him, and asked, "Why didn't my parents complete their trust?"

A swift changing of gears registered for a second on his face, then vanished as if she'd imagined it. "They meant to, I'm sure, but they didn't get around to it."

If she hadn't known the truth, Hayley would have believed him. He was that good. Why was she surprised? When she'd first caught him cheating, he'd denied it and she'd foolishly believed him. The second time Chad hadn't been able to weasel out of it. Maybe she wasn't as good at reading people as she liked to think.

"What about it?" he asked, unfazed. "Dinner tonight?"

"Not tonight. Not any night. I've found someone." She walked away without a backward glance.

There was chaos at the booth when Hayley arrived with the Grim Reaper clothes she planned to sell. Clerks from Surf's Up as well as Trent and a local group of surfers were there.

"Do you know all these people?" asked Ryan.

"Most of them." She opened the door and let Andy out of the back of the SUV where the retriever was crammed in with the boxes of clothes. "It's always like this. People chip in to help. When it's set up, which is usually around sunset, we order pizza to reward all the workers."

Ryan didn't say anything, but he appeared worried. He believed a lot of strangers represented a threat to her. They pulled boxes out of the car and trudged across the sand to the booth. Andy romped ahead of them, his tail held high like a golden plume.

"Let me help," called Courtney, coming toward them wearing a white bikini that emphasized her deep tan.

"You've met Ryan," Hayley said, recalling what Ryan had told her about the reception following the memorial service.

Courtney gave him one of her deer-in-the-headlights looks, then nodded as she took two boxes from Hayley. She couldn't tell if Trent's wife was high or simply didn't remember Ryan. As soon as the thought hit her, Hayley discounted it. Ryan wasn't the type of man a woman would forget.

"Aunt Hayley, Aunt Hayley!" Timmy rushed up to her and flung out his arms.

Hayley put down the box she was carrying and scooped him into her embrace. He was too heavy to pick up as she once had but he returned her hug with surprising strength. Andy hovered at her side, wagging his tail at the little boy who often played ball with him.

"I thought you'd died," Timmy said. "Then you came back. I'm so happy!"

"So am I, sweetie." She gazed into his tear-glazed eyes and thought how precious Trent's son was. "I'm back now and I'm not going away again."

Timmy refused to let go of her hand as

they tromped through the sand with Andy to the white canvas booth facing the ocean. Across the top was the Surf's Up sign with the signature triple-wave logo and two flags signaling dangerous swimming conditions. The sight brought the sting of tears. This was the first Board Wars since her parents' deaths.

Hayley thought of the initial competition. She had been a little girl when Russell Fordham and his friends organized the event. Their first booth had been nothing more than a canvas-covered tent held up by plastic pipe. Everyone had pitched in to sell the T-shirts, shorts and swimsuits her mother had designed.

Hayley had planned to bring Lindsey to this year's exhibition to show her how the family business had grown. She'd told her friend about designing clothes for Surf's Up, but Lindsey hadn't seen the flagship store or the Board Wars. Now she never would.

How could a life be so cruelly cut short? Knowing Lindsey had been killed by accident and that she was the intended victim didn't diminish Hayley's sorrow. If anything, it made her more upset. Lindsey had been killed just as she was getting her life back together.

Or had she?

Steve Fulton seemed so believable. Ryan certainly bought his story and wondered if Lindsey had made up the abuse for some reason. Once, Hayley would have been totally certain Lindsey had not deceived her, but she no longer trusted her judgment. Chad had fooled her. It was possible Trent had as well. Her stepbrother might not have been as broken up about her "death" as he'd seemed.

She resolutely put this from her mind and concentrated on what she'd come to do — see how MMA gear sold. Other booths lined the sand, but theirs had the best spot near the pier and bleachers.

"My father was one of the guys who organized the first Board Wars," she told Ryan. "We've been a sponsor ever since."

"Great," Ryan said, but he didn't sound very impressed. His attention was focused on the long pier, then shifted to the workers setting up the temporary bleachers.

Several surfers came up to congratulate Hayley on her narrow escape. She put down the box and began chatting with old friends. They weren't family or close friends but acquaintances who were thrilled to see her. Over and over Hayley explained the short version of her trip to Costa Rica that had caused the misunderstanding.

Ryan left to bring more boxes and signaled her to stay in the booth with Andy. Trent showed her where to place the Grim Reaper products. The Wrath's logo had already been attached to that corner of the booth.

Hayley directed Timmy and several others as they helped her set up her goods. She was so busy that she didn't notice Farah at first. Trent walked up with his sister; both were smiling.

"Hello," said Farah, "it's great to have you back."

"I didn't know I was missing," Hayley said with more sarcasm than she'd intended.

"What a mess. Your aunt was so worried." Farah glanced around. "This your new line?"

"Yes. The Wrath will be here tomorrow with posters and he'll autograph them for fans who buy any of the Grim Reaper products."

"Good idea." Farah honestly sounded as if she meant it. "I'm down here with Kyle. He's been surfing. Now he's hanging out with some of the guys. I thought I'd see if I could help. Tell me what to do."

Hayley almost fell over. When had Farah *ever* offered to help? Come to think of it, when had Farah *ever* been to the Board

398

Wars? Never.

"I could use the help," Hayley replied as brightly as possible, considering this woman might very well have been behind the plot to kill her. "I need to hang up these dog leashes and collars so people will know they're available." She bent down and put one on Andy but didn't take off his own leash since it had ID tags.

"How about using big safety pins and putting them here?" Farah pointed to the side wall of the tent just above the bank of onesies and bibs with the Grim Reaper logo on them.

"Good spot. See if you can find a few pins. We just have to put up a couple of samples. We'll keep the others under the table."

Farah trotted off. Hayley took a deep breath, relieved to see her go. She trusted Trent but she didn't quite trust Farah. If she had to make a bet, Hayley would say Farah and her mother had been behind the car bombing.

"Aunt Hayley," Timmy said, tugging at her arm. "Why doesn't Aunt Farah like me?"

It took a second to realize that Farah had greeted Hayley warmly but she hadn't even acknowledged Timmy's presence. She quickly thought back to all the family get-togethers over the years. Hayley had always spent time with her nephew, but Farah never had. Hayley assumed Farah didn't really know how to relate to young children because Timmy was the only one in the family. Hayley hadn't considered how Timmy must feel.

"Your aunt loves you, but she has a lot on her mind." It was a lame response and Timmy seemed to realize it, because he merely shrugged.

Before Hayley could come up with something more reassuring, Kyle appeared. His usual boyish smile reminded Hayley of the day she'd first met him on the beach not far from there. He'd been several years older — about fifteen — and Hayley had been a gawky twelve-year-old whose breasts were just beginning to appear. She'd been so "charged" that Kyle noticed her that she'd floated through the rest of the day.

Over the years, Hayley had come to see Kyle as one of a limitless number of surfers who hung out at the beach. She knew he'd joined a group of guys who were developing real estate locally. They'd been successful when the economy had been going gangbusters, but the slowdown had hit them hard. She wasn't sure how he was earning a living these days.

"Where's Farah?" Kyle asked with a goofy grin.

"She's hunting for pins," Timmy said as he petted Andy.

"Pins?" Kyle directed his question to Hayley. He, too, ignored Timmy.

Hayley put her hand on Timmy's shoulder. "He's right. Farah is looking for pins to use to put up the collars and leashes."

"Tell her I'm looking for her." Kyle left.

Hayley wondered if Kyle had helped Farah with the bomb. They'd assumed it was a professional job but there were instructions available on the Internet. Hayley always thought of Kyle as a dumb surfer but perhaps she'd underestimated him.

"Aunt Hayley, what can I do now?"

Hayley thought a moment. "We're almost done here. Help me put away the stuff Ryan is bringing then you can take Andy down to the water. Tomorrow I'm going to ask your father if you can help me sell T-shirts." She reached for a child's medium T-shirt. "I'll need you to wear this." She shook it out.

"Way cool!" Timmy cried with a grin. "The Wrath's the best."

"Do you know who The Wrath is?" she asked, more than a little surprised.

"Of course, everybody knows. I've seen him on TV."

401

"Your father watches?" Trent hadn't seemed to know who The Wrath was when they'd been approached to sponsor him.

"Nah," Timmy said. "Kevin's father watches with us."

"The Wrath will be here in the booth tomorrow. You'll meet him."

Timmy stared at her blankly for a moment, then cried, "Wow!! Wait 'til I tell Kevin."

"Tell Kevin what?" Courtney reappeared, now wearing an oversize T-shirt with the Surf's Up logo.

Hayley sensed Timmy's hesitation. "I need Timmy to help me in the booth tomorrow. The Wrath will be here signing posters. Timmy thinks his friend Kevin will be envious."

Now Courtney hesitated. "I don't know. Trent expects him to watch the competition."

Hayley knew how much Trent wanted to have his son follow in his footsteps. She also knew Courtney had different ideas. What did Timmy want?

"I can make do on my own," Hayley said. "You can stop by and meet The Wrath and he'll sign a poster for you. Or you can help me. It's your choice."

"I wanna help you."

"Great," Hayley said with a smile for Timmy. She looked at Courtney. "Then it's settled. I'll explain to Trent."

CHAPTER
TWENTY-SIX

Ryan glanced back over his shoulder into the booth set up for the Board Wars, which had started two hours earlier. All morning he'd been on the lookout for someone stalking Hayley, but so far he hadn't spotted anyone except for a guy who resembled Steve Fulton. The man disappeared in the distance, walking away from the competition area. The nice thing was most people were wearing swimsuits or skimpy shorts. Hard to hide a weapon.

It was after eleven and the Reaper clothes were just beginning to sell. The dog collars and matching leashes weren't going at all, despite Andy prancing around, sporting one.

"What's happening?" he asked as Trent rushed up.

"I'm totally stoked!" Trent grinned, breathless. "ESPN just called. They'll be here at noon. They want to film the booth and the junior competition this afternoon."

"Great," Ryan responded. "That should help your business."

"I can't believe it." Trent shook his head. "The Water Channel and the Outdoor Channel film us, but ESPN hasn't shown any interest in this event. ESPN covers Huntington Beach's U.S. Open and the Hurley competition at Lower Trestles in San Clemente but never us. That'll put the winners in the big leagues and bring them to the attention of mainstream audiences."

Ryan didn't respond. Obviously, Trent's mind was on the competition, not on the boost this would give Surf's Up. Ryan thought for a moment about the trust. Maybe the reason Hayley's parents had left her the business was simple. Her mind was often more on the business than Trent's.

The Fordhams knew Hayley would keep Trent in the business so he wouldn't have been cut off from a career he loved. But he couldn't have blown it and destroyed all his father had built with poor business decisions. Trent had done exactly that after the destruction of the trust.

"I gotta tell Hayley." Trent dashed toward the booth.

Ryan noticed Laird McMasters watching from his booth nearby. Not many people were buying anything. Ryan hadn't noticed much activity in Laird's booth all morning.

Ryan saw Hayley swipe at her forehead with the back of her hand as she listened to Trent, a smile on her face. It was hot under the canvas tent, unusually warm for the beach. She poured a little water from a bottle onto Andy's head to cool him off.

The oppressive heat meant the concession stands with soda, water and Sno-Kones were doing a great business. A troop of gorgeous girls wearing skimpy silver-lamé bikinis with temporary tattoos on their backs that read *Evian* were parading around the crowded beach, spritzing everyone with the well-known bottled water.

Ryan wished they'd make their way over and blast him. Ryan was wearing a Reaper tee and khaki shorts, but he was still warm. Cooling off left his mind as he saw Hayley racing his way with the retriever at her heels. She stood up on tiptoe and kissed him on the cheek.

"How do you predict fashion trends?" he asked. "In case ESPN wants to know."

"Can you believe they're coming? I can't!" She sounded as excited as Trent had a few minutes ago. "This could be huge for Surf's Up."

"Huge," he agreed. Hayley had instantly

understood what Trent had not. That was just one facet of her intelligence. She was much more complicated than he'd originally suspected. Ryan needed to protect her at all costs.

He congratulated himself on planting a tiny GPS chip in her tennis shoe last night. No one was going to snatch Hayley away from him. He could find her no matter what.

"The Internet has changed the world. Kids go online and show pictures of what they're wearing or clothes they like that they've spotted somewhere. Teenagers blog nonstop about clothes. Lots of designers listen to them. Now's the time to expand Surf's Up's Web site."

Hayley's heart might be with art but she did have a good head for business. "I notice how many kids have on shorter shorts, not the floppy-knee kind. You pointed it out at the exhibition fight."

"A lot of them are my designs. Some sold at the shop, some at other shops and some online."

"How can you tell which is which?" he wanted to know.

"It's the size of the logo on the waistband. The really large ones are from the shop, the medium size comes from other shops that sell our line and the smallest of the logos means they bought it online."

"Whose idea was that?" he asked, although he had a pretty good idea.

"Mine." She winked. "This year I'm seeing a lot more online gear. It's not a scientific study, mind you, but it tells me to keep in touch with fashion bloggers and keep our Web site updated constantly."

"How's Timmy doing?" He watched the kid show a woman a child's T-shirt.

"Great! He loved meeting the The Wrath and PimpIt. They treat him like one of the gang. He's eating it up." Hayley grinned. "I need to get back. I want to see what I can do with the display before ESPN arrives." She tugged at Andy's Reaper leash and the retriever trotted off at her side.

He enjoyed watching her flounce back into the booth. What he felt for Hayley was off the charts. He didn't know how to handle the situation. A bikini-clad bimbo whipped up to him, spraying the air with Evian and interrupting his thoughts. A blast of ice-cold water misted Ryan's face.

"More?" The pretty girl bobbed up and down in front of him, jiggling breasts that were too large to be original equipment. The sun glinted off the lamé bikini.

His cell phone vibrated. He turned away

and pulled it out of his pocket. The screen said Twelve Oaks was calling. Ryan's heart dropped; this couldn't be good news or his father's number would have appeared, not the central number.

"Mr. Hollister?" a female voice asked. "This is Molly Stern, head of nursing at Twelve Oaks."

Ryan put his hand over his other ear to block out the cheering of the crowd for a surfer who must have locked onto a killer wave. "My father?"

"He's having some problems. We've taken him to UCI Medical Center. It may be a stroke."

"UCI, not Hoag Hospital?" Ryan asked. He knew Hoag was the best regional hospital in the area. University of California at Irvine had a newer facility but it wasn't as close.

She verified his father had been sent to UCI. Ryan shoved his phone into his pocket. A shudder vibrated up through his stomach and into his chest. He glanced up and saw Hayley handing a smiling customer a leash and collar.

Could be a trick, Ryan suddenly thought. A ploy to separate him from Hayley. He pulled out his phone again and speed dialed the main office at Twelve Oaks.

He half-expected them to say there wasn't a Molly Stern on staff, but instead they put him through. The same woman's voice came over the line. "Was my father conscious when he left?" Ryan asked.

"I'm not sure."

Ryan hung up, his thoughts spinning. He should take Hayley with him, he decided as he headed toward the booth to tell her what happened. But ESPN was expected soon and this could be a big break for her, for Surf's Up. Trent would be here, of course, but he was likely to muck up things. Trent would keep the attention on the surfers, not the store. Hayley would know better.

Ryan pulled Hayley aside and told her, downplaying the seriousness of the situation. He should have been totally honest, but decided it was better if he went alone. He might have to make a heart-wrenching decision.

The Wrath came over to them. "What's happening?"

"Ryan needs to check on his father. He's been taken to the hospital."

"Could you take care of Hayley?" Ryan asked. The MMA fighter knew the situation and realized the danger to Hayley.

"Sure," The Wrath replied. He put his arm around Hayley in a way that would have irritated Ryan normally, but his mind was on his father.

"PimpIt and I will keep Hayley with us. Nothing can happen to her."

It took Ryan a second to again evaluate the situation. He didn't see how anything could happen to Hayley if she stayed in the booth surrounded by people with two fighters guarding her. She had the tracking device imbedded in her tennis shoe. If something crazy happened, he could find her.

"Don't leave the booth," he told Hayley. "Promise?"

"I swear," she responded.

Hayley watched Timmy stand beside The Wrath and take orders for T-shirts. He would tell her the size and she would reach into the appropriate bin and grab a shirt. A clerk from the store handled the money.

Timmy was more lively and happier than Hayley had ever seen him. He loved having something to do and being responsible. Standing next to his hero didn't hurt, either.

What a great kid, Hayley thought. In many ways Timmy reminded Hayley of herself. Trent and Farah had been just a few years older, but back then it seemed as if they were grown up and she was a mere baby.

411

Trent could skateboard and surf. She really wasn't interested in either, but tried hard — to please her father. That's what Timmy wanted as well.

But pleasing Trent wasn't as easy because Timmy didn't have any aptitude — or interest — in board sports. Hayley thought she could help Timmy by explaining to his father that Timmy had his own interests. Trent listened and finally consented to Timmy spending time in the booth with Hayley and The Wrath, but she could tell Trent didn't like it and he let Timmy know how he felt.

What would it take to make Trent a more caring father? she wondered. A better marriage, for starters. Courtney was in a fog most of the time. She tried her best to help Timmy but she didn't work with Trent to be a team.

How well Hayley remembered her own parents' teamwork. You couldn't play them off against each other. If her mother said no to something, Hayley learned early on not to go to her father in an attempt to get a favorable response. Russell Fordham would just ask, "What did your mother say?"

Hayley couldn't decide if Courtney needed an intervention or if someone should talk to Trent about parenting skills. Both, probably. She realized this was a father's job. Their father had successfully raised three children. Hayley had never been a parent. It wasn't her place to criticize Trent, but she saw the damage this was doing to Timmy.

Maybe she should talk to Farah. She'd been much nicer yesterday but she hadn't seen her today. Hayley stopped herself. What was she thinking? These people could be plotting to kill her. *Just keep your mind on figuring out your own mess. Then you can concentrate on helping Timmy.*

Still, she couldn't stop noticing Timmy, seeing how cute he looked when he was happy. She wished she had her sketchbook to capture his expression. She'd secretly done several charcoals of Ryan when she'd been alone in his father's house.

Her thoughts suddenly shifted. She'd like to have children. Not one child — she'd been lonely growing up — but two or maybe three. She couldn't help wondering how Ryan felt about children.

Stop! Don't get ahead of yourself. She realized how wrong she'd been about Chad. *Give this new relationship plenty of time and space.*

She recalled the concerned look on Ryan's face when he'd said his father had been taken to the hospital. She hoped it was nothing serious. *Don't let something happen to Conrad now,* she thought. At times like this, Hayley wished her aunt wasn't so antitechnology. Aunt Meg didn't have a cell phone. It probably didn't matter. Aunt Meg wouldn't have a phone on in a hospital — assuming she was with Conrad. Ryan would contact Hayley as soon as he had news.

"Hayley, look!" Timmy pointed to the wave of people scrambling out of the bleachers and getting off towels, heading toward the area where the booths and concession stands were located.

"It's the noon break," Hayley told Timmy. "We'll be busy now."

"It's broiling in here," The Wrath announced with a mischievous smile. He shucked his Grim Reaper T-shirt to reveal a huge tattoo of the Grim Reaper on a smooth, tanned torso that had obviously been waxed.

"Awesome!" cried Timmy.

"Cool," agreed Hayley. It was a new tattoo that hadn't been there at the exhibition fight. It committed The Wrath to the logo she'd created. It pleased her enormously. Soon those tattoos would be seen everywhere, especially after the ESPN film ran.

"It's hot in here," PimpIt said as he, too,

removed his T-shirt. "Aren't you sweating?" PimpIt asked Timmy. "You can take off your shirt, too."

"Naw, I'm okay."

Hayley couldn't help smiling. Timmy had to be as warm as everyone else, but there was no way he'd take off his Grim Reaper T-shirt.

"There's Aunt Farah," Timmy cried, pointing into the crowd.

Hayley looked but didn't see Farah. It was difficult to be sure with all the people and many of them wearing hats or sunglasses. "I don't see her, honey. It's probably another woman who looks like her."

"I guess." Timmy didn't sound convinced.

Hayley was uncomfortably warm and itchy. She poured more water on Andy's head to cool off the dog who had to be suffering in his fur coat. It would be great to take a dip in the ocean, but she'd promised Ryan she wouldn't leave the booth. And the crush of people coming toward them would be the test for her new line.

She mustered a smile and stood behind Timmy, ready to help answer questions. Nearby, the Evian-spritzing beach bunnies in their silver-lamé bikinis frolicked through the crowded spraying appreciative spectators with ice water. Laird McMasters had

415

left his booth and was flirting with one of the bunnies.

"We could use a misting in here," The Wrath yelled.

"No kidding." Hayley looked up at the canvas roof of the booth where a ceiling fan that had been temporarily installed was swirling the air without helping cool off the booth much.

The wave of humanity seemed to crest at the front of their booth. The Wrath was a huge draw. Trent had been concerned that people would cluster around the fighter but not buy anything. That wasn't the case. They scooped up the autographed posters but also purchased anything with his logo on it.

Hayley wished ESPN could be here to film this. Where were they? She checked her watch and saw it was after twelve. On a good day traffic crawled along Newport Boulevard onto the peninsula where the contest was being held. They were probably stuck in a slugfest of cars.

She thought about Ryan as she reached for a T-shirt and bumped into Andy. Ryan would just be getting to the hospital. It might be as long as an hour before he called her.

It was becoming hotter — if possible. She

swiped at her forehead with her forearm. The people crowding the open area at the front of the booth blocked what little ocean breeze existed.

She was dressed in short shorts and a Grim Reaper tank top but it felt as if she was wearing a coat. Her tennis shoes seem unusually heavy and hot. If Ryan hadn't inserted the tracking device, she would go barefoot.

Get a grip! It wouldn't be long before the afternoon session started. By then they would have sold out of most of the Grim Reaper merchandise. Trent wouldn't believe this.

Where was Trent? Courtney wasn't here, but Hayley had known she wouldn't be. Courtney had a voice lesson that wouldn't be over until one. Hayley decided Trent was probably helping the ESPN crew find a place to park. She wished he could see this — along with the television crew. Trent had been so sure MMA gear wouldn't attract surfer fans.

The lamé-bikinied bunnies began spritzing the crowd jammed around the front of the booth. People were loving it. This had to be one of the hottest days of the summer and some of the highest surf of the season, thanks to a hurricane south of Baja.

"Spray him!" Hayley pointed to Timmy. Sweat was beaded across the poor little guy's forehead.

A bunny reached across the low table of T-shirts and gear, giving The Wrath and PimpIt a close look at breasts the size of soccer balls as the girl liberally sprayed Timmy. Another girl took care of the two fighters while still another blasted Andy.

The retriever backed into Hayley and shook, sending droplets of water in all directions. Unexpectedly, the dog began to growl.

"It's okay, boy," she told him. He was usually very playful and wouldn't mind getting sprayed, especially when he was accustomed to having water dumped on his head. Now he was snarling, baring his teeth, which wasn't like Andy at all. She grabbed his collar to keep him from lunging forward. A beach bunny with dark sunglasses and a red bikini misted Hayley's face and doused her T-shirt.

Hayley stepped back, gasping at the shock of the ice cold water directly in her eyes and on her overheated body. The dog continued to snarl, then began to bark. People were looking at them. The Wrath moved closer to her and the bunnies scampered away.

"It's okay, Andy," Timmy told the dog.

418

"Water will make you cooler."

Suddenly the sunlight coming from behind the people clustered at the front of the booth blinded her. Hayley squinted, her vision blurring, and searched beneath a table for her purse, which was next to Ryan's laptop. He'd forgotten to take it with him in the rush to see his father.

Hayley had sunglasses somewhere in her bag. She shuffled through her things. For a moment she didn't remember why she'd unzipped her purse. Oh, yes. Sunglasses. The bright sunlight was giving her the mother of all headaches. No longer barking, Andy nudged her with a nose like a cube of ice.

As she stood up with the sunglasses, the booth began to spin like an out-of-control Ferris wheel. The rattan mat placed on the sand for a floor tilted upward, threatening to smack her in the face. She grabbed the table displaying children's board shorts to steady herself.

Heat stroke, she thought, half-panicked. Her eyes were burning. She was scorching hot now, sweat pouring from her skin. She had to get to the water. A dip in the ocean would cool her down.

But she couldn't move; her body was as rigid as a slab of granite. A whoosh like the wind rushing in from the sea filled her ears. Voices seemed to be far away and garbled.

What was wrong with her? Heat had never bothered her like this. Her entire body was quaking and a sob lodged in her throat, cutting off her air supply.

"Lee! Lee! Lee!" Someone was yelling in her face.

The Wrath.

Dark spots danced across her field of vision. All she could see was one of his eyes. Like Cyclops, The Wrath stood nose to nose with her yelling, "Lee!"

He must be saying Hayley, she dimly realized.

"Wauk! Wauk," she screamed. She was trying to say *water,* to let The Wrath know she needed to get to the ocean, but the word came out scrambled. No wonder. Her mouth was dry, her tongue felt like sandpaper.

A killer wave of dizziness crashed over her, bringing with it another wrenching bout of vertigo. She couldn't tell which way was up or down. What was happening? The world pitched from side to side as though she were being maytagged under a collapsing wave and getting battered against the ocean floor. Trapped there, unable to escape.

Her breathing ceased. Her heart no longer

thundered in her ears. The booth no longer swirled. She no longer felt Andy's frosty nose against her leg. Darkness engulfed her, as if she'd plunged straight into hell.

CHAPTER
TWENTY-SEVEN

Ryan took out his cell phone as he waited at the reception desk in the UC Irvine Emergency Room for the woman to locate his father on the computer. He clicked the app for the GPS tracking software he'd installed after he put the chip in Hayley's tennis shoe. A small map of the Newport Beach area appeared on his screen. The red icon blinked, showing Hayley just where she was supposed to be — out on the peninsula.

The map was very small on the phone's screen. The peninsula was a wormlike squiggle around Newport Beach harbor. The red light said Hayley was halfway out on the sandy beach, not moving. No doubt she was in the booth. If Ryan used his computer, the map could be larger and reveal Hayley's slightest movement.

"Son of a bitch," he muttered under his breath. He'd taken off without his laptop. It was still back in the booth under a table near Hayley's purse. Christ almighty! What if he needed to access the Internet to obtain more information about his father's condition? He'd be S.O.L.

"Sir," said the woman behind the counter. "We don't show an admission for Conrad Hollister."

"Maybe he hasn't been checked in yet." He glanced around the crowded waiting room. "Do the ambulances arrive at another door?"

"Yes, of course. But as soon as the E.R. team receives them, their name and status is logged into the computer." She frowned, looking down at her monitor. "He's not showing up yet."

Yet? Ryan murmured thanks and hurried toward the entrance. He shouldered his way through the double doors to the sidewalk. On the left he saw the service bay for the ambulances. One vehicle was idling near the open doors. He sped over and saw a young boy being lifted out of the ambulance. A male nurse with a clipboard was waiting just inside the doors.

"Have you admitted an elderly man in the last hour or so?" Ryan asked.

"No." The nurse checked the clipboard. "What's the name?" Ryan gave him his father's name and the man ran a stubby finger down the list. "No Hollister. Are you sure he's here? Could he have been taken to Hoag?"

Ryan shrugged, thinking Hoag would have been more logical because his father's cardiologist used that facility. But Molly Stern had distinctly said UCI. He hit the button for the speed dial for Twelve Oaks and asked for Molly.

"I'm so sorry," she said when she finally came on the line. "There was a change. Your father's gone to Hoag Hospital."

Ryan clicked off without thanking her. The woman should have called and saved him a frustrating, time-consuming trip. He dashed to his car.

It took him over half an hour to cross Newport and arrive at Hoag Hospital. If he'd known, he'd been just down the peninsula — less than five minutes from the hospital. He parked in a handicapped spot and raced into the Emergency Room.

He caught his breath while another woman tinkered with a computer, searching for information on his father. Again, Ryan checked his phone, still on the GPS app, to see about Hayley. The screen was blank.

Hadn't he fully charged it last night? So what else was new? These techie gadgets weren't as reliable as people liked to think.

Maybe the concrete walls of the newly remodeled hospital were blocking the signal.

"Sir, I'm not finding a Conrad Hollister."

"You're sure?"

When she nodded, a chill tiptoed up his spine. He charged through the room crowded with emergency patients and barged outside, his phone in hand. He clicked again. Still no light on the cell's screen. Shit! He jabbed at the phone again. Nothing.

Ryan sprinted through the parking lot to his car. Before he even sat in the driver's seat he had the phone connected. He waited for the cell to power up. Still nothing.

How was that possible?

The pit of his stomach churned. He ran back into the hospital and turned left just inside the doors. On the way in he'd spotted a bank of pay telephones. With all the cell phones around there were fewer pay phones, but the hospital had half a dozen in a row. None were in use.

Ryan called Information; without his cell or computer, he didn't have the phone numbers he needed. Talk about being a prisoner of technology! He got Twelve Oaks number and dialed it. When a woman cheerily answered, he asked for Molly Stern.

"I'm sorry. You must have the wrong

number. There's no Molly Stern employed here."

"What? I just called half an hour ago and you put me through to her. She's in nursing." It occurred to Ryan that the shift must have changed. This didn't sound like the same woman.

"You must be mistaken, sir," the woman replied.

"Put me through to nursing." He leaned against the wall, numb with fear now. The woman who answered in nursing assured him that no Molly Stern was employed there. A shudder passed through him as he managed to ask to be switched to Meg Amboy's room.

Spasms of fear erupted in his brain, making him shake as the telephone rang. It was possible to hijack and reroute cell phone calls. Actually, it was much easier than anyone would suspect, but few people knew how to do it. Shutting down a telephone was also a lot simpler than the average user would expect.

It was relatively easy to commandeer a cell phone so its calls could be redirected. When he'd believed he was calling Twelve Oaks, Ryan's cell must have been rerouted to the killer's number.

It all went back to the technology that sent

messages out over air waves rather than on land lines. With the right equipment, someone could easily tap into conversation. That's why law enforcement insisted on using land lines, or specially encrypted cell phones, which made tampering nearly impossible.

Obviously, that's what had been done. He was dead certain this elaborate scam had been pulled on him as a way of getting to Hayley. But he had to check on his father — just to make sure he was safe.

While he waited, Ryan threw change into the telephone beside the one he was using. It would take too long to call Surf's Up and get the cell number of someone in the booth. Instead he needed to reach Detective Wells. The police had officers patrolling the beach. With luck one of them could get to Hayley before something bad happened.

One phone wedged between his jaw and sore shoulder, Ryan used the other telephone to call the Newport Beach Police and ask for Detective Wells. He was put on Hold.

"Ryan," Meg finally answered. "Looking for your father? He's right here."

"Is he all right?" Ryan asked, although he knew the answer. It was Hayley in trouble. He hung up without speaking with his father. No doubt Meg thought he'd lost his last marble.

"Detective Wells," he said into the other telephone. When the detective came on the line, Ryan briefly explained the situation. "We have to hurry. There's no time to waste."

The bitch would get hers, the killer thought, strolling the beach at the Board Wars. The fun part — the planning, the anticipation — was over. Now for the legal high — the execution of the plan. Better than any narcotic available.

Hayley was as good as dead.

Moving like a ferret, swift and silent, the killer approached the Surf's Up booth. Check the commotion! There was no getting near the front where Hayley could be seen.

This was it. Enough false starts and unforeseen getaways.

Hayley, death is the flip side of life. It's just one short step behind you. Time to die. High time.

"Unfuckingbelievable!" Ryan shouted as he slammed his balled fist against the steering wheel. The police had the street to the peninsula blocked off just beyond the Lido Bridge. When he'd spoken to Detective

Wells a few minutes ago, the guy hadn't mentioned a damn thing about the road closure. He probably hadn't known about it; traffic police not homicide handled traffic jams. There wasn't any way — except by water — to get on or off the peninsula.

His frustration became scalding fury — at himself. What a dickhead he was! He'd smelled a rat from the second he'd received the phone call about his "ailing" father. Had he followed his nearly flawless instincts? Hell, no!

He could only hope Detective Wells' radio call to the patrolmen on the beach had come in time — or that The Wrath and PimpIt had been able to protect Hayley. But this killer was bizarre. He relied on attacks no one would expect. A car bombing. A drug-induced heart attack.

What was he up to now?

Ryan yelled out the window to a driver who'd gotten out of his car several vehicles ahead of him. "What's going on?"

"Too many cars out on the peninsula. There's no place to park." The guy in baggy faded denim shorts pointed to the traffic going in the opposite direction — off the peninsula. "They're directing cars to the light, then having them turn around and leave unless you have ID showing you live on the peninsula."

Ryan nodded; roadblocks to halt peninsula traffic jams weren't uncommon. The Fourth of July, busy summer weekends, the boat parade at Christmas usually triggered a roadblock. He couldn't sit there and wait until he made his way twelve or so cars to the front of the line, where he could flash the FBI shield he hadn't yet turned in for access onto the peninsula where the booth was located.

Christ! Between tech screwups and traffic jams, he couldn't get a break. Ryan decided he wasn't waiting. It was four — almost five — long blocks to the booth. He could get there faster on foot. He yanked his T-shirt out of the waistband of his shorts. He opened the glove box and removed his gun. He placed it at the small of his back where it would be concealed by the T-shirt. He left the keys in the car — someone else could move it — and raced toward the beach.

Sweat was pouring off Ryan and he was breathing like a marathoner when the Surf's Up booth came into sight. Two patrol officers in shorts were standing in front talking to PimpIt. The bare-chested fighter saw Ryan and waved. Relief rushed through him like a tidal wave. The police were on the scene; PimpIt was waving. Everything must be all right.

As Ryan raced closer, he spotted The Wrath, who'd also taken off his shirt. Where was Hayley? With so many people around it was difficult to spot someone as short as Hayley.

"What happened?" he yelled as he thundered up to them.

The Wrath shook his head. "I dunno, man. Hayley had sunstroke or something. She passed out. The paramedics took her to the hospital."

"You didn't go with her?" Ryan was just inches from the fighter but he couldn't help shouting the question. *Please, don't let Hayley be alone with strangers.*

The Wrath shrugged, his shoulders tense, his stance belligerent. "I tried, right?" he said to PimpIt. "The EMT guys wouldn't let anyone go."

Ryan's heartbeat skyrocketed. "Did they put her in an ambulance?"

"Yeah, sure. I guess."

"What do you mean — you guess?" Ryan was shouting again; the patrolmen moved closer.

"In case you haven't noticed," PimpIt said calmly, "we aren't next to the street. The EMTs took Hayley away on a stretcher. We had to look after Timmy. He went nuts."

The small fraction of Ryan's brain that was still functioning normally realized yelling at these guys wasn't going to help. *The facts,* his training instructed. *Get the facts.* "Tell me exactly what happened."

"It was really hot in the booth," The Wrath explained. "The Evian girls came by and sprayed everyone with ice water. It cooled us off. Next thing I know Andy's barking like crazy, Hayley's gasping for air and —"

"Ryan! Ryan! Auntie Hay-Hayley fell down," cried Timmy as he flung himself into Ryan's arms, sobbing. Andy came up behind the boy; for once the dog's tail wasn't wagging. With one arm he cradled the boy, while he signaled for The Wrath to continue with the other.

"Hayley collapsed. PimpIt raced for the lifeguard station where the paramedics are," The Wrath told him.

"Somebody must have called 9-1-1 on a cell," PimpIt added. "By the time I returned, they'd taken Hayley to the hospital."

What was really going on? The question hammered at him. How could Hayley have become so ill so quickly?

"After she collapsed, was she breathing?" he asked The Wrath.

The fighter nodded emphatically. "If she

hadn't been, I know CPR."

"Did you see what happened?" he asked Timmy, reasoning the boy might have been closer to Hayley.

Timmy nodded, still crying but quietly now. "Sh-she f-fell."

"What was she doing before she fell?"

Timmy gulped for air, then said, "Trying t-to stop Andy from biting the lady."

Andy bite? Ryan hadn't known the retriever long, but from what he'd seen and what Hayley had said, the dog wasn't a biter. Andy was a lover who lived to be petted. "What lady?"

"One of the babes in the silver bikinis spraying Evian." This from PimpIt.

"No," Timmy said, his eyes full of tears. "The lady had a red bathing suit and sunglasses."

The Wrath said, "I didn't see who sprayed Hayley."

Of course he didn't, Ryan thought, recalling the eye-patch-sized lamé bikinis. The fighter had been distracted by a nearly bare breast bouncing right under his nose.

"I didn't see it, either," PimpIt added.

"I did," insisted Timmy. "The lady had a red suit and sunglasses."

Ryan squeezed Timmy, thankful one of the guys in the booth hadn't been blindsided by boobs. "How long ago was this?"

"Fifteen minutes, max," The Wrath responded after checking his watch.

Ryan released Timmy and rushed inside the booth. His computer was exactly where he left it, but Hayley's purse had been dropped in the middle of the booth. It took a few seconds to boot up the laptop.

While he waited, Ryan considered his options. He'd already decided the woman in the red bikini had sprayed something on Hayley that caused her to pass out. It could be a number of substances, but it probably wasn't deadly or the so-called paramedics wouldn't have taken her away.

He was also certain that no ambulance had left the peninsula. The only route to Hoag Hospital — the closest to the beach — was down the blocked road. She must still be somewhere on the peninsula.

Thank God he'd thought to insert the latest Starcraft GPS device. Unless they'd removed her shoes, he could locate her.

Detective Wells charged into the booth, saying he'd taken the ferry.

"Hayley's been kidnapped," Ryan shouted to Wells, who looked like he's taken a shower in his suit.

Timmy, his arms around Andy's neck, began sobbing again. No telling what the

434

boy imagined when he heard the word *kidnapped.*

"They say EMTs took her away. She had heatstroke," Wells responded, walking closer.

The screen was glowing now; Ryan worked under the table to keep the sunlight off the screen so it would be easier to pinpoint the blinking red dot generated by the GPS device.

"Check Hoag, then check with the EMT command station here at the beach. You'll find Hayley wasn't taken by real paramedics and she isn't being treated at Hoag."

"Are they going to kill her?" Timmy asked.

"Not if I can help it," Ryan said, his jaw clenched tight.

CHAPTER
TWENTY-EIGHT

"Turn right here," Ryan shouted to The Wrath over the roar of the Harley's engine and the honking of horns and screech of police sirens. The motorcycle swerved around a group of teenagers walking in the street, jumped the curb and shot down the sidewalk. Over his shoulder Ryan saw the three policemen on motorcycles following them.

Ryan had his computer case on a strap over his shoulder to keep from dropping it. He cracked the lid and peered in again. Hayley still hadn't moved. With luck, she was in a building nearby and the tracking device would lead them to her.

"Now go right," Ryan yelled when they came to El Ranchito café. The smell of tortilla chips being deep-fried in the kitchen facing the side street filled the air. He looked around frantically, panic mushrooming inside him. The computer showed they were very close to the blinking dot. Hayley had to be in the building complex just ahead.

He raised his arm and shot two fingers into the air in a vee sign. This was the signal for the cops following them to kill the sirens. The sirens had been necessary to clear a path down crowded Newport Boulevard. They didn't want to alert the kidnapper. He might panic and kill Hayley.

"Pull in here." Ryan directed The Wrath to a space near the curb. The motorcycle cops roared up beside them. Detective Wells was riding behind one officer. These were the only cops available on the peninsula. The others were in traffic control and weren't trained for investigation even if they could have been spared. More officers were on the way, but no telling how long it would take to get here with the traffic jam and roadblock.

"This where your tracker shows Hayley?" Detective Wells had left his jacket slung across the back off the motorcycle and had rolled up his shirtsleeves. Butterfly stains of sweat marked the underarms of his blue shirt. Droplets of moisture sheened his brow.

"Yes." Ryan's voice was calm but his mind was moving at warp speed as he looked around. Could they find Hayley before the kidnapper figured out the police were on the scene and decided to kill her?

A panda car roared to a stop beside them. Ryan didn't bother to wonder how they'd made it here through the crush or how they knew not to blare their siren. Five uniformed officers got out and rushed up to Detective Wells.

"She's in that building," Ryan said, moving closer to Wells. "The tracker shows she hasn't moved in the last five minutes. She must be tied up or confined somehow."

The group eyed the waterfront complex. It was one of the newer, more innovative structures in the area that had once been home to a fishing industry that had long ago moved north. The area had fallen into decay. It had been taken over by boat shops and repair yards. In the last few years the real estate boom had transformed it into swank offices and expensive condominiums. It was only a few blocks away from Hayley's waterfront loft, which was one of the newest SoHo-style developments.

Above the subterranean garage in the complex where Hayley was being held were first-floor offices — mostly attorneys and real estate agencies according to the sign. The next two floors were private condominiums with premium views of the water.

"Does the tracker tell you what floor?" Wells asked.

"No. It's not that precise, but if I turn it to face the water like the building —" he positioned the computer and showed Wells "— we can see that she's in the far corner, but we don't know which floor."

"There's nothing much in the garage but a few cars," The Wrath told the group in a low voice, "and they're on the other side of the building from the tracking light."

"Here's what we're going to do," Wells said, obviously accustomed to taking charge at crime scenes. "Disable the elevator. Start searching with the top floor." He pointed to two officers. "Guard the bottom of the stairs."

"What about us?" Ryan asked when the group began to move away.

"Stay here. Other units will be arriving. Tell them I said to surround the building so the perp doesn't escape."

"Check the closets," Ryan called as they walked toward the building. The noose around his heart tightened. Hayley's tracker had been stationary for so long that he imagined her unable to move — possibly unconscious. He was thankful for the gun concealed at the small of his back by the T-shirt.

"What do you think?" asked The Wrath. "The officers are guarding the stairs, but could the guy jump from one of the balconies in the middle where they couldn't see him?"

Ryan shook his head. It didn't seem likely — the drop was too far — but you never knew. This guy had proven how cagey he could be. "Let's look around front."

They headed to the left with a wave to the officer off to their right, guarding the staircase. It bothered Ryan that Wells hadn't assigned anyone to secure the front of the building facing the bay. As soon as he rounded the corner of the complex, Ryan saw why. The building was set flush against the water. It was impossible to run around the front of the building. No one could jump from a water-facing balcony — the private condos — without landing on a boat moored in front of the building and being killed or seriously injured.

They hurried back toward where they'd parked. Ryan looked down into the subterranean garage. The Wrath had been right. Nothing on this side, where the tracker showed Hayley. A dozen or so cars were parked on the other side.

Ryan silently nudged The Wrath down the

steps into the garage. It had a dank smell as if water had leaked in through the sea wall, but he didn't see anything other than mold growing on the cinder block wall. In one corner was a trash can like something found in an office. His sixth sense kicked in. Holding his computer in front of him, Ryan walked up to it.

"Oh, shit!"

In the trash can was a single tennis shoe. Hayley's left shoe — the one with the GPS tracker.

"Her shoe?" The Wrath said. "Where's the other? Why leave the one?"

Ryan retrieved the tennis shoe. "He ditched the shoe with the tracker. Somehow he knew it was there." He showed The Wrath the shoe and pointed inside to the heel section where Ryan had removed the inner liner to insert the device. To anyone looking at the shoe, there wouldn't be any trace of the tracker.

"How'd he know it was in there?" The Wrath asked.

Out of the blue, the answer hit Ryan. "Hayley was sprayed in the face with something just before she became sick, right?"

"Yeah. Water. The Evian g —"

"The woman in the red suit wasn't spritzing Evian. It was scopolamine. It's used to treat nausea, motion sickness, and eye problems. It dilates the pupil, keeps you from focusing. If the spray went up her nose or into her mouth, which it undoubtedly did, it causes hallucinations and difficulty speaking. You pass out."

"She was trying to talk," The Wrath said as he followed Ryan out of the garage.

Ryan snapped his laptop shut and realized what must have happened. "Scopalamine in liquid form can be put in drinks or sprayed on an unsuspecting victim. They pass out." He held up the shoe and stared at it. His thoughts rocketed into a new trajectory. "Christ Almighty! The military used it as a truth serum. The killer asked Hayley and she told him about the tracker."

"Without knowing what she was doing?"

"She'd be too out of it to realize." Ryan covered his eyes with one hand and tried to open his mind, to think like a lunatic. He commanded his brain to go into game mode. Block out the opposing team the way he'd always done when playing pro ball. Ignore the noise of the crowd, disregard anything distracting. Focus. Concentrate.

After a moment, he asked, "How would you get away from this crowded peninsula with a semi-comatose woman?"

"By boat," The Wrath instantly responded.

"But Wells had Harbor Patrol close the exit from the bay and search boats that try to leave. Same with the ferry."

"Exactly, but who says this prick's leaving the harbor? He could take a boat to one of the islands or across the bay to a number of public docks."

"We know he was here. How far would he risk going, dragging or carrying a woman?"

"Not far," Ryan replied. "There may be several of them. At least two were posing as EMTs. They might have a boat waiting at a dock or one in a slip near here. Let's look."

"What about the cops?"

Ryan's intuition said to go it alone. He'd ignored his instincts earlier. He wouldn't with Hayley's life at stake. "We'll call them if we spot anything," he replied. "Could be a wild-goose chase."

He rushed around the corner of the building to the waterfront. Several boats were moored there but the only way down to the boat slips was along the gangway one building to the left.

He sprinted down the gangway and saw a young guy washing a huge yacht called *Long Tall Sally*. The kid had probably been at it for the better part of a day. He might have seen something.

"Did you see a man and a woman come

this way?" he yelled.

"Yeah." The kid stood up to wring out the towel he'd been using to dry the chrome railing. "She had too much sun. He was taking her home."

"Where was his boat?"

"In front of Mirage." He pointed to the nearby waterfront restaurant that wouldn't open until evening.

Just as he suspected, Ryan thought. "What kind of boat was it?"

"A Sunseeker," the guy said without hesitation. "A sixty-footer."

Wow. Ryan didn't know a lot about boats but this one was very expensive. "What's its name?"

"Didn't see a name. It was facing the other way."

Of all the damn luck! "Hey, can we borrow your dinghy?" The tender to the yacht was in the water behind the boat.

"No, it's not mine. I'd get in a lotta trouble. Hey —" He spotted The Wrath.

"Aren't you —"

"I'm The Wrath," the fighter said. "How about ringside seats to my next fight to use your dinghy for a few minutes?"

"Sure. Key's under the seat."

Ryan and The Wrath raced for the tender, *Short Fat Fanny.* In a heartbeat, they were in the boat and churning water as they sped away from the yacht.

"Which way?" called The Wrath over the roar of the outboard motor.

"Damned if I know." Ryan tried to think. Even with the exit to the harbor blocked, there were lots of ways a boat could go. The only thing he was certain of — the boat wouldn't be speeding. That would attract too much attention from a Harbor Patrol already on high alert.

"Call Wells and tell him where we are. See what he can do about backup." Ryan wasn't too confident the detective could help much with a water search. Technically, the harbor was in the sheriff's jurisdiction. They had only two boats to patrol one of the largest harbors on the West Coast.

Hayley's life depended on him.

Hayley's eyes were gritty, as if someone had spooned sand into them, but she finally managed to open them. Where was she? Why was it so dark?

She struggled to think, tried to swallow, but her mouth felt like wads of cotton and her throat was as sore as the time she'd had strep throat. Without saliva she couldn't run her tongue over her parched lips. She vaguely detected a familiar smell in the air

445

but couldn't decide what it was.

Hayley inhaled deeply and fluttered her eyelashes to make certain her eyes were really open. Yes. They were open, but all she could detect was a pitch-black oblivion. There were no shadows, no hint of any light at all.

She couldn't recall ever experiencing blackness like this. Was she dreaming? Yes. That would account for this all-encompassing darkness and the familiar yet unidentified smell.

What was that sound?

Her ears didn't seem to be working much better than her nose. She realized that she knew what the sound was . . . but no name came to mind. It seemed her senses were functioning — partially — yet her brain didn't comprehend or it would tell her what the smell was, what the noise was.

Her vague feeling of alarm became full-blown panic. A rumble like thunder over the ocean sent another wave of terror through her like a deadly poison. This seemed too vivid to be a dream. What she was experiencing felt . . . real.

"Hello! Hello!" she tried to call out but didn't hear any sound come from her sore throat. What was happening? She had spoken, hadn't she? With strep throat, she couldn't talk — only whisper. If she whispered, no one would hear her.

In a remote corner of her perplexed brain, scattered images returned in bits like a shattered mirror she needed to reassemble from jagged pieces that didn't fit. The Wrath yelling in her face. Fighting dizziness and nausea. The booth spiraling out of control.

Someone asking her questions. About what? The answer was trapped in the rubble that once was her mind.

When had these things happened? Not long ago, she reasoned, although she couldn't say why. What happened next? Why couldn't she remember? It was as if she'd fallen through some crack in the universe into a Black Hole.

She lifted her hands to touch her face, but it was hard work. Her numb arms were like cement logs — difficult to move and unbelievably heavy. Her fingers finally managed to prod her face with jerky little movements. Her head seemed to be all right, if hot and wet with perspiration wasn't troubling. Her eyes were open, she knew when an errant finger poked a dry eyeball and pain registered somewhere deep in her head.

Next she tried wiggling her numb feet. Her legs were another set of cement logs but her feet seemed much lighter and tingled as if they'd been asleep. The toes on one foot actually wiggled! Encouraging. What was wrong with the other foot?

Then she groggily realized one foot had on a shoe while the other didn't. With this thought came a fleeting memory of answering a question just before a shoe was yanked off her foot.

What would anyone want with her shoe?

If only she could see a shadow . . . or something, she could think. But it was hard to concentrate when you were in darkness as black as hell. For some reason, hell made her think of death. And an underground coffin. That would account for the darkness. Could she be dead? Or left for dead?

What kind of nightmare was she trapped in? A fresh wellspring of fear surged through her. She had been abandoned. No one was around to help her. She couldn't function well enough to save herself. She was going to die.

Think! Don't give in to panic! Be logical. There's an explanation.

Am I sitting up or lying down? she asked herself to keep from going nuts. Focusing on determining the extent of her predicament might help. Panic certainly wasn't doing her any good.

With an effort, she moved her carcass that

felt like an arthritic old lady's body and determined she was lying down on something firm — but not hard — and narrow. A bed? She didn't remember going to bed.

How could she forget something as exciting as sleeping with Ryan Hollister? Where was he? From somewhere in her foggy brain she recalled Ryan promising not to let her out of his sight. Why not?

She couldn't remember. Something to do with danger, she thought with a tremor of unease. Oh, yes. Now she recalled. Ryan had gone to the hospital. His father wasn't well.

All right, concentrate, she told herself again. *You're not in a bed,* she decided, *but maybe a sofa or something like that.* Good news. She wasn't in a coffin. She was in a place larger than that. Some loony hadn't buried her alive.

She forced herself to remain still with her eyes open to let them adjust to the darkness. Time passed. A minute, maybe two. Nothing. Her eyes didn't register the faintest glimmer of light.

Closing her eyes, Hayley let her mind drift. A thought popped into her head unbidden: ESPN was coming any minute. Oh, my God! Were they already here? They couldn't be. She didn't hear any voices, just a muffled rumble that was too steady to be thunder.

She must have been in the booth not so long ago for the image to be so vivid, Hayley reasoned. So why couldn't she remember how she'd gotten here?

In frustration she lashed out, kicking both feet. And hit a wall or something with the one shoe she seemed to have kept. *Thunk! Thunk!* She kept kicking the wall. It was a relief to hear a sound she could identify.

Tears welled under her lids and she blinked rapidly. They stung as if someone dropped acid into her eyes. Straining to see something — anything — she realized she was still suspended in darkness.

Her senses were gradually becoming more acute, she realized. Thank God! She was drifting or floating or something. She wasn't in bed; her muddled brain had already confirmed that. A hammock? No! The word was on the tip of her tongue. It was . . . what?

A boat! Yes! Yes! That accounted for the slight rocking sensation and the rumbling noise of the engine. And what she smelled had to be diesel fumes.

A boat? Whose boat? What was she doing on a boat when she should be in the booth? Was she in the hold of a boat? No. There wouldn't be a bed or sofa down there, but it would be dark like this.

"Oh, my God," she cried. If she could hear and smell, why couldn't she see anything? Even deep in the hold, she should be able to distinguish a shadow or something. Right?

Suddenly a gust of air blew over her, and she realized a door had been opened.

"Hayley? Hayley? Are you awake?" asked a muffled male voice that she couldn't quite identify.

Something told her not to answer, but her kicking must have given her away. He knew right where she was. She sniffed again, ignoring her sore throat and picking up the scent of imminent danger. Any second might be her last.

She heard him but still couldn't see even a shadow or a ray of light. Like the blow of a bat to the head, the extent of her peril overwhelmed Hayley.

She was blind.

CHAPTER
TWENTY-NINE

"Detective Wells said to come back to the dock and pick him up," The Wrath reminded Ryan. The fighter had called Wells to let him know about the Sunseeker they were after.

"I'm not taking the time! They could have Hayley off the boat and into a car or something, if I turn around now."

"You're right," The Wrath agreed. "We're finding Hayley together."

Ryan wished he could be as confident as the fighter sounded. He knew the harbor from back when his father had been better and kept a thirty-five foot Tiara at the Balboa Yacht Club. They'd cruised the harbor often and Ryan had learned its channels and secret coves like a local.

Lido Isle, the largest island in the harbor, was in the middle of the bay not far from where they'd found the shoe. The Sunseeker they were after could have gone around either side of the island. The boat Hayley was imprisoned on could be at any dock on Lido or going to several other islands. Since it was such an expensive boat — close to a million dollars — it stood to reason that it was headed to one of the more luxurious homes at the tip of Lido, on Bayshores near John Wayne's old home, or on either of the two most exclusive islands, Harbor and Linda.

"The prick wouldn't go to one of the yacht clubs," said The Wrath.

Ryan had already decided as much. Going down a gangway carrying Hayley had been a risky move, but to bring her up from a boat in front of a club's restaurant that faced the docks would be downright stupid. And if Ryan was dead certain of one thing, it was that this monster was as clever as they came.

"I'm thinking he won't use a public dock, either. Too many people around washing boats, hanging out, you name it. A private dock —"

"They're pretty close together. Would he risk being seen?"

"I doubt it." Ryan ground the words out between his teeth. "But you never know. I wouldn't have expected anyone to snatch her from the booth the way he did. He must have a plan." Again Ryan went into game mode and tried to think like the killer. "He doesn't know we're after him. He's likely to keep her on the boat until it's dark. Then he'll move her."

"If he hasn't already killed her by then."

The Wrath spoke slowly as if he was a foreigner or a young child yet each word hit Ryan like a blow. It was exactly the way he'd analyzed the situation. "He was ready to blow her up. I can't imagine why he'd allow her to live for long. That's why I've got to find her."

"Why'd he take her? Why not shoot her or something less risky?"

"We've had her surrounded, kept her whereabouts when she wasn't at the store a secret. He had to take the chance." But why? Ryan asked himself. Out of nowhere the answer came. "He'll leave the body where it can be found. Hayley won't simply disappear. They need to prove Hayley is dead or the estate will be tied up for years until the court declares her legally dead."

"They?" The Wrath asked.

"This has to have something to do with her parents' estate. Nothing else makes sense."

If The Wrath knew about the estate or had an opinion, he didn't voice it. Ryan didn't have time to explain.

"Call the Sunseeker dealer. Give my name and pretend this is an official FBI call. Get a list of Sunseekers in the harbor in the forty- to seventy-foot range in case the boat-wash kid was off a few feet."

The Wrath pulled out his cell phone while Ryan scanned the docks as they neared the tip of Lido Isle. Lots of yachts, but the only Sunseeker he saw was too small and there were two women sunbathing on it.

He gazed across the water at Bay Island. Now there was an exclusive address. The house on the point — considered to be the best view in the harbor — once belonged to Roy Rodgers and Dale Evans. It faced across the water toward where their old friend John Wayne had lived. Bay Island was unique because it didn't allow cars. Access to the island was over a small bridge by foot or golf cart.

Ryan thought not having a garage with your home would be a pain, but there were over thirty homes on the island. Few of them changed hands and when they did they sold for millions. He scanned the docks he could see on this side of Bay Island. Lots of luxury yachts but no Sunseeker.

That figured. How would the killer get a body off Bay Island? On a golf cart that everyone could see? Not likely. The creep must have gone to one of the other islands . . . or something.

For a second, Ryan's mind drifted to Hayley. He'd been enthralled by her face, but when he'd actually met her, Hayley's smile captivated him. It ruled her other features and made her more attractive than photographs revealed. Her smile brightened her face, drawing attention away from a nose that was a bit too small.

Get a grip, he silently ordered. Stay focused. Remembering how she looked, how she felt in his arms, wasn't helping a damn thing.

"Great. Thanks," The Wrath said. He turned to Ryan and told him that there were seven Sunseekers in Newport Harbor in the size category they wanted. The Wrath rattled off the names of the owners. At the third name, bells went off.

"Son of a bitch!" Ryan changed direction and revved the dinghy's motor.

"Come on. I know you're awake."

Hayley stubbornly remained silent, the words magnifying her power to resist. Her body was chilled by the fresh air that had drifted over her and evaporated the sweat sheening her skin.

She longed to feel more in control of her

body. Not that she stood a chance when she couldn't see a damn thing, but she intended to fight to her last breath. Her pulse accelerated at the thought of dying.

The idea of never seeing Ryan again tore at her heart. Why hadn't she told him how she felt? Letting that jerk Chad Bennett ruin her relationship with a good man was just . . . unforgivable.

"I don't have time to fool around."

She kept her eyes closed as if she was unconscious. Her feet seemed almost normal and her arms were now tingling. The man speaking could kill her but she would be certain traces of his DNA were under her fingernails. She'd yank out his hair by the root so it, too, could be IDed. With any luck, she'd leave a mark on his face that Ryan would notice.

She wasn't sure of Ryan's love; he might not be over his wife's death. But she knew he wouldn't give up until he found her killer. She smiled inwardly at the thought of scaring this lunatic.

But who was he? Not Trent. She knew his voice too well. Not Chad, either. She would have recognized his voice by now. This man sounded familiar but her brain wasn't functioning well enough to come up with a name. It seemed to take forever to get a thought to register and send back a response.

"I can kill you now or I can kill you later," the threatening man told Hayley.

Around her, the air shifted and she knew he was leaning closer. If she started talking now, he might postpone killing her. Surely by now Ryan must be looking for her. What made her think that?

The shoe. From some dark, remote crevice in her brain resurfaced the memory of Ryan inserting the tracking device in the heel of her left tennis shoe. The missing shoe! Oh, my God! She'd told Laird about the shoe.

Laird McMasters. Her befuddled brain had finally managed to provide the monster's name. Why would he want her dead? Simply because she didn't want him for a partner?

Start talking, urged an inner voice. She tried to speak but the words stuck to her dry tongue and her throat burned as if she'd swallowed acid. *You're as good as dead if you don't say something — anything — to distract this nut.* She tried again, but failed.

Open your eyes. Let him know you're awake. She fluttered her eyelids as she opened them to make certain he noticed.

"That's better," he said. "Didn't expect to see me, did you?"

It took a second to realize Laird didn't know she was blind. How was that possible?

"N-n-n." She struggled to speak but still nothing intelligible came out.

"Can't talk, can you?" From the self-satisfied tone of his voice, she would bet the lunatic was smiling. "That's to be expected. Don't remember much, do you?"

She jerked her head from side to side to indicate she didn't remember. She *had* to keep him talking. Buying time was her only hope.

"Scopolamine does that. It's a surefire way to induce amnesia. That's why criminals like it so much. Slip it into a drink, spray it on someone and *wham* — they forget who you are, what you look like. Perfect for robbing people."

"Naaaah," she managed to utter, meaning no. No, she didn't remember anything.

"The Russians and the Nazis believed scopolamine was a truth serum. Didn't work on everyone, but it worked on you. I asked about a tracker and you pointed right to your shoe."

How could she have been so stupid? Hayley wondered. If she'd just kept her mouth shut, Ryan could have found her. Now it would be impossible. She was on her own. There wasn't much hope of saving herself since she couldn't see, but she intended to inflict as much damage as possible on Laird. "W-w-w-aah?" She tried to form the word *why.*

Laird understood; he chuckled softly, a grating sound that filled what suddenly seemed to be a small room. "Why do I want you dead? Curious, aren't you?"

Again, she jerked her head from side to side. Keep him talking. Her arms had to move in order for her fingers to scratch his eyes out.

Or die trying.

He ran his finger along the line of her cheek and down to her neck; edging still lower he stopped at the top of her breast. She inhaled sharply at the contact. "I guess you deserve to know."

Hayley couldn't stop a grateful gruntlike sound from escaping her lips. A reprieve. How long would it last? She'd given up any hope of rescue, but she needed circulation to return to her arms, hand and legs in order to launch herself at him and draw blood. She didn't stand a chance against him, but she was going to do her best.

"I need to merge Surf's Up and Rip Tide. I can make a killing selling them together to WaterExpo. Or I can do an IPO."

Hayley understood. WaterExpo was one

of the original surf companies that had gone public. They were enormous and had an international name much bigger than Surf's Up. They'd once approached her father, but a huge company with layer after layer of management wasn't her father's style.

"Trent went for it. He saw the possibilities and could have convinced your father. But you —" his fingertip slid down another inch "— wouldn't go for it."

Not true, she wanted to shout, but the words lodged in her throat. She would have said no, but Trent had never asked her. Of course not. It was easier to blame Hayley and stay on Laird's good side. But even if she had been in favor of it, her father — and mother — wouldn't have wanted to be dictated to by corporate types.

"Surf's Up was desperate for money, thanks to your brother's greediness. He thought he'd corner the surfboard market in SoCal. He came to me and I agreed to help, even though I was tight for cash myself. What happens? You little bitch! You went to your aunt and cut me out."

The venom in his voice took her breath away. She'd known Laird for years but never suspected he felt so intensely about this. This deal would have meant millions to

Laird, she reflected. To some people money was their God.

"With you out of the picture, the estate will be divided two ways. Farah doesn't give a shit about the business and Trent needs the money. I'll get the company."

"Umm-hmm," she managed to mumble. The extent of Laird's enmity toward her was stunning. She'd dated him — briefly — but often saw him at parties and around town. She'd never suspected how much he hated her.

"What I can't understand," Laird continued, "is why your father had so much faith in you. He left you the company."

Laird McMasters was behind the destruction of the trust. She took a quick breath of utter astonishment. Hayley could go to her grave knowing the half siblings she'd been raised with hadn't been the ones to destroy the document. They didn't hate her.

"C-c-chaa." She tried to ask about Chad but the word wouldn't pass her lips.

"Chad? Is that what you're asking?" His laugh sounded like a death rattle. "He's easy. Money talks. His business hasn't gone so well since his old man kicked the bucket. The house on Harbor Island, a brand-new Sun-seeker in its dock. Oh, that's where we are by the way. Chad's place. He's down in

San Diego on a deposition. I 'borrowed' his boat."

Chad! She trembled with impotent rage. Did he kill Sylvia Morrow to keep her quiet? Or had he gotten Laird to do his dirty work? If only she could talk. She tried to ask but merely sputtered.

"Chad loved you, Hayley. Really adored you. But he couldn't keep his zipper closed. When you threw him out, poor guy knew it was over because you are so fucking stubborn."

Now, facing death, Hayley was thankful she hadn't taken the skunk back. If she had, she would never have met Ryan. Never have known what it was like to be with a good man, someone she could truly love.

"What I need to do," Laird said, as if he was discussing a new boogie-board design, "is to get you topside. I don't want to kill you down here and leave a lot of blood and evidence."

He slid his hands under her. Hayley made a split-second decision. She could try to fight him now or she could wait. She decided she had a better chance of getting away if she allowed him to carry her topside.

"You're no featherweight," he said as he trudged up the stairs. "This is an awesome boat. Right out of *Architectural Digest* — all clean lines and contemporary Italian furniture. Blood will show on the white carpet."

Good, she thought. He walked a few steps and she realized they were no longer on the stairs. From his comment, they must be in the main salon. She couldn't see anything, but in her mind's eye a stretch of Arctic white carpet was at his feet.

Now! A juggernaut of adrenaline jolted through her body. She clawed at his face and bit his shoulder at the same time. Kicking with all her might, Hayley scratched where she thought his eyes must be. She struck the side of his cheek, then found an eye.

"Shit!" he bellowed and dropped her.

Her tailbone hit the carpeted floor and fire shot up her spine as if she'd been seared by a blowtorch. She ignored it; she didn't have time for pain. Flailing with both arms, she found his ankles. He grabbed her hair, but Hayley bit him again. This time she hit the fleshy part of his calf. Since he was in shorts, her teeth sank into unprotected skin.

"Stop it, bitch!"

He yanked harder on her hair, but she didn't let loose. Warm blood — his blood — poured into her mouth. Yes! Yes! She silently applauded herself and bit with even more tenacity. She would spill his blood on the white carpet for the police to find and analyze.

He hauled her to her feet, kicking and thrashing. She had a clump of bloody skin in her teeth. She spit it in the direction of his face — she hoped.

"It's over." His words were calm but his breath was coming in ragged gasps. "You're dead."

The cold steel muzzle of a gun pressed into her temple. She closed her eyes. *I love you, Ryan. Love you, Aunt Meg. Take care of Andy.*

Her life was finished.

CHAPTER
THIRTY

Peering into the yacht's salon from the windows on the main deck, Ryan drew the gun from the waistband at the small of his back. For a gut-cramping second, the earth froze. He saw Laird McMasters' head coming from the cabin area. The bastard hadn't spotted him! Ryan choked back a curse.

He'd expected to find Chad Bennett, since he was the owner, but the attorney didn't seem to be around. Ryan motioned for The Wrath to stay low and circle to the other side of the boat where there was a second entrance from the deck to the luxurious living area.

Was Hayley still alive? Her body was slack but Ryan didn't see any blood or signs of strangulation. His pulse beat erratically and the gun trembled in his hand. *Get a grip!*

Suddenly, Hayley was flailing in McMasters' arms — kicking and biting and scratching at his face. *Go, Hayley!* Arms, legs, hands flew in all directions at once. The tumult was an unfocused attack with limbs thrashing wildly but it worked. Laird was caught off guard.

"Shit," screeched Laird and he dropped Hayley.

She hit the floor with a thud that made Ryan flinch. She hadn't broken her back, had she? No. Not at all. She grabbed McMasters' leg and ferociously gnawed his calf with a bite worthy of a lioness.

Ryan took aim, ready to shoot the prick and save Hayley the trouble. Aw, hell! Why had he told The Wrath to go around to the other side of the boat? He could see him at the window on the opposite side of the salon. Right in his line of fire. If Ryan's shot missed by less than an inch, he might kill The Wrath. But on the plus side, Hayley's unexpected attack had distracted McMasters. He still hadn't noticed Ryan, and he had no clue The Wrath was behind him, easing into the salon's doorway.

"Stop it, bitch!" hollered Laird.

Hayley had a death grip on the jerk's leg with both arms and her teeth. She'd ripped a sizable gash in his leg. There was no sign she intended to let go. Laird grabbed Hayley's long mane of hair. After several vicious jerks with both arms, he hoisted Hayley to her feet by her hair, a piece of his flesh still in her mouth. She spit it in his face.

Quick as a snake, McMasters drew a gun from the pocket of his cargo shorts. Shit! Shit! The Wrath was still in the line of fire. Ryan couldn't risk shooting. He silently cursed himself for not taking more time at the range. A trained sniper could make the shot.

"It's over." Laird's ragged breathing distorted the words. "You're dead."

Ryan launched himself into the room, gun pointed at Laird, roaring, "Let Hayley go."

"What?" Laird sounded incredulous at seeing Ryan, but he didn't release Hayley or lower the gun pointed at her temple.

"R-Ryan. I-is-s that . . . you?" Hayley croaked out the words.

She must have blood in her eyes or something. Couldn't she see it was him? Maybe the ordeal had her in shock.

Blood pooled on the floor, gushing from the ferocious bite on McMasters' leg, but he didn't seem to notice. The Wrath had moved into the open doorway behind the lunatic. Still no clear shot, but at least McMasters' attention was riveted on him. With luck, Ryan and The Wrath could overpower him.

"Let her go. The police are coming." This was a fact. The Wrath had called Wells as soon as they realized the Sunseeker belonged to Chad Bennett and was probably at his home on Harbor Island. They'd been wrong about Chad, but at least help was coming.

"Get out of the way or I'll kill her." McMasters sounded calm but fireworks flared behind his eyes and his tight expression revealed his anxiety. He inched forward, dragging Hayley with one arm. Ryan held his ground, his gun still aimed at Laird's face. McMasters' gun was still flush against Hayley's temple.

"Watch where you're going," Ryan yelled. Not that he gave a crap if McMasters tripped over the huge glass coffee table that had to be some outrageously expensive decorator's idea of chic. But any jolt could cause Laird to accidentally squeeze the trigger.

"Move!"

"Are you nuts? You can't get away." Ryan heard the distant wail of a siren. It sounded as if it was coming from the water, which meant it was the Harbor Patrol. He wasn't sure those officers were armed. They usually encountered speeding or inebriated boaters — not gun-wielding lunatics.

"Y-you'll never get Surf's Up now." Hayley's voice was almost unrecognizable.

"Is that why you want Hayley dead? Gimme a break! Of all the stupid-ass ideas, this beats them all." It was impossible to argue with a sick mind, but Ryan kept talking as The Wrath moved up closer behind Laird. If the fighter grabbed or hit him, the gun might go off. Christ Almighty! The Wrath was smart. Surely, he realized the danger to Hayley.

"Laird's after our name and my father's custom molds," Hayley said, her voice still not normal. And she wasn't looking at him, either — just gazing wide-eyed in his direction. Could scopolamine sprayed in the eyes blind you?

Laird McMasters smile flickered. "Hayley's smarter than she looks."

"Can't you hear those sirens?" Ryan struggled to keep his tone level. "They'll catch you. Let her go."

"No. She's my insurance." He sounded almost cocky now, which was truly frightening. Didn't the guy know when to give up? "I'll be on a plane and out of the country in no time."

It was possible, Ryan realized. John Wayne Airport was ten minutes away. The private field adjacent to it had lots of planes. It was

470

a short flight to the Mexican border.

"I'll let her go when I refuel in Mexico," Laird said in a tone that sounded reasonable, lucid.

Ryan knew better than to go for it. His FBI training had stressed one thing. Never let a hostage be taken to another place — no matter what you're promised. Criminals say anything to get away. Nine times out of ten they killed the victim. Anyone insane enough to plant a bomb just to get a business couldn't be trusted to keep his word.

"No way! Let her go. I'll give you time to get to your car," Ryan said, certain Laird must have his car parked in front of the house a short distance away.

"Fuck off —" Laird's curse was obliterated by The Wrath's swift karate chop to the back of the neck. His gun dropped out of his hand, his other arm released Hayley. His eyes glazed over and he slowly began to crumple.

Hayley scuttled forward like a crab. Ryan rushed to her and dropped to his knees, his gun still trained on Laird. *Crash!* McMasters collapsed onto the glass coffee table and it shattered. The nutjob was out cold.

"Are you okay?" Ryan asked Hayley over the sound of sirens coming up beside the yacht.

471

"I — I can't see anything." She felt his face.

"It's okay. We'll get you to the hospital. I'm —"

"Holy shit!" roared The Wrath. "I think he's dead."

Cradling Hayley in his arms, Ryan turned and saw Laird bleeding now from a cut on the side of his head. He'd hit the sharp corner of the glass-top coffee table with all his weight. A death-blow.

Meg rushed into the E.R. waiting room without waiting for Conrad to follow her in his wheelchair. There was a crowd of people, but she spotted Ryan standing with Trent and Farah in the far corner. Feeling light-headed, she hurried across the room, ignoring the pain in her knees.

"Meg," Ryan called as soon as he saw her. "Don't be upset. Hayley's going to be okay."

She gasped with relief and slowed her pace. "Thank God."

Ryan met her and put his arm around Meg's shoulders. "What happened? All that Wrath person said on the phone was that Hayley had been taken to the hospital."

"He saved Hayley from Laird McMasters," Ryan told her.

"Laird!" Meg's mind reeled as if short-circuited. She'd believed the Fordhams were behind this mess — not a man that they never even considered. Now it registered that Trent and Farah were here and looking more concerned that she could ever have imagined.

"Ryan isn't taking the credit he deserves," Farah told her as she and Trent joined them. "He figured out where Hayley had been taken."

"I have to see her," Meg cried.

Ryan hugged her, saying, "The doctors are treating her right now."

Meg didn't want to wait, but Conrad wheeled up and put his hand in hers.

"What happened, son?" he asked Ryan. "We heard Hayley had been kidnapped, then suddenly she was at the hospital."

Meg listened, clutching Conrad's hand, as Ryan explained about the scopolaminc that had been sprayed in Hayley's face.

"I've never heard of it," Meg said. Trent and Farah said they hadn't, either.

"Isn't that the active ingredient in Trans-derm patches for motion sickness?" Conrad asked.

"That's right," Ryan said. "Patches have minute amounts of it."

"Isn't it the stuff called *burundanga?*" Trent wanted to know. "They put it on business cards and anyone who touches it blacks out. Then they're raped or robbed but can't remember anything about it. I hear it's used a lot on tourists in South America."

"That's an Internet myth." Ryan sounded exhausted. "Scopolamine can be in a pill or liquid form, but powder doesn't penetrate the skin and cause the same reaction."

"The EMTs who took Hayley away were impostors. It was part of Laird's elaborate scheme." Rancor sharpened Trent's voice. "He even went so far as to have someone call me and say ESPN was coming to film so I wouldn't be in the booth but out looking for them."

"He was very clever. Conniving." Farah's lips thinned with anger. She explained about the shoe and the escape on the yacht.

"Why?" Meg asked, unable to fathom any reason Laird would have done this.

"He wanted Surf's Up," Trent said.

"What?" Meg turned to Conrad. "That doesn't make any sense, does it?"

"No," Conrad agreed. "It doesn't."

"There must be another reason," Meg insisted.

"No, it makes sense — in a convoluted way," Farah said. "With Surf's Up and his own company combined, Laird would have the best custom-board molds available and a brand-name surfers respected. Add that to his own business —"

"You're forgetting Laird's company doesn't have the reputation for clothing designs and the new MMA stuff that we do," Trent added.

"Still, to go to all the trouble to make a car bomb and stage an elaborate hoax is . . . so farfetched," Meg concluded.

"Not really," Farah said. "He hoped to sell the combined company to one of the big guns like WaterExpo or he could arrange an IPO. There's a lot of money involved — millions.

"An Initial Public Offering?" Meg couldn't help sounding skeptical. "In this market?"

"IPOs are staging a comeback," Farah assured her.

"Well," Meg replied, still not convinced. "When the police question him, I bet they discover another reason." Personally, she thought Laird had been attracted to Hayley — for years — and couldn't stand being shunted aside yet again after Hayley went out with him last year after she broke her engagement to Chad.

Suddenly she was aware of everyone looking at her. "What's wrong?"

"The police aren't going to be questioning Laird," Farah said. "He's dead."

Meg gazed at Ryan. She'd known from their first meeting that this was the man for her Hayley. He'd killed Laird to save her.

"I didn't kill him. No one did," Ryan said quietly. "It was an accident. The Wrath clocked him with a karate chop to the neck. Laird blacked out, fell and hit the coffee table. The blow to his head killed him."

Meg's shoulders sagged as she tried to imagine the scene. "Where was Hayley during all this?"

"He'd been holding a gun on her," Ryan answered. "She got away from him when The Wrath hit him."

Meg listened while Ryan provided additional details of her niece's ordeal. She almost laughed when he told her about how Hayley fought back and bit a chunk out of that maniac's leg.

"There's just one problem," Ryan concluded, his voice filled with concern. "Hayley's temporarily blind."

"What?" Meg couldn't believe anything else could possibly happen to Hayley. Hadn't she suffered enough? "How? Why?"

Ryan explained blindness was a side effect of a scopolamine overdose. Laird had used way too much in the solution that he'd persuaded some girl to spray in Hayley's face. "It should wear off in the next day or so, and she'll be able to see again."

"Oh, Hayley, sweetheart," Hayley heard her aunt say, tears in her voice.

It was late in the afternoon. Hayley had spent hours being prodded and checked physically. She'd taken heaven-only-knows how long to give a statement about the kidnapping. Most of her memory was fuzzy before waking up in the boat.

"A-Aunt-ie, don't cry. I — I'm okay." She'd heard the catch in her hoarse voice and realized she, too, was close to tears. Her composure had been a fragile shell since Ryan had gathered her in his arms. She felt safe with him, knowing Laird was dead and no longer a threat. But how protected could she feel when she couldn't see anything?

Aunt Meg hugged her and Hayley could feel the dampness of her aunt's cheek. She was a second mother, Hayley decided. She was one lucky girl.

A jumble of rustling noises and whispers filled the hospital room where Hayley was on a bed. Her world was still darkness. The doctors guaranteed her sight would return in another day or so, but in the interim, her other senses were becoming sharper. There were more than two other people in the room. More than three, her ears assured her.

"Wh-ho's there?" she croaked out the words.

Aunt Meg had released her. Hayley could feel her weight on the bed and knew her aunt was sitting down beside her. Another arm slipped around her. From the strength of the grip and the woodsy scent lingering in the air, Hayley knew it was Ryan.

"Don't strain your voice," he told her. "My father, Trent and Farah are here with your aunt. They were worried about you."

"I'm so sorry," Trent said, sounding genuinely upset. "I never thought Laird would do something like this."

Hayley was tempted to say that Trent blaming her for not wanting to sell the business had contributed to the problem, but she didn't. Laird was certifiable. Who could have predicted the lengths he'd go to in order to take the business away from them?

"I'm not surprised," Farah unexpectedly said. "You know how much Laird wanted to show his father that he, too, could be a huge success. He had something to prove. It obsessed him."

Hayley supposed Farah was right. Laird had admitted to her that he'd coveted Surf's Up for some time. He'd tried to get it —

legally — but she'd been instrumental in keeping the business in the family.

"Ch-aad?" The single word came out like a raspy sound. She knew she shouldn't be talking. The doctors had explained the overdose of scopolamine could damage her vocal chords. Time would take care of her voice, her sight. But it was difficult to just lie there, helpless.

"Chad was conducting a deposition in San Diego," Ryan said. "The police have a warrant out for his arrest."

"Why?" Farah sounded shocked. "Just because Laird used his boat?"

"No," Ryan explained. "I told Detective Wells that I found evidence on Alison's computer that there had been a trust. Laird and Chad destroyed it. Apparently, McMasters thought that he could persuade you two to sell if Hayley was out of the way."

There was a full minute of what Hayley imagined was stunned silence before Trent asked, "How did you know what was on the computer?"

"W-w-we —"

"I'll explain, Hayley. Save your voice." Ryan's arm tightened around her for just a second. "I hacked into her files and found it in the trash bin. They thought it had been wiped clean but it was there. I found another copy in the clouds."

"Clouds?" Farah stared at Ryan as if he were about to reveal the whereabouts of the Holy Grail.

Hayley listened to Ryan explain about cloud computing and how some information was stored on a server nowhere near the actual computer. She wished she could see them to analyze what they were thinking. They were probably asking themselves why she'd had Ryan hack into her mother's computer. They must realize she'd suspected them. It would take a thousand words for her to explain. Now wasn't the time, but she couldn't help feeling guilty.

After an awkward silence, Trent said, "Wanna bet Chad hightails it to Mexico? What's left for him here? He'll be disbarred."

"I think you're right," Farah said with characteristic sarcasm.

"I'm sure the police have considered this," Conrad said, speaking for the first time. "San Diego is so close to the Mexican border."

Hayley listened to the group discuss Chad's duplicity, how he was financially overextended, and Laird must have promised him a chunk of dough to forget he'd ever seen the trust.

"A-nd-ee," Hayley interjected.

"Andy's with Timmy and Courtney," Farah said. "They'll take care of him."

Hayley smiled and nodded to save her voice. She wanted to tell them how Andy had tried to warn her about the woman in the red bikini, but decided it would have to wait. She had something more pressing to say.

"I — I wah-nt go h-home." Hayley botched the sentence, but hoped they would understand.

"The doctors want to keep you overnight," Ryan said gently. "You should be starting to regain your eyesight by then."

"N-no!" The word came out like a shot. "Home."

"Hayley, be sensible," her aunt said. "Stay the night."

She shook her head, determined. She wanted to go home now! To sleep in her own bed. "M-my loft."

"I'll talk to the doctor," Ryan said in a resigned tone. "But I have to go out for a short meeting tonight."

"Can't you postpone it?" Conrad asked.

"I need to tell my boss that I'm resigning. I should have told him days ago, but I didn't want to leave Hayley." Ryan paused for a moment, then added, "I'll be as fast as possible. My boss is at the Marriott for a conference. I don't want him to hear about my involvement and think I'm still with the Bureau. I've violated a lot of their rules."

"Isn't hacking against the law?" Farah wanted to know.

Hayley battled the urge to make an ugly remark. Then she reminded herself that she'd misjudged Farah and Trent. She should be apologizing, if anything.

"I'll go speak with the doctor," Ryan said, breaking the uncomfortable silence. "We'll get you out of here."

She felt Ryan leave her side and walk out of the room. For a moment no one spoke. Hayley tried to imagine what they were thinking.

"Won't you have trouble getting around?" Farah asked.

Hayley shook her head. "K-know m-my place."

"I could come over and stay with you while Ryan's at the meeting," Aunt Meg volunteered.

Again, Hayley shook her head. "Sl-sleep."

"She'll be asleep," Farah interpreted. "She won't need anyone for such a short time. I'm sure Ryan will keep his meeting brief."

CHAPTER THIRTY-ONE

Hayley eased back into her own bed. Her own bed! Not that she didn't like Conrad's oceanfront home, but when you can't see *anything* the familiarity of your own place is unbelievably comforting. She knew where everything was — even though Ryan refused to allow her to stumble around on her own. He'd undressed Hayley and found a nightgown. He'd already guided her across the bedroom to the adjacent bathroom.

"Are you sleepy?" Ryan asked.

She shook her head and reached out her arms. Emotionally shaken, she eked out a whisper. "H-h-old m-me."

The bed gave and she knew he'd sat down beside her. A rustling of the sheets meant he'd stretched out. He took her into his arms, gently as if he might hurt her.

"I've never been so damn worried in my whole life," Ryan whispered, and a knot formed in her throat. "I don't know what I would have done if anything happened to you."

A shiver rippled through her as Hayley realized how close she'd come to death. She would never have seen Ryan again. The thought disturbed her then and even more now. She decided all the questioning by the police and knowing Laird had been killed made everything much too real.

"I — I w-as . . . t-errified," she managed to whisper.

"Forget about it." He kissed the top of her head. "You're safe now."

She buried her face against his powerful chest and relaxed, sinking into his embrace. Her world finally felt . . . right. Well, almost right. By tomorrow she should be able to see and speak without her throat aching. Then her world would be perfect.

"Are you okay? This isn't hurting you?" he asked.

"N-no." She could hardly lift her voice above a whisper.

The warmth of his body was so male, so comforting. At the hospital, she'd been tired but now she felt better. A familiar surge of awareness rippled through her. She'd been through a terrifying ordeal but her body didn't seem to care. It wanted Ryan, and it wanted him now. She snuggled even closer but he didn't seem to get the message.

"Detective Wells told me he'd consulted the San Francisco PD. They said a previous girlfriend had complained about Steve Fulton. I don't think Lindsey was making up anything. I just think Fulton's an accomplished liar."

Thinking about Lindsey almost destroyed her good mood. No matter what Steve had done, things would have turned out differently if Hayley hadn't insisted Lindsey come stay with her. A wonderful, talented person would still be alive.

One of Ryan's hands rested on the curve of her waist. Through the silky fabric she felt the heat of his hand as it coasted upward, a scant inch at a time. Guilty feelings were replaced in a heartbeat by anticipated pleasure. She reached up and fumbled around for a moment until she found the curve of his neck. She brought his head down to meet her lips. He kissed her carefully, as if for the very first time.

Giving herself to the passion of the kiss, freed something in Hayley that she hadn't realized existed. For some reason she'd been holding back, waiting to be sure she had the right man. Now she was certain and the knowledge lifted a weight.

She wanted to scream: *Yes! Yes! Yes!* But

her throat still hurt and Ryan would only tell her to be quiet.

As he kissed her, his hand continued to slide upward until it found her breasts. Cradling one in his warm hand, Ryan rubbed his thumb over the taut nipple. Pleasure spiraled through her and moist heat centered in her upper thighs.

"Perfect," he told her. "Absolutely perfect."

Before she could attempt a croaking response, he was kissing her again, harder this time. New spirals of ecstasy surged through her. She returned his kiss with reckless abandon. This was what she'd been waiting for even though she'd never realized she *had* been waiting. She wanted to be swept away — to forget almost being killed, seeing a dead man, knowing she'd caused a friend's death.

Ryan released her, and Hayley thought about protesting but the swishing noise and the metallic zipping sound told her that Ryan was taking off his clothes. She wiggled out of the sheer nightie she was wearing and tossed it aside. He drew her against his powerful body again and she was immediately engulfed in his heat.

She sighed deeply and inhaled the woodsy fragrance of his aftershave and reveled in

486

the smoothness of his skin and the prickling
sensation where hair covered his chest, his
sex. She ran her hands over him, memoriz-
ing every curve and firm plane. Not seeing,
relying on touch and smell, heightened her
desire in a way she never could have anticipated.

And hearing! She could actually hear the
thud-thud of his heart. It pulsed beneath
the palm of her hand. She'd never noticed
the sound before, but his ragged breathing
was familiar.

His erection jutted into her tummy, rock-
hard and hot. She ran a finger across the
smooth tip, and he moaned. Her hand
closed around him, squeezing. A low growl
rumbled from his throat.

"Are you sure you're okay?" he asked, his
voice husky. "You've got a lot of bruises. I
don't want to hurt you."

"I'm okay," she whispered.

His mouth closed over hers and she parted
her lips. Her tongue brushed his and another jolt of heat suffused her body. He
tasted faintly like coffee. His lips were firm
and moist. She arched against him, moving
provocatively as his hand on her hips
pressed her flush against his rigid penis.

Hayley couldn't remember ever being this
aroused as her pulse kicked into overdrive.

She was almost desperate to have him inside her, but Ryan didn't seem to be in any hurry. She speared her fingers into his thick hair and clutched a fistful of it. She eased one leg between his, then moved her knee — just a little.

Ryan muttered something under his breath. He could have been cursing or praying. She was reasonably certain he wasn't consulting God. She giggled at the thought. When had a man *ever* made her laugh during sex? Well, come to think about it, she'd giggled a lot the last time they'd made love.

"What's so funny?" he asked, his voice gruff and barely above a whisper.

"You must have been cursing," she whispered, "but for a minute, I thought you were praying. That made me laugh."

"I was praying. Praying I can hold on until I make you climax."

She wanted to say he'd never had any trouble before, but he smothered her words with a searing kiss. Her whole body quivered with anticipation. She didn't know what he was concerned about; she was ready to climax any second.

She tried to whisper, "Hurry," but it came out a croaking word. Soon she'd be talking normally, she realized. She could tell him how she felt about him.

Ryan eased her onto her back and moved over her. She felt the heat of his body — but not its weight. He kept his heavy torso supported by his forearms. He kissed the nublike nipple and caressed it with his tongue. The light prickle of his emerging beard rasped her sensitive skin. She wiggled beneath him, urging him to get on with it.

His mouth played with her nipple, sucking hard. Blood thundering like jungle drums in her ears, Hayley arched upward. A puff of cool air swished across her bare backside but did nothing to chill her overheated body. Her breath rushed out of her lungs in a long moan.

"Like that, huh?"

She could reply; it had nothing to do with her sore throat. She was too close to climaxing to utter a single word.

Ryan brushed the velvet tip of his penis against the soft folds of her sex. He wriggled his rigid shaft into her a scant inch at a time, slowly stretching her. With a powerful thrust, he was deep inside her. Hayley bit her lip to keep from exploding into minute convulsions of pleasure.

"I don't want to hurt you."

Again, she was afraid to speak except to herself. *It hurts sooo good.* Slowly, rhythmically, he rocked back and forth, drawing his body in and out of hers. Each thrust brought a surge of pleasure as potent as any narcotic. She moved with him, lifting her hips to meet his each time he withdrew.

Pummeling her now, Hayley held on by wrapping her legs around his hips, arms around his neck. A few seconds later, her world dissolved into a series of spasms of pleasure so intense she cried out, "Ryan! Oh, Ryan!"

She felt him throw his head back. With a final surge he powered into her as if he couldn't get deep enough. A split-second later, he collapsed on top of her, his breath coming in wrenching heaves. Still buried to the hilt, Ryan quickly rolled onto his side, taking her with him.

Still linked, they lay there winded, facing each other. Hayley snuggled against his chest, thinking she'd never made love to a man like this. She'd never given herself fully — until now.

How did Ryan feel?

She knew he cared about her, but he'd mourned his wife for so long. His love for her must be deep and lasting. Was there room for Hayley in his heart? Was he ready?

She wanted to ask him, but now wasn't the right time. He was still panting deeply, trying to catch his breath. Hayley thought she could talk, but she wasn't positive. She had managed to get out a few actual words — not grainy whispers — during sex. But this might develop into a long discussion. She should wait until she could speak normally and look him in the eye to gauge his reaction.

Ryan started to say something but the *brr-ing brr-ing* of his cell phone interrupted him. He rolled off her and a faint whoosh of air drifted across her naked body and chilled her. She fumbled for the covers as she felt Rob sit up. She found the sheet and pulled it over her.

"Hollister," she heard him say. Then he listened for a minute before adding, "I'll be right there."

She felt his weight leave the bed. "Gotta go. That was Tom Dawkins. My boss finished early."

"T-time is — ?"

"Eight-thirty." He kissed the nape of her neck, then said, "I wouldn't go, but I need to see him to explain why I'm resigning."

"O-okay. B-be . . . h-here."

His weight left the bed. "I won't be long." Rustling sounds told her Ryan was putting on his clothes. "I was going to pick up Andy afterward, but I think I'll leave him with Timmy until tomorrow."

Good idea, she thought. She needed to talk to Trent about Timmy.

"O-o-h-h," she screamed as she realized what was happening.

She felt Ryan's weight hit the bed. "What's the matter?"

"I — I c-can . . . *see!*"

"You're kidding. Just like that, you can see?"

The room wasn't pitch-black the way it had been. She pointed in the direction of the ghostly blur. "L-light."

"Light's coming through the window on the bay from the exterior lights and a full moon."

"Oth-er lights?" She croaked out the question.

"No. There wasn't any point in turning on the lights, since you can't see, and I thought you were going to sleep."

"O-on . . . n-now." She was speaking again, but her words sounded as if her tongue was sandpaper.

Hayley felt his weight leave the mattress and a second later heard the click of the bedside lamp. She turned toward it and saw a blurry glow and next to it a tall, dark form that must be Ryan. "S-see light . . . not m-m-uch . . . more."

The shadow moved closer, then blotted

out the lamp's light. She felt Ryan's breath on her cheek. He kissed her lightly on the lips. "You're getting better just like the doctors said. By tomorrow you should be back to normal. Get some rest now."

Ryan turned out the light and pressed a wad of silky fabric into her hand. Her nightgown, she realized, and slipped it over her head. She sank back onto the pillow, suddenly exhausted.

"I won't be gone long," he promised again.

Hayley closed her eyes and allowed herself to relax. It had been a harrowing experience, but everything was going to be okay. They'd find Chad, arrest him, and the jerk would get what he deserved. She'd be maid of honor at her aunt's wedding. She drifted into sleep with a contented smile.

Hayley awakened some time later — alone. She groggily blinked her eyes. Yes! She was seeing even better now. Moonlight filtered through the large window facing the bay. It was an unfocused blur, as if she had Vaseline in her eyes, but she could make it out now better than she had when Ryan had been here. Blobs of what she knew to be furniture crouched in the shadows.

Ryan? Where was he? Oh, yes. He'd gone to explain his resignation to his boss. How long ago had that been? She turned to where she knew her digital alarm clock was on the bedside table. Nothing but a red blur.

Ryan couldn't have been gone long, she reasoned. His meeting was at the Marriott, which wasn't far away, and he'd said he'd be right back.

Suddenly, her ears detected a noise. Out on the water? No. The sound had come from inside the loft. Another squeak.

It had to be the free-standing staircase that led up from the lower level to her bedroom. The stainless steel wasn't attached as tight as it should have been on certain stairs. It wasn't dangerous so she'd put off having it repaired.

Was Ryan back? She doubted it. A man of his size would cause a louder squeak. If it wasn't Ryan, who was it?

She strained to see through the darkness to her bedroom door. She recognized the outline of the door, but nothing else was visible — even the palest suggestion of a glow. If it had been Aunt Meg or Courtney returning with Andy, they would have turned on the downstairs light.

They wouldn't sneak up the stairs in the pitch dark.

Chad was her first thought. The police hadn't captured him — last she heard. He might blame her — in the same crazy way Laird had — for his troubles. She considered slipping out and hiding, but there was nowhere to go except under the bed or into the closet. Any idiot would think to check there.

She squinted into the darkness beyond her bedroom door and detected a pinpoint of light. A flashlight, she realized. It made sense. The stairs were treacherous. A fall from this level — the third floor — could mean death or serious injury.

Who would come up using a flashlight? Chad, she thought again. He'd been here many times when they'd been engaged. He'd always warned her that the stairs were dangerous. As a precaution, he would know to bring a flashlight.

Chad had destroyed the trust and had killed the secretary who'd worked for the firm for years. She realized he'd been behind the car bombing as well. He knew where she lived, where she went. He easily could have placed the GPS tracker found after the bombing. He'd waited for the right moment, the right place.

And he'd killed the wrong person. How terribly sad, Hayley thought. She didn't want to make this easy on him, but she didn't know what she could do, considering her condition.

A form appeared in the doorway, barely visible in the faint light from the window and misshapen by her distorted vision. Not a man, she realized with the next shaky breath. Too small. A woman. Who?

Scream or pretend you're asleep, she asked herself. The walls were too thick for a scream to be heard from outside the loft unless someone luckily happened to be in just the right spot. But if she played dead, a bullet to the brain might end her life — this time for good.

She forced herself to remain still and waited, watching through slitted eyes as the figure crept across the room with all the stealth of an experienced cat burglar. Did she still have the strength to fling herself upon the intruder once the woman came close enough? It had caught Laird off guard; it might work again.

As the woman crept closer, Hayley slowly slipped her foot out from under the sheet. The last thing she needed to do was become tangled and fall. The woman stopped beside the bed.

Hayley squinted so hard — afraid the whites of her eyes would give her away — that she could barely see anything but wavering patterns of dark and light. Her other senses told her the woman had stopped beside the bed and was gazing down at her.

Something cold and hard prodded her ribs. The flashlight? No. A gun.

"Wake up, Hayley." The loud voice was unmistakable. Farah!

"U-u-h-h," Hayley moaned, feigning sleep, buying time.

"Get up!"

Hayley jolted upright and saw the flashlight was off. The only light came from the large window. It was Farah, all right. She appeared to be dressed as if she was a surgeon. Cap, gown, shoe covers. Uh-oh. Her pulse skittered alarmingly.

"W-ho . . . i-s it?" Hayley asked, deciding it was wisest to pretend she still couldn't see or speak.

"Get out of bed or I'll shoot you right there."

CHAPTER THIRTY-TWO

Ryan met Tom Dawkins in the lobby of the Marriott. The older man appeared tired, paler than Ryan remembered. Heading the white collar unit of the FBI in L.A. was a tough job. White-collar crime took longer to detect and usually meant hours in court battling expensive attorneys.

"How's the shoulder?" was Tom's first question.

"Almost as good as new," Ryan said. Even though his shoulder ached now, his adrenaline level had been so high all day that he barely noticed it.

"Let's get a drink." Tom gestured toward the lobby bar.

One quick drink, Ryan told himself. He needed to get back to Hayley, but he didn't want to appear rude. This was the man who'd directed the most interesting cases Ryan's way.

They found seats in the crowded bar and

ordered from a perky waitress who tried her best to get Ryan's attention with a come-on smile. He asked for a gin and tonic while Dawkins wanted a dirty martini.

"I hear there was a lot of excitement here today and you were right in the middle of it."

Ryan attempted a smile. He wasn't proud of Laird's death. It would have been much easier to tie up the loose ends if he'd lived. What was important, he reminded himself, was that Hayley had survived.

"Strange story," Tom commented as the waitress arrived with their drinks. "One of the local cops at the conference filled me in. Did you know the police in San Diego found Chad Bennett?"

Ryan shook his head.

"Looks like suicide."

"You're kidding," Ryan said, torn by conflicting emotions. He hated what Bennett had done to Hayley, but he wanted him to be questioned by the police. It was unclear just how involved he was in the plot against Hayley. Most assuredly he'd known about the destruction of the trust, but had he helped Laird try to kill Hayley? Who killed Sylvia Morrow? "How did Bennett die?"

"Shot himself."

"There was quite a case against him."

"How'd you get yourself in the middle of this?"

Ryan didn't want to take time to explain, but he couldn't think of a polite way to kick back the rest of his drink and leave. Besides, he hadn't even gotten to his resignation yet. He gave as concise a version of events as he could manage.

"Good work," Dawkins said. "If you weren't so good on the computer, I'd send you into the field."

Ryan took another swig of his drink. This was the point where he should tender his resignation and thank Tom Dawkins for all he'd done for Ryan.

Before Ryan could speak, Tom said, "Ed Phillips sent you this. I guess you asked him to run a check on remnants from a private plane crash."

Ryan sheepishly nodded. He shouldn't have asked Ed to use the facilities but he had. He was a little surprised Ed had told Tom.

Dawkins pulled an envelope out of his jacket pocket and handed it to Ryan. "Long story short. A bomb caused the plane crash. The same type that blew up Hayley Fordham's car."

Ryan nearly dropped his drink. "Goddammit!" His thoughts spun and his instincts immediately told him Aunt Meg had been correct. Laird going to such extremes to get the company didn't make sense. Ryan didn't really know the man — having met him once — but bombing a plane and a car seemed radical. Too radical.

Conveniently, Chad Bennett was dead. Just as conveniently, Laird McMasters was dead.

Ryan vaulted to his feet. "I'll come see you soon. I've got to go. Hayley's in imminent danger." How could he have been so stupid?

"Up! Now!" ordered Farah.

Hayley stumbled out of bed, her hands flailing in front of her as if she couldn't see. Which wasn't a stretch. All she could make out were shadowy forms.

Farah grabbed her arm and yanked Hayley forward. "Hurry!"

The gloves that must be latex were whiter than the rest of Farah's clothing. They reflected the light as did the gleaming barrel on the gun. Hayley knew she didn't have nine lives. This time she was dead . . . unless. A thought formed in her mind.

"W-hy . . . d-do-ing this?" Hayley asked in a thick, unsteady voice. Her throat hurt with each word. "Y-you . . . w-won't get away . . . with it."

"Oh, *pul-eeze!* I got rid of my father and —"

"No!" Hayley cried. "D-Dad loved . . . you."

"No. He loved you and he loved my brother. He tolerated me because I was his child. He never had any time for me."

The deep-seated animosity put a shrill note in Farah's voice. It was as if she'd been holding in this statement for years. Hayley's suspicions had been on target. The plane crash hadn't been pilot error. "H-how —"

"A bomb. Like the one that blew up your Beamer, only this one worked on a timer. That way my father and your bitch of a mother would be blown to kingdom come over the mountains where search and rescue would play hell getting to them. I was betting the Civil Air Patrol would blame it on the pilot, which they did."

For a moment, horror rooted Hayley to the spot and her heart lurched wildly. How could Farah brag about killing someone — especially her own father? Tears filled her eyes. Hayley thought she might break down and sob. Suddenly, in her mind's eye, she envisioned the stylized Grim Reaper she'd created. With it came the familar slogan:

"We took out Sylvia without any problem," Farah bragged, nudging Hayley forward with the barrel of the gun.

"W-we?" Hayley shuffled her feet, but didn't move ahead.

"Trent helped me." There was a ring of satisfaction in Farah's voice now. She must realize Hayley had bought Trent's story and hadn't believed he was involved.

"T-Trent wouldn't kill . . . Daddy. Th-they were s-so close." A sense of desolation swept over her. In her head she saw Trent and her father huddled over one of the surfboard molds — laughing, talking.

"Trent kill?" A cold edge of irony filled her voice. "You've *got* to be kidding! I planted the bomb. He didn't know until after the funeral. When I told him . . . Trent cried like the baby he is at times. Then I showed him a copy of the trust that I'd taken off your mother's computer."

Hayley knew exactly what the trust said. She could only imagine how betrayed Trent must have felt — seeing in writing that his father had no faith in him.

"Well, let's just say Trent saw the light. He was still squeamish. He wanted you to live. He was quite sentimental about you. I got tired of waiting. I couldn't count on him, so

I planted the bomb under your car without telling anyone."

Hayley's chest hurt so much it felt as if it would burst. Lindsey died because this insane woman thought she was killing Hayley. And now she would get what she'd been after all along.

"W-w-w . . . whe-re?" Hayley could barely get out the word.

"Where did I get the bombs?" Hayley saw the light flash off Farah's white teeth and knew she was smiling. Gloating, most likely. "That's the good part. I fell into them. Remember my trip to Puerto Vallarta with Kyle? We drove down the coast to some out-of-the-way beach so Kyle could surf. Our car broke down on the way back. We spent the night in some shit-hole village. At the *only* cantina we met some guys. Kyle bought dope while I had a good time with the boys."

Hayley didn't have to stretch her imagination to realize Farah meant sex. Even in high school, Farah — brainy though she was — had gotten herself a reputation. After college and her return to Newport, rumors said she was more than a little wild. Hayley had chosen to ignore the gossip.

"One of the *muchachos* bragged that he made car bombs for some cartel. I didn't believe him for one second. The other guy had passed out and Kyle was sleeping it off so I let *macho* man demo one of his bombs." Farah giggled. "He woke up the whole damn village when he blew up some clunker."

"N-n-o." Hayley choked out the word, thinking not of the old car but of her parents being blown to bits.

"Yes," Farah said with pride. "I showed macho man a few kinky tricks he'd never seen and persuaded him to give me two bombs. One for you and one for dear old Dad and your bitch of a mother."

Hayley gasped, unable to say a word. Facing Laird had been a dreadful experience. Being alone in the dark with someone who was pure evil was terrifying. *Kick Fear — Believe.* There had to be a way out of this.

"W-why Laird? Ch-chad?"

"Move!" Farah shoved the gun into Hayley's ribs. "I don't have all night to chitchat. Dear old Ryan will be back soon. He'll find you in a heap at the bottom of the stairs. Neck broken in a fall. You were up wandering around — unable to see — and had a fatal accident."

So that's what she planned. Hayley would be better off to force Farah to shoot her right here. Then, at least, there would be a murder investigation. Ryan wouldn't rest until the crime had been solved.

The telephones in the loft rang simultaneously. The closest one was on Hayley's nightstand but there was another in the kitchen and one more in the entry.

"Th-that's R-Ryan."

"Let's not disappoint him. Answer the phone."

Hayley couldn't believe Farah was going to let her do this. Holding her arm in a clasp like one of The Wrath's death grips, Farah marched her into the bedroom. She grabbed the receiver and handed it to Hayley.

"H-hel-l-lo?"

"Hayley —"

Farah snatched away the phone and hung it up. Hayley had recognized Ryan's voice.

"He believes you're all right. You dropped the phone because you can't see shit. When he calls back, he'll get a busy signal. But he won't worry. He heard your voice. He knows you're here."

Clever, Hayley thought. This woman could really think on her feet. Would Ryan see through the ruse? She couldn't count on it. Even if he did suspect something, Ryan was too far away to help. Should he call the police, they wouldn't get here in time, either. She had only herself to rely on.

"March unless you want me to shoot," Farah said.

There might be a way, Hayley again thought. If she failed, Hayley could scratch Farah the way she had Laird and the police would have DNA evidence. She'd be dead but — they might catch Farah. There was a slim chance this would work, but it was her only hope.

Hayley edged forward a foot or so. "T-tell me what Chad . . . L-Laird had to gain."

"Money. Money talks as they say." There was a trace of laughter in Farah's voice. "Laird had a scheme to combine the two businesses and sell them to a big gun or go for an IPO. Either way, we'd all make a bundle."

"Ch-Chad wouldn't . . . make any money," Hayley said, just to keep her talking while she mentally reviewed her plan.

"It was worth a lot to us to have the trust destroyed. We compensated your fiancé." Farah told her with pride. "Money up front and more to come after the sale of the company."

Her tone was mocking now; she clearly believed Hayley had fallen off the proverbial turnip truck. And maybe she had. Trusting Chad and Trent had been a miscalculation that could cost her life.

"I-is Tr-Trent . . . here?"

"No. Start walking." Farah jammed the gun into Hayley's back. "Trent's in San Diego. He took care of Chad. If we'd let him live, Chad would have rolled over on us. Now it's a win-win situation."

Stalling, Hayley cried, "Ch-Chad's . . . dead?"

"Suicide plain and simple."

"Y-you won't get away —"

"We've already been through this. I'm a whole lot smarter than anyone suspects." She shoved Hayley forward. "Why do you think I wore all this gear? I'm not leaving any forensic evidence behind. Just one dead body. Understand?"

From the light now coming through the floor-to-ceiling windows facing the bay, Hayley could make out the silvery rungs of the stainless-steel banister. She knew Farah would have to get her to the edge to push her down the stairs. Or over the top of the banister.

Over the top, Hayley decided. A plunge straight down the stairs might mean she would fall only as far as the landing. Pushing her over the top of the banister meant a direct fall to the lobby level and the hard tiles on the entry floor.

"Do you want to jump or should I push

you?" Farah asked with saccharine sweetness.

Hayley paused a moment, calculating. If only she could see more than a shadowy shape, she would have a better chance of pulling this off. *Kick Fear — Believe.*

Hayley swung to the right — not away from Farah but into her, making a grab for the gun. And contorting her body.

Ryan left his car double-parked a building away from Hayley's loft. As usual there were no parking places. He sprinted up the street, his gun in his hand. The moment he'd realized Hayley's parents had been killed, Ryan knew that Laird was only part of the conspiracy.

Who would benefit from these deaths?

Trent and Farah. Possibly their mother as well. It didn't matter who was behind it, he had to get to Hayley before they killed her. True, she'd answered the phone, disconnected the line.

It could have been the accidental result of her eye problems, but Ryan didn't believe it. Getting the busy signal several times confirmed his suspicions. He'd called the police and alerted them.

Where were they? No sign of them in the street near Hayley's home. No sirens coming down Newport Boulevard. Just like the saying went — the police were never around when you needed them.

The unmistakable boom of a gunshot split the night as loud as a cannon shot. A second later glass shattered as if a department store window had been hit. The huge window facing the bay, Ryan decided as he reached the front door.

The door was locked, the way he'd left it. He put his good shoulder against the door and shoved with all his might. Nothing. No sounds from inside, either.

Sweat ran down his temples. He backed up. This time he took a running start and charged the door. It gave and he landed on his back in the entry, dazed.

He jolted upright, then felt for his gun. His fingers encountered a pool of liquid. What in hell? Blood, he realized as he found the gun in the darkness. His eyes were adjusting to the light now.

A woman's crumpled form was sprawled across the entry floor. Was he too late?

"Hayley?" he called, moving on his knees to the body.

"I'm up here."

For a second, he couldn't think beyond — Thank God!

"Careful," she cried. "Farah's got a gun."

A wild flash of happiness swept through him like a riptide. "Don't worry about her. It's over. You're safe."

EPILOGUE

Hayley stood at the altar and inhaled the scent of roses filling the air. Candles infused with essence of rose flickered around her. She smoothed the skirt of the pale lavender-colored dress that fell in loose folds to her knees.

She couldn't help looking at Ryan. The muscles of his shoulders strained at the black silk of his tuxedo. His shoulder had healed and he'd been working out again. Not that he needed to. Ryan had a rugged physique and a slow grin that made him the most attractive man she'd ever met.

They smiled at each other as "We've Only Just Begun" began to play. Conrad, standing next to Ryan, was beaming. Ryan had wheeled his father to the altar, but Conrad wanted to stand up beside Meg to be married.

"Regal. Positively regal," Hayley whispered to the men when her aunt walked up the aisle. Aunt Meg's silver hair was swept up into a cluster of loose curls at the top of her head. On The Wrath's arm, she moved with elegance and grace that came naturally to her. The Wrath didn't know Meg well, but he really liked her and insisted on escorting her.

When Aunt Meg reached the altar, the pastor cleared his throat and began the ceremony. Blinking back tears, Hayley listened. She couldn't remember when she'd ever been happier for anyone.

It had taken Aunt Meg a lifetime to find Conrad, and now nothing could part them. They were going to make the most of the time they had together. After the ceremony and reception, they were going to Tahiti. She let her mind drift as the ceremony continued.

"I now pronounce you man and wife," the pastor concluded. They kissed and everyone clapped uproariously.

Slowly Conrad inched around, with Ryan at his elbow to make sure he didn't lose his balance. Aunt Meg turned beside her new husband and offered him a shy smile.

"Friends," the pastor said, "I give you Mr. and Mrs. Conrad Hollister."

"What's going through that beautiful head?"

513

Ryan asked as he guided her around the dance floor at the reception.

"Nothing . . . really," she hedged.

"You weren't thinking about the business again, were you?"

"Not exactly." She gazed into his intelligent eyes. "I was wishing my parents could be here to see Aunt Meg." She glanced over to the head table where Aunt Meg was sitting, holding hands with Conrad and laughing.

"They're happy . . . despite everything," Ryan said.

Hayley knew he was obliquely referring to Farah's death and the scandal surrounding her parents' plane crash. The Fordhams had been in the news daily. Now Trent was in jail awaiting trial for shooting Chad.

"Yes, they are happy," she agreed. "And they deserve it."

The music stopped and Ryan escorted her out to the Balboa Bay Club's upper terrace overlooking the harbor.

"Let it go," Ryan said. "Forget everything that's happened."

"That's impossible. Even though it's been a month, I can't get over the extent of Farah's fury, her absolute hatred for her own father. It's . . . shocking."

"Look." Ryan slid his arm across her bare

shoulders. "She was mentally ill."

"But Trent —"

"He could have said no, but he didn't. He was too weak."

Hayley nodded and tried to put the situation out of her mind. They'd discussed this several times since Hayley had managed to get the better of Farah. She shouldn't be dwelling on it during such a festive occasion. "Every cloud has a silver lining."

"You referring to the jujitsu move The Wrath taught you? It saved your life."

"No," Hayley replied. Even now she couldn't believe she'd managed to hook Farah's leg and shove her over the railing. Farah had managed to fire her gun — and shatter the glass window before hitting the tile headfirst. "I'm thinking about second chances."

"I'll bite." Ryan's mouth twisted with amusement. "What second chances are we talking about?"

"Me, The Wrath, PimpIt. We're all taking a second look at our careers."

The Wrath had been so disturbed by killing a man — even accidentally — with an MMA maneuver that he'd decided to devote himself to promoting his gear. With Trent out of the picture, Hayley had been thrilled to have The Wrath join the team at Surf's

Up. It was a package deal. PimpIt, who'd never been much of a fighter, was going to work in the shop, too.

"Have you decided about your art career?" Ryan asked.

She hadn't brought up this subject because she didn't know how she felt. It had been the elephant in the room for the last few weeks. Today as Aunt Meg strolled down the aisle, Hayley had made her decision.

"I'm putting it on hold." Her voice was shakier than she would have liked. "Well, not hold exactly. I'll still paint. I'll make time somehow, but I have to keep Surf's Up going. I suspect it will head into new areas like MMA gear, but I don't want all my parents struggled to build to fail or be sold."

She allowed her subconscious thoughts to surface. "Mom and Dad had so much faith in me. I never realized how much. I was stunned that they'd left me the business."

Ryan's arms encircled her, one hand at the small of her back that was left bare by the deep vee of the gown. Her skin tingled under his fingertips.

"Hayley, I'll back you no matter what you want to do." His grip tightened and his expression became more serious. "Just save some time for us."

"Of course," she assured him. "People count the most. You are even more important to me than my aunt. You're the best."

His lips pressed against hers, then gently covered her mouth. She quivered at the tenderness of his kiss. A moment later, Ryan pulled away. "Talk about second chances. I'm getting one. I love you more than you can imagine."

Her heart pounded erratically. Ryan had never used the "L" word before. He'd told her how much she meant to him, how frightened he'd been at the thought of losing her, but he'd never said he loved her.

"I'm crazy about you, too," she whispered.

"Does that mean you love me?" he asked in a low, husky voice.

"Yes. I love you."

Reclaiming her lips, Ryan crushed her to him. There was a dreamy intimacy to their kiss, a realization that what they shared was special.

"What do you say we wait until the happy couple returns from their honeymoon in Tahiti, then we exchange vows?"

Hayley had hoped Ryan would ask her to marry him. "Mrs. Ryan Hollister has a nice ring to it."

"Speaking of rings." He pulled a blue box out of his pocket and opened it. The diamond winked at Hayley. "You're the second chance at love that I never thought I would find."

The employees of Thorndike Press hope you have enjoyed this Large Print book. All our Thorndike, Wheeler, and Kennebec Large Print titles are designed for easy reading, and all our books are made to last. Other Thorndike Press Large Print books are available at your library, through selected bookstores, or directly from us.

For information about titles, please call:
(800) 223-1244

or visit our Web site at:
http://gale.cengage.com/thorndike

To share your comments, please write:
Publisher
Thorndike Press
295 Kennedy Memorial Drive
Waterville, ME 04901